BRITCHES GET STITCHES

A MUSIC CITY ROLLERS NOVEL

ELICIA HYDER

ISBN: 978-1-945775-16-1
Inkwell & Quill, LLC

Cover Illustrations by John Woolley
www.derbygirlart.com

Edited by Nicole Ayers

For More Information:
www.eliciahyder.com

Special Thanks to everyone who made this book possible:

To Lady Fury, Electra Cal, and Mista Cal for your wealth of knowledge and help while writing this.

To Bleeding Heartland Roller Derby in Bloomington, IN for letting me borrow the B-Cup for this book.

To the *Name that Dog!* contest winners: Sue Lopp, Debra Hetland, Leisel Tuck, Carolyn Redden, and Terry Bregin. Jackie's dog's name is Freckles!

To Michele Hartley for naming Grace's parents Graham and Sheila Evans.

To the world's greatest office manager, Jenni Vaught. Thanks for helping me keep my sh*t together so I can write.

To my own badass, sexy, third-shift cop. I love you, Mr. Spouse.

TO MY AWESOME LAUNCH TEAM, THE BOOK SUMMONERS. Thank you all for showing up time and time again to help me get these books off the ground.

To my Fan Club members, HYDERNATION. You guys make my job so much fun!

And as always, thanks to all my readers who show up time and time again to enjoy my hard work. YOU are the reason why I do this. Well...*you* and bills. ♡

Derby Disclaimer

For current skaters:

I've worked really hard to keep this book derby-factual, but some parts have been embellished or stretched for the sake of fun fiction. Just wanted *you* to know that *I know*.

Also...if I tried to keep up with all the rule changes each year, I'd go mad. Am I right?

So read. Have fun. And know...YOU are a badass.

— eL's Bells, a.k.a. Author Elicia Hyder

Other novels in the Music City Roller series:

Lights Out Lucy: Roller Derby 101

Accident-prone Lucy Cooper puts her life and her heart on the line to catch the attention of the Music City Rollers' top sponsor —construction tycoon, West Adler. But will she skate off with the heart of Nashville's Most Eligible Bachelor? Or will she get herself killed in a sport that promises, "It's not a matter of if you'll get hurt—but of how bad and when."

For Addy.

Be Brave.
Be Strong.
Be Badass.

Love, Mom.

ONE

THE WHOLE HOUSE smelled like eggs.

Not the best way to start off girls' night. I pushed open the window letting the cold Nashville night air rush into the house. Sure, the gas heat was going right out into the neighborhood, but did I care? Nope. No longer my bill. No longer my problem. I threw open the sliding-glass door too.

Heavy paws thudded down the hallway as the sliding wheels of the patio door announced canine freedom throughout the house. Bodhi bounded past me, water dripping from his golden snout. He'd probably been drinking from the half-bath toilet again, his preferred water bowl over the expensive filtered fountain I'd had installed in the laundry room.

As I drank the last drop of the 2013 Chateau St. Jean Cinq Cépages we'd been saving for a special occasion, I watched Bodhi romp unbridled through our backyard. Well, Clay's backyard. Err... Make that Clay and *Ginny's* backyard.

Dr. Virginia "Ginny" Allen, MD—or as my friends and I had taken to calling her, "Dr. Vagina"—was the cardiologist, quite obviously, now occupying my bed. Lab coats and mall-bought dresses hung in my closet, and a PhD*iva* mug sat by the coffeemaker.

Bitch. I hoped she *was* a diva.

In hindsight, I should've seen the affair coming. But to my embarrassment, I'd sexistly assumed "Dr. Allen" was a man for the first few months my husband rattled on about her.

"Grace, you would love Dr. Allen in the new TennStar office."

"Dr. Allen told me the funniest story about a patient today."

And, oh let's not forget: *"Grace, you and Dr. Allen would really hit it off. You've got so much in common."*

Yes. The same shitty taste in men, apparently.

I tried to drink from the glass again, but alas, empty. I leaned on the doorway for support. Emotional and vertical.

Bodhi lifted his leg on the corner of Clay's toolshed. I appreciated the canine solidarity.

The backyard had always been my favorite part of the house. With the vintage lights strung between the ancient oak trees and the vine-draped pergola built by my father's own hands, it could have been a fairy's paradise. Ripped straight from the pages of *A Midsummer Night's Dream.*

Our first year in the house, Clay and I had spent the warm summer evenings snuggling on the wicker chaise lounge under the pergola. Me sprawled against his side, my head on his chest as he read to me.

The Martyr's Wife by C. E. Frost had been our favorite. That wine-soaked memory now so acute I could almost feel the warmth of his breath against my blonde hair as he'd read aloud. *"This moment in time is ours, completely ours. Even if for but a moment, I will hold you as though the light of the sun may not burn tomorrow."*

We'd made love right there without bothering to go inside.

Only happy meant-for-each-other couples do that sort of thing, right?

I wonder if I can strap the pergola to the roof of my car?

Except for the victorious holes it would leave in the sod, Clay wouldn't mind, even if the pergola hadn't been listed among my assets in the divorce. The happy couple would probably need the room for a swing set or a sandbox anyway. For the baby.

Their baby.

I could steal bungee cords out of the garage.

I needed more wine.

Pushing back from the door casing, I stumbled a half step. Maybe more wine wasn't the best idea. I had practice the next day, and the team had a strict policy about sobriety on the track. Which, in all honesty, was probably the only thing that saved me from going full-blown Amy Winehouse during my divorce.

Thank God for roller derby.

I also couldn't afford to be sloppy. Not this night. My very last night in the house I'd worked so hard to make a home. The house where I was now a guest, only allowed in to gather the last of my things.

Seven years, gone.

"Bodhi!" I whistled, and the dog froze on the grass, letting the tennis ball he'd found drop from his mouth. His big head flopped to the side as he stared at me. "Come on. Let's go inside!"

He picked up the ball again, slung it sideways across the yard, then fetched it.

"Come on, boy!" I slapped the side of my leg, and he ignored me.

The doorbell rang.

Bodhi jerked to attention, then charged, nearly knocking me out of the doorway like a bowling pin. He barked all the way to the door. I followed, depositing my empty glass on the marble countertop with a scraping *clink* as I passed. The bell rang again.

"I'm coming!" I grabbed Bodhi's collar with one hand and pulled open the heavy wood-and-iron door with the other. It was a vintage piece we'd found in Franklin during the house's remodel.

A party horn sounded in my face, followed by the flash of a Polaroid camera. Then my friends began to sing off-key. "*Ding! Dong!* The jerk is gone! *Ding! Dong!* The jerk is gone!"

"Oh my god!" I was laughing as they carried in fuchsia and black balloons, champagne, and a cake. I released Bodhi, letting him sniff and tail-whip my friends who were all in matching black T-shirts with different sayings scrawled in pink.

Monica's shirt: I NEVER LIKED HIM ANYWAY.

Zoey's shirt: SHE'S FREE AT LAST.

Lucy's shirt: GOODBYE, MR. WRONG!

Olivia's shirt: SHE GOT THE RING. HE GOT THE FINGER.

Tears spilled down my cheeks. "You guys!"

"Wait, we have one for you too!" Monica thrust a bright fuchsia shirt toward me.

I held it out as everyone read it aloud. "We now pronounce you single and fun!" I pulled it to my chest. "I love you guys."

They all gathered around me for a group hug, Bodhi tangling himself in the middle of our legs. "We love you too," they echoed back.

After a second, Olivia sniffed over my shoulder. "Grace, why does it smell like eggs in this house?"

I wiped my eyes as we all stepped back. "It's a long story."

"And I'm sure it's a great one." Monica held up a bottle. "But first, champagne!"

Lucy grabbed my arm. "No, first, Grace has to put on her shirt."

"Yeah, we all changed in the driveway," Olivia agreed.

"OK, OK." I unzipped the Music City Rollers hoodie I was wearing and slipped the T-shirt over my camisole.

Monica twisted off the cork's metal cage and handed me the champagne. "Grace, you do the honors."

"Smile for the camera!" Lucy said, holding up the Polaroid again.

I smiled, and she snapped the picture, then grabbed it when the camera spat it out. Gripping the bottle by its neck, I put both thumbs on the cork and pushed.

Pow!

The cork zoomed across the living room, catching a lampshade and knocking the three-hundred-dollar mouth-blown glass lamp off the end table. It shattered on the floor.

The girls gasped. Bodhi barked and ran a lap around the kitchen island.

Laughing, I handed the bottle back to Monica and grabbed Bodhi's collar as he passed so he wouldn't run through the shards. "Clay got that in the divorce. Oops." They all cackled behind me. "Who's thirsty?"

I let Bodhi back outside, and Olivia helped me sweep up the glass while Monica poured the champagne. When we were finished, Monica held her flute high into the air. "A toast, shall we?"

I smiled and raised my glass with the others.

Monica, my best friend, smiled gently. "To Grace, may this be the beginning of the very best years of your life. I love you."

I mouthed the words "I love you" back to her as everyone shouted, "Cheers!"

Without pause, I drained the champagne, then punctuated the moment with a tiny burp. The girls laughed.

The best years of my life...who knew I'd be in my thirties before those would roll around?

"Where's your mom? I thought she'd be here." Monica was looking around like she might spot my mother hiding in a corner.

"She offered to come. So did Garrett, but I told them I would be in good hands with you guys."

Lucy sat down at the island in the kitchen with her camera. "Who's Garrett?"

"My brother," I answered.

"He owns a badass brewery out near Nolensville," Monica added.

"Which one?" Olivia asked as she nosed around my kitchen.

"Battle Road," I answered. "What are you looking for?"

"I serve Battle Road at the restaurant. They have a beer called Hops on Pops." Olivia lifted the lid of the pot on the stove, and her eyes widened as if to say, "*Ah-ha!*" She looked over at me. "Grace, are we dyeing Easter eggs?"

Not a bad guess, actually.

"Sort of." I joined her at the stove and moved the pot off the burner. "I've decided to have a little fun with that hateful, cheating ex of mine."

Olivia cocked an eyebrow as she sipped her champagne.

"I'm going to write a message on them and hide them all over the house."

Champagne dribbled down Olivia's chin when she laughed. "That's epic. I want to help."

Zoey gasped and covered her mouth. "You're not really, are you, Grace?"

Lucy's head tilted toward our friend. "I don't think she's making egg salad, Zo."

I picked up my sewing kit off the floor and plopped it down on the counter. "I'm not just hiding them around the house either. I'll sew them up inside the furniture. That way, when he finds them a few months from now, they'll be nice and ripe with mold and maggots."

Olivia laughed.

Lucy made a vomiting noise.

"Aren't you afraid you'll get into trouble?" Zoey asked.

I patted her head, which was soft with the regrowth of her post-chemo curls. "You gotta live a little, my tiny friend."

Olivia pointed to the mocha-colored sofa. "You could put them in the couch pillows."

Monica walked over and lifted one of the cushions. "No, you need to put them inside the frame so they won't break."

Olivia had an evil grin. "Ooo, that's good."

"The only room that's off limits is the nursery." I refilled my champagne one more time. "It's not the kid's fault her parents are assholes."

"Her?" Monica asked.

"Judging from all the Pottery Barn pink in what used to be my home office, it's either a girl or they're really bucking the gender norms."

Monica visibly deflated. Her shoulders sagged, and she lowered her glass down by her thigh. "Grace..."

I aimed the rim of my glass at her, slowly shaking my head with a warning. "Don't. I refuse to be sad."

Monica blinked and forced a fake smile. "I was just going to ask if we can close the windows. It's freezing in here."

God bless her.

In the six months since Clay had dropped the bombshell on our breakfast table in the form of a positive pregnancy test sealed in a sandwich baggie, I'd cycled through a *lot* of emotions. Hatred. Betrayal. Devastation. How could he have done this to us? To *me*? Seven years, and he threw us away. Threw *me* away.

But resentment was the reigning feeling as of late, especially since I was practically toeing the poverty line. The divorce settlement barely covered the cost of renovating my new home—the tiny apartment above my couture children's boutique, Sparkled Pink. And I'd blown my entire life savings on one failed round of

IVF. Now Dr. Vagina had the baby *and* my house. Where was the justice in any of that?

"Who wants cake?" Zoey's question snapped me back to the present, and I realized despite Monica's attempt to change the subject, angry tears had pooled in my eyes. I quickly blinked them away before they spilled.

Lucy raised her camera. "Let me get a picture before you cut into it."

"Why? What does it say?" I asked.

Lucy snapped a photo, then turned the cake around for me to see. I read the bright pink icing out loud, "Better to have loved and lost...than to be stuck with an asshole." I laughed, just what I needed. "Amen to that. You guys are the best."

Zoey picked up a knife. "Who wants a slice?"

"Me!" Lucy said.

"Me too," Olivia echoed.

"Me three." I put my glass down on the counter. "I need something to soak up all the booze."

Monica went to where she knew I kept the plates in the cabinet.

Lucy fanned her face with the photo to help the picture develop. "Aside from the Easter egg hunt from hell, what's on the agenda this evening?"

Monica handed the plates to Zoey and retrieved a knife from the drawer in the island. "Yeah. Did you say you need to move some more stuff? What's left of yours? You haven't lived here in months."

I sat down beside Lucy. "A box of old college basketball trophies I forgot in the attic and the rest of the stuff I got in the divorce. The record player and the vinyl collection. The KitchenAid mixer and the velvet Elvis. They're really the only material objects in this den of sin worth fighting for."

"Not the velvet Elvis," Monica said with a laugh.

"Always the velvet Elvis." I smiled and put my hand on Lucy's. "I really just wanted you guys here for moral support."

Lucy smiled. "You've certainly got that."

"Thanks. I know I do." I pointed toward the back door. "I also really want to move the pergola. Think I could strap it to the roof of my car?"

"Jesus, Grace, do you want to go to jail?" Monica asked.

I rolled my eyes. "You're so dramatic. They don't send people to jail for moving pergolas."

"They will when it breaks loose on I-440 and kills a pedestrian!"

"West says we can borrow his truck if you need to move anything big." Lucy's cheeks flushed at the mention of her new boyfriend's name.

"That's really sweet. Thanks, Lucy," I said.

Monica leaned over the bar toward me. "You need to leave the pergola here. I know you love it, but you don't have a yard at your apartment, remember?"

I sighed. "You're right."

"Grace, have you moved into your new place yet?" Olivia asked.

"Last week, actually. It's small, but I like it."

"She really likes not living with her parents anymore," Monica added.

"Definitely. I appreciate them letting me stay for a while, but it's nice to be back in a home that's mine. And it's even nicer to only have to walk downstairs to go to work."

"I bet," Olivia said. "I keep thinking about doing the same thing at the restaurant, but I'd have to buy the building first."

Olivia owned one of our favorite restaurants in East Nashville, a trendy farm-to-table place called Lettuce Eat. The names of her menu items were as creative as the food. My go-to dish lately was the smoked salmon with honey-glazed butternut squash. Or as she called it, Sofishticated.

"Check the zoning laws before you build above the restaurant," I warned. "We had to get a special permit."

"Good to know. So you own your building, then?" Olivia asked.

"Sort of." I looked up as Zoey put a piece of chocolate cake down in front of me. "Thanks, Zo."

"You're welcome, Grace."

I picked up a fork. "My parents own that section of the building. Mom ran a bridal salon out of it before she retired. I'll inherit it someday, but for now, they rent it to me for far less than it's worth."

And I could hardly pay that.

Olivia looked impressed as she picked up a slice of cake. "That's nice."

"It is. Trust me, I know how fortunate I am."

"I need to stop by and see your shop," Lucy said.

Olivia narrowed her eyes. "Why? You're not thinking about babies already, are you?"

"Noooo," Lucy said, dramatically drawing out the word. "Grace is my friend, and I want to be supportive."

Olivia looked at me. "She's thinking about babies."

I groaned and reached for the champagne bottle again. "Ugh."

"No." Monica snatched the bottle out of my reach. "You've got to drive home sooner or later, and we have practice tomorrow."

I frowned, but I knew she was right.

"Your first practice without me and The Prodigy," Zoey said, smiling at Olivia.

"You can really stop calling me that. The Prodigy wouldn't have been my derby name even if I was playing." Olivia took the champagne and refilled her glass. "And Zoey, you'll make the team on your next go round. We all know you will."

"That's true," I agreed.

Zoey smiled. "I know I'll make it eventually. I won't quit."

I glared at Olivia. "Like *some people*."

She shrugged. "I was there to help Lucy. She made the team, so mission accomplished."

"We'll really miss skating with you," Monica said.

Lucy wilted in her seat. "Seriously miss you."

"It's not like I won't be involved with the team. You guys will see me at the awards thing next month," Olivia said.

My head tilted. "The what?"

"Oh! I forgot to tell you." Monica slapped her own forehead. "The Slammy Awards has been scheduled for the first weekend of December. Shamrocker told me to tell you we are invited."

"What are the Slammy Awards?" I asked.

"It's the team's annual awards-night celebration," Zoey said.

Monica nodded. "There was a post about it on the app, and I asked Shamrocker if it was open to us newbies too."

"We have an app?" This was all news to me, but to be fair, I'd been so consumed with the finalization of my divorce that I was lucky to have passed my basic-skills test.

"I just found out about the awards this week too," Lucy added.

"Are you and West going?"

"Yeah. They do some sort of appreciation thing for all the team sponsors." Lucy's new boyfriend, West Adler, was one of the biggest donors for our team. To say it had caused some drama when they started dating was an understatement.

I wrinkled my nose. "It's a couples' thing?"

Monica put her hand on my arm. "If you go, I'll tell Derek to stay at home."

"Aww, Monica." I formed my fingers into the shape of a

heart. "Thank you, but Derek should be there. He's sacrificed a lot of time with you for the sake of the sport. It's only right to let him have some fun with it too."

"Are you sure?"

"Positive." I cut another bite of cake with the side of my fork. "Besides, who knows? Maybe I'll ditch my therapist's advice and find myself a date."

Monica smiled. "That's my girl."

"I'll be there too," Zoey added with a bright smile. "I'm volunteering as an NSO, non-skating official, until the next round of Fresh Meat. And they invited all the volunteers."

Lucy clapped her hands. "Yay! The whole group together at derby again."

"Here, here," Olivia said, holding up her glass.

"So you and Styx are good?" I pointed my fork at Olivia. "Things looked a little tense with you two at the Monster's Brawl."

She shrugged. "We're OK now, I think. I got a little too excited that night about seeing an old friend of mine—Hale Damage, your coach for the B-team, the Rising Rollers."

"You know Hale Damage?" Zoey asked, surprised.

"We went to college together, but we lost touch. I heard she played a while ago, but I didn't know she was still there."

"It didn't come up with you and Styx?" Monica asked. "You've been seeing her for weeks."

Lucy grinned over a bite of cake. "She and Styx haven't done a lot of talking since they've been together."

Olivia pointed at her. "You're one to talk, Ms. Screwing-Around-with-a-Team-Sponsor."

Lucy's cheeks flushed again. "Yeah."

"And yes, we did talk about Styx's friend *Hale Damage*"—Olivia said with extra emphasis—"but I didn't know what Haley's derby name was. And she wasn't at any of the practices when I was there."

"She travels a lot with her job," Zoey said.

"I know that now." Olivia turned back to me. "Anyway, Haley and I have some *history*, and it didn't go over very well with Styx. We're working through it though."

"Look at you. Not even on the team and still causing shit." I playfully shoved Olivia's arm, but it threw me off-balance on my chair instead. I caught the edge of the countertop and laughed. "Whoa. Yeah, no more booze for me."

Bodhi scratched the back door, and I moved carefully off my stool and across the room to let him back inside. "Good boy," I said, scratching his ear as he trotted through the door.

"Weren't you guys fighting over the dog in the divorce?" Lucy asked. "Who won?"

I scowled and sat cross-legged on the floor with Bodhi. "Clay did." I patted the hardwood and Bodhi flopped down beside me. "Word of advice, if you ever want to have dual ownership of something, don't give it as a gift for a birthday or a holiday. Bodhi was a birthday present."

"Oh, I'm sorry, Grace," Zoey said.

Monica nudged her with her elbow. "Yeah, but Grace's anniversary diamond was also a gift. A two-carat gift."

I raked my nails through Bodhi's fluffy golden fur. "I'd rather have my dog, even if I did sell the ring to pay off my car." I kissed the top of his head and tears threatened to spill again.

"Enough sadness already!" Olivia theatrically gripped the sides of her head. "Geez. I'm going to slit my own wrists over here!"

I cracked a smile and the tingling of my tear ducts faded.

"She's right." Monica walked over and stood in front of me. "No more tears tonight." She reached down, grabbed both my arms, and hauled me up to my feet. "Come on. This is a party.

Let's celebrate by hiding these damn eggs all over the cheating bastard's house and praying for maggots!"

———

Two hours later, there were twelve hard-boiled eggs stashed ingeniously around the house. Two were sewn inside the frame of the sofa. One was hidden in the pillow headrest of Clay's recliner. Two were behind the drawers inside his desk. One was carefully placed inside each of the four hollow wooden legs of our farmhouse bed. One was in the mattress. And the remaining two were brilliantly hidden by Monica inside the hollow decorative balls that capped the ends of the curtain rod.

Olivia had marked each egg with a letter. And someday, if Clay ever found them all, he'd be able to spell out exactly what we all called him many times during our malevolent game of egg-hunt revenge. A twelve-letter name that rhymes with Mother Trucker.

The only time I cried was saying goodbye to Bodhi. As I crouched and hugged him at the door, I lost it when he laid his snout across my shoulder. "I'm so sorry. I don't want to leave you here with that awful man."

Monica reached down and gently took my arm. "It's going to be all right, Grace. You've got to let him go."

When I stood, I realized all the girls were teary-eyed as well. Zoey was flat-out crying for me. I dried my eyes on my sleeve and sniffed back painful sobs. We walked outside, and Bodhi whimpered as I closed the door behind us.

I froze and shook my head. "No. Screw this."

Throwing the door open again, I marched back inside. Bodhi jumped up and down like I'd been gone a year.

"Grace?" Monica asked cautiously.

"Someone come help me grab his bowls!" I called out.

"Yes!" Olivia cheered. "I'm coming!" She and Lucy ran in after me as I grabbed Bodhi's leash and a few toys from the laundry room.

"Come on, boy." I snapped the leash to his collar, and he trotted outside beside me.

Zoey's wet, red eyes were now wide and frightful as I led my dog to the car. "Is this a good idea?"

I laughed as I opened the door to the back seat and Bodhi jumped in beside the record player. "Are you kidding? This is the best idea I've ever had."

She looked down the street like the cops might already be on their way to haul us all downtown.

Olivia handed me the dog's bowls, and Lucy was behind her with both arms wrapped around a giant bag of all-natural, no-additives dog food. My choice, not Clay's.

"Thank you," I said, putting the bowls and food in the passenger's seat up front.

"Are you sure about this?" Monica asked hesitantly as I straightened out of the car.

I took a deep breath and held it for a second. "You know, I've slept alone for the past six months. Completely not by my choice. That stops now. Even if only for tonight."

"Clay's going to be pissed."

I smiled up at the star-speckled sky. "I hope he is."

TWO

ALL HELL WAS ABOUT to break loose.

That was evident from the buzzer sounding through my apartment, ripping me from the shallow dreams I'd just drifted off to. I rolled over and grabbed my phone. It was 12:47 a.m., and there were three missed calls and five text messages.

Very funny. Bring Bodhi back now.

What were you thinking?

You know what the judge said.

Are you going to make me call the cops???

Damn it, Grace.

All from Clay.

Someone pounded on the door downstairs.

I groaned and pushed myself up. My head throbbed. Definitely too much wine. Bodhi barked and darted off the bed, his back paws sliding with the comforter. He nearly face-planted on the floor, but he recovered and scrambled out of the room.

As I trudged across the room, I grabbed the short, fuzzy pink bathrobe hanging on the door to my bathroom. There was no way in hell I was about to confront my demon ex wearing a see-through tank top.

I crept to my front window to see exactly what I was in for. Was it just Clay or was Dr. Vagina and the swollen uterus in tow as well?

"Shit."

It was the cops. A white and blue Metro patrol car sat at the curb in front of my store downstairs. The rest of Twenty-First Avenue looked mostly empty.

"Shit. Shit. Shit." I was wringing my hands as I shuffled in my socks back to the foyer. I pressed the button on the wall for the call box to the front door downstairs. "Hello?"

"Grace, it's Jason. Open the door."

My head snapped back. Jason Bradley was Clay's best friend and old roommate from college. "Clay called *you*?"

"Would you rather him call the station? Let me in."

"Are you here to arrest me?"

"Of course not."

With a groan, I pressed the button to unlock the outside door. There was another loud buzz and then heavy footsteps on my stairs. He knocked, and I bent to grab Bodhi's collar with one hand as I pulled open the door with the other. When I looked up, I froze.

I'd rarely ever seen Jason in his black uniform, and I hadn't seen him *at all* in well over a year. Since before the separation and before Clay's schedule got so busy juggling a job, a wife, *and* a mistress.

As I straightened, I gathered the neckline of my robe that was gaping in the front. "What are you doing here?"

His brow crumpled, and he folded his thick arms over his plated chest. "You know what I'm doing here. And you're lucky it's me and not someone else. Clay's really pissed."

"Good! That was kind of the idea."

"Grace, it's in the divorce decree. He could legally press charges."

I rolled my eyes. "You and I both know he doesn't have the balls for that. If he did, he'd have to explain to even more people what he did to me."

Jason's mouth twitched like he wanted to say something but thought better of it. Instead, he reached down and scratched Bodhi behind the ears. The dog's tail whipped from side to side so violently I worried he might dislocate a hip.

"How'd you get involved in this anyway?" I asked.

"Clay called me wanting advice. He said Ginny—"

"Dr. Vagina," I corrected.

His mouth twitched again. "She wanted to have you arrested."

"No surprise there."

"They could have, you know? Like it or not, Bodhi belongs to Clay now. This is theft."

"Are you going to take him?" I asked, emotion rising in my throat.

Jason's face softened. "No. I told Clay I'd talk to you, and for him to come get Bodhi in the morning. Try not to make a big deal out of it."

"But this *is* a big deal. You know it is."

"Just don't make this worse for yourself, Grace. Please."

Nausea churned in my stomach. Maybe it was the wine, but I doubted it.

"Sorry you have to be involved in this mess, Jason."

He stopped petting Bodhi. "I'm sorry you've had to go through it. You didn't deserve any of this."

I knew that already, but it was nice to hear it from someone in Clay's camp. Before I could thank him, Bodhi took off through the space between Jason's legs and the front door frame.

I sighed. "He thinks it's time to go out and potty." Bodhi's heavy paws thudded down the hollow stairs in the hall.

"I can take him out if you want," he offered.

"Thanks, but I can do it. You've handled enough of our shit tonight."

He cracked a grin, and I stuffed my feet into the fuzzy UGG boots sitting in the foyer. I grabbed Bodhi's leash off the hook on the wall, then followed Jason out into the hall. Bodhi was whining at the bottom of the stairs as I closed the door behind us.

"I guess it would be pretty dumb to ask how you've been," he said.

"I'm better now than I was. Honestly, I'm just glad it's over. It's been a long year. How are you? I don't think I've seen you since..."

"Clay's birthday trip to Tahoe."

"Has it been that long?"

"A year and half."

I hooked the leash to Bodhi's collar before pushing the downstairs door open. Just as the cold air hit my bare legs, I straightened and patted the empty pockets of my robe. "Oh no."

"What's the matter?"

I looked up the steps. "I think I just locked myself out of my apartment."

Dragging Bodhi behind me, I jogged back up. Sure enough, the knob lock was engaged. I thumped my forehead against the door.

When I turned back to look down the stairs, Jason was biting down on the insides of his lips to keep from laughing.

I trudged back down. "Don't say a word."

"I wouldn't dare." But he did crack a grin.

Bodhi barked and scratched at the door. Jason pulled it open for us, and the biting cold air blew through the slit in my robe. "Is it safe to close this door? I'd hate for you to be trapped on the street."

"It's fine. I can open that one with the code. Good grief, why didn't I get a coat?"

"Or your keys."

I shoved his arm.

"Think we can jimmy the other lock with a credit card?" he asked.

I blinked. "Breaking and entering advice from the police?"

"It's worth a try."

"My dad installed one of those you can't easily open."

"Does Clay have a key? Should I call him?"

"Hell no! I'd rather lose my face to frostbite and die of hypothermia."

He chuckled and unclipped his phone from his utility belt. "How about a locksmith?"

"If I can borrow your phone, I'll call my dad. He can be here in about five minutes without traffic." Jason handed me the phone as Bodhi dragged me around the side of the building to the only patch of grass in three blocks. I dialed my parents' house phone. They'd had the same phone number as long as I could remember.

Confused and groggy, Mom answered after a few rings. "Hello?"

"Mom, it's Grace."

"Grace, honey, is everything OK?"

"Yes, I'm fine. Just stupid. I'm sorry to wake you, but I've locked myself out of my apartment. Think Dad could come let me in?"

The speaker crackled with static as Mom obviously held her hand over the microphone. After that, her voice sounded a lot like the teacher from a *Peanuts* cartoon. I couldn't understand her. "*Wah wah, wah wah wah. Wah, wah wah wah. Wah wah.*"

Bodhi squatted, and his paws teetered as he pooped beside

the fire hydrant. I grimaced toward Jason, who was now leaning against his patrol car, watching with amusement. "I don't have any bags. Are you going to arrest me if I don't pick that up?"

He grinned wider. "I'm considering it."

"Who are you talking to?" my mother asked in my ear.

"Jason Bradley."

"Who?"

"He's a police officer."

"A police officer?" Her voice jumped up an octave.

"Calm down. He's here to help. And he's an old friend from college. I'm safe and, so far, not under arrest."

Jason laughed.

Mom sighed with relief. "Thank God. Your father's getting dressed. He'll be there soon."

"Thanks, Mom. Sorry again for waking you up."

"It's OK, honey. Accidents happen. How did you lock yourself out in the middle of the night?"

"Bodhi needed to go out, and I shut the door behind me without grabbing my keys." I left out the part about how I'd stolen my dog and we were awakened by the police. "Try to go back to sleep, Mom. I'll talk to you tomorrow."

"All right. I love you, Grace."

"I love you too." I disconnected the call about the time Bodhi was wiping his paws on the grass. "Dad's coming." Bodhi and I walked back to the sidewalk in front of my building.

Jason motioned me over. "Come on. My car's warm," he said as I handed him his phone.

"That's OK. I don't want to leave Bodhi out in the cold."

Jason opened the back door of the cruiser. "Then I guess I'll have to detain him for defecating in public." He clicked his tongue. "Come on, Bodhi."

I released the leash, and my dog happily bounded into the back seat of the car. When he closed the door, I laughed, looking at my dog under arrest. "I wish I had my phone. That deserves a picture."

"I've got this." He tapped his phone's screen a few times and snapped a picture just as Bodhi licked the back window. Jason turned the screen around to show me the image. It was hilarious. "I'll send it to you. What's your phone number?"

I rattled off the digits, and he tapped them into his phone. When he finished sending the picture, he walked around and opened the passenger-side door. I followed. He leaned inside, pushed a mounted laptop out of the way, and picked up the Red Bull cans from the seat. "Sorry it's kind of a mess."

"It's perfect. Thank you," I said, sitting down.

He closed the door and walked around to get in behind the wheel. When he closed the door behind him, he slid open the window in the safety glass that barricaded the back seat. Bodhi immediately stuck his wet snout through it.

"I'm sorry. Again. You must think I'm totally ridiculous. What kind of idiot locks themself out on the street?"

"I've seen worse. Got a call once about a girl who'd locked herself out on her apartment's balcony wearing only a towel. It was snowing."

"Why was she in a towel?"

"I think she was getting out of the shower when her phone rang. She didn't have good cell service in her apartment and went outside to answer it."

I laughed as I looked around the car. There were more buttons and gadgets than I could count. "This is like being inside a spaceship. I wish you could turn on the lights and siren."

"I don't think the neighbors would appreciate that. You've never been inside a patrol car before?"

"Never. I haven't exactly lived a life of crime. I've never even had a speeding ticket."

He jerked his thumb over his shoulder. "What about Bodhi? How's his criminal record these days?"

Bodhi licked the side of Jason's face.

I laughed. "I almost forgot about that? Did Clay tell you?"

"Yeah. He dug up a flower bed, right?"

"Mrs. Livingston's begonias next door. Twelve plants. He was covered in all sorts of evidence. Flower petals and dirt all over his face and paws."

"She really called the cops?"

I nodded. "To be fair, it wasn't the first time he'd done it. We put up a privacy fence after that. How's Brady?"

His face fell. "I had to put him down in the spring. He had lymphoma, and treatment didn't work."

"Jason, I had no idea."

"You guys have had a lot going on this year."

"Does Clay know?"

He laughed, but there was no joy in it. "Honestly, I have no idea. I told him, but I think it went right over his head."

If Brady had died in the spring, Clay would have been *very* preoccupied.

"I'm really sorry. Brady was the best dog ever."

He looked out his side window. "Yeah. What about you? How's the shop?"

"It's frilly."

"Looks like it. Lots of ribbons and shit, from the looks of it. Is it going well?"

My head bobbed from side to side. "It's still open, which some days is quite the miracle. I'm hoping it picks up around the holidays."

"You make all that stuff yourself?"

"A lot of it. The dresses for sure."

"Do you enjoy it?"

I sighed. "I enjoy the process. Not so much the product anymore."

Jason didn't comment. He didn't have to. I was sure he was well-aware of my struggle to conceive.

"Ever think of making other stuff? Everybody needs clothes, not just kids, right?"

"I've thought about it, but I don't know what I'd do. And I've invested so much to make this place what it is, it'd be really expensive to change it."

"I hear ya. I just remodeled my house. It was crazy expensive."

"Are you still in Crieve Hall?"

"Yep. Still taking care of Mom."

"How is she?"

He shrugged. "Same old, same old."

Our senior year of college, Jason's mother had been beaten almost to death by his stepfather. We'd all known there had been abuse, but not that it was so severe until that night.

His mother was in a coma for three weeks and was completely unresponsive for over two months. Her head had been bashed repeatedly into the family's stone fireplace. She would never regain the ability to walk or fully speak. And as far as I knew, his stepdad was still in prison for attempted murder.

Jason had given up a baseball scholarship to drop out and take care of her full-time. He became a police officer instead of pursuing a very real shot at the major league. It was hard to believe that was a decade ago.

"How long has it been since you've talked to Clay?" I asked.

He thought for a moment. "Before tonight, he texted me to let me know about the divorce when he first filed. I offered to take him out for a beer and never heard back."

"Typical."

Again, Jason kept his mouth shut.

"Did you know?"

He shook his head. "I kinda suspected something might be up, but he denied it when I asked. Then it blew up really quickly after that. I don't think they were together *together* for very long before you found out."

"He says they weren't, but he *says* a lot of things."

"If I had known, I would've told you."

Sure, he would've. I was internally rolling my eyes.

"What else have you been up to?" He was obviously ready to steer the conversation away from his best friend. Bros before hoes, and all that.

"I play roller derby now," I said.

He turned toward me in his seat. "No shit?"

I nodded. "For the Music City Rollers. Have you heard of them?"

"I've worked security at a few of their games. Those chicks are intense. I didn't know you had it in you."

"Me either. A lot has changed over the years."

"You can say that again."

We exchanged gossip on all the mutual people we'd known over the years until Jason's eye darted to the rearview mirror. "There's a truck pulling up behind me. Your dad?"

I turned in my seat to look just as my father shut off his headlights. "Yeah, that's him."

Dad was dressed in blue striped pajama pants, loafer shoes, and a winter coat when I met him on the curb. Jason opened the back door and grabbed Bodhi's leash before he jumped out.

"Thanks, Daddy."

"Are you OK?" he asked, looking at the police cruiser.

"I'm fine. You remember Clay's friend, Jason Bradley, right? He was in our wedding."

Dad stretched out his hand toward Jason. "Of course. Good to see you again, Officer Bradley."

Jason smiled at me as he shook it. "You too, sir."

"Are you on duty tonight?" Dad asked.

"Yes, sir. I was in the area when Grace locked herself outside."

Dad's eyes narrowed. He obviously wasn't buying the story. "Well, she's very fortunate you were here."

Jason handed me Bodhi's leash.

"Grace, what's Bodhi doing here?" Dad asked.

Jason and I exchanged a glance. "He's just visiting. Clay's coming to pick him up tomorrow."

"Today," Jason said, looking down at his tactical watch.

Dad cocked an eyebrow. "Grace, did you steal the dog?"

I didn't answer.

Dad sighed and shook his head. "Thanks for not hauling her off to the slammer, officer."

Jason chuckled. "I wouldn't dream of it."

With a yawn, Dad turned and walked to the door. "Is it the inside or outside door you're locked out of?"

"Inside."

"All right. Thanks again, Jason."

"You're welcome, sir."

When Dad had gone inside, I smiled up at Jason. "Again, I'm really sorry you got dragged into this."

"Don't worry about it. I'll check in with you tomorrow."

"That's really not necessary. I've inconvenienced you enough."

"It's no trouble. I can even come in the morning for the exchange if you're at all worried about it."

"I'm not afraid of Clay. It'll be fine. Unless you feel like just arresting him for being a total assworm."

Jason laughed. "I wonder what the ten code for that would be." He bent and scratched Bodhi behind the ears. "It's good to see you again, Bodhi."

It was evident from the tail wagging that the feeling was mutual.

Jason straightened and opened his arms for a hug. I stepped into the embrace and awkwardly smushed myself against his body armor. "Take care of yourself, Grace."

"You too, Jason. Tell your mother I said hello."

"Will do."

I stepped back but not before noting that he smelled like alpine aftershave and peppermint.

He waved before turning back to his patrol car. I stood there with Bodhi until he pulled away from the curb. And as he did, Jason flipped on the flashing blue lights.

I smiled.

———

ENNNGGGG! ENNNGGGG! ENNNGGGGGGGGGGG!

The front-door buzzer was like a warning bell just a few short hours later, but it was worth it though to wake up with Bodhi's wet nose on the pillow beside me. For the first time in months, I hadn't slept alone. And it was glorious.

Bodhi started to spring from the bed, but I rolled over and curled my arm around his fluffy neck. He whimpered and wriggled, wanting desperately to run to the door.

ENNNGGGG! ENNNGGGG!

With a groan, I released my dog and he bounded off the bed.

Clay banged on the door downstairs.

I took my sweet time. Brushed my teeth. Pulled my hair up in a pile on top of my head. Put on a bra. Then I started a cup of coffee in the Keurig before inching my way to the intercom on the wall.

My finger was almost on the buzzer to let Clay into the building when he yelled outside. "Grace, open the door!"

Hmm. I turned and walked back to my bedroom where I carefully, and slowly, chose a Music City Rollers hoodie to put over my tank top. My cellphone was ringing on my nightstand, and his hateful voice was echoing off the brick outside.

"Grace! I know you're in there! Your car's in the lot!"

I finally walked back to the call box and pressed the button. "Hello? May I help you?"

"Let me in the damn building!"

"Who is this?"

Clay swore.

I laughed and pressed the button to release the lock on the front door. His angry feet pounded up the stairs to my apartment. When I finally opened the door, Clay was red faced from the cold and probably his fury. He was wearing the gray peacoat I'd bought him for Christmas and the shoes I'd gotten on sale at Off Broadway. His dirty blond hair needed to be cut and was beginning to curl around his collar.

"Good morning, douchewaffle." Bodhi darted between my legs and the door and pummeled Clay's chest with both paws.

He pushed our dog down without so much as a hello. "Ginny said I should've called the police and let them deal with this."

I shrugged. "You *did* call the police."

"I could have had Jason arrest you."

"You should have. I'd much rather be in jail than looking at your stupid face right now."

"I mean it, Grace."

"Trust me, I do too." I leaned against the door. "Tell me, Clayton, how long did it take you to realize he wasn't home? We were gone for hours before you started calling."

He snapped a leash onto Bodhi's collar. "I was trying to calm down before I decided how to handle it. So you're welcome."

"How did you know he didn't run away? Or that he wasn't dognapped?"

Clay's hazel eyes narrowed, and an angry vein throbbed in his forehead. "Really? A dognapper who takes his food bowl and his rubber chicken?"

"Yes. You couldn't have been sure."

"Shut up, Grace."

I stormed out of the apartment with my finger aimed right at his eyeballs. "Tell me to shut up one more time."

He caught my wrist. "If you pull this dognapping shit again, I'm going to press charges. Do you understand?"

I wanted to punch him. It would feel *so* good to slam my fist into his infuriatingly handsome face. Mess it all up for the home wrecker no doubt asleep in my egg-infested bed.

"Say goodbye to Grace, Bodhi."

With a huff, I took a knee beside my dog. I hugged his neck and kissed his scruffy face. "It's OK if you pee on their stuff when they're at work," I whispered loud enough for Clay to hear as I scratched behind both of Bodhi's ears one more time. "I love you."

Clay tugged the leash toward the stairs. "Come on. Let's go home."

"You need to get his stuff!"

"I'll buy new stuff."

"At least take his chicken—"

"Goodbye, Grace."

I glared at his back, then slammed the door. "I hope we're doing hits at practice today."

THREE

"I'M JUDGING from your glower that the exchange with Clayton didn't go so well this morning." Monica was approaching my car when I got out at roller derby practice later that morning.

"He actually called the police on me."

Her eyes doubled. "Really?"

"Yeah, but it was a friend of ours we've known for years. He just told me to give the dog back this morning. It was so worth it though." I opened the trunk and lifted out the heavy skates' bag before slamming the trunk's lid with a little more force than necessary. "Clay was such an ass this morning. I thought about hip checking him right off the staircase."

"I'm sorry."

I sighed and fell into step beside her as we crossed the parking lot to the Music City Rollers' Sweatshop, the practice space for our team. "I wish someone had told me all those months ago to prepare for the waves that come with a divorce. Just when you think you're over it, you sign the papers and get sucked into the undertow all over again."

She linked her arm through mine. "I'm here for whatever you need."

I smiled at her. "On a brighter note, look at this." I pulled out my phone and showed her the picture Jason took of Bodhi in the back seat of his car.

Her head fell to the side. "Why is the dog under arrest?"

"Pooping in public."

"What?"

"It was a joke. I actually locked myself out of my apartment, and Jason let us wait for my dad in his car."

"Who's Jason?"

"Our friend, the cop. Really nice guy."

The hinges of the heavy metal door creaked as Monica pulled it open. Inside, the room was loud with chatter echoing off the concrete walls and floor. Our teammates were seated in the bleachers rather than gearing up for practice. I looked at Monica. "What's going on?"

"Britches Get Stitches, over here!" someone shouted.

Monica tapped my arm.

"Oh, that's me." I looked around. Shamrocker, one of our Fresh Meat coaches, was waving from a folding table piled with bundled shirts. Her pixie cut was dyed a pale blue, and she wore a unicorn T-shirt. Monica and I walked over. "Sorry, the derby-name thing is going to take a while to get used to."

"I feel ya, girl." She handed me a stack of black-and-teal tank tops. "Britches Get Stitches, number 6-ft-2. Correct?"

"Yeah. What are these?"

She smiled up at me. "Your practice jerseys. Welcome to the team."

"Practice jerseys? Should I change?"

"Not unless you want to. They're for scrimmages," she said.

I held the shirts to my chest. "I kinda want to wear it now."

Shamrocker laughed. "By all means then."

"When do we get our bout-day jerseys?" Monica asked.

"We'll order those in January to be here for the preseason doubleheader in late February."

"Thanks, Shamrocker."

She winked.

"Come on." Monica nudged me forward. "Lucy is saving us seats."

Lucy held up her jersey as we approached. The back of it read: Lights Out Lucy, #LoL. "Isn't this great? It finally feels official."

Monica held hers up by the collar displaying her derby name and *actual* name, Dr. Hooker, $100. I pointed to it. "You were smart, Monica. You're going to know when people are calling your name."

"Smart? My legal name is Dr. Hooker. I changed my name voluntarily when I got married. There's nothing smart about that."

I laughed as we sat down on the left side of Lucy. "Valid point. Speaking of, I have some very important marriage advice for you, Lucy."

Monica frowned and rolled her eyes. "Excellent. Advice from the week-old divorcée to the girl in a week-old relationship."

"This is important, and you would tell her the same thing," I said.

She lifted an eyebrow.

I looked at Lucy. "Don't change your name when you get married."

"Oh!" Monica put her hand on my arm and leaned across me. "For sure, listen to that advice. Especially if you marry a guy named Hooker."

We all laughed.

"West's last name is Adler." Lucy blushed. "Not that I'm thinking about marriage or anything."

"Whatever his name is, legally changing your name is a pain the ass. I thought it was bad the first time, but changing my name back this week was even worse."

"You took your maiden name back?" Lucy asked.

"Yep. I'm Grace Evans once again."

"How does that feel?" Monica asked.

I groaned. "It feels like a lot of paperwork."

The girls giggled.

"What happened with the dog last night?" Lucy asked.

Monica leaned forward to look across me. "Grace almost went to jail."

"Really?"

I rolled my eyes. "No. Not really."

Someone up front whistled, saving me from the awkward conversation. It was Midnight Maven, the only one in the room already on her skates. It was obvious from the sweat glistening on her chiseled abs that she'd been hard at work already that morning. We were all slackers by comparison to her and the skaters standing next to her: our former team captain, Medusa, and Susan, the league president.

Maven cupped her hands around her mouth and yelled. "Listen up, bitches!" The room instantly fell silent. "We've got some housekeeping business this morning before we start practice, so the sooner you all shut up and pay attention, the sooner we can get geared up and out on the track."

God, I loved Maven. Hated her sometimes too, but only when it was her turn to lead our workouts. Maven had a thing for burpees. Reason enough to occasionally hate anyone.

She turned toward Susan. "Madam President."

Susan stepped forward. "Good morning, everyone. For those of you who are new, typically, our monthly league meeting is held on Monday night in the auditorium at MacKay University." She lowered her voice and smiled. "Because they have cushioned seats."

"And they a have a bar next door," Medusa added.

Everyone laughed.

"But we were notified yesterday that someone tripped the sprinkler system in the auditorium. That means we won't have our meeting space while they repair the damage. So we've decided to have an abbreviated meeting this morning and recon-vene as scheduled in December.

"If this is your first league meeting, this is when we handle all the business for the team. As president, I preside over the meet-ings. I'll try to make this as quick as possible. I know everyone here is anxious to run some suicides with Maven."

Everyone laughed. Someone behind me made a puking sound.

Susan continued. "Our first order of business is for me to introduce you to our new team captain." She gestured toward the front row of the bleachers. "Everybody, give it up for Riveter Styx!"

Monica, Lucy, and I exchanged a surprised smile. "Did you know?" I asked Lucy. Since she lived with Olivia, Styx's current girlfriend, Lucy should've known if any of us did.

"I had no idea." She made a sour face. "Things with the two of them have been a little tenser than Olivia let on last night."

Styx stood up in front of the group. Her short dark hair was freshly cut, spiked in the back, long in the front. Her bangs had bright red streaks and were tucked behind her left ear. She wore black booty shorts and had a large tattoo on her thigh of a skull formed out of black roses. Styx's cheeks looked a little pink while we clapped with the rest of the room.

She waved and everyone began to quiet down. "Thanks, everyone. I'm honored to have been voted in. I certainly have big skates to fill." She flashed a smile over at Medusa.

"Bet your ass you do," Medusa said with a wink.

Styx laughed and turned back to all of us. "I'm really honored to have been elected. I'll do my very best for you guys this season."

Everyone cheered.

"We know you're going to be amazing," Susan said as Styx returned to her seat. "Now, we have some other skaters to recognize today. All of us on the board of directors have agreed, we've just seen one of the best Fresh Meat groups come through training. We're so excited to have you all as part of this league. So if you just passed your skills test and this is your first practice as a team member, please stand up!"

Monica and I stood, and I pulled Lucy up by her arm. The other newbies popped up on the benches around us: Roxsee Rolls, 5 Scar Jeneral, Electra Cal, Goldie Knocks, and Slugs Bunny. It was a little sad I had an easier time remembering their names than my own when it was called.

All the veteran skaters around us were clapping. Medusa gave a loud, "Woohoo!"

Not gonna lie, my chest puffed out a little. We'd busted our asses (literally, a few times) to make the team, and it felt amazing to stand there among these women I'd admired so many times from the grandstands.

I gave a little wave and sank back onto my seat.

When the room settled back down, Susan continued. "For all you newbies, each team member is required to serve on a committee or hold a position on the board, so I'm going to run through all the available committees where you can get plugged in. Committee leaders, when I call your name, please stand up so they know who you are."

She looked down at the paper in her hand. "If you'd like to be involved on the marketing committee, please see our marketing coordinator, eL's Bells."

A girl with blue hair stood on our right side.

I nudged Lucy with my elbow. "That's your team. You know that, right?"

She smiled. "Of course. I can't wait."

"If you'd like to help out with merchandising, please see Bad News Baroness. If you're interested in event and bout-day coordination, please see our gaming director, Black-Eye Candy. For community outreach, please see Midnight Maven. For recruiting and Fresh Meat training, see Shamrocker. For fundraising and sponsor relations, see Medusa.

"We also have a director's position and a coaching position coming open for the juniors' team now that Full Metal Jackie is retiring. If anyone is interested in those jobs, please talk to me after practice. The sooner you get plugged into a committee, the better, but if you're not involved by the start of the season, you will not be allowed to play on game day. We are a volunteer-run organization, and everyone has to carry their weight."

I looked at Monica. "What are you going to do?"

She just shrugged.

"Now, we've had some good news and some bad news this week," Susan continued. "The good news is the Rising Rollers have been invited to participate in Bleeding Heartland's B-Cup Tournament in Bloomington, Indiana."

Most of the girls clapped. Some of them cheered.

I raised my hand. "What tournament?"

"It's an invitational tournament just for roller derby B-teams. They base their selections on stats from the prior season," Susan said.

Black-Eye Candy turned around in the row in front of us. "It's a lot of fun. The winner wins a golden-bra trophy."

"The tournament is being held very early next year as a preseason kickoff event." Susan looked down at her notes. "It's scheduled for the third weekend of March. Saturday and Sunday.

If you are a Rising Roller and want to be rostered, please let me know after practice."

Looking down the line at Lucy and Monica, they were both nodding with wide smiles.

I pulled out my phone to check my calendar. There was a missed call and a text from my mother. *Just checking to see how you're holding up this week. Call when you can. Maybe we can do lunch? xoxo*

I swiped the message to bring up her text thread. *At practice. Call you later. Love you.*

Then I pulled up my calendar and swiped to the weekend in March for the tournament. No conflicts, as usual.

"Listen up, newbies!" Susan shouted. "The B-Cup Tournament is the fastest way for you to make the chartered team. The All-Stars is our travel team that competes in sanctioned games at the international level. We have a tradition, whenever we're invited to the B-Cup, that the MVP for the Rising Rollers automatically qualifies for a spot on the All-Stars. So this is your chance! Are you ready to work hard and prove that you're ready to skate with the best of the best?"

I responded "Yes!" at the same time Monica said a drawn-out "Nooo." She was shaking her head beside me.

The girls in front of us looked back and laughed.

"Mon?" I asked.

With a horrified look, she gestured toward the front of the room. "You've lost your mind if you think I'm ready to skate with Maven or Medusa."

"I'm with Monica," Lucy agreed quietly. "But you've got a real shot at it, Grace."

We'll see.

"What's the bad news?" someone down front asked.

We all looked up.

Susan sighed. "The Rising Rollers are now officially without a coach until a replacement is found."

Whispers rippled through the room.

"What happened to Hale Damage?" someone else asked.

"Hale Damage resigned for personal reasons," Susan said, keeping her eyes firmly fixed on the paper in front of her.

Monica, Lucy, and I exchanged a knowing glance. The coach resigned because of Olivia and Styx. It was a full-blown roller derby love triangle.

Susan raised her voice over the noise of speculation flying around the room. "We've got some leads on a new coach already, but until we choose a permanent replacement, chartered team members will take turns leading the Rising Rollers. Are there any more questions?"

About twenty hands shot into the air.

Susan frowned. "Any questions that aren't related to the reasons why Hale Damage left?" All hands but one went down. "Doc Carnage?" Susan asked, pointing to her.

"Are you going to be tapping current skaters for the permanent position?" Doc Carnage asked. She was a real-life neurologist.

"We haven't had time to make any decisions, but if you or anyone is interested, come talk to me or any of the other board members when we're done here," Susan said. "Anyone else?"

No one else spoke, so Susan moved on. "On to a happier subject, who's excited about the Slammy Awards?"

The room erupted with excitement.

Susan held up a hand to quiet everyone back down. "The celebration is Friday, December second, at seven o'clock. This year, it will be at The Drunken Nun in East Nashville. Please plan to Uber home or have a designated driver. The Slammy Awards are a lot of fun, but we want everyone to be responsible.

"Another incentive to not overindulge is everyone has to be

up bright and early the next day for the Nashville Christmas Parade. This is a mandatory event for all team members. The juniors will be skating with us, and we'll all be handing out flyers and swag. If you don't have a game-day jersey, please wear a Rollers hoodie or T-shirt."

Monica squealed quietly beside me. "I can't wait for the parade," she whispered.

I smiled and looked back at Susan.

"The final thing we need to discuss is our holiday schedule. Starting the week of Thanksgiving, we won't have Saturday practices again until the new year. Mondays and Wednesdays will continue as scheduled, and you must attend fifty percent of practices each month."

Princess Die, another veteran skater, raised her hand. "Will we scrimmage on Wednesday nights?"

"Yes. Our weekday practice plans will stay the same." Susan pulled her phone out of her pocket and held it up. "You can find all the information on the team app. Newbies, if you don't have the Music City Rollers app, you can download it from any app store. Our password to access the information is NOBALLSRE-QUIRED. All caps. No spaces."

I chuckled as I navigated the app store on my phone. When the app loaded, I entered the hilarious password. There was a section for team news, the schedule, events, a chat message board, and more. I tapped on the button that said "Rising Rollers." A flashing post at the top read, "Welcome to our new skaters: 5 Scar Jeneral, Britches Get Stitches, Electra Cal..."

I smiled.

Suddenly, everyone around me was clapping, and because I'd been distracted by my phone, I had no idea why. I looked up in time to see the league's head coach, The Duchess, entering from the locker room.

She raised her arms in question. "Why are you all still sitting down? Did you come here to talk or to skate?"

Susan grinned. "You heard her, ladies. Gear up and get on the track!"

"The Duchess is leading practice?" I asked no one in particular as we all got up.

"She usually leads at least once a week," Black-Eye Candy answered as we walked down the bleachers. "She took some time off while Medusa was leading practice after nationals."

"How are her practices?" Monica asked. "Are they tough?"

Candy smiled.

"They can't be worse than Medusa's," I said.

Candy's head tilted. "I don't know. Guess you'll find out today."

"Great," Lucy muttered behind me.

By the end of the "warm-up," the trashcan was looking like a probable receptacle of my morning coffee. We started with five laps of skating while doing squats. I was plenty warm enough after those, but it was only the beginning.

Squat-skating was followed by more laps filled with toe-touches (Lucy fell twice), lunges (I may have pulled my groin), and jogging on our skates (Monica tripped over her wheels and crashed into Maven). We did so many laps of "sticky skates" that I lost count, and then did "drunken crossovers" until I actually felt drunk.

Near the end of the drills, Candy skated past me while I was doubled over, gripping my knees, and trying not to vomit on the track. She just grinned. I shot her the bird.

The Duchess blew her godforsaken whistle, then shouted with her gravelly voice, "Who's ready for some endurance trials?"

Oh, the grumbling and murmuring that ignited.

The Duchess laughed. "Just teasing. Get some water and divide up in teams. We scrimmage in ten!"

———

After practice and a quick and healthy lunch with Monica, I drove back through downtown Nashville. It was a trek that grew more difficult with each new day as tourists and transplants flocked to middle Tennessee. I read somewhere that a hundred people a day were moving to Nashville, and judging from the traffic on Twenty-First Avenue, I believed it.

It was a Saturday, for god's sake.

The only upside to the traffic was the ample time motorists would spend staring at the backlit, glittery rose-pink sign above my shop's front window displays. Sparkled Pink, my custom children's clothing boutique, had become my baby when I couldn't have a real one.

The shop began by accident, really. Sure, my mother taught me how to sew before she taught me how to write, and I did have a fancy degree in fashion design from the best program in the Southeast. But neither of those things had been the springboard into the fashion world that I thought they would be. In fact, as many people with fancy degrees would probably attest, I ended up in a completely unrelated field for the better part of a decade: hotel management.

I'd taken a job as a front-desk clerk at the Belle Meade Hotel and Spa my sophomore year of college. About the same time I met Clay at a frat party. The job was only supposed to be temporary to help fund my inevitable move to New York, Paris, or Milan.

Then Clay and I started dating.

Then he proposed.

Then we got married.

Then we bought a house.

Then we wanted to have a baby.

Fashion just never made sense.

Fortunately, even though I hated it, I was good at the hotel business, and my last promotion to Director of Hospitality came with a hefty pay bump and a nice corporate office.

But then Clay started to worry that me being on my feet so much could be counterproductive to trying to conceive. He reasoned that he made enough money so that we really didn't need my income. He said I should just stay home. Start preparing to have a family...

That's right, ladies and gentlemen. I even gave up the safe, shitty job for what my husband went and found with someone else.

Didn't I warn you I was bitter?

Stop. Count to ten. *1...2...4...5...10...* And focus on the positives—like I'd promised my therapist I would do.

One positive was that Sparkled Pink almost started itself. When I left the hotel, I worked part time for my mother at the bridal shop. She was cutting back her hours and taking fewer clients since my dad had retired, so I took over almost everything but the bridal gowns themselves.

In my downtime, I spent a lot of time making dresses for my own little girl, the one I didn't have yet but who was certainly forthcoming.

One day at the shop, a bride's mother saw me working on one of my creations. She asked if she could buy it for her granddaughter. As they say, the rest was history. Mom retired later that year and handed the store's keys to me.

Sparkled Pink carried everything from infant pantyhose to 100 percent couture children's fashion. I carried a few high-end brands that I hand-selected at different fashion shows, but the bread and butter of my store were my custom designs.

The first dress I ever sold was called "The Sophia" because that was the name I was planning to use if Clay and I ever had a girl. More dress designs followed, some named in homage to family members, other names plucked at random from my *Big Book of Baby Names.*

The Sophia.

The Gabrielle.

The Charlotte.

Those dresses and others covered the back wall of my store. And while I kept some of the best sellers in stock, most of the named dresses were custom-made to order.

The process was simple. The customer picked out the design then hand-selected their favorite fabric, lace, and beading. Afterward, we took their measurements and half of the final cost up front. The turnaround time was two-to-six weeks, depending heavily on our workload, the complexity of the dress, and if we had any of the pieces pre-assembled.

Clay always said it was like a build-your-own burrito station for little girls' couture.

Up until my world had so sensationally imploded, I'd loved everything about it. But these days, it was getting harder and harder to work with toddlers and their mommies. Hmm, I wonder why?

But back to the positives...

Even from the street, I could count several heads bobbing through the clothes racks inside my store. That was definitely a good thing. Especially because it was the first of the month, and every bill I had was coming due. That included the property tax invoice, which loomed in the future like doomsday.

(Insert vomiting noise here.)

Property taxes had gone up, up, and up in Hillsboro Village. It was one of the old-school trendy spots in the city, connecting the Vanderbilt University campus and Music Row. My shop and apartment were nestled between A Village of Flowers and The Pancake Pantry, making it the olfactory sweet spot on the block. My store always smelled like heaven.

I parked in the back parking lot in my designated space, then walked around to the trunk and opened it. A smell like rotten cheese puffs smacked me in the face. I shuddered as I reached for my skates' bag. "Definitely time to wash my gear. Gross."

I lugged the bag around the building to the red door that led to my apartment. I needed to check on the shop but not before at least changing my disgusting clothes. Otherwise, no amount of maple syrup and roses wafting through the air would keep the patrons in my store.

Before going up, I stopped at the metal mailbox attached to the wall. Both the store's mail and my personal mail came to the same box. Most of it was junk, except the water bill was due, as was the electricity. Behind them was a menacing envelope stamped with "Final Notice" in thick black ink. I already knew it was an overdue invoice from my fertility doctor. Talk about insult to injury.

I'd hoped the judge would stick Clay with the bill in the divorce.

He didn't.

With a sigh, I shoved the bills into the stinky bag where they belonged. Then I glanced back at the street, to the spot where Jason's car had been cozy and warm the night before.

I can't believe that asshole wanted to have me arrested.

When I finally hauled my bag into my apartment, I was greeted by Bodhi's half-eaten bowl of kibble and his rubber chicken. I dropped the bag, and all my resolve, with a heavy thud in the foyer.

The tears came before I could even close the front door. Leaky, snotty tears that couldn't be beaten back with hatred for Clay—or averted by a dognapping plot.

My dog was gone.

My *ex*-husband was an asshole.

And I was really, really alone.

I slumped against the wall and cried. Wailed, if I'm being honest. And when the maniacal snot-fest slowed to erratic hiccup-sobs, I blew my nose into the front tail of my practice jersey with a loud *honk!*

Peeling myself from the wall, I realized I'd been leaning against the intercom button. As I stepped away, the buzzer sounded. I pressed the button again. "Hello?"

A panicky voice came through the speaker. "Grace? Grace, are you all right?"

It was Jason Bradley.

FOUR

WHAT THE HELL is he doing here? was my first thought.

My second was, *Grace, you have snot all over your shirt.*

I raced back to the buzzer and pushed the button. "Hello?"

"Grace, it's Jason. Are you in trouble? I thought I heard—uhh —I heard you crying."

He had heard me honking my nose like a goose with sinusitis. I thumped my forehead against the wall. "Yes, I'm fine," I lied. I was pretty sure my heart had flatlined. I probably should have requested he call an ambulance...or the coroner.

"Can I come up? Is this a bad time? Maybe I should have called first, but I was already in the area..."

"No, it's OK. Give me two seconds."

Shit, shit, shit, shit, shit.

I hurried through my apartment, yanking my smelly tank top off over my head. The fabric caught on the tiny hairs at the back of my neck, ripping them with blinding pain from the follicles. I yelped and stumbled into the coffee table with my shins.

Staggering through the pain, I said a lot worse bad words and limped into my room to grab my Music City Rollers hoodie off the end of my bed. I stuffed my arms into it as I walked back to the foyer, then decided to walk down to let him in rather than using the buzzer. As I plodded down the steps, I zipped the hoodie to cover my sports bra. Or I thought I did, at least.

I pushed the door open, and the icy breeze smacked against my bare midsection. Jason's eyes fell to where my zipper had split at the bottom, all the way up to my chest.

His eyes darted away, but he couldn't keep the grin off his lips or the heat out of his cheeks.

I gathered the fabric in my hands to cover my squishy middle. "Oh, good grief."

"I'm sorry. I should have called," he said again, finally able to look me in the eye.

"No, it's fine. And it's only appropriate that I'm a complete disaster again, right?" When I looked down, one of my knee-high rainbow socks was flying at half-calf, and my right lime-green Converse was untied.

We both laughed.

Clearly, he was off duty, judging by his blue jeans and fitted black T-shirt. Partially hidden by an army green leather coat, the Punisher skull (ironic for a man of the law) stretched across his chest.

"Grace?"

I hadn't realized I was staring. Maybe it was the lack of sleep from the night before. "Sorry. You wanna come up?"

He glanced up and down the street behind him. "Sure. Thanks. You're not locked out again, are you?"

"Ha. Ha. Ha," I said with a smirk as he followed me. "Sorry I'm a mess. I've been at roller derby practice all morning. Hence the sweat, the shorts, and the ridiculous socks."

"That does explain a lot," he teased.

At the top of the stairs, I opened the door. "Come on in. As long as you don't mind the mess I just made." Crap. Or the smell of rotting dairy; my derby gear was still in the foyer.

"Not at all."

You say that now.

He followed me inside, and I snatched my derby bag off the floor as soon as we walked in. I whisked the bag to my bedroom and stashed it in the closet.

When I returned, he was looking around his feet at the dog stuff, my discarded jacket, my keys...

"Would you like some coffee? Or a beer, maybe? I've got some of my brother's craft stuff in the fridge," I said.

"I'm off duty today. I'd love a beer." Jason carefully stepped over my stuff as I walked to the refrigerator. "This is a great apartment. Is it new?"

"Thank you. Yes, it is. It was just finished a few weeks ago." I opened a Battle Road IPA with my magnetic bottle-opener-slash-mermaid-tail that was stuck to the fridge.

When I handed it to him, he studied the label. "I forgot your brother owns a brewery."

"Have you been there?"

"Yeah. Clay took a few of us there for a tour when they first opened." His mouth immediately snapped shut, like he worried Clay's name might be some sort of a trigger word. He tilted the bottle up to his lips. "This stuff is really good."

"Thanks. Glad you like it." I glanced back toward my bedroom. "Can you give me a second to actually put on a shirt?"

He chuckled again. "Sure. Mind if I sit?" He gestured toward the living room.

"Of course not. Be right back."

"Take your time."

I didn't take my time. I put on a pull-over sweatshirt, straightened my socks, and tied my shoe. I did stop to glance in the mirror and retie the knot of hair on my head. When I reemerged from my bedroom, Jason was peeling the label on the beer bottle and looking up at the wall.

He pointed to the framed painting of Elvis Presley on black velvet. "You got the velvet Elvis in the divorce?"

"It was the second most heated custody battle after Bodhi."

"Nice." He scooted over and patted the cushion beside him.

I sat down. "So what's up?"

He turned to face me. "How did the exchange go this morning?"

"There was a lot of swearing, and I may have contemplated knocking him down the stairs."

He balanced his beer bottle on his thigh and settled back against the armrest. "That's fair, but I'm glad you didn't. I'd have a hard time trying to talk you out of *those* charges."

"It really sucked having to give my dog back." Tears prickled the corners of my eyes again.

"I'm sure it did. I'm really sorry." He put the beer on the coffee table—and used a coaster. "He called me again today."

I groaned. "What now?"

"Nothing, except he mentioned a broken lamp and some missing wine."

"The lamp was an accident. And that was *my* wine. I bought it in Sonoma last year," I said.

"Were you awarded it in the divorce?"

I frowned.

"Then it wasn't yours anymore. Is there anything else I should be aware of?"

I thought about the eggs.

"No."

He put his hand on mine. "This will get better. Just lay low, and I'm sure he'll calm down."

"I hate him so much, Jason."

"I know," he said, squeezing my fingers.

I took a deep breath and let it out slowly. "Thanks for letting me know. You didn't have to come all the way over here."

"The place where I buy my cop gear is a couple of streets over. I needed to be out here anyway." He stood. "I should probably get going."

"Me too. Have to check in on the store. I'll walk you down."

When we reached the foyer, I looked around on the floor for my jacket. It was now hanging on the coat hook beside Jason's. Bodhi's stuff was also missing. "Did you tidy up?"

"Figured you might not want to see it right now. I washed the bowl and put the toys and food under the sink in the kitchen. Hope that's OK."

My shoulders wilted, and I had to stop myself from whimpering. "Thank you, Jason."

He winked as he stuffed his arms into his coat. Then he reached for the door handle and opened the door for me. "Wait."

I stopped and looked at him.

He grinned. "Do you have your keys?"

"Oh, shut up." I laughed as we walked out and started down the stairs. When the door closed behind us, Jason double-checked that it had locked. No one besides my dad had ever checked that my doors were secure. Not even Clay.

Jason stepped sideways and looked at the front of my store. The old brick storefront had a new wooden facade with beautiful crown molding. The whole thing was painted a light minty blue with a bold black-and-white awning over the white front door.

"Mind if I take a peek inside?" he asked.

"Of course not." I pulled open the door, and the welcome bells jingled. "Welcome to Sparkled Pink."

Jason looked around the shop, taking in its gleaming wooden floors and built-in wooden shelves and clothes racks. A crystal chandelier hung above the custom check-out counter built by my dad.

"This place is nice," he said, looking genuinely impressed.

"Thank you. It was a lot of work." I didn't tell him that Clay and I had done most of the work ourselves, ripping out the old carpet and knocking down the walls that had once divided the storefront into sections.

His eyes narrowed like he was trying to remember something. "What was it before you owned it?"

"Sugar Drop Bridal. My mom made custom wedding gowns."

"Right!" He formed his hands into a rectangle. "Big white sign."

I nodded. "Yep." I touched my chest. "That sign, which is a total rusty tetanus risk now, is still hanging in my parents' garage."

"That's cool. It was here for a really long time."

"Twenty-five years. They opened it when I started kindergarten. Have you always lived here?"

He picked up a pink tutu—one I'd made myself—and tested the width of its elastic waistband. "Since I was four. My family moved here from Knoxville when my real dad was hired on with the highway patrol and sent to Davidson County."

"Your dad was a cop too?"

He was smiling as he put the tutu back on its hanger. "Yeah."

"I never knew that."

"Grace?" The chipper voice of my assistant, Kiara Washington, made us both turn as she walked out of the back workroom. She wore a white blouse with a red scarf and fitted black pants. A shocking red flower was poised in her jet-black curls that matched the bright lipstick slathered across her full smile when her eyes landed on Jason. "Well, hello."

"Kiara, this is Officer Jason Bradley, an old friend of mine."

She extended a perfectly manicured hand. Her nails were painted with tiny red flowers to match her outfit. "Hello, Officer Bradley. Kiara Washington."

"Call me Jason, please. It's nice to meet you."

"Kiara is the only reason I have any sanity left. I couldn't run this place without her," I said.

And it was true. I had several other seamstresses, including occasionally my mother, who worked part-time for me from home, but none of them lived and breathed the fashion industry quite like Kiara.

She was a design student at MacKay University just down the street, and I was lucky to have snagged her as an intern at the start of the fall semester. Her enthusiasm was the number one thing I loved about her, followed closely by her amazing eye for design and her steady hand with a needle and thread. She was a natural talent and an extremely hard worker.

Even as a student, she was so good with the business side of things that I immediately hired her to help me in the store. Now my website was up and running, my Etsy shop was bringing in orders, and my workroom didn't look like a nuclear warhead had detonated. She really couldn't have come along at a more perfect time. Despite my recently-departed enthusiasm for all things related to kids and babies, business was up almost 20 percent.

Kiara reminded me a lot of myself when I was twenty-two. Back when I was young and eager. Before I'd had my hopes and dreams ripped out of my defunct uterus.

Sadly for me, I was certain to lose her as soon as she graduated to the high-fashion world. Her graduation date was set for the end of spring.

"It's really nice to meet you, Jason." Kiara was beaming. Her constant wealth of positivity was truly one of her superpowers. "Grace, are you here for a minute? If so, I need you to sign off on the two orders Margaret turned in today—"

I waved my hand to stop her. "You can sign off on them. I trust you."

"Really?"

"Of course."

"Great." Her face quickly fell. "I also have some questions about Sylvie's latest order. She stopped by earlier. I told her you were at practice."

"Sylvia was here today? On a weekend?"

"About ten minutes before you walked in the door. It can totally wait as long as you don't mind suffering the wrath of the underworld on Monday." She held up two fingers like horns at her temples. "She said she'd be in to see you first thing Monday morning."

Jason waved his hand. "Do what you've got to do. Don't let me keep you. I need to go anyway."

I smiled. "OK, well it was good to see—"

The front bells jingled again. "Gra-ace!"

I froze. Only one woman in the world could make my name have so many syllables.

"Good god, we said her name too many times," Kiara whispered behind me.

I slowly turned around, my metaphorical balls withering like raisins.

Sylvia Sinclair, my best and absolute worst customer, leaned in the front door of my shop and slid her massive designer sunglasses down the bridge of her nose. "Grace, be a dear and come help me unload my car, please."

I looked past her to where her Bentley sedan was parked illegally at the curb.

Jason turned before I could start toward the door. "I've got it."

"Aren't you a handsome dear?" she said, eyeing him carefully over the top of her glasses. Her dyed auburn bob was a little frizzier than normal, and she wore a black coat with thick shoulder pads and silver earrings so big they seemed to make her head sag.

I double-stepped to catch up with them as they walked outside. "What's in your car?"

Sylvia opened her back door "Fabric, Grace. Fabric." She had a raspy southern accent that sounded odd, even to my Tennessee-born ear. Like society had tried to whip the drawl out of her but had only barely succeeded. Everything sounded sarcastic or annoyed, like *"What else could I have in the car besides fabric, Grace? Duh."*

Maybe I should have known, however. It wasn't the first time she'd shown up with a ream of something fresh off the loom.

She was the only daughter of Lord Barton Sinclair, a prominent figure in the textile industry. Note, "Lord" was his first name, not an actual title, which really summed up well the whole of her personality, in my opinion. Like true American royalty, the family business had roots dating back to the Industrial Revolution of the 1800s. I'd actually studied them in college.

A Google search once revealed that Sylvia, or "Sylvie" as she insisted we call her, was eighty-one years old. No one would ever believe it though, as she was somewhere on the plastic scale between Dolly Parton and Barbie.

The only thing telling of her age was the cane she sometimes carried. Today, it was one with a diamond-encrusted handle; it matched her two-inch *high heels*. No matter the outfit, I'd never seen her in flats—with or without the cane.

"Fabric for what?" I asked.

"The dress I ordered for Alexandria last week." She stepped back as Jason lifted two large reams of periwinkle satin from her leather back seat.

My head snapped back. "You mean the dress I already started working on?"

"It's not a problem, is it?"

It was hard to keep my mouth from falling open. "Of course

not." Why would it be? It was only four days of work, after all. *Sigh.*

"You know I'll make it worth your time," she said, closing the door when Jason straightened with the reams.

Of that, I had no doubt. Sylvie was a regular in my shop. In the year that I'd known her, I'd made nine dresses for her grand-daughter Alexandria. All of them unique. All of them expensive. All of them freaking periwinkle blue—a color she was deter-mined to make me sick of.

Even so, my personal jury was still out on deciding if her unshakable presence was a blessing or a curse. A blessing because she'd hooked me up with her company's distributor and a deep discount on fabric. A curse because...well, she was a regular in my shop.

At least once a week, Sylvie would park in front of my door and saunter inside. Despite the "No Pets Please" sign on the door and my multiple requests to not bring the dog inside, she usually had her dog, Miss Taylor—named after Elizabeth Taylor—in tow. Sylvia would fondle every piece of clothing in the store, detailing to me what was wrong with each of them.

"Pink pearls would have been so much more delicate for this beading."

"You know, Grace, there is such a thing as too much tulle."

"This dress would be prettier in periwinkle."

She'd ask questions about my life. Offer legal advice about my divorce—she'd been through a few. And she was simply fasci-nated by the fact that I played roller derby, which I found kind of hilarious considering her snobbish attitude. Mostly, however, she complained and nitpicked my shop and my designs until I wanted to scream.

But I had to remind myself that the rolls of fabric Jason was holding would be more than enough material for a rack full of dresses.

As she closed the door, he looked over the mound in his arms at the "No Parking" sign her car was almost nestled against. "Should we wait for you to move your car?" he asked.

She waved him off. "I'll just leave it running. It'll be just a sec."

I doubted that.

Jason looked from her to the "No Parking" sign again, obviously debating whether or not to insist. He was the police, after all. I wondered if he might write her a ticket.

He didn't.

Someone (probably *not* from Tennessee) laid on their horn as they were forced to go around Sylvie's car.

"Are we going to stand out here all day or what?" Sylvie leaned on her cane as she crossed the sidewalk in front of us, her heels *click-clacking* unrhythmically across the sidewalk. "I need to pick up Miss Taylor in twenty minutes."

"Where is she today?" I asked, rushing past her—she was waiting for me—to open the door.

She stopped so suddenly Jason almost ran into her. Then she pointed a ringed finger down the street. "She's getting her Estée Lauder fix."

My eyes must have gone blank.

"She's at the groomer's," Sylvie clarified with a huff as she went on inside.

Jason turned sideways to carry the fabric through the door.

"I'm so sorry," I mouthed.

"Are you kidding? I haven't been this amused since...last night."

I groaned and followed them in.

Jason put the fabric on the counter, then stepped cautiously out of the way. He was watching Sylvie carefully with a look of suspended amusement, like she was a show pony about to do a trick.

She grabbed my hand and slammed it down onto the ream. "Feel this blend, Grace. It's a new fabric we're calling Sinclair Satin. Isn't it glorious?"

"It's exquisite." It really was. Silky and smooth, cool but cozy. I couldn't begin to imagine how much it would cost by the yard if I had to buy it myself. "Sinclair Satin? Is it proprietary?"

"Of course. It's a silk charmeuse imported from China with just a touch of spandex"—she patted her hips—"for a little forgiveness around the holidays."

I blinked. "Wow. I wish I could just make up new fabrics as I needed them."

"All you need is a loom and credit card."

"Right."

She leaned toward me, and the unmistakable scent of Elizabeth Arden caught my nose. "It's worth starting the dress over, I think. Yes?" Before giving me time to answer, she squeezed my hand. "I know! You can sell the other dress you started to someone else. You can even call it The Alexandria."

"That's a lovely idea," I said with a pinched smile.

She released my hand. "Of course it is. Goodbye, Kiara."

Kiara stepped over beside me and waved. "Goodbye, Sylvie!"

Sylvie paused by Jason, who had resumed his spot on the couch. "Thank you again, handsome."

He winked at her. "You're quite welcome."

"Oh, and Grace?" Sylvie looked back, leaning heavily on her cane. "Can you have the dress ready by Thanksgiving instead of the first of December? I'm willing to pay double for the rush and to cover the cost of the fabric you already used."

Double. The dress was already more than most car payments. I thought of the "Final Notice" bill that was sitting in my apartment. "Sure, Sylvie. I can rush it."

She smiled as much as the fillers around her mouth would allow. "Thank you, Grace."

"You're welcome."

"I'll be sure to bring Miss Taylor over to say hello sometime this week!" she called on her way to the door.

I reached toward her. "That will be quite—"

"See you then!" The doors chimed and closed behind her.

My shoulders slumped with a sigh.

Jason looked back toward the door. "I have new retirement goals now."

I laughed. "It's like she lives on a different planet. I'm sorry."

"Definitely not a big deal. Who was that?"

"Are you familiar with the seven rings of hell?" Kiara asked, leaning against me.

I laughed. "Her name's Sylvia Sinclair."

"I feel like I know her."

"I'm sure you've written her plenty of citations. I think she believes that 'No Parking' sign was put there to hold her spot."

"You're probably right. Well, I guess I'll take off."

I walked over and gave him a side hug. "Thanks again."

"Don't mention it." He paused and looked at me seriously. "Don't ever hesitate to call if you need me, Grace. I'm your friend too."

I smiled. "Thank you."

"Kiara, it was nice to meet you," he said, waving to her.

She waved back. "You too."

When the door closed behind him, Kiara spun toward me. "Hello, Officer Eye Candy. Who the hell was that?"

"A friend of Clay's."

"You oughta be making that man a friend of *yours*. He's beautiful."

"It's definitely not like that. He almost had to arrest me in the middle of last night for stealing my dog."

She squinted and turned her ear in my direction. "Excuse me?"

"Clay got Bodhi in the divorce."

Her jaw dropped. "No!"

"Yes."

"So you dognapped him?"

I pressed my lips together.

"Girl, you're crazy. That's hysterical."

I picked up the reams of fabric.

"Here, I'll help," she said, following me to the workroom. "You're really not going to name that stupid periwinkle dress The Alexandria, are you?"

"Hell no."

"Thank God. Did that old bird just say she'd pay double for the new dress?"

"She sure did."

"Wow. I wonder if she would adopt me," Kiara said.

I laughed. "You'd sell your soul to be a Sinclair?"

She put a hand on her hip. "With that kind of money, I could buy a new soul."

I laughed and hoisted the reams onto an empty space on the shelf.

"Speaking of money, I was wondering if I could pick up some more hours around here," she said.

I thought for a moment. "Well, I could honestly use all the help I can get. I'm absolutely swamped between my derby schedule and getting ready for the holiday rush. Black Friday will be here before we know it."

"I was thinking the same thing. And it would really help me out. I'm trying to save up to go to New York over Christmas break."

"To plan your escape from Tennessee?" I asked with a smile.

"No. To visit my cousin in Brooklyn. I've always wanted to see the city at Christmas."

"I went once with Clay. I dragged him all over Manhattan looking at the Christmas displays in the store windows."

"I've only seen them in pictures."

"You're going to love it."

She gripped my arm. "We should do that here."

"You're serious?"

"Yes! We'll pick a theme, decorate the front window, and the customers will pour in!"

"Kiara, didn't I just say I don't have time for *anything* right now?"

"Let me do it. Maybe I can get some friends to help me. It would look great on my resume if we can make it a success."

I leaned against my work desk, tapping my finger over my lips as I considered it. "I do need to decorate for the holidays."

"And what could it hurt? You know I have an eye for these things."

That was true. "What about the money? I'll level with you. I'm strapped right now."

"Let me come up with a plan and a budget before you say no. If we can't afford it, we can't afford it. And I'll put the hours toward my internship."

Truth be told, I really needed all of her remaining internship hours spent making dresses, but it would be good for her to learn something different. After all, she could already make my gowns almost as well as me. She'd also already mastered the most cutting-edge avenues of retail marketing, so I figured a little old-school advertising might be good for her.

And her excitement was inspiring. It almost sparked a little joy and hope inside my shriveled heart.

"OK. Come up with a plan, and if I can swing it, the answer is yes."

She clapped her hands together. "Can I get started on it right now?"

"What were you working on before I got here?"

"I just finished those bloomers you asked me to do."

"All of them?" I asked, surprised. I'd only shown her the day before how to make them.

"Three of each size up to eighteen months, correct?"

I nodded.

"All done."

"Impressive."

"So is that a yes?" she asked.

"After you do a quality control check on the dresses Margaret turned in."

She clapped her hands excitedly.

"And keep an eye on the store while you're at it." I looked at the periwinkle fabric again. "I've, unfortunately, got a lot more work to do."

FIVE

"SO CLAY CALLED the police again on me yesterday," I told Monica the next morning. We were gearing up in the parking lot of Centennial Park, home of a true-to-scale replica of the ancient Parthenon in Greece. Random, I know.

We'd skated the paved loop every Sunday morning since we started Fresh Meat. Except once when it rained and once when her oldest daughter, Maisie, had the flu.

She tied the laces of her left skate. "You're kidding me."

I snapped the chin strap of my shiny black helmet. "Nope. He was pissed that I broke the lamp and drank that bottle of wine."

"What a dick."

"Right?"

"How'd you find out?"

"His friend Jason came by again to tell me." I looked up toward the building as a thought occurred to me. "And I think to check on me after the exchange with Clay."

"That's nice."

"Yeah. He even put away Bodhi's stuff so I didn't have to see it."

"How thoughtful," she said, putting a hand on her chest.

"I know."

She turned toward me. "You don't think he likes you, do you?"

"God, no. That's just the kind of guy he is."

"Maybe that's the kind of guy you need in your life."

I laughed. "Kiara thinks so too. She's calling him 'Officer Eye Candy' now."

Monica stood on her skates. "He's cute then?"

"Yeah, I guess. Never really thought about him that way before. He and Clay are really close."

"He's obviously not so loyal to Clay if he's coming by to check on you. Maybe you should see where it goes. Be a little spontaneous. I think it would be a very healthy thing for you." She tapped her chest. "I should know. I'm a doctor."

"You're a doctor of *music*, Monica."

"Still, I am pretty smart."

I couldn't argue with that. Monica was the most intelligent person I'd ever known. She had a bachelors and masters in music history, and had recently completed a PhD in musicology, whatever that was. I'd once tried to read her doctoral dissertation, something about sounds and memory and cognitive processing. I failed.

"Your gear stinks," she said, scrunching her nose.

"I know. I was going to wash it yesterday when I got home, but then Jason came by and I got busy at the store. I'll do it tonight." I stood from the bench and skated with my bag across the sidewalk to my open trunk. I dropped it inside and slammed it.

I skated back to Monica and pointed to her bag on the ground. "You done with this?"

She strapped on her helmet. "Yeah."

I toted it back to her SUV, and when I stuffed it in the back and closed the hatch, she hit the lock button on her keys from the bench. She stood and straightened the sleeves under her elbow pads as I skated back over. "You know, it's about to be too cold to skate out here," she said.

"Yeah. I hear it's supposed to be in the mid fifties by this time next week."

She shuddered. "I'm not looking forward to that. I don't have so many layers of insulation anymore."

"No you don't," I said, shaking my head.

"Feel this." She poked her thigh. I did the same. "Feel how tight that muscle is now? I'd forgotten there were even muscles under there!"

That was one of the things I loved most about the sport. Derby was about what our bodies could *do*—not what they looked like.

"How much weight have you lost now?"

Monica turned to the side, put her hands on her hips, and cocked a knee forward. "Seventeen pounds."

I clapped my wrist guards together. "I'm so proud of you."

"Thanks."

"Come on. You ready? I've got lunch at my parents' house at noon, so I can't stay too late today."

"I can't either," she said as we started down the path. "I have choir practice this afternoon."

I grabbed her wrist. "Oh my god, I need to buy tickets!"

"You'd better hurry. They do sell out, you know?"

"I know. I'll get tickets today. I don't know how you do everything that you do, Mon."

"To be honest, it helps that we're down to two practices this time of year. Between the school concerts and my chorus group, this is my busiest season."

"I'll bet, and you have Derek and the girls to take care of."

"Well, Derek certainly carries the load of the family."

I sighed. "You guys are all my relationship goals wrapped up in one happy couple."

She laughed. "How so?"

"He's perfect."

"He's really not. I mean, he's great, but nobody's perfect."

I started counting on my fingers as I skated in front of her to pass an old man walking his dog. "He supported you through your bazillion years of school. He packed up his practice and moved out of state when you were offered the job here. He keeps the girls all the time—"

"He's a good dad, and he supports me like an equal. That's what marriage is."

We were on a clear part of the path, so I practiced a 180-degree turn and then skated backward to face her. "Not all marriages." I turned forward again.

"Was it all bad with you and Clay?"

I wanted to say yes, but that would've been a lie. "No. We didn't fight a lot or anything. In fact, if it had gotten *bad* maybe I wouldn't have been so blindsided by the end of it. You know, the day he told me about the baby, I actually thought he was going to surprise me with a trip to Bora Bora. Can you believe that?"

Monica didn't laugh.

I turned around again and slowed to skate beside her. "Maybe if I hadn't been so hyper focused on the shop and my ovulation cycle—"

"Don't do that to yourself, Grace. There's no excuse for what he did to you."

"I'm not making excuses for him. I just should have seen it. And I should have realized sooner that we were investing every-thing into *his* future instead of *ours*."

"What do you mean?"

"Look at me now. What do I have to show for the last decade besides a business that I no longer love? I don't even have Bodhi."

"I thought you loved the shop."

"In the beginning I did. I had baby fever, and it was exciting to make tiny dresses and suits, and dream about whether or not we would have a girl or a boy. Now? Let's just say all those oozy-goozy feelings are shot all to hell."

We skated toward the small lake beyond the Parthenon to where there was a circular track of concrete.

"I can understand that, but are you thinking of closing it?"

"And put my mother in an early grave? God, no. I'll get over it. I have to get over it. It's what I'm good at, and I've invested so much into it."

She pointed at me. "Grace Evans, I swear, if you waste the next seven years doing something that doesn't make you happy, I'll kick your ass. And I have the thigh strength to do it now!"

We both laughed.

"But I'm good at clothes, and I *do* enjoy the process."

"Why not make a different end product?" She thought for a second. "How about brides? You could probably capitalize on your mom's success."

I made a gagging noise.

"OK. No brides."

I jumped over a small stick on the path like it was a foot tall so I could practice sticking the landing. "No wedding stuff at all. Have you met my mother? There's a reason she's so scatter-brained now."

"What about couture women's fashion? I love the stuff you make for yourself."

"I don't know. That would probably be almost as stressful as brides."

"I'll keep thinking on it."

"What up, derby bitches!" a voice called behind us.

Monica and I both spun on our wheels to see Full Metal Jackie walking down the path. She held the leash of a strange-looking mutt with the black-and-white spotted body of an English setter and the head of a beagle.

"Hi, Jackie," Monica said as we rolled to meet her.

"Hey, Monica. Grace," she replied. "I didn't realize that was you."

I laughed. "Are you shouting profanities at a lot of random people today?"

"Only the ones wearing quad skates and pads." She wiped sweat off her forehead and shortened her dog's pink leash by wrapping it a few times around her hand.

Jackie had been one of my favorite veteran Music City Rollers from the very first time she led Fresh Meat practice. Like me, she was Amazonian in height, pushing six four or six five when wearing skates. Unlike me, she was newly pregnant and happily married. She'd recently retired from derby, citing her "nine-month injury" as the reason.

I dropped onto my kneepads to pet her dog. "Hello there."

The dog jumped and slammed both paws against my shoulders.

"Freckles, down!" Jackie shouted, tugging on the leash.

I laughed. "She just wants a hug." I hugged the dog and let her lick my cheek.

"She's a nightmare. Sorry, Grace."

I stood, using my toe stops to push myself up off the concrete. "No worries. She's cute."

Freckles was wagging her tail like she knew I was talking about her.

"How are you feeling these days, Jackie?" Monica asked.

Jackie smoothed the front of her thin jacket over her midsection. "Better these days. I finally pushed through all the morning sickness of my first trimester."

"Girl, I feel your pain." Monica put her hand over her heart. "I was so sick with my first daughter that I lost nine pounds in the first three months. I couldn't keep down water."

"I know. And who decided it was *morning* sickness? In my experience, it's been all-day sickness," Jackie said with a laugh.

Freckles, perhaps sensing my awkward silence, nuzzled my hand with her wet nose. I scratched behind her ears. "You're a sweetie." I've always believed dogs have the ability to read human emotion. I know Bodhi does...when he isn't too busy drinking from the toilet or playing fetch with himself.

"How's derby retirement treating you?" Monica asked.

Her eyes widened. "I have so much free time now. I guess I didn't realize how much time I spent at the Sweatshop." She started counting on her fingers. "Or community events or fundraisers or parties."

I looked at Monica. "Or places like this, skating."

"Exactly. Derby's a full-time job. I'm still helping out with the juniors' team, but I'm hoping that will be passed off before the baby comes."

"Oh yeah, Susan mentioned that in the team meeting. They're looking for your replacement," I said.

"Yep, but I don't think anyone volunteered. Have you guys joined a committee yet?"

We shook our heads. "Still thinking about it," I said.

"Well, the junior girls are the very best, just saying."

Monica's face soured. "I am *so* not ready to be responsible for anyone else playing this sport. I barely know what I'm doing myself."

"That's not true. You had one of the highest scores in team history on the written exam," Jackie argued. "You know more about the rules than some of the All-Stars, I think."

I looked at Monica. "She has a point."

"What about you, Grace? Those girls need a new coach, and I've always had a soft spot for you."

"Because we're both six-foot-seven in our skates?" I asked with a laugh.

She smiled. "Yes, ma'am."

"I don't know about coaching. I didn't even come close to a perfect score like Monica."

"There's no better way to learn something than to teach it to someone else, and you have the technical skills almost mastered."

I narrowed my eyes. "I feel like you should go into politics, Jackie."

"Well, I do work in the governor's office..."

Monica laughed. "Really?"

"Really. And we could seriously use the help. We're so short staffed that I'm already filling two positions, coach and president."

"Why are you so short on help? The team has a lot of skaters," I said.

"Yeah, but the juniors' team is brand new. They haven't even played their first bout yet, so it's not really high on the league's priority list." She grimaced. "It also probably takes the most time commitment out of all the volunteer committees. It's hard when we all have lives outside of derby to add in a whole second practice schedule."

I grinned and crossed my arms. "You should have stopped while you were ahead."

She laughed. "It's really rewarding though. The kids are great. Just think about it, and if you're interested, come watch us practice sometime. Tuesday and Thursday nights at the Sweatshop."

I looked at Monica. "OK. We'll think about it."

"Cool. You guys just started practicing, right? Are you enjoying it?" she asked.

"Absolutely," I said.

"I haven't felt this good in years," Monica added.

Jackie smiled. "And it's a great community to be part of. I already miss it. You're coming to the Slammy Awards, right?"

"Oh yeah," we said together.

"Excellent. I'll be there, probably as the designated driver for half the team."

I laughed. "That sounds about right."

"Well, I won't keep you guys. Freckles and I were on our way to the car when we saw you. Thought we'd come say hello."

"So glad you did," Monica said.

"Yeah. It's good to see you, Jackie. We're going to miss you at practice." I bent to pet the dog. "And it was nice to meet you, Freckles. I hope to see you again sometime."

"Bye, girls," Jackie said with a wave as she turned back toward the parking lot.

When she was gone, I looked at my watch. "It's almost ten thirty."

"All right, no more talking. Let's get this done. What's our fastest time around the loop?"

"With this many people out here?" My head bobbed side to side. "I'd guess nine or ten minutes."

"Skate two laps and call it a day?" she asked.

I smiled. "Two? In under thirty minutes?"

"Yes," she said confidently. "No breaks. We can do this."

"All right."

Monica pushed her sleeves up her forearms. "Go!"

———

The first Sunday of every month was now the designated gathering of the Evans clan at the homestead. This was a post-retirement ritual started by my mother in an effort to reclaim some of the lost family time of our younger years. Growing up, both my parents had been very successful business owners—Mom in bridal wear, Dad in construction—which left little time for home-cooked meals and conversations around the dinner table.

Mom was hell-bent on making up for lost time. Problem was, Sheila Evans wasn't exactly *Suzy Homemaker*. A seamstress, absolutely. A cook? Not so much. During meal prep was almost the only time we ever saw our mother angry. It was like road rage, but over the stove.

The reassurance that she *was* human was comforting as of late. Especially since lately I wasn't having much luck living up to her legacy in the couture-design department. She'd made running her store look so easy. All I wanted to do was quit.

My brother Garrett's brand-new, king-cab truck was beside my car in the driveway. It was a glaring reminder that, unlike me, he *had* inherited the golden thumb of entrepreneurship. The truck had an iridescent-blue paint job and flashy chrome trim that could be used to signal space if he needed to.

Meanwhile, the clear coat was peeling on my eight-year-old sedan, and it was eighteen hundred miles overdue for an oil change. These days, a loud whirring noise was coming from the engine. I had no idea why.

With a heavy sigh, I opened my door and got out. The hinges croaked like a bullfrog.

"Hello! Hello!" I called when I walked in the front door without knocking. A faint haze of smoke hovered near the ceiling. I grinned.

"In the kitchen!" Mom replied.

Garrett's eight-year-old daughter, Hope, was coming down the wooden staircase. "Aunt *Grathe!*" She ran the rest of the way with open arms and collided with my midsection, nearly toppling me over.

Her long blonde hair was braided in pigtails, and she wore a burgundy floral print dress and black ballet flats. Her two front teeth were missing.

"My goodness, have you grown since last month?" I asked, bending to rest my chin on her head.

"I dunno."

"I think you're going to be a giant like me, kiddo."

She beamed up at me. "*That'th* what *Popth thayth.*"

"I said what?" My dad, aka "Popsicle" or "Pops," walked through the dining room to where we were standing in the foyer.

"You *thaid* I *wath* going to be a clodhopper giant like Aunt Grathe." Hope was still hanging off my waist.

I gasped. "A clodhopper giant?"

Dad's eyes widened. "I said no such thing! Tall, strong, and beautiful like your Aunt Grace is what I said."

"Nuh-uh!" Hope argued, laughing.

He pointed at her. "That's it. No cake for you, toothless."

She swatted his hand away. "Don't call me *toothleth!*"

Dad growled and reached for her. She squealed and ran away. Still laughing, he turned toward me and opened his arms for a hug. "The child lies, Grace."

"Sometimes you're a shockingly terrible person," I said, stepping into his embrace.

"I know." He kissed the side of my head. "How are you, honey?"

I sighed. "It's been an interesting week."

"I'll bet. We've thought about you a lot. You holding up OK?"

"Yeah. It's nice to have some closure, at least. And my name back. But I miss Bodhi."

"You gave him back to Clay, then?"

I nodded. "He was pretty pissed off the next morning."

"I'll bet he was." Dad put his arm around my shoulders and turned me toward the dining room. "You'll get through this. The worst of it is over."

I leaned my head against him. "Thank you, Daddy."

"Your mother made you a surprise." He grimaced and lowered his voice to a whisper. "Try to be excited about it."

I laughed as we turned the corner into the kitchen. On the counter, I saw it. A misshaped Bundt cake with black crumbs mixed into the white frosting. I bit down on the insides of my lips.

"Grace, you made it!" Mom cheered from where she was stirring a pot of *something* on the stove. "You're late. We were getting worried."

"No, we weren't," my brother, Garrett, said from the breakfast table.

I shot him the bird, making my mother gasp and put her hands on her hips like she'd never seen me do it before.

Garrett laughed and leaned back in his chair, crossing his boots out in front of him. He'd grown a beard since I'd seen him the month before, and he was wearing a new hoodie sporting the Battle Road Brewing label. Unlike me, Garret had inherited the golden entrepreneurial gene from our parents. The astronomical success of the brewery was evidence of that.

Mom came over and hugged me. "How are you, Gracie?"

She was tiny compared to me, Garrett, and Dad. I had to bend to put my arms around her. "I'm OK. Staying busy."

"That's the best thing for you these days. How's the roller derby?"

A true southerner, my mother put "the" in front of everything. *The* roller derby. *The* Walmart. *The* Facebook.

"It's good. I just finished my first week of practice as an official team member."

She looked over at my dad. "Graham, we should watch her one night this week."

"Oh no. I'm not ready for spectators just yet. But I am skating in the Nashville Christmas Parade in a few weeks. You should definitely come watch that."

"You're still playing that crazy sport?" Garret asked.

"I just made the team last week. It's not like it's old news."

He pointed at me. "Well, thanks to you and that stupid game you took us to—"

"*Bout,*" I corrected him.

"Whatever. Ever since the 'bout'"—he actually used air quotes—"the girls haven't shut up about roller skating."

"You should have told me. I'd love to take them skating sometime."

Garrett cocked an eyebrow. "Are you offering to babysit?"

"Anytime."

Mom laughed from the stove. "We're lucky to get you here once a month, Gracie."

"No, I want to. Let me check my calendar." I pulled out my phone to check my calendar, but on the screen was a picture message from Jason. I swiped it open.

The photo was a mirror selfie of him in a department store's dressing room. He wore a long, pink, fuzzy bathrobe over his clothes. The caption read: *If I buy this, we can be twins.*

I laughed out loud.

"Earth to Grace," Garrett said, waving his hand in front of my face.

"Sorry. What was I doing?" I asked, still staring at the picture.

"Not earning the title of Aunt of the Year, apparently. What are you looking at?" Garrett reached over and snatched my cell phone out of my hand.

"Hey!" I shouted.

"Well, well. Who is this?"

"Give me my phone!" I lunged for it, but Garrett caught me by the forehead and held me at his long arm's length.

"Dad, tell him to stop!"

"I swear, you two are in your thirties now, right?" Dad grumbled.

"Is that Clay's friend? The cop?" Garrett looked at me.

I groaned. "Give me my phone."

He handed it back to me. "Scandalous, Gracie. I'm proud of you."

"There's nothing scandalous going on."

"Is this the same guy who was at your apartment in the middle of the night?" Dad asked.

Both my brother and Mom "Ooo"ed at the same time.

"Yes, but it's not like that. Clay wanted to have me arrested. Jason stopped him."

"And now he's sexting you," Garrett added.

"Garrett!" my mother yelled.

"He is not sexting me."

"Who's sexting you?" Garrett's other daughter, Gabby, asked as she came into the kitchen.

Dad twitched. "How do you know what that is?"

"Pops, I'm twelve. I'm practically a grown-up," Gabby said.

"No, you're not, young lady," Mom said, pointing a slotted spoon covered in gravy at her.

"I'm not sexting anyone." I sighed and turned off my phone's screen without responding to Jason right away. "He's just a friend."

"How good of friends are you?" Garrett asked.

I thought about it.

"Do you talk on a regular basis?" he added.

"Well, no…"

"Does he date your friends?"

"No, but—"

"Is he gay?"

"No!"

Garret shook his head. "Then this is the first baby step into sexting, sis."

Mom whirled around. "The next person to say *sexting* in my kitchen gets zero cake."

"Sexting!" Garret and Dad said at the same time.

Mom's mouth dropped open, but her face quickly shifted from shock to a blush. Then, much to my relief, she started laughing. "Oh, shut up! Extra helpings for both of you!"

"Poor Mom," I whimpered. "I'll still eat the cake."

"That's why you're my favorite, Grace," Mom said, turning back to the stove. Whatever she was cooking—gravy? Motor oil, maybe?—was boiling over onto the burner. *"Shht! Shht! Shht!"*

It wasn't until I was an adult that I realized my mother swore a *lot*. Her favorite curse word was *shit*. But I guess she figured it didn't count as long as she omitted the letter *i*.

"Need some help?" I asked, trying to stifle a laugh. Garrett didn't even bother. His forehead was on the table, and his shoulders were shaking as he cackled.

"No, I'm fine." Mom carried the bubbling pot to the sink. Black tar sizzled on the burner, sending more black smoke into the air.

While everyone was focused on the fire hazard in the kitchen, I texted Jason back. *I think the robe looks better on you than me.*

My brother didn't notice.

"Grace, did you tell Gabby you'll be skating in the parade?" Mom asked, obviously trying to change the subject.

I turned toward my niece and opened my mouth to speak, but Gabby excitedly waved her hands in front of my face. "I already know about the parade. Can I come with you?"

"No, you can't go with her, and how do you already know about the parade?" Garrett asked.

Gabby put a hand on her hip. "It's on the Rollers' website, Dad." If we'd been in the nineties, she would've tacked a "duh" and an eyeroll onto her answer.

"You've been on our website?" I asked.

"All the time."

I leaned toward her. "Did you know they have a brand-new junior roller derby team?"

Her eyes quadrupled in size. "No way!" She spun toward her father. "Dad, can I join?"

"Absolutely not," my brother replied.

Gabby's mouth dropped open. "But *why?*"

"Gabrielle, do you remember that girl getting her nose broken when she plowed through the crowd?" Garrett shook his head. "I don't want to pay your medical bills. Hell no."

"Son, watch your language," Dad said.

"Maybe sometime you and I could go skating, and I could show you some tricks," I said, directing the conversation away from a full-blown meltdown.

She leaned toward me and lowered her voice. "Will you try to convince Dad?"

I winked. "I'll do what I can, but don't get your hopes up."

"I won't. I gotta go tell Hope!" She ran off toward the family room.

Garrett groaned. "Don't encourage them, Grace."

"Why not? What's so wrong with being part of a sport that teaches girls to be confident and fierce? She could use some strong women in her life, you know."

"Because her aunt's too busy for her."

"Hey!"

He put his hands up in defense. "It was a joke. Calm down."

"You can make it up to me by letting her join the team. Derby's a family. It would be good for them."

He sighed. "I'll think about it, but don't say anything else to Gabby until I've made up my mind."

"Deal."

My brother was single, a widower actually. His wife, Jamie,

had died of breast cancer after stopping chemo when she found out she was pregnant with Hope. Jamie died just before Hope's first birthday. Garrett hadn't dated anyone seriously since.

I was the only Evans, immediate and extended family included, to ever get divorced. Granted, we weren't an enormous family, but still. It was a legacy I wasn't exactly keen to break.

"Aunt *Grathe!*" Hope ran into the kitchen with Gabby on her heels. "Gabby *thaid there'th* a junior roller derby team! Can I play too?"

My brother slid me an annoyed glare.

"Girls, we're not going to say another word about it until your dad's had a chance to really think it over. OK?"

Her shoulders dropped with a heavy huff. "Fine. Are you really going to *thkate* in the *Chrithmath* parade?"

"Yes! Will you come watch me?"

She looked back at Garrett. "Dad, can we?"

With a sigh, he nodded.

I smiled at him.

"Will Riveter Styx be there? Or Full Metal Jackie?" Gabby asked.

"How about Midnight Maven?" Hope added.

"Or Medusa." Gabby gripped my forearm. "She's my favorite."

Hope looked a little dreamy-eyed. "Mine too. *The'th thooo* cool."

Garrett leaned toward Dad. "What's with these names? Sounds like a metal band."

"Kinda looks like one sometimes too, now that you mention it," I said.

"Have you been to watch it yet, Dad?" Garrett asked.

"Not yet, but I'm sure we'll go see Grace play," Dad said.

Gabby went around the table to Garrett. "Dad, let me see your phone. I want to show Pops the team."

"Mom, want me and Garrett to set the table?" I asked, slipping my phone back into my pocket.

"That'd be great. Thank you."

Garrett turned his palms up with a confused look that asked, *"Why would you do that?"*

"You're such a bum, Garrett. It won't kill you to help out," I said, walking to the dish cabinet across the kitchen. "Get the glasses. I'll get the plates."

As I reached into the cabinet, my phone buzzed twice, and as much as I hate to admit it, my heart torqued with excited agony. I cradled two plates on my forearm, then pulled out my phone.

I looked at the screen.

Not a chance.

"Busted," Garrett said behind me.

I yelped and dropped the dishes. They shattered with a loud crash on the tile floor.

"Grace!" Mom yelled.

Garrett laughed.

Dad covered his mouth with his hand.

I groaned and knelt to pick up the biggest pieces of ceramic. "I'm really sorry, Mom. I'll replace them."

"I bought them in Nantucket twelve years ago, dear," Mom said with an eye roll.

My nose scrunched. "I'm really sorry."

"You hold the dust pan. I'll sweep," Dad said as he carried over the broom.

"Gabby, you'd better get the plates. Your Aunt Grace's hands seem a little slippery today," Mom said.

"I'm sorry," I said again as Dad swept the last of the dish fragments into the dust pan.

"So what'd the cop say?" Garrett asked me as he passed us with an armful of tea glasses.

"He said, 'Your brother's an asshole, Grace.'"

Garrett and Dad laughed. Mom swatted me from behind with a dishtowel and huffed. "I swear if I could still ground you, I would."

When we were finished, I put the silverware out in the dining room and took my seat at the table—china-cabinet side, to the right of Mom's seat. In the kitchen, Dad turned on the electric carving knife, so I pulled out my phone and texted Jason again. *Full disclosure: I'm saving this photo in case I ever need blackmail.*

My phone buzzed immediately.

Jason: *You wouldn't dare.*

Me: *I might even make it my screensaver.*

Jason: *Do what you must. I'm rocking this pink robe.*

I laughed.

Wait. Were we flirting?

"Hey, do you know what the plan is for Thanksgiving?" Garrett asked directly across the table from me.

I shook my head.

"Hey, Mom! What are we doing Thanksgiving Day?" he called to the kitchen.

"*Linner* here at two o'clock!" our mother answered.

Dad had coined the term "linner" when we were kids because he refused to call a meal in the middle of the afternoon lunch or dinner.

"Think Granna is cooking?" Garrett whispered to Gabby with a grimace.

She made a sour face and then laughed.

Mom carried a huge bowl of mashed potatoes into the dining room. They looked normal, which was encouraging. Dad carried the plate of roast beef into the room and placed it in the center of the table.

Once everyone was seated, Dad said a blessing, praying for

each of us specifically. At the end of the prayer, we all said "amen" together, then dove in different directions for the food.

"Grace, do you have a big sale planned for Black Friday?" Dad asked over the sound of clinking spoons and china.

"Yeah, but I'm not doing anything crazy like opening before dawn."

Mom wasn't looking at me as she passed Garrett a bowl of creamed corn. "I never opened my shop at all on Thanksgiving weekend."

Oh great. Here we go.

I nodded and plucked a biscuit from the bread basket. It was burned on the bottom. "But you didn't exactly have a retail store. Nobody buys wedding gowns as gifts for Christmas."

Garrett picked through the roast beef slices with his fork, probably searching for the biggest one. "And, Mom, you worked *every* holiday."

I laughed. "Right? Do you remember that Christmas morning when we had to open presents in the kitchen because she moved her workroom to the den?"

"That was only because Jenny Hayes was getting married on New Year's Eve and I wasn't finished with her gown yet." Mom pointed a butter knife at me. "But I was home, wasn't I?"

"And I'll be home too. Just not from nine to six that one day. I'll be closed the rest of the weekend, I think."

"If you do flyers or something, get me some and I'll put them out at the bar," Garrett offered.

"Thanks." I smiled. "You know, when you aren't being a jerk, you're very nice and generous."

Garrett winked at me. "I try. Occasionally. How's business going?"

I groaned.

"That good, huh?" he asked with a grin.

Dad looked over, concerned. "Is everything OK with the store, Grace?"

"Truthfully?"

Everyone looked up.

"It's suffered with all the divorce drama, and it's harder and harder to have a storefront when so much retail is being done over the web. Kiara has helped boost the store's presence online, but I'm starting to fear it's too little, too late. I'm hoping to get sales back on track during the holidays. It just doesn't help that my motivation to make children's clothing is kind of lacking lately."

"Wonder why," Dad said, shaking his head sadly.

"You could always make wedding gowns," Mom suggested.

I dragged my fork around in my mashed potatoes. "Yes, because being part of matrimonial bliss is right up there on my priority list with celebrating babies."

Mom stopped mid chew and looked at me. "I'm sorry. I didn't think about that."

"It's OK," I said.

"You could make Barbie clothes," Hope suggested.

I raised my eyebrows. "That's a great idea."

"Or stripper clothes," Garrett said with a rotten smile.

"Garrett! In front of the girls?" Mom said, pointing to his daughters.

Gabby was laughing behind her hand, probably to keep herself from spewing her mouthful of food all over the table.

"In all seriousness," Garrett said, plucking three half-burned rolls from the bread basket, "you can always come boil hops with me."

"Thanks, brother. I might have to take you up on that."

Silently, I prayed I wouldn't have to.

After dinner, when Garrett and I had helped Mom clean up,

Dad came up to me tapping an envelope against the palm of his hand. The look on his face told me everything that was inside it.

My heart sank. "Is that the property-tax bill?"

"After our conversation at dinner, I'm terribly sorry to give it to you."

I took a deep breath. "It's OK. I've been saving for it."

He handed it to me. "Smart girl."

Inside was the bill. I pulled it out and carefully unfolded it. My chest tightened. "Oh."

"It's higher this year because of the added square footage of your apartment. Do you have enough to cover it?"

Sure didn't.

"I'll get there," I said, hoping it was true. "I've got until March, right?"

"Yes." He put a hand on my shoulder. "You'll let me know if you need help?"

"Of course." I held up the paper. "But if I can't do this, I don't have any business keeping the store."

"I respect that, Grace." He pulled me into a tight hug. "You'll find a way."

"I know, Dad. Thank you."

I really hoped he was right.

SIX

I'M CRAVING *pancakes* was the message waiting for me when I woke up on Thursday morning.

Jason and I had been chatting all week long, like I needed anything else to distract me from work. We talked about our friends and our families. He wanted to hear all about roller derby, and he told me stories from patrol. I whined about dressmaking; he whined about working third shift.

None of our conversations had been about Clay.

I rubbed my eyes and texted him back. *That's very random. Good morning to you too.*

Jason: *I think I need some Pancake Pantry. I have court downtown today. How about an early lunch?*

Me: *What time?*

Jason: *11?*

Me: *Perfect.*

I inhaled, only realizing then that I'd been holding my breath. Holy shit. Were those butterflies? Smiling, I jumped out of bed.

After taking extra care getting ready that morning, I walked down to the store. The lights were already on when I opened the door. "Hello?" I called, a little confused, when I cautiously went inside.

Kiara stepped into the doorway to the workroom. She wore black pants and a polka-dot blouse with a Peter Pan collar. "Hi!"

I put my hand over my heart. "You scared me. What are you doing here so early?"

"Come here! Come here!"

"OK," I said slowly.

I walked to the workroom, and what I found made me stumble back a step. Bags of white cotton. Boxes of pink glitter. Cans and cans and cans of pink, white, and gold spray paint.

"Tada!" she announced, her arms extended into the air.

"Um..."

"What do you think?"

I put my hand on my forehead. "I think I'm really confused."

"It's going to be a *sparkled pink* winter wonderland." She pointed back to the front of the store. "For the window!"

"Oh!" I looked at all the stuff again. "But where did all this come from? You didn't buy it, did you?"

"God no," she said with a laugh. "You know the big craft store off Franklin Road in Brentwood?"

"Yeah."

"My boyfriend's parents own it."

I blinked. "Wow."

"Yeah. I told them I needed some supplies for my internship project and they said I could have whatever I wanted."

"You're kidding?" I walked over and looked inside a box full of glittery pink ribbon. "Did you tell them it was for a store window? Like a commercial store? I don't want to get sued, Kiara."

"I told them all about it. And my advisor at school loved the idea. She said if I can really make something of it, she might be able to pull some strings with the newspaper to get it featured."

"Are you serious?"

"As a sale at Barney's."

"Why would she want to put it in the paper?" I asked.

"To get it on the radar of other businesses. She thinks she might be able to make it part of the curriculum next year and let design students compete for scholarship money."

My eyes widened. "Hey, that's a great idea."

"I think so too." She clasped her hands together. "So do I have your permission to do it?"

I laughed and looked around at the packed workroom. "I can't very well say no now, can I?"

"No, you can't." She stepped toward me. "But are you happy? Is this OK?"

Putting my hands on my hips, I nodded. "Yes, I'm happy. Do I have to help?"

"I'll do it all."

I gave her two thumbs-up. "Then I'm ecstatic. What else do you need?"

"I'll need some white Christmas lights. Those tiny wired ones that look like fairy lights. You know what I'm talking about?"

"Yeah."

"I found some online. I'll need about eighty dollars to get enough strands for what I want to do."

I considered it. "I can do eighty. Is that all?"

"I kinda want to buy a pink Christmas tree."

I smiled. "How much?"

"A hundred...*ish.*"

"Is it online too?"

She nodded.

"Send me a link."

"Can I get started on it today?" she asked.

"Yes, but you're going to have to move this stuff off my table. One of us still has to make gowns."

Kiara removed everything that was currently in the front display, then she used brown craft paper to "gift wrap" the front window. With pink and white window markers, she wrote on the glass: *Santa's elves are working hard on a big surprise. Come on in, we're open!*

Even that was pretty cute.

Later that morning, I was in my workroom cutting out the pattern on the periwinkle satin when I heard the front door bells jingle. My breath hitched with excitement. I stood, paused, and took a deep breath.

"You OK?" Kiara asking, looking up from where she was making snowflakes out of tissue paper.

With an excited smile, I nodded and stepped over the piles of art supplies she'd scattered across the floor. "I have lunch plans."

"Gra-ace!"

Oh great.

"With Sylvia?" Kiara asked with a chuckle.

I hung my head and trudged out to the storefront.

"Good morning, Sylvie." Her shih tzu was under her arm. I gritted my teeth. "And hello, Miss Taylor."

Sylvia was using her cane again today, with her two-inch patent black heels. She also wore a deep bluish-black fur coat— fox fur, I think and definitely real—over a white turtle neck with a heavy-beaded necklace. I shuddered for the fox. She was like Cruella de Vil's wicked stepmother.

Miss Taylor wore a diamond-studded collar, also presumably real.

"Grace, what on earth happened to your front stindow?"

"Kiara is decorating it for the holidays."

"In brown paper?"

"No. That's temporary. She wants it to be a surprise."

"It looks ridiculous."

I sighed. "How can I help you, Sylvie?"

"I was just coming by to check on my dress." She shoved the pooch into my arms as she hobbled past me toward the checkout counter.

I held Miss Taylor at arm's length like she might be rabid. I loved dogs, but she had bitten me twice before.

Sylvia looked behind the desk. "Is it in the back?"

"It is, but it's not ready to be seen yet. It's going to take a while. You know it's a process." I was turning in circles, looking for some place to put the dog down.

"I know. I'm just excited. Have you got anything new?"

I blinked. "Since Saturday?"

She pushed her thick glasses up the bridge of her nose. "I'll take that as a no." Her heels clacked across the floor toward the dress-up corner, a spot I'd created for kids to play while their parents shopped. "This could do with some tidying up, Grace."

I laughed awkwardly and carried Miss Taylor to the corner. "We had a few kids in this morning. They love to make a mess."

Using her cane, she picked up a plastic tiara and lifted it for closer inspection.

"It's from Target," I said as if I needed to clarify.

"Hmph." She hobbled over to a table covered with accessories for little girls. "How's your roller derby thing going? When do you start playing in something I can come watch?"

I was surprised she remembered. Or that she'd want to come see me play. "It's going well. I made the team not long ago, and the season starts in the spring."

"The spring," she repeated as she reached into a glass jar full of beaded elastic bracelets Kiara had made. Pulling one out, she stretched it between her index finger and her thumb.

The front door bells jingled again. This time it was Jason, dressed in jeans and a sweater. "Hey, Grace, there's a purple town car out here parked in front of the fire hydrant. Do you know—"

"That's mine," Sylvia said. Just then, the elastic band shot off her finger toward Jason's head. He conjured up his old baseball skills and caught it with his free hand. The other was holding his black uniform.

Sylvia gave a raspy laugh and clapped her hands. "You're a regular Mickey Mantle, aren't ya? Nice catch, handsome."

Jason looked too confused to thank her for the compliment. He lifted the front of his T-shirt to display the badge pinned to his belt next to his holster. "Ma'am, I'm going to need to ask you to move your car. It's a safety hazard."

"All right, all right. I was only popping in for a minute." She hobbled over to me and took the dog from my hands. "Come on, Miss Taylor. Officer Killjoy says we've gotta go."

Jason shook his head. "I didn't say that."

"It's OK, son. No need to apologize for harassing the elderly."

"Ma'am, I wasn't—"

"I said no need to apologize."

He looked at me with wide eyes as she passed by him. Then she stopped, hooked her cane over her forearm that was cradling Miss Taylor, and squeezed his bicep. "Oh, how nice."

Jason's eyes widened. "Wow. Um, thank you, Mrs. Sinclair."

Her head snapped back at the mention of her name. She pushed her glasses up as she studied his face. "Have we met?"

"Yes, ma'am. I helped you carry in some stuff here just the other day."

"That's right. Well, you call me Sylvie." She looked over at me. "This one's a keeper, Grace."

My cheeks flushed with heat.

She waved to me. "I'll come by later this week to check on my dress. Have a good day, you kids!"

When the door closed behind her, I pointed in her direction as I walked to greet him. "Can you come by every day and do what you just did? She's never been in and out of here so fast."

"Get myself felt up by your geriatric clientele? Sure." He laughed and handed me the bracelet Sylvia had fired across the room. "Are we still on for lunch?"

"Yeah. Let me grab my coat. What's with the uniform?"

"I was hoping I could change here after we eat."

"Afraid of spilling something on your shirt?"

"Afraid of someone spitting in my food. I try to never eat in public wearing my uniform."

"Eww."

He nodded. "Exactly."

"Would you like me to hang it up in the back?"

He walked over and handed it to me. "That'd be great." When I took hold of the hanger, he didn't let go. "It's good to see you again, Grace."

My heart thumped in my chest. "You too."

With a smile, he released the hanger and I turned to carry it to the back. That was when I saw Kiara's head poking around the corner. "You're such a creeper," I whispered as I walked past her.

"Officer Eye Candy again, huh? You go, Grace."

"He's taking me out for pancakes."

"Pancakes? Pshh... If I were you, I'd be taking him upstairs."

"Kiara!"

"What? That man is too hot for pancakes." She peeked back out to the storeroom. "Although, I'll bet you could melt butter on that six-pack. Slather him up in some maple syrup and—"

"Kiara! Oh my god, you're insane." I reached for my jacket hanging on the rack. "I'll be back in about an hour. Can you mind the store while you make your mess back here?"

"This is art, honey. And you just wait. You're going to thank me."

I slipped my arms into my jacket. "I certainly hope so."

She followed me to the front. Jason was looking at a rack of hand-tied hair bows when we entered the room. He glanced over and smiled at Kiara. "Hello again."

"I think a blue one would go best with your eyes," she said, pointing.

He lifted a blue bow off the rack and held it to the side of his head. "Yeah?"

She laughed. "Oh yeah."

I walked over to him. "I'm ready if you are."

He put the bow back and waved to Kiara. "It's good to see you again."

"You too," she replied.

"Want us to bring you back some lunch?" I asked as we walked to the door.

"Nah. I'll go out and grab something when you get back. Have fun."

"She's nice," Jason said when we were outside. "How much does she work for you?"

"She's actually an intern-slash-employee. A design student at MacKay. She was so good working for me for free that I hired her to come in on the weekends while I go to derby. Now, she's usually here Thursday through Saturday."

"Does she make dresses too?"

We walked next door to the Pancake Pantry. "Probably better than me."

He held the restaurant door open. "I doubt that. The two of you make all that stuff in the store yourselves?"

"Well, I have two other seamstresses who work part-time, Margaret and Carla. And some of the stuff in the store, like the blue jeans and the shoes, are wholesale items I buy and resell."

The girl at the hostess stand smiled when we walked in. "Hi, Grace!"

"Hello, Maggie."

Jason turned toward me with a cocked eyebrow and a teasing grin.

"Yes, I'm on a first-name basis with most of the staff here. And the girl at the ice cream shop. And the bartender at the tavern. You know I just went through a nasty divorce, right?"

He chuckled.

"Two today?" Maggie asked.

"Yes," I said.

"Would you like your usual table?"

Jason laughed again.

"Don't judge me. That'll be great, Maggie."

She plucked two menus from the rack. "Right this way."

He touched the small of my back, urging me to go ahead of him, and a tingle rippled down my spine. "I'm totally judging you," he said quietly.

I laughed as we followed her through the maze of tables. "I can't believe there's not a line today," I said to Maggie when we reached my favorite four-top near the window.

"Today's your lucky day. You've hit the sweet spot between the breakfast crowd and the lunch rush." She put the menus down on the table. "Your server, Alex, will be here in just a moment."

"Thanks, Maggie," I said.

Jason thanked her as well and then pulled out my chair for me. "Wow. Such a gentleman. Thank you."

"You're welcome." Rather than sitting across the square table, he sat beside me. He must have noticed my surprise because he gripped the side of the tabletop. "Is it OK if I sit here? I like to be able to see the doors."

I blinked. "Oh. Yeah, of course." I picked up my menu and would have ducked my disappointed face behind it if it would've blocked his view. I'd thought he just wanted to sit beside me.

"You eat here a lot, then?" he asked.

"All the time, and I'm not even ashamed of it."

He grinned. "Can't blame you. I'd be here every day myself. What's your favorite?"

"My very favorite is the Georgia peach crepes, but lately, I've been ordering the whole-wheat pancakes. They're amazing, and I can more easily justify cleaning my plate."

"Makes total sense." His eyes were scanning the menu. "So many choices."

With his attention diverted, it was easy to study him from my seat. Unlike me, it didn't seem he'd aged much since college. His hair was lighter than I remembered, without the slightest hint of gray. And where I was well on my way to a perfect pair of crow's feet, he only had faint crinkles at the corners of his deep-set eyes. They were the color of winter ale. My gaze drifted down his strong, clean-shaven jawline, the kind perfect for trailing fingers—

"Hello, folks."

I jumped, realizing the waiter had appeared like Houdini at our table. "My name is Alex, and I'll be taking care of you today. Would you like some coffee?" He held up a stainless pot.

"Please," Jason and I said together.

Alex poured our cups full. "There's cream and sugar on the table. Do you know what you'd like to order?"

Jason looked at me. "Grace?"

I hesitated for only half a second. "I'll have the Georgia peach crepes and a side of grits, please."

"Good choice. And for you, sir?" Alex asked.

"I'll take the pecan pancakes and a side of bacon."

"You got it. If y'all need anything else, let me know."

"Thanks, Alex," Jason said, handing him our menus.

Jason ripped open a packet of sugar and poured it into his coffee. "Sylvia's interesting. Is she a friend of yours?"

Interesting question. "I'm not sure. She usually talks *at* me, like I'm stupid, but she keeps coming back, so who knows? She's a good customer though."

"I can tell from the car alone. She has the town car *and* a Bentley?" He let out a deep whistle.

"She has others too. I've seen at least two other fancy cars."

"I'm kind of surprised she drives herself," he said.

"She doesn't always. I've seen a man and a woman bring her to the store before."

"Do they park in designated parking areas?" he asked.

"How do you think I knew someone drove her?"

He laughed through a yawn and covered his mouth.

"Tired?" I asked.

"Always. I'm not meant for the night shift."

"Do you always work nights?"

He nodded. "Monday through Friday."

"That's got to suck."

"It's only temporary. I accepted a promotion, but that came with this shift until the new year."

"Well, congratulations then. What kind of promotion?"

"I made sergeant."

"Nice." I started doing the math in my head. "I guess you've been there for, what? Five, six years now?"

"Seven, actually."

That didn't seem possible, but I remembered he was starting the police academy the week after my wedding. So seven years would be right. "Wow. Do you like it? Being a cop."

He stuffed his fists into the pockets of his jacket. "I do. It's stressful always, but it's never boring. Like today, in court, is *definitely* not going to be boring."

"How come?"

"Halloween night, I got called to a bar down off Demonbruen. There was a drunk guy there threatening the bartender. He was dressed as a six-foot-tall penis."

I clapped my hands over my mouth.

Jason closed his eyes. "It was horrifically well detailed. Veins, hairs, two giant balls down around his ankles."

"Oh my god," I said, laughing.

"It's all on YouTube. Just search for 'cop in Nashville wrestles giant penis.' I'm pretty sure I might wind up on *Jerry Springer*."

"Wrestles?"

"The guy literally bent over and charged me with his penis head. I had to tackle him to the ground to handcuff him. It was humiliating. And hysterical."

We were laughing so hard that the ladies at the table next to us looked over.

"The costume was about seven feet tall, so you can imagine what it looked like when I put him in the back of my patrol car. I don't think I'll ever hear the end of it from the guys at work."

"I'll bet you won't."

"Today is that guy's day in court. I really can't wait to hear this one be explained to the judge."

"I'm tempted to close the shop and come with you."

He chuckled. "It is open to the public."

"As much as I would love to be there, I'm swamped with work. This month starts the busiest shopping season of the year."

"You're not telling me anything I don't know. I usually end up working the Bellevue shopping district every Black Friday. Last year, I had to arrest three people on assault charges for fighting over discounted televisions."

"People are crazy."

"It's a good thing you're a tough roller girl now, I guess. You can serve as your own store's bouncer if you have to," he said with a smile.

Dear god, he has dimples. How had I never noticed that before?

"Grace?"

I blinked hard to try to reboot my brain. "Uh...well, nobody in my store ever fights over anything, but yes, I suppose if I had to, I could hip check someone to the curb."

"I don't think you've told me. How did you start playing?"

"My best friend, Monica, and I saw them skate in the Nashville Christmas Parade last year. They were handing out flyers for their next scrimmage that was open to the public a few weeks later, and we've been hooked ever since."

"It's kind of a jump from watching safely in the stands to actually playing, right?"

I smiled. "I guess. At their last bout of the season a few months ago, they announced they were recruiting new members for their 'Fresh Meat' group"—I used air quotes—"so Monica and I signed up. We officially made the team a couple of weeks ago."

"Throw in the divorce and it sounds like life has been pretty eventful for you lately."

"It has been. Doors closing, windows opening and all that. When you did security, did you get to watch the Rollers play at all?"

His eyes widened. "Oh yeah. It was pretty badass. I'll admit, I didn't understand a whole lot of what was going on, but it was a blast to watch."

"Maybe sometime I can explain it to you."

"I'd like that. When's your next game?"

I held up a finger. "First lesson of Derby 101 is they aren't *games*, they're *bouts*."

He grinned over his coffee. "OK. When's your next bout?"

"The season doesn't start back until spring. My first bout is actually going to be an invitational tournament in March called the B-Cup."

"The B-Cup? Like..." He put his coffee down and cupped two hands under his pecs.

"Exactly. Apparently, the winner gets a golden-bra trophy."

He laughed. "I love it. Can't wait to see that."

"It's in Indiana."

"Oh." He sat back and shrugged. "Who knows? Maybe I'll still make it."

"What about you? What are you doing for fun these days?"

"I do a little cage fighting on the side..."

"Really?"

He shook his head and chuckled. "No. That's a total lie. I'm a complete wuss."

My mouth fell open.

"How am I supposed to follow up you playing roller derby? That I'm the third baseman for our intramural softball team at the station?" We were both laughing. "That I coach Little League?"

"You coach kids' baseball?" I repeated, my giggles fading.

"Yeah. It's a volunteer program through the police department. It's nice to be part of a team again, even if I am four feet taller than all the other players."

His eyes were sweetly sad.

"Do you ever regret not going all the way with baseball?"

He took a deep breath and sat back in his seat. "Who says I would've gone all the way?"

"Jason, you were so good. We all knew you were headed to the majors."

He smiled. "I wouldn't have done anything differently."

I believed that. Jason Bradley could never have been accused of being anything other than a great guy. But it was clear, he didn't want to talk about the glory days or what might have been.

"Do you like Little League?"

"I love it. Kids are funny, man. The ones on my team are five and six. Half the time, they don't know which way to run or who to throw the ball to. The first day of practice, this one boy took a leak in the outfield. It was hysterical."

"Oh my god, that's funny."

"His mother didn't think so. I thought that woman was going to lay an egg on the bleachers."

"I'll bet. My mother would have died," I said.

"Mine too. What about you? Do you still play basketball?"

"With my brother sometimes in the driveway at my parents' house. But other than that, never."

"That's a shame. You were really good. Have you ever thought about coaching?"

I curled my hands around my coffee cup. "Not ever. I'm so rusty now, I cheat when I dribble the ball."

He chuckled. "That's too bad. Coaching is one of the most rewarding things I do. I love kids."

Three simple words, and my heart fell about a thousand feet through the floor. I wondered if Clay had told him about our struggle to have children. After years of trying, it was hardly a secret. Still, I wondered if he knew.

Time to change the subject.

"I wouldn't have time for basketball these days even if I wanted to play or coach. I barely have enough time for work with my derby schedule. It's becoming a problem."

"So you practice on Monday and Wednesday and Saturday, and you skate with your friend every Sunday. Do you really enjoy it that much?"

I smiled. "I really do. It's fun and exciting. Not to mention, I get to feel like a total badass."

"Feel like? Grace, badassery isn't a new thing for you." He leaned on his forearms. "I'll never forget that game you played against Montgomery State. The one where you nailed the three-point shot, then intercepted the inbound pass, backed up, and hit another three-pointer."

I blinked. "You remember that?"

"Are you kidding? *Everyone* remembers that."

"It was a lucky play."

"Bullshit."

My cheeks felt warm. "Thanks."

Our waiter returned with a large round tray. "Georgia peach," he said, putting my crepes down in front of me. "And a side of grits."

I smiled, thankful for the diversion. "Thank you."

"And the pecan pancakes and a side of bacon." He put Jason's plate down in front of him. "Can I get y'all anything else right now?"

"I don't think so," I said.

Jason shook his head. "We're good. Thanks, Alex."

"No problem. Flag me down if you need anything."

When he left, Jason leaned close to his plate and inhaled. "I could take up gluttony as a hobby."

"Right?" I asked, scooping up a mound of peaches and real whipped cream. I moaned with pleasure when the warm sauce hit my tongue. When I looked at him, he was staring at my mouth. "Want a bite?"

He cleared his throat and laughed, his eyes darting to his own plate. "I wouldn't dare come between you and those peaches." He picked up his bacon and bit off a large piece.

After a few heavenly bites, a phone rang at our table. It wasn't mine. Jason looked down and unclipped his cell from his belt. His shoulders fell when he looked at the screen.

"What's the matter?" I asked, my fork mid air to my mouth with another loaded bite of crepes.

He put the phone face up on the table for me to see.

Clay.

I groaned.

Instead of answering it, he pressed a button on the side that made the screen go black. Then, as he clipped it back in place on his waistband, I saw an unmistakable flash of guilt in his eyes.

"You can take the call. I don't mind."

"Nah. I'll call him later." He turned his eyes and attention to his plate and sliced through his pancakes with a little more force than necessary.

I sat back in my seat and put my hands in my lap. "Jason, what are we doing here?"

He swallowed, then looked at me. "What do you mean?"

"You and I talking so much and now eating lunch together."

With a sigh, he laid his fork down. "I don't know, Grace, but I like talking to you." A small smile crept across his lips. "More than I like talking to your ex these days. I feel guilty as hell, though. Not gonna lie."

I put my hand on his. "That's because you're a good guy, and Clay's decided that he's not."

"That's the truth." He was staring at our hands on the table. Then he looked at me. "But maybe it's best if we cool it and keep this in the friend zone, huh?"

"Maybe. There's no way this isn't going to get messy, and I've had enough drama this year to last a lifetime."

He nodded. "Yeah. You certainly deserve a break."

I squeezed his hand and released it. "Better eat your pancakes before the syrup gets cold. I'd hate to send you off to battle the giant penis in court on an empty stomach."

He laughed. "Definitely can't have that."

We finished our breakfast in loaded silence, speckled with small bits of polite small talk. Then he paid for our check, added a generous tip for Alex, and we left.

When we turned the corner toward my store, Jason suddenly stopped walking.

I stopped too. "What is it?"

He pointed up ahead. "Isn't that what's-her-face's car again?"

"Shit." Sylvie was back.

The front bells chimed and her loud voice carried out onto the wind. "Don't forget to tell Grace, Kiara…"

I panicked. "She can't see me, or she'll be here all day telling me everything that's wrong with my store."

He looked around, then grasped both of my arms and guided me backward into the covered kitchen entryway to the restaurant. My back flattened against the door, and Jason's rock-solid chest pressed against me.

Heat radiated between us as his body vibrated with soft laughter. He smelled delicious, like fresh cologne and sugar. Or maybe that was coming from the kitchen door behind me.

Whatever it was made my insides tingle, an intoxicating feeling I really didn't need right then with us having just decided to keep things friendly. Still, common sense didn't stop me from gripping two fistfuls of his supple leather jacket to hold him close.

"I'll tell her, Sylvie," Kiara was saying around the corner of the wall. "I know she'll be very sad she didn't get to see you again."

"Of course she will," Sylvie said.

Jason laughed harder, and I clamped my hand over his mouth to keep him quiet.

"Wave goodbye to Kiara, Miss Taylor."

I had no doubt Sylvie was waving the dog's paw at her.

"Goodbye, Miss Taylor," Kiara said. "Goodbye, Sylvie."

"I'll see you tomorrow!"

I dropped my forehead against Jason's shoulder.

The bells on the door jingled again, presumably as Kiara closed it, but we stayed frozen for a moment longer. We waited for the rumble from Sylvia's engine, and finally relaxed.

Then someone knocked on the glass behind me. I jumped. And screamed. That time, Jason laughed out loud.

I turned and saw a man in a white apron holding up his hands as if to ask, "What are you doing?"

"Sorry," I mouthed.

Jason's hand slid down to mine, and he took a step back to look down the street. "Looks like the coast is clear." He pulled me toward him onto the open sidewalk. "You all right? I was afraid your heart might have stopped just now."

"That guy scared me to death."

"I know. I thought I might have to administer mouth-to-mouth."

Still holding his hand, I took a step toward him. "Keep it up, Officer Bradley, and no one is going to believe that 'keep things in the friend zone' line you spouted off earlier."

"Yeah, well..." He grinned as he held the door to my store open for me.

"I'll grab your uniform," I said when we walked back inside. "And you can change upstairs in my apartment unless you want to use a dressing room that was designed for three-foot princesses."

He laughed. "I think I'll use the apartment if you don't mind."

"Of course not. I cleaned it last night and everything." I'd cleaned my apartment with the thought that we might wind up there together at some point. It looked like that wouldn't happen after all. Not ever.

With a forced smile to cover my disappointment, I walked to the back.

Kiara was plugging in a hot-glue gun. She looked at the sparkly watch around her wrist. "Those were some speedy pancakes."

"Yeah," I replied flatly and reached for the uniform hanging on the coat rack.

"Sylvia came back to see you."

"Hold that thought," I said and carried the uniform back to

where Jason was waiting, checking something—probably Clay's message—on his phone.

I pulled my keys from my purse and handed them to him with the hanger. "Here you go. The code to the door downstairs is twenty-seven, twenty-seven."

He smiled as he accepted them. "Twenty-seven for your old basketball number?"

My head snapped back. "Yeah. God, you have a good memory."

"Is that your derby number too?"

"No. My derby number is six-foot-two."

He laughed. "That's hilarious." He jerked his thumb over his shoulder. "I'd better get changed. Can't be late."

I stood there as he walked outside and sighed heavily as the door jingled closed behind him. "Well, doesn't this suck?" I asked out loud.

"What sucks?" Kiara asked behind me.

"It's over even before anything began, and I really don't want to talk about it."

"OK," she said, stepping out of my way as I walked back to the workroom.

I sank down at my desk. "What did Sylvia want?"

"She wants a sash around the dress. Preferably somehow incorporating roses."

"Of course. Why wouldn't she want roses?" I said with a heavy sigh.

Kiara looked like she wanted to ask if I was OK, but she didn't. And for that, I was grateful.

While Jason was gone, I sewed together a few of the pieces of the periwinkle dress...and fantasized about different ways I could kill my ex-husband.

I could sneak into the house and put cyanide in the Keurig.

Or put amoeba-infested water in his neti pot.

Or force feed him shards of glass and make him wash them down with laxatives.

Whoa.

Maybe it's time to follow up with the therapist, Grace.

The front door bells saved me my from own horrific thoughts.

"Want me to get that?" Kiara asked from the floor.

Shaking my head, I stood and walked back out to the store room. Jason was in his black uniform, all drool-worthy and distracting.

Clay who?

He gestured toward the door. "I'd better get going."

"Yeah. Thanks again for breakfast," I said, walking over to say a proper goodbye.

"Thanks again for joining me." His eyes fell to the floor. "I'm sorry that—"

I waved my hand to stop him. "Jason, don't. It's OK."

He smiled gently. "I really like you, Grace." He sighed. "I've always really liked you."

My breath caught in my throat. I swallowed hard all the emotions trying to erupt out of me. This conversation needed to be diverted. Fast. "Have fun with the giant penis in court today."

He burst out laughing. "Ha. Thanks. I'll try." Then he put his arms around me, kissed the top of my head, and lingered for a second. "I'll see you around, Grace."

I waved as he stepped away. "Goodbye, Jason."

SEVEN

THE UPSIDE to the missing male distraction in my life was that I'd been incredibly productive for the week and a half following my non-breakup with Jason. I completed three new holiday dresses for the Black Friday inventory, made a custom-order party dress for one of my regulars, and had just finished Sylvia's periwinkle gown that morning before practice.

The gown turned out pretty spectacular, if I do say so myself. The Sinclair Satin had been used to make the bodice, and over a hundred pieces of wired, iridescent periwinkle tulle had been rippled and curled to fill out the skirt. I'd added a pleated chiffon waistband and a hand-tied, rose-shaped bow for the back.

All of that had been done in the middle of the whirlwind Kiara had created in my workroom. As I walked into my final Saturday practice before the holidays, she sent me a text.

Let me know when you're on your way back.

"Please be done with the front window. Please be done with the front window," I prayed aloud as I texted her.

Will do.

I dropped my stuff on the floor beside Lucy and Monica. "Good morning, girls," I said, looking around the room.

"Morning. Who are you looking for?" Monica asked.

I sat down. "I need to talk to someone about having to miss practice. Know who that is?"

"Why? Where are you going to be?" Monica asked. We'd never blown off practice before.

"I'm going to skip Monday so I can get ready for Black Friday. It would be better than missing the scrimmage on Wednesday."

Monica nodded. "That makes sense. You need to talk to Shamrocker, I think."

"I need to talk to her too," Lucy said.

"Is everything OK with you, Lucy?"

"Yeah. West and I took the week off to go spend with my dad in Riverbend, so I won't be here."

My head snapped back. "This sounds pretty serious with you two."

"It's going really well," she said, unable to hide a smile.

"Good for you. I'm happy for you, Lucy." And I was. Even if my own love life was in the toilet, she deserved to be happy.

"I have other news too. Guess who's going to be with us at the parade," Lucy said.

We both looked at her. "Who?" I asked.

"Jake Barrett is supposed to be performing. They announced it Thursday in my team meeting at work," she said.

Jake Barrett was one of country music's hottest superstars. Lucy worked in the office that managed him, and he'd shown up to watch her skate in her very first public bout, our Halloween Monster's Brawl. He'd come in costume, dressed as Jason from *Friday the 13th*.

"I'm going to try to introduce him to the team."

"That's exciting," Monica said.

I nodded. "It would be really cool to meet him."

"Don't say anything in case I can't pull it off. Jake can be a little flaky."

I pretended to zip my mouth closed. "My lips are sealed."

"How was your week, Grace?" Monica asked. "I haven't heard from you much."

"I've been crazy busy at work. There hasn't been much time for anything else. Which reminds me, have you guys joined a committee yet?"

"I met with the marketing team this week. It was pretty cool," Lucy said.

"I won't even be able to think about it until after the holidays. I can't take on anything else right now," Monica said.

"Me either. Shopping madness is upon us, and I don't know how I'm going to keep juggling practice and work as it is."

"I hear ya. I am thinking about letting Maisie play on the juniors' team if she wants to. If she does, I'll probably help out there," Monica said.

"Is Maisie old enough?" I asked. Monica's daughter had just turned nine.

"The website says they take girls from eight to eighteen," Monica said.

"Whoa. That's young. But it's not full contact, right?" Lucy asked.

"No. It's full contact," Monica said.

Lucy's mouth fell open. "Shut up."

I tied my sneaker. "I'm trying to talk my brother into letting my nieces play. They're obsessed with derby now."

"That's so sweet," Lucy said. "Their hero is their Aunt Grace."

I pointed across the room to where Medusa was chatting with Maven and Styx. "Their hero is *Medusa*."

Monica chuckled. "Can you blame them?"

"No," Lucy and I said together.

We all stood and pushed our bags to the side. Monica nudged my arm. "Have you heard anymore from Officer Eye Candy?" she asked with a hopeful smile.

"Who?" Lucy asked, perking up.

I sighed and shook my head. "No one. I told you, Monica. It's over."

I hadn't talked to Jason again since our fateful pancake lunch. I wished I hadn't thought about him either, but my brain simply wouldn't cooperate. And now, thanks to Monica, he was front and center in my mind for our off-skates warm-up.

Maven took over practice when we'd finished warming up with Medusa, and I was pretty sure if anyone on the team could cure me of daydreams, it was Maven.

"Everybody spread out for fast feet!" she called, draping a whistle around her neck.

"What are we doing?" Monica asked no one in particular.

Shamrocker was a few feet in front of us. "We're about to die. That's what's going to happen."

"Why?" Monica's voice sounded a little panicked.

Beside Shamrocker, Princess Die looked back at us. "Have you done her burpees?"

I groaned. Monica nodded.

Princess Die smiled. "They're a vacation by comparison."

Monica seemed like she might break down and cry.

"When I say go, you'll sprint in place as fast as you can for ten seconds." Maven sprinted in place, her feet pounding the floor a thousand times per nanosecond. "On the whistle, you'll drop to the floor, all the way flat on your belly, then pop back up and sprint in place again." She dropped to the floor, then jumped back up on her feet and kept running.

"What the actual hell?" Monica asked.

"Get ready!" Maven yelled. "Go!"

The sound of all our feet slamming the ground was deafening. Then Maven blew the whistle, and we all dropped down onto the cold painted concrete. I jumped back up and ran as hard as I could.

After three rounds, I could no longer feel my feet. Four rounds in, I left a sweaty body print on the floor. I'd slowed to a jog by round six, and I couldn't get off the floor by the time most everyone else finished round ten.

Frog jumps came next. We literally jumped like a frog—touching the floor between each hop—all the way across the room. Then we did the same thing backward all the way to the starting line. Lucy fell once. Monica walked backward most of the room. And my legs were knotted like sailors' ropes by the time the jumps were over.

Our resting period was a series of dynamic stretches. Knees to chest, ankle rotations, hip rotations, torso twists...All I wanted to do was lay on the floor and drink my weight in cold water. But alas, the torture continued.

And I didn't think about Jason Bradley another time.

———

I went home and straight to the shower after practice. Kiara had given me very specific instructions to not come to the store one second before two o'clock and to not even glance at the storefront as I entered my apartment.

Of course, I didn't listen. But I couldn't see anything either. The front window had been freshly recovered in brown paper.

She'd written on the paper this time instead of the window: *Grand unveiling today! Hot cocoa and Christmas cookies at 2 p.m.!*

Had I agreed to hot cocoa and Christmas cookies?

I texted her, as promised, before I left my apartment to come down. When I walked inside, she was ringing up a customer, a woman with a toddler on her hip.

To my right were two college-age boys, each holding the corner of a large strip of brown paper in front of the window. One of them smiled at me, and his corner lowered just enough for me to see a flash of white behind him.

Kiara snapped her fingers. "Uh-uh, Davion! Don't you get lazy on me now!" Davion. I recognized his name. He was Kiara's boyfriend.

Davion quickly straightened, snapping his eyes forward toward the wall.

My head fell quizzically to the side, but before I could ask, Kiara spoke. "There's the genius of whom we speak."

I walked toward the cash register.

Kiara had a bright smile. She wore a fuzzy cowl-neck white sweater and bright blue pants. "We were just talking about you, Grace. This is Megan and her daughter, Riley. She just bought the Charlotte dress."

I beamed. "That's one of my favorites."

"You made them all?" the woman asked, adjusting the little girl on her side.

"Kiara and I made them, but all the gowns are my designs."

"They're beautiful," she said.

"Thank you. Have you been in before?"

"No. I had no idea this was even here until we had breakfast next door."

"Yes, I swear their pancakes are our best advertisement!"

She laughed. "That may be true."

"Megan, if you have a moment, we have a very special surprise for Grace. I'd love for you and Riley to see it," Kiara said, walking around from behind the counter.

"OK. Sure," Megan answered.

"Riley, do you like hot cocoa?" Kiara asked.

Riley nodded with her thumb in her mouth.

"Speaking of hot cocoa," I said. "When did we decide to—"

Kiara wagged her finger. "No, no, no. This is my surprise."

"And ours," a voice said from the back of the room.

Mom and Dad walked out of my workroom. Dad was carrying a bright orange drink cooler with a spout on the front.

"You called my parents?" I asked Kiara.

"I did."

I laughed as Mom came over to give me a hug. She held up a strip of periwinkle satin. "I'm in charge of the blindfold."

"Blindfold?" I asked, giving Dad a kiss on the cheek.

Kiara walked toward the front of the store. "Yes. Blindfold."

The boys holding up the craft paper were starting to visibly tremble. "Kiara, how long have these poor guys been here?" I asked.

"Since about nine this morning," she said.

My eyes doubled. "Holding that thing the whole time?"

"Of course not, silly. And as soon as you put on that blindfold, they can lower their arms." She walked over and plugged something into the wall.

Mom held up the satin. I turned and she put it over my eyes, tying it behind my head. The fabric reminded me of Sylvie. "Kiara, did Sylvie pick up the dress this morning?"

"I haven't seen her since last week," she said.

"I haven't either. That's weird. Remind me to try to call again before I leave."

"You got it."

"Kiara, should we go outside?" my mother asked, holding onto my arm.

"Yes, please. Davion, you and James take the table and the cookies outside," she said to the boys. "Don't forget the cups!"

The paper crumpling echoed around the room as my mother guided me to the front of the door and outside. "Stay here," she said, releasing me. The door bells jingled, and I assumed she was holding it open for my dad.

It was freezing outside. I wished I'd worn a thicker coat.

"She's really a good find," Mom said a moment later.

"Kiara?" I smiled. "Yeah, she's amazing."

"She's an intern?" Dad asked.

I nodded. "Part-time employee too."

"Maybe you should make her full-time," Mom said.

"I'd love to, if she sticks around after college. I'm sure that won't happen though. She's too good for Nashville."

"Did I miss anything?" a woman's voice said behind me.

I turned, not really sure why since I was blindfolded.

"Hi, I'm Grace's mother, Sheila," mom said.

"Nice to meet you. I'm one of Kiara Washington's professors from MacKay. Imogen Sleight. Is this Grace?" she asked.

My back was to the window, so I pushed the blindfold up over one eye. The woman in front of me was smiling. Imogen Sleight was pale with wiry white hair and glasses with thick dark rims. She wore a faux-fur-lined black puffer coat—Michael Kors if I wasn't mistaken.

"Hi, I'm Grace Evans," I said, offering her hand. "Excuse the blindfold."

"No excuse needed. I'm glad I didn't miss the big unveiling. Kiara's been so excited about this."

"She certainly has been," I said.

"You're a professor?" Mom asked.

"The department chair, actually."

"That's wonderful. It's so nice of you to show up here to support one of your students," Mom said, noticeably impressed.

"She's a very special student."

Before I could agree, the front door bells jingled again behind me. I tugged the blindfold back down quickly. I heard Kiara moving people around and giving orders to the boys.

"Professor Sleight, you made it!" Kiara said.

"I wouldn't miss this," the teacher said.

There was a faint rustle of paper, probably inside the window, and I heard my mother gasp softly beside me.

"Mama, look!" I heard little Riley say.

"I know. I see it. It's so pretty," Megan agreed.

"You ready?" Kiara said behind me.

My heart was thumping with excitement. I nodded, and she pulled off the blindfold. I covered my mouth with my hands. The window took my breath.

She'd created rolling hills of snow with the cotton and had painted large shimmering snowflakes that hung from the top. The pink Christmas tree—which I hadn't been so sure about—was decorated with white ornaments and white lights and placed on a rotating stand that turned slowly.

A glittery snowman wore a scarf and earmuffs (sold inside), and two child-sized mannequins were reaching up to catch the snowflakes. They were wearing two of our new limited-edition winter designs: the Holly and the Noël.

The whole thing was set against a backdrop of a million twinkling fairy lights.

Everyone on the street was clapping.

Tears filled my eyes. "Kiara, it's just..." I had no words to complete the sentence, so I hugged her. "Please don't ever leave me!"

She laughed. "Aww...are you crying?"

"No!" I said, covering my watery eyes with my hand. I sniffed and hugged her again. "I love it."

"It's absolute breathtaking," my mother agreed.

"Nice work," Dad said.

"Welcome, everyone. We have hot chocolate and cookies!" Kiara announced to the crowd of passersby who had gathered to check out the commotion.

The unveiling turned into an impromptu open house. Patrons were in and out of my store for the rest of the afternoon, renewing my hope that the holidays might indeed save the store from going under. The property-tax bill wasn't going to pay itself.

My parents stayed for a little while. So did Kiara's professor. A few regulars stopped in as well. Still, no Sylvia. I tried to call her again before we closed.

A man answered the phone.

"May I speak to Sylvia Sinclair, please?" I asked.

"I'm sorry, Mrs. Sinclair is not available. May I take a message?"

"My name is Grace Evans, from Sparkled Pink children's boutique. Sylvia ordered a dress from me and asked for rush delivery before Thanksgiving. I left a message with someone yesterday but haven't heard back. She's generally in my store a few times a week, but she's not been in lately."

"Oh...well, Mrs. Sinclair has been in the hospital for the past few days."

I sat down at my work desk. "Oh no. Is she OK?"

"They are letting her come home today. I'll be more than happy to send someone to pick up her order."

"Thank you. I know she was really wanting it before the holiday," I said.

I gave him the address for the store, and he promised to send someone early the next week. I told Kiara the bad news as she put tiny pairs of blue jeans out on a table. "When was the last time she was in here?" she asked.

I thought for a moment. Then heat rose in my cheeks as memories of being sandwiched together with Jason in the alcove next door flooded back to my mind. God, he'd smelled so good. Felt so warm and strong.

"Grace?"

I blinked. "Over a week ago."

"I hope she's OK."

"Me too." And I did. Suddenly, I felt very guilty about avoiding her that day. As crazy as she made me, I'd sort of gotten attached to her.

Kiara stopped working and pulled her phone from her pocket. "I just got a message from Professor Sleight."

"Was she impressed?" I asked.

"Absolutely. She wants to know if we would be available for an interview with the newspaper early on Wednesday. The article will run on Thanksgiving."

"Absolutely. A newspaper interview before Black Friday, are you kidding? I'll be available at two in the morning if they need me to be."

She smiled. "I'll tell her yes then." When she finished texting, she pulled more pairs of jeans from the box.

"This could really turn into something for you, Kiara." I walked over to help her. "I've seen things like this snowball to get national attention."

"Really?"

"Yep. Back before flash mobs were a thing, my best friend organized a spontaneous concert in the middle of Rockefeller Center with the choral department at her school. To this day, she puts that experience on her resume, and everyone in her business knows it. She said it's come up in every interview she's ever had."

"Was this Monica?" she asked.

"Sure was. Now she's got a fancy-schmancy job at Lockwood Academy. All because of an idea she had in college."

"That's good to hear. But right now, I'm just trying to make it through this semester."

I laughed. "I hear ya."

"What's your plan for next week? I don't have school at all."

"We'll only be closed on Thursday. We need to get ready for

Black Friday before then, so if you want to work all week, you can. I'll probably be working late a lot."

"Won't you have roller derby practice?" she asked.

"I'm going to skip practice on Monday, but I don't want to miss Wednesday night's scrimmage. So if I'm not there, I'll be here each day and night. You're welcome to join me."

"Good deal. Thanks, Grace."

"How's planning for your New York trip coming along?" I asked.

"I'm about halfway to my goal. I have enough for plane tickets. I just need food and spending money."

"You'll get there." And I was sure she would. Looking at the window again, I could see a nice holiday bonus in her future, even if I had to sell my soul to give it to her.

———

It was weird skipping practice on Monday. Kiara and I worked together until eight o'clock when I sent her home. Then I didn't quit until almost two in the morning. On Tuesday, I started the whole routine over. But, by the time I left in the wee hours of Wednesday, three more gowns were complete, all the extra Black Friday stock had been unpacked and put on the shelves, and the rest of the store was decorated.

Kiara brought me coffee when she came into work Wednesday morning shortly before opening. "Bless you," I whispered, accepting the paper cup.

"How late were you here?" she asked, carrying her stuff to the back.

I followed. "I think I left around four."

"Mercy," she said. "It looks great out there though."

"Thank you."

Just then, the front door bells jingled. "Gra-ace!"

"Sylvie," I whispered, closing my eyes. "There is not enough coffee for this so early in the morning."

Kiara laughed as I turned back toward the store.

I froze.

Sylvia Sinclair was in a wheelchair. Miss Taylor was laying on her lap, on top of a thick blanket. Sylvia wore dark sunglasses and her hair was as unkempt as I'd ever seen it. I didn't recognize the tall man with dark hair who wheeled her in.

"Grace, dear," she said, her voice shakier than usual.

"Sylvia," I said again, this time touching my chest.

Concerned, Kiara followed me out to the store room.

"How are you?" I asked as I walked over and knelt beside the wheelchair. Miss Taylor growled at me.

Sylvia reached for my hand, and I gently curled both of mine around hers. For the first time ever, she seemed fragile. Feeble, even. She weakly squeezed my fingers and nodded her head back twice to beckon me closer.

I leaned in.

"What the hell did you do to your front window?"

I pressed my eyes shut. My lips too.

Behind me, I heard a soft chuckle from Kiara.

"Didn't they tell you, Grace? Christmas colors are red and green. *Red* and *green*. What's with all the pink? What are we celebrating here? Christ's birthday or breast cancer? You really shouldn't celebrate cancer. I personally take offense."

I scratched my head. "Nobody is celebrating—"

"Its leukemia," she blurted out.

"What's leukemia?" I asked.

She released my hand and tapped her chest. "The doctors say I have leukemia."

"Oh, Sylvie. I'm so sorry."

She waved toward the window. "So if you're gonna celebrate cancer, you should at least find out the color for leukemia."

The man with her was trying not to laugh.

I wanted to ask about her prognosis, but Miss Taylor barked at me. Sylvia looked past me. "Where's my dress, Grace? I didn't come all the way down here for my health, you know."

With a sigh, I stood. "I'm so glad you're feeling like your old self, Sylvie."

As I walked toward the back, I glared at Kiara, who was barely maintaining her composure.

In the back, I found Sylvia's gown. When I carried it out to the storefront, Sylvia's manservant had wheeled her over to our holiday gowns. "This beading is gaudy, Grace."

I looked back over my shoulder and mouthed the words "kill me now" to Kiara. That time, she let a snicker escape.

"And you should really start using Sinclair Satin instead of this cheap stuff. I can get whatever color you want, you know."

"I'm sure you can. We can talk about that sometime, if you'd like," I said as politely as I could manage. It was nice fabric, after all.

"How about tonight?" She looked at the man. "We don't have plans tonight, do we?"

"I don't think so," he said.

"I can't tonight, Sylvie. I have derby practice."

"Ah yes." She weakly snapped her fingers over her head. "Andrew, did I tell you Grace plays roller derby?"

"No. That still exists?" he asked me.

"It does. It's bigger than ever," I answered.

Sylvia scoffed as only old, rich women can properly do. Then without giving me a chance to beg an explanation for her snobbery, she waved her hand in the air. "My dress, please?"

I sighed and pulled the plastic wrap up around the hanger. "Here you go."

Sylvia stared at it for a long moment, then smiled and leaned forward in her chair. "The fabric is gorgeous," she said, running her hand over the bodice.

Of course she thought the fabric was gorgeous. She made it!

"Do you like it?" I asked nervously.

Sylvia looked away and shifted in her chair. "The dress is fine, Grace."

She might as well have been talking about canned meat.

I was screaming on the inside. *The dress is fine?* From the design sketch to the rose bow, I'd invested at least forty hours into that dress. Not to mention the fact that I had to start it over after I'd already cut out the fabric.

She reached back and tugged on the man's sleeve. "Andrew, pay her and let's go home."

"Yes, ma'am," he said and reached into his suit jacket's inside pocket.

Unsure of what to do or how to react, I stood there paralyzed until my mother's voice echoed in my head. "The customer is always right, Grace. And at the end of the day, all that matters is that they write you a check."

Or hand you a black credit card in Sylvia's case.

With a clenched jaw, I covered the dress back up in its pink plastic (I hoped that it bothered her), and exchanged the dress with Andrew for the credit card. I walked behind the counter and punched the numbers into the digital point-of-sale system.

"Are you OK?" Kiara whispered.

"Mmm-hmm," I hummed an octave above my normal range without meeting her eyes.

The front door bells jingled.

Kiara straightened and glanced toward the door. "I'll bet that's our reporter."

"Sylvia, do you need a receipt?" I asked.

"Of course. You should always keep receipts, Grace."

I ripped the receipt tape so hard that it yanked half the roll out with it. When I turned to carry it back to her, I saw a woman in a crisp gray pants suit with a guy holding a camera and wearing jeans and a sloppily buttoned shirt.

I took the receipt and the credit card back to Andrew and Sylvia. I handed them to him. "Here you are. Sylvia, it was a pleasure doing business with you as always," I lied, sounding extra chipper.

She cleared her throat. "Thank you, Grace."

"I hope Alexandria enjoys her dress," I added, hoping to hell that someone would.

Andrew paused as he put the card back in his wallet.

"Grace, are you ready?" Kiara called from the front of the store.

I forced a sweet smile to Sylvia. "I hope you'll excuse me. We have a reporter here who'd like to feature the store in the newspaper."

I wasn't sure why I'd added that last bit, except for wanting to make a statement that, damn it, somebody thought I was pretty important. OK, maybe they were here for Kiara and not for me, but still.

"I hope you're fully recovered soon." I did mean that part. She was a mean old hag, but I wouldn't wish cancer on anyone.

She waved as Andrew rolled her out the front door. I watched them go, my eyes fixed on her wheels as the door closed behind them. I wished her disapproval didn't hurt so much.

"Grace?" Kiara asked. "Are you ready to do this?"

I nodded. "Sure am."

EIGHT

"ON YOUR INSIDE!" someone screamed as I cut left to enter the pack during our scrimmage that night.

Seemingly out of nowhere, Electra Cal came at me in the middle of a turn. Her shoulder missed my upper arm and slammed into the soft spot just beneath my collarbone. The impact spun me around on my skates, and I went down hard on my knees just off the track.

"Call off the jam!"

"Call off the jam!"

Stunned and in pain, it took my brain a second to realize those voices were shouting at me. I double-tapped my hips with my hands until the jam whistle blasted four times.

Monica skated over and looked down on me. "You OK, Grace?"

I was panting, but I nodded. "I'm OK."

Medusa joined her. "You've got to keep your head on a swivel, Britches. You didn't even see Electra Cal coming, did you?"

I groaned in response.

She offered me a hand and pulled me up. "Your stance needs to be lower too. Your center of gravity is way off."

"Thanks," I said, checking to make sure I hadn't cracked a knee pad.

"And pay attention to your bench coach. Goldie scored a few points before you called off the jam."

I nodded.

She slapped my helmet. "You'll get it next time."

I wasn't so sure. Everything hurt. My body was exhausted, and my brain couldn't focus.

Monica and I skated back to our team's bench together. "You OK? What's going on with you tonight?"

"I'm just off my game. Haven't slept much this week." I picked up my water bottle and drained what was left of it.

"It shows. Maybe you shouldn't scrimmage when you haven't had enough rest."

I tossed the water bottle toward the trash can and missed. "You think?"

Shamrocker took my place as jammer for the next jam. I reached up to remove my jammer panty, the star cover on my helmet. Medusa pointed at me from the end of our bench. "Britches, if we run another jam, you're back in as jammer. You're up next. Get ready."

I swore quietly and dropped my hand, leaving the star in place. A minute and a half remained on the period clock. I silently prayed the current jam would last the full two minutes.

Monica grinned at me. "It's almost over."

"It's going to be an Epsom salt bath kind of night." I winced as I stood on my skates.

Doc Carnage, the other jammer, called off the jam early.

"You've got this, Grace," Monica said as I skated back out to the track.

"Keep your eyes on me!" Medusa yelled.

I gave her a thumbs-up and took my place on the jammer line next to...oh god, Maven. "Good luck, *Britches*." The way she said my name made it sound like a curse.

After a few seconds, the jam whistle blew and we took off. My opponents—Rocksee Rolls, 5 Scar Jeneral, and Bad News Baroness—had formed a tight triangle to hold me back. Black-Eye Candy, their pivot and fourth blocker, was their final line of defense, lurking beyond them in case I broke through the wall.

Maven was somewhere behind me, but I knew it wouldn't likely be for long. I had to get through the pack before her to claim the title of lead jammer. Only lead jammers could call off the jam early to prevent the other team from scoring.

I cut to the right, and the blockers headed me off.

I darted back to the left, and Candy spun around to stop me.

I pushed against 5 Scar and Baroness's melded arms; they didn't budge.

Maven caught up with me.

The wall of blockers holding me back made a hole for her on the inside line, and I took the opportunity to bust them apart. Maven and I collided, and I knocked her sideways.

My teammates stood and cheered.

But she didn't fall or go out of bounds, and just as I passed her team's final blocker, Maven caught me in the middle of the turn. She angled, and I ducked my shoulder as she slammed into me. I sailed off the track, all eight wheels airborne, and landed on the side of my hip.

Cackling like a witch, Maven skated backward in the wrong direction *toward* the pack we'd just escaped. She stopped close to her line of blockers—the ones I'd barely been able to pass—because she knew I had to reenter the track behind her. I swore as I did.

"Nice try, newbie," she hissed before skating off again.

Then her blockers swarmed, reforming their wall in front of me.

"What the hell kind of play was that shit?" I shouted, pushing against them.

"That was called Eating the Baby," Bad News Baroness answered, laughing.

The referee's whistle told me Maven made lead jammer. Finally, my blockers came to my rescue. Styx hip checked 5 Scar out of the way, and I skated past them around the track.

As I rounded the third turn, something caught my eye near the front door. A black police uniform. I straightened.

Jason?

A sharp shoulder caught the middle of my upper arm, and Maven let out a guttural scream as she knocked me out of bounds again. This time, I landed on my butt and slid halfway to the front door.

I pulled my skates under me and pushed myself up. Good god, my muscles were screaming. Trying to catch my breath, I skated back onto the track.

Just as I caught up with the pack, Maven double-tapped her hips to end the jam, and thereby the scrimmage, before I could score my first point.

I swore again.

"Back to your benches," someone yelled.

As I skated over, I looked toward the door again. Jason gave a small wave and mouthed the word, "Sorry."

What's he doing here?

Several of the other girls noticed him too. That was obvious by the hushed whispers happening around me.

"Is that...?" Monica was pointing toward the door when I plopped down beside her.

"That's him," I said, wiping my sweaty face on the front of my jersey.

"I thought you decided not to see each other anymore."

"I thought so too. We haven't talked in a couple of weeks."

"Good practice, ladies!" Styx called as she skated out in front of us. "Congratulations, newbies, on surviving your first scrimmage!"

Several of the other skaters clapped. Maven wasn't one of them.

"Don't forget!" Styx shouted. "Saturday is our last weekend practice of the year. Next weekend is the parade—"

Medusa cupped her hands around her mouth. "Next weekend is also the Slammy Awards!"

Even for that, everyone was too exhausted to really cheer.

"Yes, the Slammy Awards too. Anybody have any questions?" Styx asked.

No one responded.

She nodded. "See you guys this weekend!"

"Here. You need this," Monica said, handing me her water bottle. "And you might oughta skate into the bathroom and wash your face before you go over there."

"What's wrong with my face?"

Her nose scrunched. "It looks sticky."

I drank half her water. "Then it's a good thing he and I aren't dating. Thanks for the drink." I handed it back to her and got up, my muscles threatening to split down the middle. I groaned and skated slowly across the room.

Jason grimaced as I rolled toward him. "I feel like I almost got you killed out there."

I laughed, but I was in too much pain to really find it funny. "You did. What are you doing here?"

"I have some news." He gripped his utility belt. "Clay called me today."

"Did he tell you that he caught Ebola at the hospital?"

His head fell to the side. "No."

"Does he have an infestation of worms feeding on his few remaining brain cells?"

Jason's eyes narrowed. "No. Given this a lot of thought, have you?"

"It keeps me up at night." I crossed my arms. "If he wasn't calling to tell you he's dying a slow and painful death, I can't imagine what phone call would be worth you coming to see me in person."

"Grace, Clay asked me to dog sit starting tomorrow through this weekend."

I froze. "He what?"

"He asked me to keep Bodhi while he goes out of town for Thanksgiving. Tomorrow morning through Sunday night." He smiled. "He didn't say I couldn't outsource the job."

"Jason, are you serious?"

He nodded.

Suddenly more energized than I had been all day, I squealed and threw my arms around him. I smushed my hot, sweaty body against his—and certainly not in a good way. "Oh my god!" I was bouncing on my toe stops against him. "I think I love you!"

Then I realized what I'd just said.

I stopped and dropped my arms. "I mean...I don't *love you* love you...I just mean..."

I'm getting my dog, I thought.

"Ha!" I laughed loudly. "Screw it! I'm getting my dog. I do love you!" I hugged him again.

He laughed and hugged me back. "Grace?"

I pulled back enough to look at him. "Yeah?"

"You're gross."

"I don't even care." I bit my lip with excitement, then slowly backed away from him. "Thank you, Jason."

He bowed his head. "You're welcome. But it has to be our secret."

I held up my pinky finger. "Pinky swear."

He laughed and interlocked his pinky with mine. "I told him I'd pick Bodhi up when my shift ends. Would seven be too early to bring him by your apartment in the morning?"

"Not at all. The earlier the better." I was still holding his pinky. "Thank you again. A thousand times, thank you."

He released my hand and backed slowly toward the door. "You're welcome. I'll see you tomorrow."

I covered my mouth with my hands and squealed into them. He winked and walked out the door. I turned back toward the track, raised my fists into the air, and screamed so loud it echoed around the Sweatshop.

———

Despite my exhaustion, I could barely sleep that night. I was wide awake when my cell phone buzzed at 6:47 in the morning.

It was a message from Jason. *On our way.* Attached was a selfie of Jason in his patrol car with Bodhi in the back seat behind him.

I saved the picture to my phone and sent back three red hearts. My boy was on his way!

My front door buzzed twenty-three minutes later. I pressed the unlock button, then stepped out into the hall as Jason pulled the door open downstairs.

"Bodhi!" I called.

Jason released the leash, and Bodhi ran up the stairs. I knelt down and let him clobber me over the threshold to my apartment. He licked my face, his tail wagging so violently that it rocked his back legs.

"Sorry it took so long," Jason said, coming up the stairs. "People tend to lock down their brakes when they get in front of a police car."

"It's OK." I pushed myself up. "I'm just so glad he's here. You have no idea."

He followed us into the apartment, carrying Bodhi's bowls and dog food. Clay didn't send any toys or treats. "I have a pretty good idea. I'm going to have to take this uniform to the cleaners to get the stench out of it."

I laughed and stuck my tongue out at him.

Bodhi trotted through the apartment, sniffing the baseboards and rugs, probably checking for signs of canine infidelity.

"Where do you want me to put this stuff?" Jason asked.

"On the floor right there is fine. I'll put it away later."

He put the stuff on the floor by the door. "Happy Thanksgiving, by the way. Do you have big plans today?"

"Happy Thanksgiving to you too. I'm having linner with my whole clan."

"Did you just say 'linner'?" he asked.

My face felt hot. "Yes. Ugh. It's one of those family words that make no sense to anyone outside our little haven of craziness."

He smiled and shook his head. "No. I get it. It's not lunch. Or dinner—"

"It's *linner*," we said together and laughed.

"What are you doing for Thanksgiving?" I asked.

"I have to work tonight, so Mom and I will eat early with my aunt and her family. I'm making sweet potatoes. Have to cook them when I get home."

"You cook?"

"Somebody in our house has to."

I lifted an eyebrow. "Are you any good?"

He folded his arms across his chest. "I can hold my own."

"That's good. Maybe you should save me a plate. Our meal is always...interesting."

"Interesting?"

"My mother thinks she's Betty Crocker, and she's *so* not."

His brow rumpled with doubt. "It can't be that bad."

"Oh, but it can be. Last year, she decided to deep fry the turkey. There was a fireball in the backyard so big the neighbors called the fire department. Dad hosed the whole thing down with the fire extinguisher."

"I think I remember that call over the radio."

"Really?"

He laughed. "No."

"It's not a joke. I'm debating on packing a sack lunch."

"I can't wait to hear the stories. You've also got your Black Friday thing this weekend, right?"

"I do."

"Want me to come over and help?"

My head fell to the side. "Help sew or help run the register?"

"Neither. Help with the dog," he said, pointing at Bodhi.

"Oh! Actually, that would be really helpful. I obviously hadn't planned on needing someone to dog sit."

"No problem. I'll just plan to come here when I get off work."

"Thank you, Jason." I looked at Bodhi's stuff sitting in my foyer. "When did Clay ask you to keep him?"

He hesitated.

"Jason?"

"Right before I came by your practice. I couldn't wait to tell you."

"You mean, he was going out of town for a long weekend and didn't even bother to get someone to watch the dog?"

"I really didn't ask."

I clenched my jaw. "I hate him so much."

"I know you do. But don't let it ruin your day. Maybe if he'd planned ahead he would have picked someone better than me and I wouldn't have the chance to let you keep him."

I shook my head. "There's nobody better than you. Jason, I

really don't know how to thank you for this." I reached up to straighten the name badge on his chest.

His eyes followed my hand, then he looked at me with soft, gentle eyes and smiled. "I'm really happy to do it."

I believed him. "Can I give you a non-stinky hug this time?"

"You can always hug me. Stinky or not." He opened his arms, and I gladly walked into them.

We stood there a moment past the "just friends" time mark. Then he turned his face into my hair and lingered there a second longer. Finally, Bodhi pushed his way between our legs, and Jason took a step back.

"I guess that's my cue," he said, taking a knee beside my dog. He scratched him with both hands behind the ears. "You be a good boy for your mama." Bodhi licked Jason's face from his chin to nose. "Oh geez. Thanks, Bodhi." He stood and wiped his face on his forearm.

"Sorry," I said with a grimace.

"Don't be."

"I'll see you tomorrow then?" I asked.

"Yeah, I'm off duty at six. I'll need to go home and help Mom get her day started, and then I'll be over."

"OK."

He turned and walked back to the door. "You two have fun."

Bodhi came over and sat down right on my feet. I laughed and knelt down to hug his neck. "We will."

———

The house smelled delicious when Bodhi and I walked inside my parents' front door. I stopped, backed up, and checked the number on the outside wall just to be sure I hadn't walked in to the neighbors.

Dad came into the foyer and stopped when he saw Bodhi.

"It's OK," I said, going inside and closing the door behind me. "I'm dog sitting for the weekend."

Dad's eyes widened. "Clay's letting you keep him?"

"Not exactly."

He scowled. "Grace."

"It's fine, Daddy. I didn't steal him." I leaned over and kissed his cheek. "Happy Thanksgiving."

"Happy Thanksgiving. Need some help?" he asked.

I handed him the bag I was carrying. It contained a chocolate pecan pie I'd picked up at the store the day before and the newspaper I'd grabbed from the gas station on my way over. I slipped off my coat. "It smells amazing in here."

"Shh." He put a finger over his lips. "I'm afraid you'll jinx it."

I laughed. "Is Mom responsible for how good this place smells?"

"Yes, and you better make a big deal out of it. She's really proud of herself."

"OK."

"Where's Garrett?"

No sooner had the words left my mouth, did the door open behind me. My brother and the girls walked in.

"Bodhi!" Hope squealed, charging after the dog. He barked and ran toward the living room, invoking a game of chase.

"No running in the house!" Garret called as he unwound the green-and-blue scarf around his neck. He gave me a side hug with the arm that wasn't carrying a load of beer, his contribution to our holiday meal. "Happy Thanksgiving, sis."

"Happy Thanksgiving to you." When I released him, I grabbed Gabby. "Come here, you." I rested my chin on her head, which was getting harder and harder to do.

Hope had finally caught Bodhi around the neck. He was panting with his tongue hanging sideways out of his mouth. "Come on, Bodhi," she said, pulling him back to the foyer.

"Hope, let the dog go," Garrett said, taking off his dark gray wool coat.

With a huff, she released him. Bodhi crouched like he was going to pounce and barked. She screamed again and took off running.

"Knock it off!" my brother bellowed.

Mom came into the foyer, drying her hands on a dishtowel. "What on earth is happening in here?"

"Hi, Mom. Happy Thanksgiving," I said, giving her a hug.

"Happy Thanksgiving, Grace. It sounds like you brought a herd of elephants with you." She stretched up to kiss my brother's cheek. "Hello, son."

"I brought the herd." He held up the beer. "I also brought the booze."

"Garrett, I asked you to bring dessert."

He held up the beer again. "It's a high-octane chocolate stout, Mom."

My mother's face soured. "That sounds disgusting."

"He's full of it, Granna." Gabby held up a plastic bag. "We brought cake too. One of Dad's lady friends baked it."

"Great. Bring it to the kitchen," Mom said.

I grinned at my brother as we walked. "Lady friend, huh?"

"He has lots of them," Gabby said over her shoulder with an eyeroll.

"Not true," he argued.

Gabby stopped walking and looked up at me. "We have two casseroles in our fridge, Aunt Grace." She held up two fingers. "*Two.* And the cake."

"From different ladies?" Dad asked.

"Not anyone I'm seeing, Dad. Gabby's being dramatic."

"We call them 'prospects' at home," she continued. "There's a list."

Garrett opened his mouth, probably for a rebuttal, but he laughed instead. "Shut up, Gabby."

She giggled.

Dad put my stuff on the kitchen table and opened the newspaper I'd brought.

"See if you can find my article in there," I said, thumping the back of the paper with my finger. "It should be in the Life and Style section."

He started flipping pages.

Garrett carried his beer to the refrigerator and pulled one out for himself. "Grace, you want a beer?"

"Is it really a chocolate stout?" I asked with a frown.

"No, it's our new winter ale."

I thought of Jason's eyes. "Sure. I'll try one."

"Dad?"

"No thanks. I'm saving all my room for that bird," he said, nodding toward the oven.

"It does smell great in here, Mom," I said.

She was almost giddy. "It does, doesn't it?"

Hope and Bodhi ran past us into the kitchen. Then she whirled around, slinging her hair across her face. "Aunt *Grathe*, think you can *introduth uth* to *Medutha* at the parade?"

I brushed the hair out of her eyes. "I think that can be arranged."

She held both hands over her head. "*Yeth!*"

When she was gone, I caught Garrett's eye. "Have you thought about junior derby?" I mouthed so the girls wouldn't hear me.

He frowned.

Then so did I.

"Oh, here it is," Dad said, straightening in his chair. "They put a nice picture in here."

I leaned over to look. It was a photo of me (looking tired) and Kiara (looking perky) standing by the window.

Dad began to read the article out loud.

The holiday shopping season is upon us, and eager Nashville consumers heading to Hillsboro Village will have a sweet treat waiting for them. Sparkled Pink, a children's couture boutique on Twenty-First Avenue, is already drawing crowds each day thanks to a senior fashion-design student from MacKay University.

Kiara Washington approached her internship sponsor several weeks ago with a clever idea: to decorate the store's front display window like those she'd studied in class. Local designer and owner of the store, Grace Evans, was happy to oblige.

"I thought it was a brilliant idea," Evans said in an interview on Wednesday. "Kiara is a wonderful designer, and now she's proven herself to be a genius businesswoman as well. I'm lucky to have her."

"Most of my classes at MacKay are focused on textbook learning and displays built inside the classroom," Washington told us. "I was very thankful that Ms. Evans and my professors in the fashion-studies department agreed for me to implement what I've learned in the real world."

Fashion-Studies Department Chair Imogen Sleight agreed. "In our program, there is a lot of discussion about the importance of getting our students out of the classroom and into the field. We hope that next year we'll be able to partner with more local businesses to make this exercise available to all our students in the program."

Professor Sleight also tells us that MacKay University is considering hosting a city-wide competition next year, where students can design window displays and win scholarship money through participating businesses.

Sparkled Pink is located at 1777 Twenty-First Avenue South in Nashville. This Black Friday, doors open at eight a.m. All in-stock merchandise will be 10–20 percent off, and the first twenty customers in the door will receive a thirty-dollar credit on any design-your-own couture gown.

My brother clapped when my father finished reading the article. Mom had stopped cooking. Even my nieces were listening intently. "Congratulations, Grace," Dad said, laying the paper on the table and putting his arm around me.

Still smiling from ear to ear, I shook my head. "Don't congratulate me. I didn't do any of this. It was *all* Kiara."

"That's an excellent article." Mom pointed a spoon at me from the stove. "I've said so before and I'll say it again: you're lucky to have that girl."

I nodded. "I am well-aware."

"She's lucky to have you too, Gracie," Garrett said. "Did that say she's an intern?"

"Yep."

"Do you pay her?"

"For the extra work she does on top of her internship hours."

Garrett drummed his fingers on the wooden tabletop. "I need to get me some interns."

I pulled out my phone and brought up a new text message to Kiara. *Just read the article! It's great. You're already a star! Happy Thanksgiving. I'm so thankful for YOU.*

She responded almost immediately in all caps. *THANK YOU!!! Happy Thanksgiving.*

"Do you have enough people to work?" Mom asked.

"Just me and Kiara. I doubt we'll need more than that. We never really have a huge rush."

"You've also never been in the paper before," Dad said.

"That's true," Garrett agreed.

"Well, I don't have the budget to bring in anyone else, so I guess we'll have to wing it." I got up and walked around the counter to Mom. "What can I do to help in here?"

"Want to drain the potatoes?"

"Sure."

Mom was chopping lettuce on the cutting board. "If it looks like you're going to need more hands tomorrow, call me. I can come by for a few hours."

"Thank you."

"Hey, Granna, want me and Dad to set the table?" Gabby asked.

Mom smiled. "That would be wonderful, Gabby. Thank you."

"Gabrielle!" Garrett raised both hands. "Haven't I taught you better than that, child? We don't offer to help. We definitely don't offer *me* to help."

She marched around his side of the table and grabbed his hand. "Come on, Dad."

Garrett went limp leaning back in his chair. "I don't want to. You can't make me."

She pulled and pulled on his arm. "Dad!"

I put the pot of potatoes down and tiptoed around behind her. "You gotta get him right here, Gabs." With my index finger, I jabbed my brother in the armpit. Hard.

With a loud yelp, he jumped out of his chair and lunged at me, laughing. He grabbed me, linebacker style, around the thighs and threw me over his shoulder. "You wanna fight, little sister?"

Mom was screaming as he spun me around in the air. "You're going to break everything! Get out of my house right now! Graham, help!"

Dad was laughing. Or at least I thought he was laughing. I was hanging upside down, looking at my brother's back. I pounded my fists against his side. "Put me down!"

Bodhi was barking and hopping around us.

Hope was attacking Garrett from the front. "Put her down, Dad!"

Garrett finally bent and settled my feet back on the floor.

"You're such an asshole," I said, laughing and panting and straightening my shirt.

He pointed at me. "You know better than to poke me. I hate that shit."

"Language!" my mother shouted.

He reached for Gabby's hand. "Come on, we'd better set the table before Granna decides to not let us eat."

Linner was finally on the table at a quarter past two. I was starving. And everything Mom had prepared looked...well, amazing.

The rolls weren't burned on the bottom.

The mashed potatoes were fluffy and smooth.

The turkey was a flawless golden brown.

Everything was so perfect that I secretly poked around in the trash looking for carry-out containers. There were none.

We all gathered in the dining room and held hands around the table. One by one, around the circle, we all said one thing we were thankful for. When it was my turn, I closed my eyes and thought about all the good things I had.

A family that loved me.

Good friends that pushed me to be better.

My dog lying at my feet.

I smiled. "I'm thankful for new beginnings, with the very best people at my side."

NINE

THE STOMACH CRAMPS started around midnight.

I rolled over, pulled my knees into my chest, and prayed they'd go away. They didn't. An hour later, in the bathroom, I was gripping the toilet-paper roll and praying another prayer—to die quickly.

The vomiting started a half an hour after that. I'll spare the details, but a trash can was involved because the toilet was otherwise occupied. At some point I woke up on the bathroom tiles in the fetal position. Bodhi was licking my face.

My phone chirped on my nightstand sometime around four in the morning. I crawled to get it. It was a text from my brother.

Garrett: *I think something was wrong with the turkey.*

Me: *OMG. I want to die.*

Garrett: *Gabby's been in the bathroom for the past two hours, and Hope threw up in my bed.*

I wanted to offer my help, but seeing as I was texting him from the floor by my bed, there wasn't any use.

My phone rang sometime later. I didn't even look at the screen.

"Grace?" It was Mom. She sounded as shitty as I felt.

"Hi."

"Are you OK?"

"I have a pulse."

She groaned. "I'm so sorry, Gracie."

"Are you and Dad OK?"

"We're both sick too. And I just talked to Garrett. He and the girls…" Her voice broke. "I think it was the turkey."

She sounded like she was starting to cry on the other end of the line. Or maybe she was holding back more vomit.

Just in case, I tried to console her. "It was an accident, Mom." I wanted to add that we didn't think she'd tried to kill us all on purpose, but I figured that wouldn't help.

"I need to go help your father. Call me later and let me know how you're doing," she said.

"I will."

"I'm so sorry, honey."

"I know. I love you."

"Love you too."

We hung up just as my stomach began to gurgle again.

I was awake when the alarm on my phone went off at six. When I turned it off, I dropped it on my mattress, too weak to return it to the nightstand.

Oh god. I had to open the store in two hours. I pushed myself up to sitting and all the blood drained from my head. My vision swirled and stars twinkled at the edges of my vision.

I flopped back down. Bodhi rested his head on my chest. Too bad I hadn't trained him like one of those St. Bernard rescue dogs. I could've really used a barrel around his neck containing some kind of fluids. My mouth felt like it was covered in sandpaper.

My phone dinged again. It was a text, this time from Jason. *On my way home to check on Mom. Be there soon.*

Me: *Major case of food poisoning over here. Not sure if I'll be able to work after all.*

Jason: *Are you serious? Do you need to go to the hospital?*

That was a fair question.

Me: *I feel like I need to go to the morgue.*

The phone rang. I tapped the speakerphone button, unwilling to hold the phone to my ear. "Hello?" I sounded like a ninety-year-old man with a three-pack-a-day habit.

"It's Jason."

"Hi."

"Should I turn on the siren and head your way?"

"Do you carry body bags?"

"No."

"Then you can't help me."

"You're worrying me, Grace."

I draped my arm over my eyes. "I'm really sick, but I'm fine. You can go home."

"I'll hurry."

"I really don't think there's any way I'll be able to work today. There's no sense in you coming."

"You're not going to be able to take him down those stairs and outside if you're too sick to open the store. I'm coming. Don't even try to argue with me."

I groaned. I *really* didn't want him to see me like this. "Jason, I—"

"I said don't argue. I'll be there soon. Tell Bodhi to cross his legs."

My cracked lips pulled as I smiled. Then my stomach wobbled again. "I gotta go." I barely hit the end-call button before the dry heaves began again over my bedside trashcan.

When I was done, I texted Kiara. *I'm almost dead with horrific food poisoning. Don't think I can open today.*

She didn't answer.

I texted Monica next. *I need advice from a doctor. When should one go to the emergency room with food poisoning?*

My phone rang again. I hit the speaker button to answer. "Hello?"

"Grace?" Monica asked.

"Yeah."

"Good lord, you sound terrible."

"I feel worse."

"I'm not *that* kind of doctor, Grace."

"I know, but you are a mom. What do you know about puking and dehydration?"

"How'd you get food pois—" She stopped herself. "Oh, your mom. Was it the turkey?"

"Does it matter? What do I do?"

"Can you keep anything down?"

"No."

"Try to get some ice chips to suck on at least. Do you need me to come over?"

"No. Jason's on his way soon."

"Really?" Her voice was full of hope and intrigue.

"Not now," I warned.

"Maybe you should call Doc Carnage."

"I don't have her number. Besides, I don't want to wake her up."

"She might already be up. It is Black Friday...Oh Grace. It's Black Friday. What are you going to do?"

"Not make any money, I'm sure." *And probably lose my store,* I added silently.

"I saw your article in the paper yesterday. I'm sure a lot of other people did too. Want me to come in and help out?"

"Thanks, but Kiara will be here."

"OK, but if she needs help, call me. Try to stay hydrated. I'll check on you in a little bit."

"Thanks, Mon."

I tried to sit up again. Getting vertical was a challenge, like my head weighed a thousand pounds and my spine was made of gelatin. When I was finally able to drop my feet off the side of the bed, I had to stop and rest. It took a moment for the dizziness to clear so that I felt safe enough to stand. Then I pushed myself up slowly, bracing against the side of the bed in case my legs buckled underneath me.

After a moment of testing my leg muscles, I zombie-walked to the kitchen. Bodhi stayed beside me all the way. I pulled a cup from the cabinet and put it under the crushed-ice dispenser in the refrigerator door. The sound blistered my eardrums, but I snagged a jagged piece of ice and put it on my withered tongue.

The buzzer for my front door sounded through the apartment. I walked over and pressed the intercom button. "Hello?"

"Grace, it's Kiara. I'm going to need you to let me in." Something in her voice sounded off. Worried? Excited, maybe?

I pushed the button to release the lock, and a second later, I heard the echo of her footfalls as she ran up the stairs. I opened the front door.

Her eyes were the size of goose eggs, but her head snapped back with alarm. She put her hand to her chest. "Oh my stars!"

"I look that good, huh?" I stepped back to let her inside but stumbled and bounced off the wall, sloshing ice everywhere.

She grabbed my arms to steady me as Bodhi lapped the ice shards off the floor. "Grace, do you need to go to the hospital?"

"That's debatable." I gripped the wall for support. "Mind if I lay down?"

"Please. I'm afraid you might pass out."

"It is a possibility."

"Hey, Bodhi." Kiara looked at him twice. Then back at me with questioning eyes.

"If anyone asks…" I slowly shook my head. "You never saw him."

"Scandalous. You've not been dognapping again, have you?"

"No." I took a few deep breaths. "Police-sanctioned weekend visitation." I finally turned to go back to my room, but my stomach lurched again. I dove for the trashcan in the kitchen. Not that it mattered; there was nothing else in my stomach to come up.

Kiara was making retching noises behind me when I stopped heaving. I lifted my middle finger over my head.

"Sorry. I'm a sympathy puker." She hooked her arm under mine and pulled me off the floor. "Are you sure this is food poisoning?"

"Could be the Ebola virus considering how I feel." I hugged my cup of ice against my chest.

"I got your text, but I was driving." She helped me back to bed and put my ice on the nightstand. "We have a problem."

"Tell me about it," I said with a moan as I rolled onto my side. Bodhi jumped up onto the bed behind me.

"Look at this." She turned her phone so that I could see the screen. It was a photo of a line. A long line at the front door of my store. "This is outside, right now."

"Holy shit. Are you serious?"

"Yes, ma'am. There are about thirty people down there, and we don't open for another hour and a half."

I covered my face with my hands. "What am I going to do?"

"I can handle a lot of it by myself, but do you have anyone we can call for help? Your mom, maybe?"

"Mom ate the same food I did yesterday. She's just as sick."

"What about Margaret or Carla?"

"Both out of town for the holiday. Monica can come, probably. Where's my phone?"

She reached for it across my bed. "Here."

I took it and looked at the screen. There was a message from Jason. *On my way. Going to stop at the store.*

"Jason's on his way here."

She turned her ear toward me. "Officer Eye Candy?"

I nodded and swiped my screen to unlock it.

"Oh no," Kiara said, walking to my closet.

"What are you doing?" I asked as I pulled up Monica's number and tapped it.

"You do *not* want that beautiful man to see you like this."

"I really don't care."

"Grace Evans, I'm pretty sure you have vomit on your shirt. Trust me."

I looked down, but then Monica answered the phone. "Hey."

"Hey. I need help. There's already a line at my store. Can you come?"

"As soon as I get dressed. I'll see if any of our friends are available too," she said.

"Thank you, Monica."

"Of course. See you soon."

When I hung up, Kiara was going through my dresser drawers. "Where are your pajamas?"

"One drawer down," I said.

A moment later, she carried over a clean pair of Abominable Snowman pajama pants and an old gray sweatshirt that would hang off my shoulders. "This is the best I could do. Can you get changed by yourself?"

"I think so." I hoped I was right.

"I'm going downstairs. Davion is here setting up the hot chocolate I made this morning."

"You made hot chocolate again?"

"Yes, ma'am. We buckled it into the back seat of my Prius."

I laughed, and it hurt. "That's hilarious."

"Text me when you safely get changed so I know you didn't fall and crack your skull open."

"OK."

She walked out of my room.

"Kiara?"

She stopped and poked her head back inside.

"Thank you."

"You owe me so big," she said with a teasing smile.

I knew I did.

I successfully managed to change my clothes *and* brush my teeth by myself. I was slumped over the sink the whole time, but damn it, they were clean. My phone beeped as I trudged back from the bathroom.

It was a message from Garrett. *Called the pediatrician. Taking Hope to the ER.*

I immediately dialed his number. "Hey," he answered on the first ring.

"Is she OK?"

"She's sick. The doctor's just worried about her getting dehydrated. Better to be safe, you know?"

"Do you need me to come over and stay with Gabby?" I asked.

"Jamie's mom is here."

"Oh good. How do you feel?"

He groaned. "I feel like we're ordering takeout next year."

"God, I know. Poor mom."

"I gotta go. I'll call you later."

"Keep me updated," I said.

"I will." He hung up the phone without saying goodbye.

When I hung up, there was a message from Jason. *I'll let myself in if you can open your apartment door.*

Me: *It's unlocked. I'll be in bed.*

I heard him just a few minutes later. I tried to sit up, but thought better of it. Bodhi took off barking toward the front door. It opened and closed behind him. "Hey, Bodhi," he said.

A moment later, he was in my bedroom doorways. His face fell when he saw me. "You look like a vampire."

I nodded against my pillow. "That was the look I was going for."

"Can I come in?"

"Enter at your own risk."

He carried in a couple of grocery bags and sat down on the edge of the bed beside me. Bodhi jumped up beside him, then flopped down across my legs. "I didn't know what flavor you liked, so I brought you fruit punch, mixed berry, and lemon-lime Gatorade." He set them out on my nightstand. "Also, some ginger ale and saltine crackers."

"Thank you," I said with a whimper.

He put his hand on my forehead. It was ice cold. Then he laughed. "I don't know why I did that. My hands are frozen."

I wanted to laugh but I couldn't. "Thank god. I thought I was dying of a fever. Is it cold outside?"

"I saw a few snowflakes on my way in. Have you been able to drink anything?"

"I had a few ice chips. So far, I've kept down about two of them."

He grimaced. "Try some of the Gatorade. Tiny sips. And I recommend the berry or the lemon-lime...they won't stain as bad if they come back up."

I nodded and tried to sit up.

He slid his arm around my back to help me. When I was vertical, stars twinkled in my vision again. I rested my face against his shoulder. And he held me there. "You OK?"

I nodded again, and honestly, could have cried he was being so nice. Finally, when I thought I could hold it upright, I lifted my head.

He pulled back and pointed to the nightstand. "Which one do you want?"

"Lemon-lime." My voice cracked. "Please."

He picked it up and unscrewed the cap. "Tiny sips," he said again as he handed it to me.

I tilted it up to my lips.

"Have you seen what's happening downstairs?" he asked.

"Kiara showed me a picture."

"You have to open the store. You know that, right?"

"We're working on a plan." I took another sip of Gatorade.

He stood. "I'm going to take Bodhi out. You good for a minute?"

"I'm good."

"Come on, boy," he said, standing up and slapping his thigh.

Bodhi scrambled against the blankets to stand, then shook the bed when he jumped down. My stomach tumbled again. I put the cap back on the Gatorade and slid back under my blankets.

My phone beeped. It was a text from Monica. *Lucy is at her Dad's, but Olivia and Zoey are both coming to the store.* Then she sent an animated picture of Superwoman.

Me: OMG. *You guys are the best. I love you so much, Monica.*

Monica: *I love you too. You're just obligated to go Christmas shopping with me now that I'm missing Black Friday.*

Me: *Of course I will. Thank you. Thank you. Thank you.*

Monica: *We'll all be there as soon as we can. I'll come up and see you when I get there.*

Me: *If you do, you can meet the hot cop. If he's still here.*

Monica: *I'll be right over.* 😉

I'd dozed off by the time Jason returned sometime later. One eye opened in time to see Bodhi do a flying leap onto my bed, landing on my ankles. "Oh," I grumbled as he walked across the bed, jostling me with every step on the mattress.

My stomach swayed. I covered my mouth and rolled off the

bed, scrambling toward my bathroom. I *refused* to vomit in front of the hot cop if I could help it.

I'd barely slammed the door behind me before I lost the little bit of lemon-lime into the commode. There was a light knock behind me a few seconds later.

I reached up and flushed the toilet before slumping down onto the tiles with a moan.

Jason cracked the door. "Grace? You OK?"

I mumbled something incoherent.

He stepped over me to get to the sink. I heard the water running, and a moment later, a cool cloth touched my face. Tears trickled down to the floor. "Want to go back to bed?" he asked softly.

I nodded.

He pulled my arm up and across his shoulders, then his other arm slipped behind my back. His strong hand gripped my ribcage, and he lifted my upper body off the floor. My legs were wobbly underneath me. "Can you walk?"

I put one foot in front of the other, leaning heavily against him. He laid me on the bed, then took the wet washcloth he'd draped over his shoulder and laid it across my forehead. Using his fingers, he plucked a piece of ice from my cup and held it up. "I washed my hands," he said and winked.

I opened my mouth, and he slipped it between my lips.

"Thank you," I whispered.

He sat down, and the bed dipped under his weight. "I'm sorry you're so sick. Just say the word if you think we need to go to the hospital. I drove the patrol car so we can get there in a hurry if we need to."

I managed a weak smile.

"Bodhi and I went for a nice walk to the park and back. He should be good for a while."

The park was near the hospital, several blocks away. "How long were you gone?"

He looked at his watch. "Half an hour, maybe."

"Thank you," I said again.

He leaned toward me. "Full disclosure, I didn't pick up the poop either. I forgot to take the bags." He put a finger on his lips. "Don't tell anybody."

I chuckled, which triggered a cough, which triggered more nausea. With a pained groan, I rolled away from him.

His hand slid down to my hip. Sick or not, I noticed.

Thankfully, the nausea passed that time after a few deep breaths. He was still sitting beside me when the front-door buzzer sounded.

"That's probably Monica. Can you let her in?" I asked.

"I can try to figure it out." He stood and walked out of the room. "He—hello?" he asked eventually. Looking out the door, I could see him bending to talk directly into the speaker.

"Hey, it's Grace's friend, Monica—"

"And Olivia!" Olivia shouted.

"Can you buzz us in?" Monica asked.

"Uh...yeah. Give me one second." He figured it out quickly and pressed the unlock button. It buzzed quietly. Monica's and Olivia's voices, their laughter, carried up the stairs.

He opened the door.

Their chatter stopped immediately.

"She's really sick, but come on in," I heard him say.

Monica tiptoed into my bedroom with Olivia close behind her. "Grace? It's Monica."

I lifted a hand, then let it flop back onto the bed.

She frowned. "You look like you don't feel so good."

"You look like shit," Olivia said.

My lips cracked as I smiled.

Monica took my hand. "You've got quite a crowd outside."

"I've heard."

She patted my knuckles. "We're going to take care of them. You get to feeling better and don't worry about a thing."

"Thank you."

"It looks like you're well taken care of." She leaned close to my face and whispered, "He's even cuter in person."

"Grace, you need anything?" Olivia asked, walking around in front of Monica.

"I'm good."

Olivia laughed sarcastically. "You are *far* from good, my friend."

"How are you and Styx?" I asked.

Her nose scrunched. "Taking a break. But that's not important right now. You need to focus on getting better."

I gave her a limp thumbs-up. "Talk soon though?"

"Of course," she said and winked.

Monica stood and turned toward Jason, who was standing by my dresser. "You promise you'll take absolute perfect care of her?" she asked him.

"I promise," he said, smiling at me.

"And you promise you won't leave her side for a second?" Monica asked.

Olivia leaned over me. "Like this side." She patted the mattress next to me. "Like, *right here?*"

"Oh my god, stop." I pushed her arm back, or I tried anyway. Bodhi thought she'd been talking to him, so he scooted closer to me.

Jason was grinning. If I'd had the strength to be embarrassed, I would have been.

Laughing, Olivia took a few steps back and pulled on the back of Monica's jacket. "Come on, Mon. We've got work to do."

"Thank you, guys," I managed.

Monica squeezed my toe. "Feel better. Please."

"I'll be fine."

She looked at Jason. "I'll come check on her in a little while. My number is in her phone if you need me."

"OK," he said.

Monica waved one more time at the bedroom door, and then he followed them out to the foyer. When he came back, he got another piece of ice for me.

"Sorry about that," I said softly.

"Why on earth are you apologizing?"

"My friends...they're—"

"Worried about you?" He smiled. "Don't worry about it." As I sucked on the piece of ice, he walked around the bed and sat down. Then he leaned toward the floor.

"What are you doing?" I asked.

"Taking off my boots." He looked back. "I can't let your friend down, right?"

"Right."

Jason stretched out beside Bodhi.

"Do you mind?" I asked and flicked my eyes toward Bodhi when Jason looked at me. "I gave up on the 'no dogs on the furniture' battle long ago."

"Not even a little bit." He patted the empty space next to him. "Come here, Bodhi."

Bodhi gleefully commando-crawled closer to him on the bed. And he smiled and panted with joy as Jason raked his fingers through his golden fur.

"Where'd you get the name Bodhi? Are you a closet Buddhist?" Jason asked rolling his head toward me on the pillow.

I reached over and picked up the dog's wavy blond ear. "Patrick Swayze, *Point Break*."

He chuckled. "The hair. I should have guessed. That's hilarious."

"We'd always planned to get another dog"—I paused and

took a deep breath—"a black Lab, and name him Johnny Utah, but this one"—I lazily tapped Bodhi's head—"has been enough to handle since day one."

"Between the begonias and the criminal record, I'd say so."

Out of all the flowers in the world, how had he remembered that Bodhi had dug up begonias?

"Mind if I turn on the TV?" he asked, pointing to the television on the dresser at the foot of the bed.

"No." I rolled to reach for the remote on the nightstand.

"Stop," Jason said.

He scooted above Bodhi's head, then rolled toward me and slowly leaned across me to reach the remote. Our noses were inches from each other. I held my breath, certain it reeked of vomit.

When he had the remote, he moved back to his side of the bed. "Be warned, it is ninety-nine percent certain I will pass out. If I do, and you get sick again, hit me or something."

"OK."

He flipped through the channels for a while before finding the on-demand movies. "Have you seen *Interstellar* with Matthew McConaughey?"

I shook my head.

He clicked play, then put the remote between our pillows. Not five minutes in, he rolled over onto his side toward me.

"You look like you're already about to pass out," I said.

He looked at me with only one eye open and smiled. "I don't know what you're talking about. Are you OK? Do you need anything?"

"I need sleep."

He pulled the comforter up around me. "Comfy?"

I managed a slight nod.

He yawned and settled back into his pillow. "Wake me up if you need me. Pinky swear?" He held his pinky up toward me.

I lifted my arm to hook my finger with his. Then he smiled and draped his arm over my dog.

And just like that, my heart did a somersault right out of the friend zone.

———

I was up and down, back and forth to the bathroom for the rest of the morning. Jason woke up and helped me for a few of the trips, though I tried—against my pinky swear—not to disturb him. Finally, we both passed out for a solid few hours.

Neither of us watched the movie.

The buzzer to my apartment woke us sometime later. It was dark outside, which meant it could be midnight or it could be five in the afternoon (thank you, daylight savings.) It was the latter, just after five p.m.

The buzzer sounded again, and Jason pushed himself up.

"I'm sorry," I said, trying to sit up.

He held up a hand to stop me. "Lay down. Don't need you fumbling around in the dark, having a head rush. I got it. I'm a master of the intercom system now."

I smiled and flipped on my beside lamp. I was sitting up, sipping my Gatorade when he let them inside the apartment. Kiara came in first, looking a little more disheveled than she had that morning. "That was crazy," were the first words out of her mouth. Then she corrected herself. "I'm sorry. How are you?"

"A little less horrible than I was this morning. Thank you for asking."

Monica and Zoey walked in behind her. "Hi, Zo. Thank you for coming," I said, reaching for her.

She came over and took my hand. "I wanted to come up earlier, but we decided you were hopefully sleeping."

"I was." I looked at Jason. "We both were. Zoey, did you meet Jason?"

She shook her head.

"Zoey, Jason. Jason, Zoey," I said.

He walked over to shake her hand.

"Nice to meet you. Thanks for taking such good care of our friend," she said.

"It was my pleasure." Jason checked my cup. "Grace, I'm going to get you some more ice, and then take Bodhi out."

"Thank you."

"Happy to."

Monica caught my eye. "Olivia said to give you her love. She had to leave earlier to open the restaurant."

"Of course." I looked at Kiara. "How'd it go?"

"I think it's safe to say that we did more business today than we have since I've been working for you." Kiara handed me the printed receipt from the point-of-sale system.

I choked.

It was enough to cover the property taxes, the rest of what I owed to the fertility doctor, and Kiara's spending money for New York.

"You have got to be kidding me!"

"This girl is a rock star," Monica said, putting her hands on Kiara's shoulders.

"You all are," I added.

Jason returned with my ice cup. Then he waved to my friends. "If you all aren't here when I get back, it was very nice to meet you. I hope to see you again."

They all echoed their thanks, then he called Bodhi to him and left the apartment. When he was gone, Monica flopped down on the bed in his spot. "Oh my god, Grace. I love him."

"He's super nice. How long have you been dating?" Zoey asked.

"We aren't," I said.

Kiara put her hands on her hips. "Coulda fooled me."

Monica raised her hand. "Me too."

I covered my face. "He has seen me puke so many times today. At one point, he even held my hair back."

"That guy *loves* you," Monica said.

"No, I think he was just afraid I was going to die." Before I went too crazy with the Gatorade, I put it back on the nightstand and settled against my pillow. "I don't know what I would have done without you all today."

"It was actually kind of fun," Zoey said. "I've never worked retail before."

"Really?" Monica asked.

"You're a natural," Kiara said. "She helped the customers and Monica rang them up. I took all the custom orders."

"How many did we have?"

"Forty-seven."

I choked on the air. "What?"

"You heard me."

"Forty-seven? Like, three shy of fifty dresses?"

"Yes, ma'am. We've got our work cut out for us. I already sent five each to Margaret and Carla."

I gripped the sides of my head. "They're not guaranteed by Christmas are they?"

She shook her head. "Oh no. I told everyone that it was a minimum of six to eight weeks, but if I got a hint that they were hoping it could be a gift for Christmas, I secretly made a note of it. I thought we could prioritize those."

"You're a genius, Kiara," I said.

She did a little curtsy. "Thank you."

"Her boyfriend is pretty adorable too." Monica propped her head up on her elbow. "He stayed all day, bagging up orders, greeting customers with hot chocolate—"

"As long as the hot chocolate lasted." Kiara laughed. "I think we need a bigger thermos."

"True," Zoey agreed. "I didn't even get any, and I was here by ten thirty."

"Really, guys. I don't know what I would do without you. All of you." I looked pointedly at each of them.

Monica put her hand on my arm. "I'm just glad you're feeling better."

"Me too," Kiara said.

"Me three," Zoey added.

Kiara jerked her thumb over her shoulder. "I've got to run. Davion went to get the car. I just wanted to tell you the good news."

"Are you still working tomorrow?"

"Yes, ma'am. I plan on coming in early, if you don't mind the extra hours. I've got lots to do."

"I don't mind at all. You can work as many hours as you want. And I don't have practice, so I'll come down in the morning."

"You rest and get to feeling better. And spend some time with Bodhi...and Officer Eye Candy." She winked and turned toward the door.

"I'll see you tomorrow, Kiara."

"Bye, ladies," Kiara said with a wave to Monica and Zoey. "It was great to hang with you. You did great today!"

"Thanks, Kiara. Bye," Monica said.

"It was nice to meet you!" Zoey called after her. When she was gone, Zoey stepped closer to the bed again. "I'm going to head out too, Grace."

"Thank you so much, Zoey. I owe you one."

She took my hand again. "You owe me *nothing*. I'll see you at the Slammy Awards next weekend?"

I touched my forehead. "I forgot all about it. But yes. I'll be there."

"You, Monica?" Zoey asked.

"Yes, ma'am."

She walked around to give Monica a hug. "OK. See you then."

"Be safe going home!" I called as loudly as I could as she walked to the door.

"I will!"

"I seriously forgot all about the awards," I said to Monica after Zoey was gone.

Her nose scrunched. "I'm going shopping tomorrow if you want to go with me."

"No, I'm spending the day with Bodhi. And I'll probably still be in bed a lot." I sighed. "That was rough."

"I could tell. When I saw you, I was so worried. Oh my god." She examined my face. "You still kinda look like a dead person, but it's a little darker in here now, so it's less shocking."

I chuckled. "Thanks. I think."

She rested her head beside mine on my pillow. "Thanks for not dying on me today."

"You're welcome."

The front door opened, and her smile widened when we heard Jason and Bodhi walk back in. "You should invite him to the Slammy Awards," she whispered.

I sighed. "I'll think about it."

"OK. Feel better, Grace." She pushed herself up, but I caught her hand to stop her. "Do you have any idea how much I appreciate you?"

She smiled and nodded her head. "Yeah, I do."

"Grace, do we have any dog treats?" Jason called from the kitchen.

"He said *we*," Monica hissed.

I rolled my eyes. "No, I tried to stop yesterday, but everywhere was closed. Then today happened. I'll get him some tomorrow. You can give him some cheese out of the fridge."

Bodhi barked. He loved cheese.

"Has he been fed today?" he asked.

"No. His food is in the pantry."

"Got it!"

Monica walked to the door and waved. "I'll call you tomorrow. If anything happens, even in the middle of the night, you call me."

"I will." I straightened in my bed. "That reminds me. I need to check on my niece." I grabbed my phone off the bed as Monica told Jason goodbye in the kitchen.

There was a missed call from my mother and several missed texts from other people.

Mom: *Just calling to check on you. Call me back...if you're still speaking to me.*

Garrett: *Hope is fine. They're giving her IV fluids and sending us home. I'm begging for them to hook me up to some too. How are you?*

Olivia: *Had to run. Hope you're feeling better. XOXO*

Lucy: *Heard you're sick. Let me know how you're doing.*

And the final message was from Clay.

Wanted you to hear it from me first. Ginny and I are engaged.

TEN

STARING AT MY PHONE, I sat there for what felt like an eternity. Finally, Jason walked back into my bedroom. "She's nice. I like your friends."

I stared at him.

"What? Are you going to be sick again?" He moved to grab the trashcan off the floor.

Yes. But for a completely different reason.

I handed him my phone. He turned it around to read it, and I watched his face morph from confused to are-you-*effing*-kidding-me? "He didn't tell you?" I asked.

Jason shook his head, then sat down beside me and put the phone on the nightstand. "You OK?"

I didn't know what I was.

Shocked.

Angry.

Hurt.

I dropped my hands into my lap. "Am I that easy to get over?"

"God, Grace. No." Jason pulled me into his arms, and for the first time all day, I was thankful for my dehydration. I may have been silently crying against Jason's shoulder, but not one single tear was shed for that asshole.

Jason shook his head against mine, his fingers tangled in my matted hair. "Don't ever think that." He turned his face and pressed a kiss against my temple. "Ever."

"It *really* doesn't feel like that right now. Ten years, Jason. We've been divorced for a month, and he's already marrying her."

"You know he's only marrying her because of the baby."

I tossed my hands up. "Is that supposed to help?"

He dropped his head. "I'm sorry. No."

"Why does she get everything that was supposed to be mine? My husband. My baby. My house. Hell, she even gets my dog." I covered my face, willing myself not to cry anymore. "I hate her, Jason. I hate him. I hate all of this so much." My chin trembled.

"Come here," he said, pulling me close again. That time, I sobbed against his chest. Still no tears, though my eyes did get a little cloudy. Jason rubbed my back and kissed my forehead. He finally sighed. "Want me to go shoot him? I have my gun."

I laughed through my phantom tears. "Please."

He held me a while longer. "Want me to call into work tonight? I could stay here with you."

"That's so tempting, but no. I need to be a big girl about this. He doesn't deserve me falling apart over him." Though I did wonder—for the tiniest of moments—if he didn't deserve me sleeping with his best friend because of it, no matter if the "sleeping with" involved sex or not.

"No, he doesn't deserve you falling apart." He tilted my face up so that my eyes met his. "He never deserved you at all, Grace Evans."

I wondered then if he might kiss me.

Maybe he would have had I not been spewing my guts out all day.

Because it was *that* moment, for sure. The one where the

relationship scales tipped very certainly from friendship to something else. For both of us.

He took Bodhi out one last time before he left, then promised he'd be back the next day. And I knew before we even said goodnight, it'd be another sleepless night for both of us. Him, because he had to work.

And me...because I'd just fallen for Clay's best friend.

————

After tossing and turning most of the night, I woke up to the telephone around nine in the morning. It was my mother.

"Hello?" My throat was scratchy.

"Hey, have you rejoined the land of the living today?"

"Barely." I rolled over and sat up. Bodhi was flat on his back with all four paws in the air. He looked over at me and blinked. "How are you and Dad?"

"We're both better. Dad still has a bit of diarrhea—"

I held the phone away from my ear. "La! La! La! I don't want to hear that!"

She chuckled. "Sorry."

"Are you trying to make me puke some more?" I shuddered and reached for what was left of the lemon-lime Gatorade. "Have you talked to Garrett?"

"Yeah. They're all fine now too. They let Hope leave the hospital around seven last night. What did you do about the store?"

I finished off the rest of the drink. "Kiara opened it, and it was a smashing success. She didn't even need me there."

"Of course she did." Perhaps she caught some kind of tone in my voice that only mothers could recognize. "Why would you say such a thing?"

"Because she wouldn't be the only one who doesn't need me anymore. Clay's getting remarried."

Silence.

"Mom?"

"He's what?"

"He's marrying that girl he got pregnant."

"That little shit." She didn't even bother to drop the *i*. "Are you OK?"

"I'll be fine."

"Yes, you will be. Better her than you, I say."

"Thanks, Mom. On a happier note, will you tell Dad he doesn't have to worry about the property-tax bill? I'll have enough to cover it."

"Of course. That's great news."

"It is. For now. I still need to figure out what I'm going to do long-term."

"I'm positive you will, Grace."

Bodhi wriggled in the covers beside me until he could flip over on to his belly. Then he stood up on the mattress and nudged me with his snout.

"I need to take Bodhi out. Can I call you later?" I asked.

"Sure, honey. Anytime."

"Love you."

"Love you too," she said and I hung up.

There were more messages on my phone. I was a little afraid to check them after having my heart ripped out the night before, but then again...one might be from Jason.

Yes! He'd texted around six thirty. *Off duty and back at home. Going to sleep for a few hours and I'll come over. Call if you're not OK, and I'll come now.*

I texted him back and prayed it wouldn't wake him. *Feeling better this morning. About to take Bodhi out.*

The next message was a picture from Monica. She'd just sent

it. It was of her in front of the full-length mirror. She wore a white dress with big black polka dots. *What do you think?*

Me: *I love it.*

I got up and had to stop and grip the nightstand. My stomach still felt a little shaky. It settled after a moment, and I went to the bathroom, then pulled on my UGGs to take Bodhi outside to potty. Monica texted me back while Bodhi marked every blade of grass on the corner. *I'm getting it. Slammy Awards, look out!*

Me: *LOL Is the party very formal?*

Monica: *Yes. Didn't you see the pictures from last year?*

Me: *Would I ask if I did?*

Monica: *It's formal. Are you sure you don't need to go shopping?*

I frowned. *I'll figure something out.*

Monica: *I'm sure it will be fabulous. As usual.*

Me: *I woke up with a hot man in my bed this morning.*

Monica: *????!!!!*

Me: *Literally hot. His normal body temp is about* 102.

Then I sent her a photo of Bodhi lifting his leg on the street sign's post.

Monica: *Aww... But I was really hoping for a real man in your bed. Could be the best way to thank Officer Eye Candy for the weekend with Bodhi.*

Me: *Oh geez.*

Monica sent back the eggplant emoji.

My head fell to the side. I texted her back. *WTF?*

Monica: *Ask Officer Eye Candy what it means. I'm sure he can explain it to you.*

I rolled my eyes. *Whatever. Something did happen last night, but I'll tell you about it when I see you.*

Monica: *Something sexy?*

Me: *Something with Clay.*

She sent back a puking-face emoji.

Me: *We'll talk about it later.*
Monica: *How are you feeling this morning?*
Me: *Much. Much. Much better. Thank you.*
Monica: *Good. Gotta check out. Chat later?*
Me: *Yep. Bye!*

Bodhi and I went back to my apartment, and I cleaned up the mess from the night before. It was frightful. I spent half an hour just scrubbing the bathroom. I also changed the sheets on my bed, though I considered leaving them because the spare pillowcase smelled faintly of Jason.

When the apartment was livable again, I went to my closet to find something to wear to the Slammy Awards. There was the gown I'd made for Clay's sister's wedding. *Nope.* There was the dress I'd worn on my last anniversary. *Hell no.* At the back of my closet was a black halter-top dress covered in red roses. I'd actually made it in college. I held it up in front of me and looked in the mirror hanging on the door.

Thanks to all the skating, and the puking of the past twenty-four hours, it looked like it might actually fit.

I hung it on the back of the door. "Bodhi, want to go see Kiara?"

He wagged his tail.

I dressed in real clothes for the first time since Thanksgiving and carried the dress downstairs with Bodhi on his leash. The front door bells jingled as I walked inside. "Hello, hello!" I called.

Kiara was measuring a young girl around the middle. There were several other customers already in the store, and it had only been open for about twenty minutes. The little girl squealed at the sight of Bodhi. "Look, Mommy! A puppy!"

Her mother turned, looking horrified at the sight of the dog in the store. Her face quickly recovered when she saw me.

"Hey there," I said, tightening Bodhi's leash around my hand.

"Oh, hi. You must be the owner. I recognize you from the paper." She walked over with her hand outstretched.

I draped my dress over my forearm and shook her hand. "I am. Grace Evans, nice to meet you."

"Amy Abrams. I believe you know my sister-in-law, Meredith."

I racked my brain for anyone I knew named Meredith.

She touched her forehead and pressed her eyes closed. "Wait, what's her derby name? Jackie something…"

"Full Metal Jackie?"

"That's her!"

"Yeah, she's great."

"It's really nice to meet you, Grace. I love your store."

"Thank you." I paused by Kiara before walking to the back.

She stood and patted the girl on the top of the head. "You're all done, Callie. Mrs. Abrams, I'll be right back and we'll ring up your order."

"Take your time," Amy said. "We're going to look around."

Kiara followed me to the back of the store. "How are you feeling?"

"Still a little off but worlds better than yesterday." I hung my dress on the coat rack.

She pulled out its skirt. "Ooo, vintage."

I scowled. "I made this dress in college."

Her eyebrows lifted with a smile.

"Oh, shut up, Kiara."

She laughed. "What are you doing with it?"

"I need a dress for a party next weekend. Nothing in me wants to go buy one, and I don't have time to make anything from scratch. I was hoping to pick your brain about this one."

"What kind of party?" she asked.

"Derby banquet." I smoothed my hand over the fabric. "What do you think?"

Her head tilted as she stared at it. "You should go Bettie Page with it." She drew a triangle on the front with her fingernail. "Maybe cut out the middle here to show a little skin, and add some red or white fabric around the collar."

"That's a good idea. I wonder if I have time."

She looked me up and down. "I wonder if it still fits."

"Don't make me fire you."

"You wouldn't dare."

I laughed because she was right. I grabbed a box of pins from the shelf and my favorite pair of fabric scissors and dropped them into a bag. "I want to try to get it done ASAP, so I can start on all those orders tomorrow."

She handed me the notebook she was holding. "We're going to have a few more. I've already done two new orders this morning, not including the ones that have come in online."

"Holy cow." I flipped through the seemingly endless pages of the book. "I might have to bring in some help."

"Your mom?"

"Yeah." I grinned. "Maybe it will keep her out of the kitchen."

Kiara laughed.

"I'm stealing this," I said, picking up an old dress form that had once belonged to my mother.

"Stealing it from who? If it's not yours, then I don't know who I'm working for."

I draped my dress over it, slung my bag of supplies over my shoulder, and grabbed the dress form and the dress around the middle. "I'm going to run this upstairs and then go to Milo's for some coffee. You want any?"

"I've already got some. Thank you." She led the way back out to the store. "I'll grab the door."

Outside on the sidewalk, I held the awkward half-mannequin around the middle as I punched in my door code. When I finally got the door open, I decided to sit it at the bottom of the stairs and tote it up later.

Bodhi and I walked two blocks to Milo's, a dog-friendly cafe that specialized in lattes and homemade organic dog treats. They had an outdoor ordering window for customers with dogs.

I pressed the service bell. It was a chorus of barking dogs.

The manager, Matt something, slid open the window. "Welcome to Milo's. Oh, hi, Grace." He looked down at my feet. "Hey there, Bodhi. Long time no see." He leaned out of the window and reached toward my dog. "Shake?"

Bodhi put his paw in Matt's hand.

"Good boy," Matt said. He reached behind him on the counter and grabbed a peanut butter dog treat and tossed it to Bodhi.

"Thanks, Matt," I said as Bodhi gobbled it up.

"Of course. What can I get for you?"

"I'll take a large hazelnut Americana with a splash of cream." Just then, my stomach rumbled like a warning gong. "Maybe make that hot tea instead."

"What kind?"

"Do you have anything with ginger?"

He looked over the tea display behind him. "Looks like we have a green ginger peach."

"Perfect. Can I get that with some honey?"

"Sure thing. Hot or cold?"

I held up my free hand. "I'm wearing fingerless mittens. What do you think?"

He smiled. "Hot it is. Anything for Bodhi? We've got a new Puppy Spice Latte this season. It's got pureed pumpkin, full of vitamins and minerals, and it's made with goat's milk to help digestion." He looked at the dog. "It tastes *doglicious* too."

Bodhi's tail was whipping a thousand miles an hour. I

scratched his head. "Sure. Sounds good. I also need a medium-sized bag of peanut butter treats."

"Anything else?"

"That's all."

Matt rang us up on his tablet. "That'll be twelve eighty-two."

I handed him a ten and a five. "Keep the change."

"Thank you." He reached into a large glass jar by the window, then handed me a cellophane bag of dog treats. It was sealed with a Milo's sticker. "Don't eat these all in one sitting, Bodhi."

"Thanks, Matt." I put the treats in my pocket and felt my phone buzzing. I pulled it out and looked at the screen. Jason. I tapped the answer button. "Hello?"

"Hey, it's me."

"Hey, me, aren't you supposed to be asleep?"

"Yes, I am *supposed* to be, but unfortunately, I'm wide awake. What are you up to?"

"I'm at Milo's cafe, down the street from my place. We just got here. Would you like to join us?"

He was quiet for a second, and I wondered if I shouldn't have asked. "Yeah. Let me throw on some clothes, and I'll be right there."

I cringed with excitement. "OK. We'll be inside. It's chilly today."

"See you in twenty minutes."

"All right. Bye."

"Bye."

"One ginger peach tea with honey and a Puppy Spice Latte for the Bodster," Matt said, passing the drinks through the window.

I hugged Bodhi's cup against my chest, then took my drink. "Thanks, Matt."

"No problem, Grace. It's good to see you again."

Bodhi and I took the second door into the cafe. There was a dog-friendly "Puppy Lounge" that was separate from the main dining room. There was a woman with a schnauzer and an old man with a black Lab. My tea wobbled as Bodhi tugged on his leash, wanting to greet the Lab with a butt sniff.

I dragged him to a table in the back corner and put his latte on the floor by my chair. He began lapping it up before I even sat down.

It was almost twenty minutes on the dot when I saw Jason walk into the main dining room of the cafe. I sent him a text message as he looked around the room. *Do you feel like you're being watched?*

He smiled as he texted me back. *Where are you?*

I got up, walked over to the glass wall, and tapped on it with my fingernail. His face whipped in the direction of the sound, and he smiled when he saw me. He came through the door that connected the two rooms. "I should have known."

Bodhi joined me to greet him. Jason bent to scratch Bodhi behind the ears before giving me a hug. "Welcome back from the land of the dead. How are you feeling?"

"So much better. I had a pretty great caretaker yesterday."

"I slept all day," he said with a chuckle.

"Not true. I was pretty worried about you last night because you didn't sleep nearly enough. And look at you now, awake again."

"Sleep's overrated."

"Do you want some coffee or tea?" I asked. "It's the best in the village.

"I actually drank two cups of coffee on my way over. If I have anymore, I might rattle right off this seat."

I picked up my empty cup. "Well, I'm all done if you want to go."

"Where to?"

"I was thinking about walking down to the market and grabbing something easy to eat. I'm hungry, but I'm afraid."

"I can understand that. Let's get you some toast and bananas. If that settles OK, maybe we can graduate to soup for lunch."

"That sounds great."

It was a three-block walk to the supermarket. "Why don't you wait here with Bodhi, and I'll run in and get the stuff?" he offered.

I lifted an eyebrow. "You're going to buy me groceries?"

"Grace, I went through your cabinets looking for food yesterday. Unless you've been starving yourself for a while, you don't buy groceries."

I laughed. "I get what I need."

"And today, you need bananas and bread. I'm going to pick out a couple of things for a soup that I make."

"You *make* soup?"

"I told you, I'm a pretty good cook. Are you good to wait out here? I'll hurry."

"I'm good."

He turned to walk inside, but he stopped suddenly by the door. "Do you have a pot?"

I put a hand on my hip. "I'm not a cavewoman. Yes, I have a pot."

He winked. "Just checking."

There was a bench beside the street. I sat down and got a treat out of the bag for Bodhi. He sat by my feet to eat it. A few minutes later, a black car pulled up at the curb in front of me, and the back window rolled slowly down.

Sylvia.

"Grace, what are you doing out here? Have you gone homeless on me?" she asked.

"No, ma'am. Just waiting for a friend. Did you have a nice Thanksgiving?"

"Never celebrate it," she said.

That was surprising with as much as she went on and on about her granddaughter, and how badly she wanted the dress by Thanksgiving.

"Oh. Were you able to give Alexandria her dress?" I asked.

"What? Oh yes."

"Did she like it?"

"Sure. Yes. Thank you for asking. We've got to go now. Miss Taylor is going to be late for her spa day. Goodbye, Grace."

I wanted to inquire more, but Sylvia was already rolling up her window. With a huff, I waved. "Bye."

"What was that?" Jason asked, walking out with a woven grocery bag. "Were you being propositioned?"

"It was Sylvia."

"Oh. Did you ever finish that dress for her?"

I stood and we started down the street. "Yeah. It was very anticlimactic. I think she hated it but didn't want to tell me."

"Really? I don't see that woman having a problem speaking her mind to anyone," he said.

"Maybe." I really didn't want to talk about it. I tried to peek into the grocery bag. "What'd you get?"

He swatted my hand away. "Don't you worry about it."

We walked against the wind back up the street toward my building. The sky was gray and blowing tiny balls of snow. "You warm enough," Jason asked when I ducked my chin into my scarf.

"No," I said with a smile.

He offered me his elbow, and when I linked my arm with his, he pulled me against his side. We walked arm in arm for the last two blocks. It was great. So easy. So comfortable. So close. As we neared my apartment, I realized I didn't want the walk to end.

"Looks like business is still rolling in," he said as we passed by my store.

I looked through the door to make sure Kiara had it under

control. She did, as always. "Yeah. We're going to be really busy for the next few weeks fulfilling a ton of orders."

"That's good, right?"

"Very good."

He looked at me sideways when we stopped at my door. "You don't look so happy about it."

I sighed. "To be honest, since everything happened with Clay, it's been hard to get excited about making stuff for other people's kids."

"That's fair." He punched in my door code. "Have you heard anymore from him?"

"No. You?"

"No."

Jason pulled open the door, then immediately slammed it. "What the hell?"

I laughed and punched in the code again. "Jumpy, officer?"

"I thought I might have to pull my gun."

I opened the door myself.

"What is that thing?" he asked, looking at the dress form.

"It's a kind of mannequin I use for making dresses." I picked up my dress that was draped over the top of it. "I'll put this on it, and it will be easier to make alterations."

"Here. Take the groceries and you and Bodhi go on up. I'll carry your fake person upstairs."

"Thanks."

Jason followed me and Bodhi up to my apartment. "That dress looks a little too big for your normal clientele."

"This is actually my dress. Our derby-awards banquet is next weekend, and I need something to wear."

"Derby awards? That sounds fun."

I nodded as I unlocked my apartment door. "I'm sure it will be. You could come with me if you want." I was glad I wasn't facing him; I'm sure my face was beet red.

"When is it?"

"Friday night at The Drunken Nun in East Nashville."

We walked inside and I flipped on the light. "I would love to."

I stopped and spun around. "You would?"

"I would." He grimaced as he set the dress form down in the corner. "But I have to work."

"Oh. That sucks." Inside, my whole body slumped with disappointment. I bent and unhooked Bodhi's leash.

He took off his coat. "Will you ask someone else?"

That was an odd question, especially coming from someone who had clearly taken dating off the table. "I don't know. Why?"

"Not sure I like the idea of you going with anybody else."

When my back was turned to hang up my own jacket, I smiled. "Then maybe you should figure out a way to get off and take me."

He smiled. "I wish." Carrying the bag of groceries, he walked past me to the kitchen and turned on the light. "While I make your lunch, do you want to find that movie we started yesterday? I'd like to finish it if I can stay awake."

"Sure." I froze in the hallway between my bedroom and my living room. *Where* did he want to watch it? The day before it had been acceptable to lay together in my bed. But now?

I stepped back into the doorway to the kitchen. "So, awkward question. Do you want to watch the movie in my bedroom again?"

He turned around and chuckled. "It is more comfortable than your couch."

"What's wrong with my couch?"

"Nothing, but your bed is awesome." He grinned. "Don't worry. I can keep my hands to myself if you can."

I wasn't sure how to answer that, so I laughed and carried the dress form into my bedroom. I put it by my sewing machine near the window, and then I found the movie we'd been watching on-demand.

Cabinets opened and closed in the kitchen. "Grace, do you have a toaster?"

"Er..." I said, slipping the dress over the mannequin.

He laughed. "You don't have a toaster? How do you cook your Pop-Tarts?"

"Pop-Tarts, really?"

"I love Pop-Tarts. What about a cookie sheet? I can broil the bread in the oven."

"Check the tall cabinet near the fridge," I said.

"Got it."

While Jason banged around in the kitchen, I started work on my dress. Using a tape measure and chalk, I outlined a triangle just below the bust, then I drew the lines on the collar that I would cut out for the new neckline.

"Ready to try solid food?" he asked, walking through my bedroom door.

My stomach growled at the thought.

He carried a plate over and handed it to me. "Whole-wheat toast with a tiny bit of peanut butter and a sliced banana."

Bodhi was lying halfway under the sewing table, chewing on his rubber chicken. He got up when he smelled the peanut butter, no doubt. I moved to my side of the bed. Bodhi followed me and Jason walked back to the door. "What would you like to drink?" he asked.

"Water would be fine. There are bottles in the fridge."

Bodhi whimpered by my legs. I tore off a corner of the bread and tossed it to him. Jason returned with two bottles of water and put one of them on my nightstand.

I bit into the toast. "This is perfect. Thank you."

"You're welcome. Try not to throw it up."

I smiled. "I'll do my best."

When he finally stretched out on the other side of the bed, I handed him the remote. "The movie's ready to go."

He moaned with pleasure as his head settled into the pillow. "This feels so good."

"It's memory foam," I said.

"I'm so not making it through this movie again. If I fall asleep, can you check the chicken on the stove after a while?"

"Sure. Do I need to do anything with it?"

"It's on low, so it should be fine. Just don't let it boil over or run out of water."

"OK."

"But wake me if I am asleep."

"Absolutely not. You need to rest. You were up all night."

"Yeah, but I also need to go home and check on Mom at some point."

I kicked off my shoes and sat cross-legged on the bed. "Does she stay at home alone when you're gone or at work?"

"Most of the time. Sometimes her sister stays with her or takes her out. Like today, they went to a crafts fair downtown."

"That's nice."

"It is. They're really close. And we have a home-health nurse who comes when I need her to. But Mom's fairly independent these days. Especially since we had the renovations done to the house. She can get around a lot easier."

"Is she in the wheelchair always?" I asked.

"Most of the time. She can get in and out of it now by herself, but it's easier and safer for her to use it."

"Is your stepdad still in prison?"

He took a long drink from his bottle. "Actually, he's dead."

"Dead?"

"Heart attack about two years ago."

"Wow. I had no idea."

"I didn't tell anyone. Not even Clay." He pointed at my plate. "Eat your toast. It's better when it's warm."

It wasn't clear what exactly he didn't want to talk about, his stepfather or my ex. Probably neither, I surmised as he started the movie.

Once again, Bodhi hopped up on the bed between us, and twenty minutes later, he and Jason were both sound asleep.

ELEVEN

"SO NOTHING HAPPENED?" Monica asked *again* the next morning. We were skating the park slowly because I still wasn't feeling 100 percent. "You've had that man in your bed twice now and didn't lay a finger on him either time?"

"I told you, he slept through the movie. Then he made me soup, we ate, and he went home. That was it."

I had Bodhi on his leash, and he was trotting beside me.

"When are you going to see him again?"

"After I leave here, actually. I told him I'd drive Bodhi back to his place. Clay's coming to pick him up at noon."

She groaned. "That sucks. I'm so sorry."

"I don't want to talk about it."

"How'd you take the news about Clay?" she asked.

I'd told her while we geared up that he was getting remarried.

"I cried, but without any tears because I was dehydrated."

"He's such a douche."

"I'm aware. I really don't want to talk about him either."

"Fair enough. Did you ever ask Jason to the Slammy Awards?"

I hopped over a rock on the path. "We actually discussed it, but he has to work. He did say he would have liked to go. And that he wasn't crazy about the idea of me taking someone else."

"Hey! That's something," she said, nudging my arm with her elbow pad.

"I guess. I did decide what I'm going to wear."

"Oh yeah?"

"Yep. A dress from college, actually. Kiara gave me some ideas, and I updated its look a bit."

Her face soured. "I hate you sometimes, Grace."

My mouth fell open.

"I can't even remember the clothes I wore in college, much less fit into any of them."

"I am having to alter it a bit. You'll see."

"I'm sure it will be spectacular."

"Thank you."

"We've got the team meeting on Monday night, don't forget" she said as we rounded the corner near the Parthenon.

"Have you thought any more about the derby-committee thing?"

Monica hopped over a clump of leaves on the path. "I actually took Maisie skates shopping yesterday, so I guess I'm going to coach the juniors."

"Seriously?"

She smiled. "Yeah. At least it will be something fun she and I can do together. I still can't start until after the concert though. What do you think you'll do?"

I shrugged. "I figured whatever you chose, we'd do together. But I'm trying to get out of the world of children these days. I think junior derby would be counterproductive. Maybe I'll go do marketing with Lucy."

"One article in a newspaper and now you're an expert?" she teased.

"Something like that." We turned the corner near the lake. "Did I tell you I got my tickets to your show?"

"Tickets? As in *plural?* Are you going to bring Jason?"

"I don't know. I was thinking about bringing Mom."

She linked her fingers together in prayer. "Please bring the hot cop."

"We're not dating, Monica."

"And we're not skating at the park right now. What other lies shall we tell, Grace?"

A flash of something gray scampering across the road ahead caught my eye...but not before it caught Bodhi's. He darted forward, sounding a chorus of gleeful yelps as he charged down the path. My left arm flailed as I tried to hold tight to his leash with my right hand *and* stay upright on my skates.

I saw the squirrel as it leapt from the path, down the hill toward the water. "Bodhi, no!"

It was too late.

He cut left, spinning my skates and pulling me sideways. I dropped the leash as I went down on all fours into the grass. I slid a couple of feet and rolled once, landing flat on my back.

I lifted my hands. A stick was jutting out of my right wrist guard, and I screamed when I pulled it out.

"Are you OK?" Monica shouted.

I ripped off the wrist guard, and blood trickled from a gash in my palm down my forearm. I swore and kicked my wheels against the cold ground. Bodhi bounded over and tried licking my face.

Pushing him away, I rolled to sit up. "No more skating with you, you big oaf."

Monica walked over, carefully stepping sideways on her skates. "You all right?" she asked again.

"Yeah. Just impaled my hand with a stick is all." The dog

plopped down directly on my lap. "Bodhi, move." I pushed him off me.

Monica offered her hand and then helped me up.

"Thanks," I said, grabbing the leash off the ground.

"Think it needs stitches?" Monica asked, leaning over my hand.

I shook my head. "No. It's just a bad scratch. I think I'm done skating for the day though."

"Yeah, you need to get that cleaned up. There's a lot of dirt in it. Want to skate down to the bathroom?"

The thought of an open wound inside the public-park bathroom made me queasy. "It's about time to head out anyway. I think I'll clean it out at Jason's."

"Well, I'm sure the good officer is certified in first aid."

"I hope so." I tugged on the leash. "Come on, Bodhi. Let's go."

I drove with one hand across town to Jason's house. I'd been there once or twice before when we were still in college. The ranch-style house looked completely different now. Its old red bricks had been painted white, and dark-wood posts supported the covered front porch. Freshly painted chocolate shutters framed the front windows, and purple and yellow mums sat beside the arched double front doors.

I parked next to Jason's squad car, then let Bodhi out of the back seat before gathering his bowl, his food, and his treats. My feet seemed to weigh a thousand pounds as I trudged up the smooth concrete handicap ramp to the entrance.

Jason pulled the door open before I even rang the bell. "Hey, Grace."

I looked around, confused. "Are you psychic?"

He laughed and stepped out of my way. "No. Mom saw you pull in through the window in the kitchen. Come on in." He took Bodhi's leash before I could even ask if the dog was allowed inside. Bodhi trotted in ahead of me, and Jason bent to unhook his leash.

The inside was unrecognizable. Where I remembered small, boxy rooms was now a completely open floor plan. There was a half wall near the hallway and a support beam between the kitchen and the dining area. That was it. The furniture was sparse, and the pieces were accessible by wide pathways. "Wow. This place looks amazing," I said as I put Bodhi's bag down by the door.

"Thank you. We lived in knee-deep sawdust for about a year, but it was worth it. Right, Mom?"

To my left, in the remodeled kitchen, Jason's mother turned in her electric wheelchair. The right side of her face twisted downward, and her right arm lay withered in her lap. She smiled with the good half of her mouth. "Hello, Grace," she said as well as she could.

Jason stood beside me, his hand on the small of my back "Grace, you remember my mom, Marybeth Bradley."

"Of course." I walked to the kitchen and knelt down beside her chair. "Hello, Ms. Bradley."

She offered me her left hand and I took it with my hand that wasn't crusted with blood. "Please, call me Marybeth. It's nice to see you again after all these years. You're just as lovely as always."

I smiled, but I found it odd that she'd ever thought of me as *lovely*. We had never really known each other well. "It's good to see you too. Your house is beautiful."

"My son did it for me." She smiled up at Jason, who was standing behind me. "He's a good guy."

"I think I'd have to agree." I pushed myself up and turned toward him. I showed him my bloody palm. "Mind if I use your bathroom? I had an accident at the park."

"Geez, Grace," he said, gently taking my wrist. "What did you do now?"

"Bodhi and I went skating." I grinned down at his mom. "Bodhi saw a squirrel."

She laughed.

Jason pulled on my arm. "Come downstairs. I've got a first-aid kit in my baseball bag."

I thought of Monica and smiled.

"Be right back, Mom," he said over his shoulder as he led me through the living room with Bodhi on our heels. A staircase hidden by the half wall took us to the basement. It had been transformed into a full apartment, complete with a small kitchen and a wood-burning fireplace. A sliding-glass door led outside to a small patio and fire pit.

"Wow. I was *not* expecting this," I said, wide eyed, as he walked to the closet.

"Yeah, it turned out really well. It's nice to have some space that feels like my own after sharing the house for so long. Mom likes it too." He grinned over at me from the closet. "It's easier for me to sneak girls in now."

"Priorities." I laughed and ran my clean hand along the back of the leather sofa. He had an old vintage trunk for a coffee table, and a desk made out of reclaimed wood. "It's really nice in here. Did you decorate this place yourself?"

He unzipped a large duffle bag on the floor. "Uh, no." There was a strange pause. "Actually, a girl I dated for a few months was an interior designer."

"Ohhh," I said, drawing out the word. "Can I get her number?"

He laughed as he started pulling things from the bag: a binder, a notebook, a few water bottles, a helmet...

"Here we go." He stood with a small white box in his hand. "Come to the sink."

I followed him to the small kitchen, where he turned on the water and handed me a bottle of hand soap. "Wash."

Bodhi plopped down by my feet, perhaps sensing the pain of the warm water burning my shredded palm. I cringed as I rubbed the cuts with soap.

Standing beside me, he looked over my shoulder. "That's one hell of a scratch."

"I pulled a stick out of it. It was jammed in there under my wrist guard."

"Ouch." He ripped a paper towel off the roll and gently dried my hands. "Have a seat at the table."

We sat beside each other at a small bistro two-top, and with his teeth, he tore open a package of antibacterial cream. "This shouldn't hurt at all." Still, I braced myself as he smeared it over the gash and the smaller scrapes. Then he covered the whole area with a gauze pad and pulled out a roll of athletic tape.

Somewhere between his carefully laid strips of tape, I got lost staring at his face. He hadn't shaved in the few days we'd spent together, and the perfect amount of chin stubble—somewhere between Adam Levine and David Beckham—covered his angular jaw line. "This looks good on you," I said, tracing my free index finger down the side of his face.

He smiled. "Think so?"

"Yeah. I like it."

"It's outside of our grooming standards for work, but it's my day off, so..." He looked up. "You're all done."

I wiggled my fingers. "Thank you. I hope you're keeping tabs on how many times you've had to take care of me this week. I feel like I'll never be out of debt to you."

He wadded up the trash and dumped it in the garbage can by the wall. "I kinda like you in my debt. I plan on collecting all at once, big time."

I laughed. "Sounds good to me. So when's my demon ex-husband supposed to show his ugly face?"

Jason looked at his watch. "About twenty minutes."

With a heavy sigh, I slid off my chair and into the floor beside my dog. "I guess I'd better go so we don't get busted." I patted my lap. "Come here, Bodhi."

He got up and padded over, then flopped across my legs. I bent over him, wrapping my arms around his fluffy neck.

Jason leaned his elbow on the table, looking down at us. "If it helps, I told Clay I'd dog sit for him anytime."

I nodded, turning my face toward the wall as tears prickled my eyes. "I love you, Bodhi," I whispered.

He lifted his head under mine, then turned to lick my cheek.

With a sniff, I dried my eyes on my sleeve and pushed myself off the floor. "Thanks again, Jason."

He got up, leaving his water on the table. "I'll walk you out." Halfway up the stairs, Jason's cell phone rang. "It's Clay."

I stopped walking and turned around. Bodhi looked up, confused, suspended on the stairs between us.

Jason tapped the screen and held the phone to his ear. "Hello?" He listened for a moment.

I crossed my fingers and closed my eyes, silently praying. *Please say you're not coming. Please say you're not coming. Please say you're not coming.*

Another thought occurred to me and my eyes popped opened. Maybe Clay was dead and someone was using his phone to ask Jason to keep Bodhi forever.

Jason brow rumpled. "Yeah. Of course that's fine. How far out are you?" As he listened, his eyes widened. "OK. See you in a second." He ended the call. "We have a problem."

"A second?"

"Yeah. Give me your keys. I'll put your car in my garage."

I pulled my keychain from my pocket and he snatched it from my hand. "There's a door to the garage beside my room. Go in there and hit the garage door button for me."

"OK."

He squeezed past me and took the stairs up two at a time.

"Be right back, Mom! And if anyone asks, you haven't seen Grace!" Jason called as I went back to the basement. Bodhi followed me.

In the corner across from his kitchen were two doors, one on each wall. I opened the first and froze when I saw his bedroom.

A king-sized, wood-panel bed was centered on the wall, unmade, like we could have just been tangled up in the charcoal comforter. A huge gun safe was beside the dresser. And a full bookcase was beyond the bed.

I may have had a hot flash.

I slammed the door and tried the other. *Bingo.* Jason's truck was parked inside. There were two illuminated buttons on the wall. I pressed the top one. The door behind his truck began to raise. "Crap." I closed that door, and hit the other button. That time, the second bay door slowly slid up.

Jason was already in my car with the whistling engine running. I really needed to get that fixed. As soon as he pulled it into the garage, I closed the door. When Jason got out, he ducked down to look out the closing bay door. "I think he just pulled in."

"That was close."

"Yeah." He jogged around the car and came in the door where I was waiting. "What's wrong with your car? It's making a noise."

"I dunno. A hole in something or other. Do you think he saw my car?"

"No. Wait down here until he's gone. I'll try to get rid of him quickly." He slapped the side of his leg as he walked through the room. "Come on, Bodhi."

Jason started up the stairs, but Bodhi sat down by my feet.

"Go. He'll take off running when he hears the doorbell," I said.

Jason nodded and went on up.

But then the doorbell rang, and Bodhi just looked up at me. I put my hands on my hips. "You know it's him, don't you?"

His head flopped to the side.

"Go on," I whispered. "You're going to get all of us into trouble."

I heard the door open upstairs, followed by muffled voices. Grabbing Bodhi's collar, I pulled him up the stairs behind me.

"We've had a good weekend," Jason was saying when I reached near the top.

"Is this his stuff?" Clay asked.

"Yeah, let me get that. Bodhi!"

I tried pushing the dog up the last couple of steps. He wouldn't budge. There was a crinkling of paper before Jason called out again. "You want a treat, boy?"

At that, Bodhi took off running. I tried to not take it personally.

"Hey, what are those?" It was Clay's voice.

"Dog treats," Jason answered.

The paper crinkled again. "Those are from Milo's."

"Shit," I whispered.

"You went to Milo's, over by Grace's apartment?" Clay asked.

"Yeah! Sure. Dogs love that place!"

Good lord. I rolled my eyes. Jason couldn't lie to save his life.

There was silence, and I didn't need to be at the front door to know that it was tense.

"Did you see Grace?"

"Just for a minute." That lie was only slightly more convincing. "She really misses him, Clay."

"How would you know she's missing him?"

There was a pause. "We talk sometimes."

More silence.

My heartbeat seemed to echo off the stairwell walls.

"Jason." Clay's voice was tight. He was trying to control his temper. "Are you seeing my wife?"

"*Your wife?*" I mouthed, screaming in my head.

"I think you mean your *ex*-wife," Jason said. "And no. I'm not. At least, not like *that*."

Jason's answer was a swift kick to the gut.

I listened hard, but there was only more silence. I could imagine Clay's eyes narrowing with skepticism.

Finally, Jason spoke again. "You're like a brother to me. I wouldn't do that."

I nearly rolled down the stairs.

"I'm sorry, man," Clay said. "Grace just makes me crazy."

"I make *you* crazy?" I whispered.

"Don't worry about it," Jason told him.

"Did you hear the news?" Clay asked.

"No. What?" Jason lied.

"I'm getting married again." Clay didn't sound happy about it, which made me feel only slightly better.

"Didn't you *just* get divorced?" Jason asked.

"Yeah, but you know...the baby will be here in a few months. Ginny thought it'd be best to go ahead and get the wedding out of the way. Hey, you wanna be my best man?"

Jason laughed nervously.

"I'm just kidding. We'll probably do something small. Maybe elope. I hear Bora Bora is nice."

My hands clenched into fists. "You son of a..."

"I hope you're happy, Clay. You and Ginny certainly deserve each other," Jason said.

"Thanks, man."

I rolled my eyes. He couldn't even tell anymore when his best friend was slamming him.

"How about a drink sometime this week so we can catch up?" Clay asked.

"Sure. Just let me know when," Jason answered. "Here's the dog's stuff. Seriously, I'll keep him anytime."

"I appreciate that. Ginny and I might be traveling some over the holidays. If we do, I'll hit you up."

"Sounds good. I'll see you later."

"Bye." Clay raised his voice. "Bye, Marybeth!"

I couldn't hear it if she responded.

The door closed, and a moment later, Jason appeared at the top of the stairs. I turned and faced the other way. He came over and sat down beside me. "You heard all that?"

I didn't answer.

"It's true, Grace. He's like a brother to me." He draped his arms across his knees and sighed. "An asshole brother, for sure sometimes, but still."

I nodded.

"Will you look at me?"

I took a deep breath and finally met his eyes.

"I really like you, and I wish things were different."

"Is that supposed to make me feel better?" I almost shouted.

"No."

"So you *intentionally* want to make me feel worse?" I asked. He reached for my hand, but I pulled away and stood. "Give me my keys."

"Grace, please don't leave like this," he said, standing up.

I held out my hand. "Keys, please."

He reached in his pocket and handed me my keychain.

Angry tears threatened to spill from my eyes. I wanted out of that house as soon as possible. "Goodbye, Marybeth!" I called up the stairs.

"Goodbye, Grace," I heard her say.

"I'm going out the garage," I said, starting back down.

Jason followed me. "I don't want you driving when you're upset."

I shook my head and didn't stop. "I'm not upset."

"Grace."

I spun on my heel to face him. "Jason, I'm fine. I've had the absolute worst year from hell. Trust me, you don't have the power to make it any worse. I won't *let you* make it any worse."

He stared at me for a moment, then he nodded.

"I appreciate all you've done for me this weekend, but it'd be really great if you don't call or text me anymore, OK?"

"OK." He stuffed his hands into his pockets.

Then I turned and walked out the garage door, slamming it behind me.

TWELVE

MONICA AND HER HUSBAND, Derek, were waiting outside The Drunken Nun when my Uber pulled up to the curb on Friday night. I gave her an excited wave through the window, then thanked the driver as I got out.

"Grace! Oh my god, you look amazing!" Monica ran carefully on her heels toward me.

I did a slow twirl in the black dress covered with red roses. "Thank you." I felt amazing. It was the first time in months I'd really felt pretty. "Too bad I don't have a hot date here to appreciate it."

"Have you talked to him at all?" she asked with a grimace.

"No. It's done. I plan on drowning him from my memory tonight."

Her nose wrinkled, but she quickly changed the subject and took both of my hands. "Let me see this creation. I swear, Grace, this dress is gorgeous."

Kiara had stayed late that afternoon to help me put the finishing touches on my party dress. I had cut out the triangle in the front of the bodice and had lowered the neckline of the halter into a deep sweetheart. As Kiara predicted, the dress was too small when I put it on. So I ripped out the zipper and put eyelet holes in the back to lace it up like a corset. She finished it off by sewing a few layers of red tulle under the skirt to make it stand out.

To finish the look, I twisted my blonde hair up in tight pin curls, and fixed a bright red rose in the back.

"You look beautiful too, Monica." I hooked my arm around her neck and turned her around toward her husband. "Derek, how does it feel to be married to the hottest woman in Nashville?"

He walked over with a wide smile. "I honestly can't wait to get her back home."

She squealed. "Derek, stop it!"

I pushed her toward him, and he caught her in his arms.

"You both need to stop it," I said with a laugh. "Why are you out here in the cold?"

"Why are neither of you crazy women wearing coats?" Derek asked.

I ran my hands down my skirt. "And cover up any of this?"

He shook his head.

"I told him the same thing," Monica said.

He took her arm. "And you've been standing out here with your teeth chattering."

"Why aren't you inside?" I asked again.

She jerked her thumb over her shoulder toward the door. "None of our friends are here yet, and I felt weird going in there with all the vets."

Couldn't blame her. The veteran skaters on our team were intimidating as hell.

A sign hung over the black door: RESERVED FOR A PRIVATE EVENT. WELCOME MUSIC CITY ROLLERS!

My heart fluttered. I still couldn't believe I was part of the team.

Monica must have felt the same because she let a tiny squeal slip.

Derek opened the door and held it for both of us.

Music rose over the chatter of the bar. A live band with a female singer was playing a jazzy version of "U Can't Touch This" with a bass cello, a drum set, and a grand piano. Monica grabbed my arm. "Oh my god, do you hear that?"

"She's really good," I said.

Derek leaned in between us. "Can I bring you ladies a drink?"

"We'll go with you," Monica told him.

The building was two levels. Downstairs was the stage and a dance floor with a long bar covering the side wall. In the back and up in the loft, tables faced the stage. The place was packed with far more people than were actually on the team.

I followed Monica and Derek toward the bar, which was already swamped with people. Only a handful of them I recognized. Lady Fury, a recently retired skater, was laughing with Midnight Maven. Doc Carnage was sipping a bright teal-blue drink and talking to a man I didn't know. She waved when she saw me.

At the far end of the bar, a small space opened up just before the wall. If we hurried, we might be able to wedge into it to order.

Derek saw it too. "Monica, Grace, over here."

When the three of us reached the empty space, it wasn't empty at all. Hidden by a group of what I assumed (by their team-spirited colors) were team Jeerleaders, a man was seated on a barstool.

"Nuts," I said, scanning the bar for holes again.

The man caught my eye. "Do you need to order?"

"Please?" It was more of a whimpering plea than an answer.

He stood, motioned to his barstool, and pressed his back against the wall. "Be my guest. This place is a madhouse."

"Thank you." I couldn't help but notice the man was attractive. Dark hair. Bronze skin. Perfect teeth. Before I started staring, I pulled Monica beside me into the space he'd vacated. "Mon, what do you want to drink?"

"Something fruity with vodka!"

My eyes widened. "Oh boy. Derek, you might have your hands full."

"I'll take it," he said, winking at his wife.

I looked at Monica. "How about a Sex on the Beach?"

"Yes, please," Derek answered for her.

She giggled.

I sighed. "You guys are too much. Derek, what would you like to drink?"

"Water will be fine. I'm driving."

I shook my head. "This is why God created Uber, Mr. Hooker." I signaled the bartender, a tall red-headed man with a beard. "One Sex on the Beach, one water, and..." I looked around the room. "What's the teal-blue stuff so many people are drinking?"

"That's the RollerRita. Like a margarita with blue curaçao liqueur."

My nose scrunched. "Not strong enough for tonight. How about a Long Island Iced Tea, please?"

"You got it," the bartender said.

"Being brave, huh?" Monica asked, leaning against the bar beside me.

"Or stupid." I smiled at the man who'd moved for the sake of our order. "Thank you again. Do you need a drink?"

He glanced down at the amber liquid in his whiskey glass. "I'm good right now. Thank you, though." He gestured to his barstool. "Would you like to sit while you wait?"

Suddenly, I was keenly aware that my legs looked far better

in heels when I was standing. And yes, I should have accepted his offer for all sorts of reasons: my soon-to-be-aching ankles or the ease of reaching the bar, but damn it, I'd worked hard on my dress —someone needed to appreciate it.

"Thank you, but I'm OK." I leaned against the bar top, straining my hard-earned derby calves at an angle. That's right. Flamingos dance. Some monkeys flash their nether regions. And derby girls flaunt their calves. When I turned my back to him, Monica caught my eye and smiled. She knew.

"You haven't seen Lucy, Olivia, or Zoey?" I asked her.

She shook her head. "But, to be honest, I barely looked around and then dragged Derek back outside to wait for you."

I held up my hands. "No judgment here."

She leaned against me. "Thank you. I felt so stupid."

"Not stupid at all." I lowered my voice to a whisper. "They're badass." I didn't need to clarify that I was referring to the veteran members of the Music City Rollers being badass and to us being...*not*.

At least, not yet, anyway.

"Sex on the Beach." The bartender handed me a stemmed glass filled with orange pink poison, which I immediately passed to Monica. "And a Vatican Iced Tea."

"*Vatican* Iced Tea, huh?" I laughed as I took it from him.

The bartender winked and pointed at the "drunken nun" on his T-shirt. "This ain't New York, sweetheart."

I took a sip through the straw. "It's delicious. Thank you."

Monica smiled. "Does it taste like bad decisions and a headache?"

"Only if I'm lucky."

"Don't forget we have the Christmas parade tomorrow."

"What time are we supposed to be there?" I asked.

She looked at my drink, then at me. "Seven in the morning."

"That should be fun." I stuck my straw into my mouth again.

"Oh look! There's Lucy and West," Monica said.

Lucy was waving from a table up in the loft and beckoning us to join her. I took a step back from the bar and turned toward the dark, handsome stranger in the corner. "Thanks again for saving the day."

He smiled. "I'll try and hold the spot if you need it again."

Monica hooked her arm through mine as we walked away, leaving her poor husband to follow us. "That guy was cute," she said in a loud whisper.

"I know. I might have to drink this extra fast."

She laughed and leaned her head against mine.

"Grace! Monica!"

We looked toward the dance floor as Zoey ran over. She was barefoot and waving a pair of blue ballet flats at us.

"Hey, Zoey." I looked down at her when she reached us. She wore a sleeveless teal dress with a kaleidoscope pattern. "You look adorable."

"Thanks. You look like a fifties pinup."

I smiled and swished my ruffled skirt. "That was exactly what I was going for."

West Adler, Lucy's boyfriend, stood when we approached the table. He pulled out the seat beside him for me, and I turned to Lucy and flashed her an impressed smile as I sat down.

"Wow. I didn't know men still did that," I said. "Thank you, West."

He smiled. "Gotta win over the friends, right?"

"Spice Girls wisdom?" I asked, cocking an eyebrow.

He laughed. "I guess so."

"He's a keeper, Lucy," I said between sips of my drink.

"I agree." She beamed at him.

Monica smiled back at her husband. "Derek only does that when he's trying to get laid."

Derek took a quick step forward and pulled out the seat

beside me. He gave a dramatic bow to his wife. "For you, my lady."

"See?" she said with a laugh. She gave him a peck on the lips before she sat. "Everybody, this is my husband, Derek." Then she pointed around the group. "This is Lucy, West, Zoey, and you already know Grace."

Derek waved and sat next to Monica. "I hope there's not a quiz later."

"It's nice to finally meet you, Derek," Lucy said.

He tipped his water toward her. "You too, Lucy."

"Is Olivia still coming?" Monica asked her.

"She said this morning she was leaving work early to be here."

"Did you find out any more about what's going on with her and Styx?" Zoey asked.

Lucy was drinking a RollerRita, rimmed with blue salt and garnished with a lime. "Some kind of love triangle that I don't quite understand. Apparently, Hale Damage told Styx that Olivia was 'the one that got away' and started this whole mess. And I guess Haley and Styx are *derby wives*, whatever that means."

"But I thought Olivia and Styx were together now?" I asked.

West leaned forward. "Derby wives are just best friends in the league. They don't have to be together, or even lesbians for that matter."

We all looked at him surprised.

He laughed. "What? Medusa's wife is Maven. Everybody knows that."

I raised my hand. "Not everybody."

West had once dated our former team captain. If anybody would know, it'd be him.

"Where is Medusa?" Zoey asked, scanning the crowd below.

"Haven't seen her," Lucy answered.

West smiled over his glass. "She's only known for her punctuality to practice."

"Oh my god, is that Full Metal Jackie?" Lucy asked, looking past us toward the stairs.

I turned in my chair. I'd seen Jackie recently, but she'd been wearing baggy workout gear at the park. Tonight, I hardly recognized her. She was in a fitted, sequined party dress that perfectly showed off her baby bump.

My heart twisted, and I took a long pull through the straw of my Vatican Iced Tea.

"Hi, Jackie!" Zoey chirped, her typical cheerful self.

Lucy stood and walked around the table to hug her. Then she pointed at her belly. "Look at you! You've really popped out since the last time we saw you."

Jackie smoothed her dress over her bump. "Almost five months now. We found out this morning that it's a girl."

"A girl!" Zoey squealed.

Lucy clapped her hands. "How exciting! Have you picked out a name?"

"Harper Elizabeth." Jackie's face was flushed and glistening, either she was "glowing," as they say, or suffering from the hike up the stairs. My cynical side—which was now being prodded by a few shots of white liquor—hoped it was the stairs.

"That's a beautiful name," Zoey said.

I sucked on my suddenly empty glass, and the air bubbling through my straw rattled the ice cubes. It was loud, even with the music, and everyone looked at me. Monica's wide eyes were asking, *"What the hell, Grace?"*

"Sorry," I mouthed.

Jackie smiled. "Thank you, Zoey. Are you doing the next round of Fresh Meat training?"

"Yes, ma'am. It starts in January."

Jackie squeezed her shoulder. "Good to hear. Hopefully, if

I'm not otherwise engaged"—she put her hands on her baby bump—"maybe I can come watch you pass."

"That would be great! When are you due?" Zoey asked.

Oh god. Kill me now.

I took Monica's Sex on the Beach and sucked down three giant gulps.

"Mid-April, so hopefully I'll make it."

Monica kicked me under the table. "Sorry," I said, sliding her glass back over.

She jerked her head toward the stairs, her eyes wide. I looked over to see the guy from the bar, hopefully coming to rescue me. God, he was cute. Like Batman—or, better yet, Batman's equally hot nemesis. "I could use a hot supervillain in my life right now."

I hadn't realized I'd said that out loud until Monica whirled toward me. Thankfully, I don't think anyone else heard.

"Have you eaten today?" she whispered, looking at my empty glass.

I shook my head and frowned.

She said something to Derek, then he looked at me, chuckled, and left the table, passing the hot guy halfway across the loft. I straightened in my seat and smiled.

Then he touched the small of Jackie's back, and she turned around.

Then she kissed him. Full on the mouth.

Monica looked at me and pressed her lips together. I wanted to thump my forehead on the table.

Jackie turned back toward us with the hot guy standing in that place at a girl's back reserved for husbands, serious boyfriends, and golf instructors. "Guys, this is my husband, Uriah." She said other things too, but I wasn't listening. I was looking at the loft railing, wondering if I could make a tumble from it look like an accident.

"Grace!" Monica hissed.

Had I said that out loud too?

"What?"

"Jackie was talking to you."

I looked back at Jackie and *her* supervillain. "Sorry. Distracted by the band."

"I was just telling Uriah that Monica might start helping with the juniors' team. I said, I was still hoping I could count on you too."

"She talks very highly of you," he added, rubbing the back of her neck.

Meh, he wasn't that cute after all. I swirled my straw around in my ice cubes. I needed more booze.

"Think you'll consider it?" Jackie asked with a hopeful smile.

I winked, clicked the side of my tongue, and gave her a thumbs-up.

"Excellent. Well, I'm going to take off and find something boring and nonalcoholic to sip on. You girls have fun," she said.

We waved as she walked away. I noticed her ankles were a little puffy. Never thought I'd be jealous of that. I took a deep breath and stood. But as soon as I was about to announce I was getting another drink...

"Grace! Britches! Whatever the hell your name is now, sit'chur ass down!" Olivia belted behind me.

I turned. She was carrying a round tray full of shot glasses filled with black liquid toward our table. "Hey! Where did you come from?" I reached to help her, but she swatted my hand away.

"Sit, sit! Celebratory drinks on me!"

As she passed out shots, I (and, no doubt, everyone else at our table) looked around for Styx. I didn't see her anywhere. What I did see was Derek returning with a glass of water and a bowl full of pretzels.

I scowled at Monica.

She pointed a bright red nail at me. "You need carbs and hydration."

"She needs a shot!" Olivia announced, handing me a glass.

"I should be buying you a shot after all you did for me last weekend," I said.

"Well, I got your thank-you card and the gift card. You really didn't have to do that."

"I know. I wanted to." I sniffed the shot glass. It smelled like black licorice and regret. "What is this?"

"Jäger, my love. Congratulations."

"Congratulations for what?" Monica asked.

Olivia offered a shot to Derek as he sat back down. "For surviving your first few weeks of big-girl practice."

"No thanks," he said. "Driving."

I reached for it. "I'll take his."

"Thatta girl," Olivia said, giving it to me.

Monica groaned.

"Olivia, where's Styx?" Lucy asked. Better her than anyone else.

She put the tray down on a nearby empty table. "She's around here somewhere. Come on! Bottoms up!"

Everyone except Derek threw back a shot. Mine burned like battery acid down my throat. I shuddered as I sat back down. Monica gagged beside me. Zoey was coughing across the table.

I put my second shot down, my eyes still watering. "I'm gonna let that first one settle," I said to Monica.

She pushed the bowl of pretzels toward me. "Eat."

I picked up the water instead.

The whole room erupted in applause. We all turned to look as Medusa walked in, arm in arm with two very large, very attractive men.

She wore a black sequined dress with an asymmetrical, skinny-strap top. It was suction-tight, like it might have been fitted with a vacuum hose, and its short skirt had a slit so high it showed off the full image of her namesake's head inked all the way up to her bikini line.

Thigh tattoos. Never understood that trend. Perhaps it was because mine were like tree trunks. Nobody wants to call attention to that.

Medusa's, however...*sigh*. It was like each snake was positioned to accentuate a different muscle.

The room was going crazy—exactly her intent, I was sure.

"She's so hot," Olivia said behind me.

Gay or straight, nobody could argue with that.

Medusa moved away from her two escorts, pushing one of them down into a chair and mouthing for him to *"Stay put."* Then she walked on stage and took the microphone from the singer of the band.

"Good evening, bitches!"

Everyone cheered louder.

"Welcome to the eighth-annual Slammy Awards! My name is Medusa, and I will be your emcee for the evening. Let's give it up for our badass band tonight, Marlena's Way, ladies and gentlemen!"

We all clapped. Some people stood. I was not one of them. I looked at Monica and fanned my face. "Is it hot in here?"

She shook her head.

"We're going to have a lot of fun tonight. Let's get rolling with the awards, shall we? To present this year's Slammy Award for Best Referee, let's all welcome our new team captain, Riveter Styx!"

As the room applauded, I scooted my chair back to sit next to Olivia. She was drinking a beer by herself. "You OK?"

She smiled, but it was forced. "I will be."

"What's going on with you and Styx? I thought you said you were taking a break."

"We were. She asked me to come, but hasn't spoken to me since I got here."

"What happened?"

"Things have been rough since Haley left the team. They are really close, and Styx has been pretty upset about it. They're supposed to be announcing Haley's replacement soon."

"Do you know who it is?"

She shook her head. "This is the first time I've seen Styx all week."

"Ouch. Think you'll break up?"

She shrugged.

I leaned toward the table and grabbed the second shot of Jäger. "Here, you need this more than me."

Olivia laughed and downed it in one gulp.

Styx held up a trophy made of gold spray-painted skate wheels and skulls. "And the winner for Best Referee is...Jessticular Fortitude!"

The room cheered as our head referee walked on stage to claim her award.

"Why are you drinking tonight?" Olivia asked.

"Man problems." I burped and it tasted like Jägermeister.

Olivia laughed. "At least I don't have those. Want to go to the bar?"

"Absolutely." I stood, then immediately sat back down. "Whoa," I said, gripping my chair.

Monica turned around. "You OK?"

I blinked. "I'm good. We're going to grab a drink. You need anything?"

"I'm OK right now. Thank you. You should drink some water, Grace."

I picked up the water. "Yes, Mom." I drank half of it before standing again. The second attempt was more successful.

"You ready?" Olivia asked.

"Ready."

We carefully navigated the stairs, and when we reached the bottom, Styx pretended like she didn't see us. She was talking to Shamrocker at a table spitting-distance away.

"Come on," I said to Olivia. "Next round's on me."

———

Near-freezing temps in a sleeveless dress with a short skirt will do wonders to sober a girl up. At a quarter past midnight, Monica and Derek waited with me at the curb for my Uber to arrive. I hugged her goodbye as Derek opened the back-seat door for me.

"Are you going to be OK to get home by yourself?" She pulled back to look at me. "We really don't mind driving you."

"It's too far out of your way. It's fine. I'm sure. Look, I'm sober." I used each index finger to slowly touch the tip of my nose.

"I think if you have to give yourself a sobriety test to prove your claim, that's proof enough," she said with a smile.

I put my hands on her shoulders. "I promise I'm OK. Enjoy the rest of your date night."

"We will. Hey, do you want to ride together to the parade in the morning? Derek is going to bring the girls later."

"It's going to be so early," I whined.

Derek leaned toward me. "And you're going to be *so* hungover."

Monica pointed at my face. "You were warned. Don't forget this is mandatory."

"Oh, I know. Yeah, we can go together. I'll pick you up so you guys don't have to take two cars."

She grimaced. "You sure?"

"Yeah, I'm sure. Six fifteen?"

"That should give us plenty of time," she said.

I looked back at the car. "I'd better go."

"Text me when you get home."

"I will." I got into the back seat of the car. "Thank you, guys."

They both waved, and Derek closed my door.

"Want me to crank up the heat?" the driver asked as he pulled away from the curb.

"Please," I said, my teeth still chattering. I pulled off my black stilettos and inspected the red splotches they'd left under my hose on the backs of my heels.

My phone buzzed on my lap. It was a text from Jason. *Just let me know you're safe, OK?*

I swiped the message open. We'd had a full text conversation at the bar that I only barely remembered.

It started with me sending a sideways and blurry selfie of me and Olivia. The caption said, *c what ur missing?????????*

Come to think of it, maybe Olivia sent that one.

He'd replied with, *Looks like you're having fun.*

Me: *Did I text you?? OMG my bad. My sorry*

Jason: *How are you getting home?*

Me: *I missssssss you, officer eye candeeeee*

I groaned. "Oh god."

Jason: *I miss you too. LOL*

My next message was nothing but eggplant emojis. Olivia had sent that one. I had no idea why.

Jason: *Hahaha. I can't wait for you to read this sober.*

"Excuse me," I asked the driver. "What's the eggplant emoji mean?"

He snickered. "Maybe you should Google that one."

I did. Then I groaned some more.

I hadn't replied to Jason after that. He'd texted two more times.

Grace? And the one that had just come through.

With a sigh, I texted him back. *Safe. In an Uber on my way home.*

He didn't answer.

My head was starting to throb by the time we turned onto Twenty-First Avenue. All I wanted was a big glass of water and my bed. "I'm never drinking again," I said aloud.

The driver chuckled. "I hear that one a lot. Is this you?"

I leaned to the middle to look out the other back-seat window. "Yes." I bent to pick up my shoes.

"I'll wait here to make sure you get inside. There's a man standing out there. Seems to be waiting for you to get out of the car."

I looked again as Jason stepped out of the shadow cast by the awning in front of my store. I sighed. "It's OK. I know him. One of Metro's finest, actually."

The driver relaxed. "Oh, good."

"That's sweet of you to care though. Thank you."

"Have a good night, ma'am."

"Thanks. You too." I picked up my shoes off the floor, then took a brave, deep breath before pushing open the door.

Jason walked over and met me on the curb. He was dressed in jeans, a sweater, and his wool coat. I was barefoot. His eyes fell to my dress. "Wow. Now I'm *really* sorry the picture you sent was blurry."

I managed a weak smile. "Thanks. Why aren't you at work?"

He looked at the ground. "I called one of my buddies last weekend when you told me about your awards thing. He switched with me so I could have the night off."

My head snapped back. "Why didn't you say anything?"

"You asked me not to call you anymore."

I swallowed hard.

"How are you feeling?" he asked.

"I'm OK. I quit drinking about an hour ago." I looked up and down the empty street. "What are you doing here?"

"I wanted to make sure you got home OK. Did you have fun?"

I reached into my purse and pulled out my Slammy Award. "I won a Slammy for Newbie to Watch."

He took it for a closer look and chuckled. "That's great. Congratulations."

I put it back in my bag.

"I'm really glad you texted me tonight, Grace."

"Technically, my friend Olivia started that."

He looked away. "Was it you that said you missed me?"

I sighed. "Yes, but I was very drunk."

"So you don't miss me?"

My shoulders dropped. "Jason, what do you want from me? I don't want to do this hot-and-cold thing with you."

"You know Clay asked me to hang out this week."

I held up a finger. "Stop right there."

"What?"

"All I wanted was to have a good time tonight. To have a few drinks and dance with my friends. To not think about my shitty ex-husband or the fact that I'll probably never be able to have kids. I *almost* got my wish. So I'd appreciate you not capping my night off with tales of the forever faithful brotherhood of you and that slimy piece of shit."

"He blew me off."

I lifted my shoes in the air. "Of course he blew you off, Jason! He's an inbred anus barnacle, or did you not get the memo?"

He grinned. "Inbred anus barnacle?"

I finally cracked a smile.

Jason reached for my hand. "I'm sorry for what he did to you. And I'm sorry that I let him stop me..." His eyes fell to the sidewalk.

"Stop you from what?"

He took a deep breath. "From this." With one step, he closed the gap between us and pressed his lips to mine.

My knees wobbled. Maybe it was the Jäger. Maybe it was him. Maybe it was the fact that I hadn't been kissed by a man other than my dad in nearly a year.

Jason pulled my arm around behind him. Then he slid his strong hand up my jaw until his fingers curled around the back of my neck, and his thumb pressed against my cheek. I gripped his soft coat as his tongue explored my mouth and his other arm held me against his hard body.

"Grace?" he asked against my lips.

"Mmm?"

"Are you still drunk?"

"Maybe a little."

His hand moved back to my waist. "Are you going to be OK with this tomorrow?"

"Yes."

"Then can we go inside? Your teeth are chattering against my mouth."

"Please," I said and sucked his lower lip between my teeth.

Lacing his fingers with mine, he led me to my door and punched in the code. My teeth *were* chattering, but only partly from the cold. My heart was pounding so hard I wondered if he might hear it as we ascended the steps inside.

I stuck the key in the front-door lock as his arms slid around my waist from behind. I pushed the door open, and he backed me up against the wall inside. As he pulled off his coat, he locked the door behind us. Then his hands started at my thighs and moved up to cup my ass.

I heard his breath hitch. "Grace..." He closed his eyes and leaned his head back. "Are you wearing a garter belt and stockings?"

"I'm wearing a pinup dress. Of course I'm wearing a garter belt and stockings."

He shuddered against me. "Can I see?" His strained voice cracked. "Please?"

Taking his hand, I pulled him into the living room. Without being directed, he moved the coffee table aside and sat down on the couch. I turned around in front of him. "I can't do this by myself."

His fingers worked the knot in the ribbon at my tailbone that held my dress together. I heard him suck in a jittery breath, then he leaned his head against my spine. "My hands are shaking," he said with a laugh.

I reached back and put my hands on his wrists. "You can do this. I promise."

A minute later, he blew out a slow sigh and pulled the ribbons through the eyelets. The dress loosened, then slowly fell to my bare feet. My heart was pounding. I had been a college athlete the last time a man saw me naked for the first time.

When I turned around, in my black bra and thong with my garter belt and thigh-highs, Jason visibly swallowed. Then he slumped back in his seat and leaned his elbow on the armrest to cradle his head. "Good god. That's the sexiest thing I've ever seen."

"You look like you might cry," I said with a relieved smile.

His knuckles went white squeezing his forehead. "I might."

I laughed and did a slow, full turn for him.

"Take your hair down," he said quietly.

I reached up and began pulling the pins out of my curls, letting them fall around my shoulders.

"You're so beautiful, Grace." He sat forward and reached for my hand, pulling me down onto his lap. I straddled his hips and kissed him, suddenly the drunkest I'd felt all night.

THIRTEEN

THERE'S something to be said for a man whose body is trained to be awake all night. Goodness. We'd certainly put his nocturnal schedule to work after my stockings came off.

They were ruined, by the way, as Jason had spent all his patience unlacing my corset. And as for my garter belt, it had come off by way of his teeth. Round one was hot and heavy, ending quickly before we made it off the sofa.

But the second...oh, mercy. Round two lasted for hours as we christened different parts of my apartment. The floor. The table. And don't even get me started on the bed he loved so much.

For the first time ever, I was grateful for those grueling months of 27 in 5s. Who knew *this* was what I'd been training for?

"I have to skate in the parade today," I said with a groan as I flopped onto my back beside him. The moon was shining through the blinds in my bedroom, casting white rays of light over my bare torso.

Smiling, he traced his finger down the center of my breasts to my belly button. "I'm sorry?"

I laughed. "No, you're not."

His hand slid down beneath the sheet, slipping between my damp thighs. "No, I'm *really* not."

I squirmed at his touch, and he leaned over and kissed me softly. On the lips. On the neck. On the collar bone. I raked my nails through his hair. "I have to get up and take a shower."

"Want some company?"

"No. I'll never leave this apartment."

"That would *not* be a bad thing."

"Except that I gave my word. And I promised I'd pick Monica up at six fifteen. What time is it?"

He reached toward the nightstand and picked up his phone. "A little after five."

"What time did I get home?"

"Around one."

"Four hours? That's impressive, Officer Bradley."

"Well, you said you wanted my eggplant."

My eyes popped open, and I rolled toward him. "Oh my god. We're never talking about that again."

"Oh, you better believe we are." On his side, he propped his head up on his elbow. "That was the funniest text I've ever received. And I really prefer the title Officer Eye Candy."

I laid on my stomach, burying my face in the pillow.

"Come on, it turned out pretty well, I think." He leaned over my back and pushed my thighs apart. "Right?"

I moaned, forcing my legs together again. "I have to go."

"If you say so." He kissed the back of my shoulder. "But you've been awake all night, so I don't want you to drive. I'll take you myself."

I turned onto my back again. "Not to pick up Monica. She has no idea that you're here, and if I roll up to her house with you, we won't have a chance for me to give her all the juicy details."

The corner of his mouth tipped up. "You're going to tell her?"

"She's my best friend. I tell her everything." For a second, my heart stuttered. "Why? Do you not want me to?"

He pushed my hair behind my ear. "You can tell anyone you want, Grace. This isn't a secret. Not for me."

I took a deep breath. "Thank you."

He kissed me again. "But if I'm not driving you, I'm at least calling you an Uber. Deal?"

"OK. Make sure you add a stop for coffee. God knows, I'm going to need it."

———

My sunglasses weren't dark enough when I walked—I use the term loosely—out of my apartment a little while later. I'd been playing roller derby for the better part of a year, and my legs had never had a workout like they'd gotten for the past five hours.

Jason was still upstairs in my bed, finally asleep after one last round in the shower. I'd admired him for a second before sneaking out, the perfect lines formed by his pecs, the way his hip bones dipped in tantalizing creases. God, he was hot.

Monica was waiting at the curb when the car pulled up at 6:22 after stopping for coffee. She wore a Music City Rollers hoodie and earmuffs. Her head fell to the side as she opened the back door. "You needed a ride? Are you still drunk?"

I yawned. "No, but I'm definitely not coherent enough to drive. Get in, I brought you coffee."

She shoved her bag into the middle seat between us and climbed inside. "You should've called me."

"I told you I'd drive." I handed her a to-go cup from Milo's. "For you, my dear."

"Thank you. What happened last night? You promised you'd text me when you got home."

I smiled behind my coffee cup. "I was busy."

She looked over as the driver pulled back onto the road. "With what?"

"Or who," I said.

She gasped and turned toward me in her seat. "Oh my god. What did you do?"

"Jason was waiting for me when I got home. He's still there."

"Shut up."

"Yeah. He apologized for choosing Clay, and then he kissed me. Then he kinda dragged me up to my apartment and didn't let me sleep all night."

"*Let you*, huh?"

I giggled. "It was so good, Monica. Makes me wonder if all normal couples have sex like that. And if you're wondering, the answer is yes, he looks even better without his clothes on."

She fanned her face. "OK. No more details. The married woman has to draw the line somewhere."

I laughed.

"So what does this mean?" she asked.

I shrugged as the driver merged onto I-40. "I honestly have no idea, but he asked to come over again tonight. I told him I'd call after the parade."

"What changed his mind? Did he say?"

"He was supposed to hang out with Clay sometime this week, and Clay didn't show. Surprise, surprise." I drained the last of my coffee. "I guess Jason decided a half-assed friendship wasn't worth it."

"How close are they?" she asked.

"They were roommates for three years in college. Jason was a groomsman in our wedding. And up until Clay lost his godforsaken mind, they hung out all the time."

"So Clay's going to be *pissed*."

"Oh yeah."

She pointed at my face. "Is that what this is about? Getting back at Clay?"

Fair question. I thought about for a moment. "I won't lie and say it's never crossed my mind, but no. I really like him, Monica."

She patted my arm. "Good. He seems like a winner."

I smiled. "He is."

As we neared the parade route and saw police blocking off the streets, Monica was almost drooling on the car window. "I'm so excited about this. This is where it all started for us, Grace, and now my girls are going to see me skate with the team!"

Monica and I had first found out about the Music City Rollers when we took her daughters to see the parade. Fast forward a year, and we would be rolling through the streets of downtown with them.

The team was meeting at a parking lot off Woodland Street, across the river from the starting line of the parade. With the traffic—thank you, Nashville—we were almost the last of our group to arrive when the Uber dropped us off.

There were a bunch of people with our group. It seemed as if everyone turned out. Skaters, refs, juniors, and of course, the Jeerleaders. They were all geared up with bright teal pom poms and tutus.

Lucy was already there with West. They let us stash our gear in the back of his truck. He was wearing a white T-shirt with thick black letters. It read:

Adler Construction ♥ *MCR*

"West, are you in the parade?" Monica asked.

He nodded. "The board invited all the sponsors to come. I said I would as long I wasn't required to be on skates. Lucy made my shirt."

"It's really cute," Monica said.

"Are you feeling as crappy as my roommate this morning?" Lucy asked with a grin.

I grimaced. "Probably not. Olivia's bad?"

"She was throwing up in the bathroom while I was trying to eat breakfast," West answered.

I made a puking sound.

"You stayed with her last night?" Monica asked.

"Yeah," Lucy said. "We were going to go to West's house, but I was afraid she might get us kicked out of our apartment if she continued the party at home. Styx did come back with her though."

"They made up?" I asked.

"Oh yes. They did," West said with a laugh.

Monica looked around the lot. "Is Styx here?"

"Yeah. She rode with us." Lucy stretched up on her toe stops to look over the heads of the people around us. "Looks like she's getting something to eat."

"There's food?" I asked.

There was indeed. Someone had organized a small table of breakfast foods: whole fruit, muffin, granola bites, and drinks. Strangely, most of us hovering around the coffee (hallelujah) had also been the ones hovering around the bar the night before.

"Grace!"

I turned and saw Jackie waving to me near a huddle of pint-sized skaters. She pointed to me and then to Monica and motioned us over. I carried a banana—hello, post-bender potassium—as we walked over.

"Girls, I need a favor," Jackie said, desperation plain on her face.

"Sure. What's up?" Monica asked.

"I'm short a few parents today. Think you could help me wrangle the juniors during the parade?"

My nose scrunched.

Monica elbowed me in the ribs. "Of course we will."

"Great. We're going to have a quick team meeting. Can you join us?"

"Sure." Monica grabbed my shirt and pulled me forward as Jackie began to speak to the crowd.

"We're going to line up behind the Rollers for the parade. K2, FrostFire, and Little Red Right Hook will go first, carrying our banner. Britches, can you stay near our banner girls?"

I was peeling my banana.

The woman standing next to me nudged my arm. "I think she's talking to you."

I blinked and looked at Jackie. "I'm sorry. Derby-name problems."

She laughed. So did a few of the girls.

"And yes, I'll stay with the banner girls." I turned back to the woman beside me. "Thank you."

"No problem," she whispered.

"If you're a level-one or level-two skater, you'll stay together in the pack behind the banner. Doc Carnage will be with you."

Oh, I liked Doc Carnage.

Jackie looked over the group. "Where are my level threes?"

Several hands went up.

"If you're a level-three skater, or if you're off-skates, please see me for some junior-derby stickers and refrigerator magnets. We need to hand them out to every kid we see until we run out. This is great exposure and an excellent chance to recruit some new members!"

Monica and I were proof that the tactic worked.

"If you're not already geared up, get on it." Jackie looked at her watch. "We're rolling out to line up in fifteen minutes."

Monica and I walked back to West's truck to put on our gear. Then we lined up with the league to start the journey across the bridge into downtown. The six-lane bridge was closed to traffic.

I turned toward the girls who were carrying the Junior Rollers' banner. "All right. Who's who?"

A girl with short blonde hair hidden under her helmet raised her hand. "I'm K2."

"Like the mountain?"

"Exactly."

I gave her a thumbs-up. "Cool." I looked at the next girl.

She was tall and had long brown hair with bright pink streaks. "I'm FrostFire."

"What's that name mean?"

"It's from a book."

I nodded like I found that interesting and looked at the last girl.

"Little Red Right Hook. I'm Doc Carnage's daughter."

"That's awesome. I love your mom. Is this all of us?" I asked.

FrostFire looked around. "Anybody seen Hellissa?"

Hellissa, I liked her already.

"She texted and said she'd be late. Her sister is in the parade too, so she's going to try to make it here to meet us," Little Red Right Hook said.

"Who's Hellissa?" I asked.

"She's one of our best skaters," K2 said.

Monica skated over to me. Her smile was as wide as her face. "You ready to do this?"

"Yep. I just hope my body is too."

Turns out, it wasn't.

Judging from the navigation app I'd checked just before we left, it was a quarter of a mile to the start of the parade. Halfway across the bridge, I was already panting.

"I never...noticed...this road...went uphill before." I laced my fingers on the top of my helmet. "Monica...don't let me...drink anymore."

"Right. It was the drinking that's got you so winded."

The junior girls were watching me with a mix of amusement and disgust.

Thankfully, I was wearing a backpack carrying what was left of one of the Gatorade's Jason had given me the weekend before. God bless him. I drained the rest of it.

Near the end of the bridge, the parade line stopped. It was another twenty minutes before the official start of the festivities. Up ahead of us, Lucy was waving her arms to get our attention. She motioned us forward. Monica told Jackie we'd be back in a minute, and we skated over to see what Lucy wanted.

She leaned toward us. "He can't come back and meet the whole team, but my boss said I could bring you guys up to the float if you want to meet Jake Barrett."

"Are you serious?" Monica asked.

"Hell yeah," I said.

"Come on, we have to hurry." Lucy led us and West to the front of the line to a parade float made to look like the North Pole. "He's over here," she said to us, then she started waving her arm again. "Ava!"

A beautiful woman with long dark-brown hair turned toward us. Jake Barrett was standing beside her. "Lucy, hi!" she said. Then she turned and said something to Jake. He nodded, smiled, and followed her over.

"Lights Out Lucy!" Jake bellowed, opening his arms. He hugged her. "I haven't seen you in a month of Sunday's, girl. How's my favorite roller derby queen?"

"I'm great. It's nice to see you."

"You too. You too. Who're your friends?" he asked, looking at the rest of us.

"You remember West," she said.

The two men shook hands.

"And these are my friends, Monica and Grace." Lucy smiled. "Or Dr. Hooker and Britches Get Stitches."

He laughed. "These names. Y'all kill me. Nice to meet you guys. Hope you're havin' a merry holiday season."

"We are. Thank you," Monica said.

Just then, a flash of something beyond Jake Barrett's head caught my attention.

A flash of periwinkle blue.

———

We said our goodbyes to Jake, and he climbed up onto the float. Monica nudged my arm. "What's the matter with you?"

I was gawking at the little girl being helped onto the float behind him. She was wearing my dress—the one with the hundred iridescent ruffles. The one made from Sinclair Satin.

I turned to Lucy. "Who are the kids on the float with Jake?"

She rolled over to me and leaned toward my ear. "They're kids Zoey has helped in the past through Hope Haven."

That was when I saw the woman who'd been with the girl in my dress walking straight toward me and waving to get my attention. She had an older girl at her side. "I'll meet you guys back with the group. Excuse me," I said to my friends, and I skated across the parade line to meet them.

This should be interesting.

The woman extended her hand. "Hi, are you with the Rollers?"

That was not what I expected.

"I am," I said.

She put her hand on the other girl's head. "I'm Sadie Worley. Melissa's mother."

"Hi, Melissa." Good lord, I was confused.

"*Hellissa*," the girl said, correcting her mom.

Her mom sighed. "Right. *Hellissa*."

I blinked. "Oh, Hellissa! The girls were asking about you." I looked at the mom again. "What did you say your last name was?"

"Worley," she answered.

Not Sinclair. I guessed it could have been a married name. But why would she have ever been part of Hope Haven? It was a shelter for battered women and their children. I mean, you never *really* know what goes on in people's private lives, but still…I felt like I was missing something.

"Listen, Hellissa's little sister is on Jake Barrett's float, and I just don't feel comfortable leaving her by herself. Could Hellissa join the team with you?" the woman asked.

"Sure." This was clearly not the time or place to ask about the little girl and her periwinkle dress.

"Thank you so much." The woman looked at Hellissa. "I'll be here. We'll wait for you at the end."

"Thanks, Mom." Hellissa turned toward me.

"No skates today, huh?" I asked, looking down at her sneakers.

"I don't have any skates yet. I borrow some from the Sweatshop."

Suddenly, I felt like the biggest asshole in the world.

"Do I need them to be in the parade?" she asked.

"No. Lots of girls are walking. Come on. We'd better hurry."

Sylvia's dog wore a diamond-studded collar. There was no way in the world her granddaughter wouldn't be able to afford a pair of roller skates. There was more going on here than I realized, and there was no way I could ask this girl about her sister's dress without looking like a crazy person.

"I really dig your derby name," I said as we reached our group.

She looked up, surprised. "You do?"

"Yeah. It's badass."

She smiled. "Thanks."

After the officials rearranged the line, placing our league behind a huge helium gingerbread man, the music started up ahead.

"Thank god we're not near the bagpipes," I said to Monica, gripping my skull.

Monica laughed.

Three of the four of my banner girls were ready to skate, but FrostFire was playing on her phone. I bopped her on the helmet. "Don't text and roll, kid."

"I'm not *texting*." She turned her phone around. "This is Instachat."

I bopped her helmet again. "Put it up."

With a sigh, she stuck the phone into her back pocket.

Monica was chuckling quietly beside me. "You're a natural at this."

"Shut up, Monica."

That was the exact moment that my phone buzzed in my pocket. I straightened and started to reach for it, but stopped. "What's the matter?" Monica asked.

"My phone's ringing."

"And you just got on to her. You know you can't answer it now."

I clenched my fists. "I know."

"I'll bet it's him," Monica taunted.

I growled as the phone continued to ring.

"I'll bet he really wants to talk to you," she added.

"I hate you right now."

"I know."

Thankfully, the parade started moving and I had something to distract me from the missed call burning a hole in my back pocket. It gave another short buzz, signaling a voicemail or a text. I clenched my teeth as we started down First Avenue. Spectators were lined up four-bodies deep on both sides of the street, waving as we passed.

Jackie came over and handed me a stack of magnets and stickers. "Can you hand these out?"

"Of course." I split the stack with Monica, and we skated to the side of the road.

My best friend's smile was as big as anyone's at the parade. She was like a kid on Christmas handing out those stickers and waving to all the kids. It was adorable.

At the corner of First and Broadway, the parade turned right up the main honky-tonk strip of downtown Nashville. In front of the Hard Rock Cafe is where I saw a big white banner with my name on it.

We ♥ Britches Get Stitches #6ft2

My brother was holding it over his head, with my nieces jumping up and down in front of him. Mom and Dad were beside them.

Waving like a madwoman, I skated forward until I saw Medusa high-fiving kids in the crowd.

I tapped her on the shoulder. "I need you!"

She looked confused, but she followed as I skated over to my nieces. Their mouths were gaping. I snapped my fingers at my mother as Medusa hugged them. "Mom, get a photo!"

The four of us grouped up, Medusa threw up the rock-and-roll hand sign, and Mom snapped our picture. She gave the girls high five's before she skated away. I started to follow her, but I heard my name.

"Aunt Grace!" It was Gabby. Her arms were spread wide.

With tears in my eyes, I skated over and grabbed her. And Hope squeezed me around the middle. "I love you, Aunt Grace," Gabby said.

I kissed the top of her head. "I love you too, kiddo." Then I pulled out my phone and snapped a selfie of the three of us. My brother may have photobombed it. "I'll see you guys later. Love you!" I called, blowing kisses.

I skated back to my banner girls in the line. They were all waving and smiling. Even Hellissa. I tugged on her sleeve. "Did you see those two girls I was hugging?"

She nodded.

I gave her two of the junior-derby stickers. "Take them these?"

"You got it." She ran over and gave them the stickers. It might as well have been hundred-dollar bills.

When Hellissa returned, I put my arm around her and squeezed her shoulders. "Thanks. You just made their day. They want to play junior derby just like you."

She smiled proudly; I knew the feeling.

"Hey, can we get a picture?" I asked her.

"Yeah!"

I pulled out my phone and snapped a selfie of the two of us. Then I took a picture with the whole juniors' team behind us. *Maybe helping out as a coach wouldn't be so terrible. I should send this picture to Jason,* I thought. That was when I remembered the missed call and message, which had been cleared from my home screen.

I pulled up his chat window. There were no missed messages from him. My heart deflated a little. That was when I saw a message from Kiara.

You're in the parade, so you probably won't get this for a while. Just thought you should know, Sylvia collapsed in the store. Ambulance is taking her to Baptist Hospital. Doesn't look good.

FOURTEEN

WHY THE HELL do parades move so slow?

I was desperate to get out of there after Kiara's message, but the parade didn't end for eight more blocks. Forcing myself to not think about it, I stuffed the phone back into my pocket without responding. It buzzed four more times before we reached Eighth Avenue.

Near the route's end, I spotted a group of Nashville police officers. Jason was waving near the center. Immediately, visions of the night before flashed through my mind. My cheeks flushed with heat.

He came over to join us when we reached the end of the parade. "I tried to text you, but I guess you don't have your phone."

"Yeah, have to set a good example for the girls. No texting while skating."

I wondered if he would greet me with a kiss. He didn't. Determined to not read too much into that, I pulled Monica over to us. "Monica, you remember Jason, don't you?"

"Yes! It's great to see you again." All smiles, she was clearly still riding the high of the parade.

"You too, Monica. You guys looked great out there," he said, shaking her hand.

"Thank you!" She spun on her wheels to the left. "My family's here! Gotta roll. Grace, do you need a ride home?"

Umm...did I?

Thankfully, Jason jumped in and saved me from a potentially awkward conversation. "I heard you were here without a car," he said with a wink. "I was hoping to give you a ride."

I smiled at Monica. "I'm all taken care of."

"See you tomorrow at the park?" she asked.

"Of course."

"Nice to see you, Jason. Bye!" she called, skating over to meet Derek and the girls on the sidewalk.

When I turned back toward him, Jason stepped forward and put his hands on my hips. "You really did look great out there. My buddies all agree."

I felt the heat rush to my cheeks. "Telling your friends about me already, huh?"

"You bet I am." Then he kissed me, for all of downtown Nashville to see. "You ready to go?"

"Let me check with the coach of the juniors' team and see if she needs anything else from me before we go. I also need to tell you something." I held up a finger. "Be right back."

Jackie was gathering all the junior girls together. I skated over to her. "Hey, Jackie. Are we all done or do you still need me?"

"No, we're all done. Thank you so much, Britches. You were a natural out there with them today."

I smiled. "It was fun." A few of the girls, including Hellissa, were watching me. I waved. She waved back.

Then her mother walked up and hugged her. The little girl wearing my dress was right behind her. I wanted to say something. To ask. But how would I do that without sounding like a lunatic? Especially now that Sylvia was in the hospital.

A hand came to rest on my side. "Everything OK?" Jason asked.

"You see that girl over there in the blue dress with all the ruffles?"

"Yeah."

I turned toward him. "Do you remember that dress I was making for Sylvia? You know, the crazy dog lady from my store who can't park."

He smiled. "I will never forget her. Is that the dress?"

"That's the dress."

His eyes widened like he was waiting for me to deliver a punchline. "And...?"

"She said the dress was for her granddaughter, but I don't think that's her granddaughter."

"So? Maybe she decided to give it to someone else."

"Possibly. It's just when I gave it to her, she acted like she hated it. Then today, I see the dress on another kid. I'm having a hard time processing what that means."

Jason looked like he was having a hard time processing why it mattered so much to me. "Why don't you ask her where she got the dress?"

"No. I need to ask Sylvia. Or maybe Zoey."

I pulled my phone from my pocket. There was a now-pointless text from Jason telling me he was waiting near the end of the parade route, and he wanted to know if I needed a ride home. The other messages were from Kiara.

Sylvia's driver called from the hospital.

The doctors think she needs a blood transfusion. He will call again when he knows more.

They admitted her and moved her to ICU. She's still unconscious.

I have Miss Taylor here. They are supposed to be sending someone to get her soon.

"What's the matter, Grace?" Jason asked.

"Sylvia collapsed in my store, and they've admitted her at Baptist Hospital."

"Because of the dress?" He asked, very confused.

"No, but I can see how you would think that. Sorry, my brain feels a little scattered right now. Can you give me a ride to the hospital?"

"I'll take you anywhere you want to go. Are you ready now?"

"I am, but I need to tell Lucy I'm leaving without getting my stuff." Thankfully, I'd had the good sense to stick my shoes in my backpack before the parade. The rest of my gear was still in the back of West's truck. I looked around for them, but didn't see them anywhere. "I'll text her. Let's go."

———

Jason had parked in a lot close by that was reserved for the Metro police officers. We were able to get to his truck quickly once I'd switched my skates for sneakers. He opened the passenger-side door for me, and when I stepped forward to climb inside, he grabbed my hand to stop me.

"I missed you when you left this morning," he said, inches from my face.

With a flirty smile, I ran the zipper on his jacket down and then back up. "You were sound asleep when I left this morning."

"But I was absolutely heartbroken when I woke up alone. Last night was amazing." His voice became low and rough. "Like, mind-blowing amazing."

Gooseflesh rippled my skin. "I can't even think about it without feeling a little dizzy."

He took that as his cue to kiss me again, long and hard, his tongue gently probing my mouth, reminding me of all the wonders of the night before. God, that man's mouth could work magic. His hands slid around to my ass and pull my hips against his.

"Ma'am, is this gentleman harassing you?" The booming voice made us both jump.

Jason swore. Then laughed. "Stiles, you piece of shit, you scared me to death."

"Don't you know better than to make out in a parking lot around a bunch of police cruisers?" the guy asked.

"We were just leaving, thank you very much." Jason looked at me. "Let's go."

I got into the truck and watched him walk around the front. Other officers were walking back to their cars around us. Jason got in and buckled his seatbelt. "Sorry about that."

"I thought it was funny."

"I'll certainly catch hell about it later. Where are we headed?" he asked as he put the truck into reverse.

"Baptist Hospital."

The hospital was only about a mile and a half away, but with the traffic it would still take at least fifteen minutes. Across the bench seat, he held my hand. "You must be exhausted," he said.

"I am. I plan on passing out just as soon as I know what's going on with Sylvia."

"Would you be interested in passing out at my place?"

I smiled. "As long as we don't do what we did last night. I don't think I'd ever be able to look at your mother again."

"Mom's pretty forgiving, and she really likes you."

"She doesn't even know me."

His head tilted to the side. "She knows more about you than you think."

I looked over at him. "What's that supposed to mean?"

"Let's just say she's heard a lot about you. Especially lately."

I squeezed his fingers.

There were nothing but red taillights up ahead of us. Jason relaxed back in his seat. "Can I talk to you about something?"

That sounded ominous. "Of course."

"You know I'm a package deal, right?"

"You and your mom."

He nodded.

"It's one of the things I really like about you. Your devotion to her, the way you take care of her. I wouldn't want that to change just because I'm in the picture."

"That's good because it won't ever change. I'll never put her in a home. I'll never send her to live with anyone else. If we're going to do this, that needs to be clear from the very beginning."

His tone made it pretty clear that he'd had an issue with this very thing in the past. I appreciated his transparency about it. It would be nice if all men were that open and honest. Clay, for example. It would've been very nice to know that he planned to have babies with other people while we were married.

"Do what exactly?" I asked.

He grinned over at me. "A man doesn't sleep with his best friend's ex-wife lightly."

"Jason Bradley, I'd like to remind you, there was zero sleep involved."

He leaned across the cab and pulled me in for another kiss. "And I can't wait to *not* sleep with you again."

"Since we're talking deal-breakers, can I bring up another uncomfortable conversation?" I asked.

"Of course."

"How much did Clay tell you about our infertility stuff?"

"I think I've gotten the general gist of it. I don't think he ever told me what the reason was though."

"Nobody knows. It says so right in our diagnosis: 'unexplained infertility.'" I used air quotes. "The doctors say there is an explanation out there somewhere, but modern medicine hasn't found it yet." I stared at the road ahead. "The problem was *obviously* not on Clay's end."

"I'm really sorry, Grace."

I nodded. "I just need you to know, I don't ever want to go through that again. Every month, praying and hoping, just to be crushed over and over. If it happens, great, but I'm done trying and winding up devastated."

"I figured as much." He gave my fingers a reassuring squeeze. "And, for the record, it isn't a deal breaker for me."

I took a deep breath and let it out slowly.

When we finally reached the hospital, Jason parked in the parking garage and held my hand as we walked inside and navigated the halls to the intensive care unit. He followed me up to the information desk. The woman behind the computer looked up at me. "May I help you?"

"I'm looking for a friend of mine. Sylvia Sinclair. She was brought in by ambulance."

"Are you a family member?" the woman asked.

"No. Just a friend."

The woman's face softened. "I'm sorry. I can only give information to a family member."

"Excuse me," a man said behind us.

Jason and I both turned.

The man was dressed in a flawlessly tailored suit made of luxurious fabric. "Did I hear you ask about Sylvia Sinclair?"

"I did."

"I'm her son." He stretched out his hand. "Benjamin Sinclair-Hoyt. You can call me Ben."

I should have guessed by his suit that he was her relative. The fabric screamed of the Sinclair dynasty.

"Grace Evans. She's a regular in my store. The store where she..." I swallowed.

"Collapsed?"

I nodded. "My assistant called me when it happened. I came here as soon as I could. How is she?"

He sighed heavily. "They are doing tests now, but given her recent history, they're sure it's a complication from the leukemia."

I put my hands over my heart. "I'm so sorry. Is there anything I can do? Do you need someone to keep Miss Taylor? She hates me, but I'd be happy to take care of her."

"Miss Taylor hates everyone. She's with the house staff now, I think. But if we need any help, I'll let you know. You've been a good friend to my mom. She speaks very highly of you."

My lower jaw dropped just enough for him to notice.

"Does that surprise you?" he asked with a chuckle.

Surprise me? Jason showing up at my apartment had surprised me. The news that Sylvia Sinclair spoke highly of me was right up there on the surprise scale with the ending of the *Sixth Sense* and *Project Runway*'s move from New York to LA.

"To be honest, I thought she hated me."

Her son smiled. "Only those who are most loved by her do."

"May I ask you a personal question?" I asked.

"I guess."

"Is Alexandria your daughter?"

His posture suddenly stiffened. "Lexi?"

"Maybe. I guess." I was nervously spinning the ring on my middle finger. "Sylvia has commissioned me to make a lot of gowns for her granddaughter."

Ben ran a hand down his face, pulling his mouth open in a look of shock. "I had no idea."

I wanted to ask, "*Seriously?*" but Ben was clearly having a moment.

He looked up at the ceiling, and when his gaze turned back to me, his eyes were wet with tears. "My daughter's name was Lexi, but my mother hated the name and always insisted on calling her

Alexandria. Even Lexi's Christmas gifts were always signed to Alexandria."

I didn't miss that he used the words *was* and *were.*

"Lexi was killed in a car accident six years ago. My mother was driving when they were hit head on by a drunk driver."

I felt Jason's hand at the small of my back.

"You didn't know?" Ben asked.

I shook my head. "She never told me anything."

"That's why my mother walks with a limp. And why she wears those ridiculous shoes all the time. Her ankles were crushed in the impact, and when they healed, they healed at an angle. High-heeled shoes are easier for her to walk in."

Tears brimmed my eyes. "Oh my god. I'm so sorry for your loss."

He bowed his head slightly but didn't respond.

"I think I remember that accident," Jason said. "I'm a Metro police officer. Was it near the West End off-ramp on I-440?"

"It was," Ben said.

The door behind us opened, and Sylvia's assistant, Andrew, walked into the waiting room. "Ben, you made it," he said.

The two men greeted each other with a hug and talked for a moment in hushed tones. When they finished, Ben turned back toward us. "Grace, this is my brother, Andrew."

Brother? I'd assumed by Sylvia's cool interactions with him that he was an employee. Maybe I wasn't so surprised that Sylvia liked me after all.

Andrew came forward and shook my hand. "Hello again. I remember you from your store."

"How is she?" I asked.

"One of the nurses told me that she semi-regained conscious-ness during the CT scan, so that's good."

"That's very good," I agreed.

Ben looked at his brother. "Did you know Mom was having dresses made for Lexi?"

Andrew glanced at the floor. "I just found out recently. She's been donating them to children in need."

My heart nearly melted into a puddle on the floor.

Ben reached into his back pocket and retrieved his wallet. He opened it and pulled out a small photograph of a little girl, maybe seven or eight years old, wearing a periwinkle blue dress with ruffles.

Tears spilled down my cheeks. "That's why she behaved so strangely when I presented her with the dress. It looked a lot like this one."

Andrew looked over my shoulder at the photo. "Oh yes, it did. The dress you made, she donated to a family at —"

"Hope Haven," I finished for him. "I saw a little girl wearing it today in the Nashville Christmas Parade." I quickly swiped the tears from my face and cleared my throat. "Ben, Andrew, I won't hold you up any longer. Please keep me updated on your mother's progress. You know how to get in touch with me."

They both nodded, thanked me for coming, and promised to update me with her condition. Then Jason and I said our goodbyes and walked out of the waiting room. Once we were safely in the hallway, I fell into his arms and cried.

———

Sunday morning, I woke up in Jason Bradley's bed. Convincing me to stay the night hadn't been difficult. Between the exhaustion, both mental and physical, he'd been very persuasive. I was downright sore the next day.

Thank God Jason had told me it was raining outside when I woke up to my alarm a couple of hours earlier. There was no way on earth I could've skated the park with Monica.

The shower was running in the bathroom. When I finally pulled myself from the delicious sateen sheets, I decided to join him. First, I'd have to get my legs to work. They strained standing up from the bed.

Putting on his discarded T-shirt from the floor, I walked into the bathroom. For a moment, I stood there silently and watched him from behind as he lathered his hair. "Knock, knock," I finally said.

He looked over his shoulder. "Good morning, beautiful. I'm surprised you're awake."

"Not as surprised as I am. Got room for one more in there?"

"Please."

"Let me brush my teeth. Where's that toothbrush you promised me last night?"

He opened the shower door and pointed to a mirrored cabinet beside the sink. "There are a couple of unopened extras in there. Help yourself."

Looking in the mirror as I brushed my teeth, I was a frightful mess. Mascara smudged beneath my bloodshot eyes, hair resembling something from the Muppets. I had to be at my parents' house for lunch. I hoped I could come up with a reasonable excuse by then that had nothing to do with the truth.

Jason was smiling when I stepped into the shower behind him. "Have I told you how smokin' hot you are?" He moved to the side to share the hot water.

"Only about a thousand times in the past forty-eight hours." I draped my arms round his neck. His hands settled on my hips. "Did you sleep at all?"

"I slept a lot, actually. So much that I'll probably regret getting my schedule out of whack when I go back to work on Monday."

"It sucks that we have to return to the real world tomorrow. I have so much work to do this week I won't even know where to begin."

"Still trying to get caught up on all your Black Friday orders?"

"I'm pretty sure I'll still be trying to get caught up on those orders the day I start drawing Social Security."

His fingers dug into my hipbones. "Well, I will go ahead and warn you that I plan on doing everything imaginable to keep you distracted."

I squirmed against him. "Yeah?"

"Oh yeah." He kissed me beneath the shower head. "Do you have plans next Saturday?" he asked when he pulled away.

I thought for a moment. "Not that I can think of right offhand. Why? What did you have in mind?"

"I was hoping we could put that dress of yours to good use again. The department's holiday party is Saturday. I'd like for you to go with me."

"Wanting to show me off to your friends already?"

"Absolutely."

"Then I'd love to. Do you have plans for the Saturday after that?" I asked.

He shook his head. "I'm off on Saturdays and it's not baseball season, so I have zero plans if they aren't with you."

I raked my nails across the back of his neck. "Would you be interested in getting dressed up and going to the Symphony Center with me? Monica is performing with the choir and I have two tickets to go see her."

"Sounds fancy."

"It is."

"I'd love to. Hey, look at us making plans for the future already."

I laughed. "I know. Two whole weeks."

He reached for his black mesh shower sponge and drizzled body wash over it. Then he dragged it across my chest.

"Can I be a girl for a second?" I asked.

He cocked an eyebrow as he slid the sponge over my shoulder and down my arm. "If you are not a girl all the time, then we need to have a very serious discussion."

I laughed. "You know what I mean."

"You can always ask me anything, Grace."

"I haven't done this in a really long time." I gestured between us.

He grinned. "Let a man soap you up in the shower? There's not a whole lot to explain."

"Not this...well, I haven't done *this* either, at least not in—" I stopped myself. "That's not what I'm talking about."

He chuckled. "What are you talking about?"

"Are you seeing other people?" I blurted out.

"No. Are you?"

"No," I said.

"Good. I'm glad we got that out of the way. Anything else?"

"Are you going to tell Clay about us?"

He looked at me. "Does it matter?"

"I'm not sure."

"It shouldn't matter, Grace."

"I know. It's just you've been friends for a really long time, and—"

"Do you want me to tell him?"

"No."

He went back to washing my arm. "Why not?"

"It will be more drama. And I'm so tired of all his drama."

Jason nodded. "When I showed up at your house Friday night, I had already decided that I didn't owe Clay anything. Even an explanation about all this. I have no plans to call him and make an announcement. But it will come up sooner or later. Nashville isn't that big."

"I'd rather it be later." My eyes drifted toward the shower wall. "Although, it would be kinda victorious to be a fly on the wall when he finds out. Watch his face melt when he finds out you and I are together."

Jason stopped lathering. "Wow."

"What?"

"You're not over it."

"Over Clay? I hate Clay."

"There's no doubt about that."

"Is that a bad thing?"

"It just means you're not over it."

I wanted to stamp my foot and argue. Or maybe list all the reasons why one could never possibly get over an atrocity such as what Clay had done to me. But Jason had resumed his work with the sponge across my collar. With his body blocking the full stream of the shower head, the suds slid slowly down my stomach. His eyes carefully followed them. Watching him watching me was one of the sexiest things I'd ever seen.

"Grace?"

"Hmm?"

"I have a favor."

My mind spun to the sexual variety. "Anything."

He was quiet so long that I opened my eyes. "Don't make me your rebound guy."

"I won't, Jason."

"Promise?"

"I promise."

FIFTEEN

"SO...HOW'S IT GOING?" Monica had saved me a seat at our first official team meeting on Monday. It was in a small auditorium at MacKay University, and we had seats right up front.

My cheeks immediately burned. "Things are going well."

She laughed and wagged her finger. "Oh no, you're not getting off that easily. Spill it. I want all the details."

"Let's just say, I'm very glad that he works Monday through Friday. Otherwise, I'd never get anything done."

"Ahh, new love. I remember those days."

"Psh, if any married couple I know still experiences those days it's you and Derek."

"I can't complain. Have you two been together since the parade?"

"On and off. I stayed at his place Saturday night, but I left in time for lunch with my family. He came back over late last night and stayed until very early this morning." I yawned. "I haven't slept much."

Laughing, she prodded my arm with her elbow.

"I won't see him again for a while though, and it's a good

thing. I'm going to be so busy fulfilling those dress orders this week that I hired my mom again to temporarily help."

"How many dresses have you done?" she asked.

"So far, Kiara and I have finished eight gowns since Black Friday. Margaret and Carla have each done two. Only forty-one more to go. More are being added every day."

"If I could sew, I would totally help out. Did I ever tell you that I failed home economics in high school because my fingers bled all over my end-of-the-year sewing project?"

"No. How did you bleed all over your project?"

"Accidentally stabbing myself with the needles."

We both laughed.

"Hey, how's the old lady who comes into your shop? Sylvia, right?"

"Yeah. She's better. Her son called last night to say that she finally woke up, and they moved her to a regular room. They're talking about letting her go home later this week." I sighed. "I don't think she has too much time left."

"That's so sad," Monica said.

Susan walked up to the podium and the front of the room. "Good evening, everyone. Let's get down to business so we can all go home. First, I'd like to thank everyone who worked so hard to make the Slammy Awards this year such a success. And I sincerely appreciate everyone behaving enough so that the Christmas parade was also a smashing success the very next morning."

Monica nudged my arm. "She's not talking to you."

I snickered.

"Our first order of business today is to discuss the next Fresh Meat training," Susan said. "Shamrocker?"

Susan sat down as Shamrocker took the podium. She had a slip of paper in her hand. "In the two days since the parade, we've received twelve emails inquiring about the next training session."

Several people clapped.

"The next Fresh Meat training is scheduled to begin January sixteenth. We are always looking for help with newbie training, so if you are interested in joining us, please see me after the meeting. As of right now, their skills test is scheduled for Saturday, March eleventh. That's the weekend before the B-Cup Tournament."

Black-Eye Candy raised her hand at the end of our row. "Are there more flyers we can take with us tonight? I'd like to hand some out over the holidays."

"Yes, we have plenty. See me after practice and I'll hook you up." Shamrocker looked around the room. "Any more questions?"

No one else spoke.

"Then that's all I have," Shamrocker said.

She sat down and Susan returned to the podium. "Next we have some good news for the B-team. You'll be happy to know we've selected a new head coach."

The room was dead silent.

Susan looked toward the back of the room. "Everybody give it up for Medusa."

Monica put her hand on my arm as everyone else clapped. "Oh god," she whispered. "I'm gonna die."

I chuckled. "You know, she's probably the best shot we have at winning the B-Cup. This is a good thing."

Medusa walked down the aisle and up to the podium beside Susan. Her black hair had a fresh set of bright purple highlights, and she wore fuchsia tiger-striped leggings and a slouchy black sweatshirt.

She waved to all of us. "I'm pretty sure that once upon a time I swore I'd never take another coaching position again, right?" A few people in the room laughed. "But I've been so impressed by this latest group of recruits that I decided to break my own rule." She looked around the room, making eye contact with several of us. "I look forward to this upcoming season, and I look forward to bringing home that golden-bra trophy in March!"

Everyone cheered.

She held up a finger. "We do have an update about the tournament. The bracket for the tournament has been released. There is a chance we will be playing Richmond in the finals."

My smile faded quickly. "Richmond, as in our arch rival that kicked our asses twice last year?"

Monica looked like she might vomit.

"So we're all going to train our hardest between now and March. Am I right?" Medusa yelled.

The cheering resumed.

All smiles, Medusa walked back toward Maven on the last row.

"It's a good thing I'll be skating with the juniors soon. I'm going to need all the extra practice I can get," Monica said.

Susan held up her arms to silence everyone. "I'm sure it will be a very exciting year for the B-team. In January, we will be booking travel for the B-Cup Tournament. It's close enough to drive, but we will be staying overnight at a hotel. Last year, I think rooms were about a hundred dollars each, and most of us slept four to a room.

"Next on the agenda, I'd like for Full Metal Jackie to come up and fill us in on what's going on with our juniors' team."

Jackie walked to the front of the room. "If you guys don't already know, our juniors' team is growing every week. We are working hard to fill a full roster by the beginning of the season. In the middle of this, you all know I've retired. This week, Doc Carnage has agreed to take my place as the president of the junior's league."

I clapped, looking around for Doc Carnage. She waved a few rows back.

"I'd also like to formally welcome Dr. Hooker to our training team. She'll be joining us full-time at the start of the year." She gestured toward Monica. Several of our teammates clapped. Monica waved. "We could still use more help. Please see me after the meeting if you're interested in joining."

I swear, she was staring at me.

Susan returned to the front. "Our final order of business is to discuss our upcoming practice schedule. Remember, for the rest of the month, we will not practice on Saturdays. There are lots of holiday conflicts this time of year, so enjoy your weekends with your families and friends. Christmas is on a Sunday this year, so we will not practice the week after the holiday. Practice will resume on Monday, January the second, right here for our next team meeting. Any question?"

No one raised their hands.

"OK. We'll see you all at Wednesday night's scrimmage! Meeting adjourned."

———

It was a very good thing that Jason worked during the week. We talked a lot and texted, but I had no time to see him, even for dinner. Every minute I wasn't at derby practice was spent behind my sewing machine. Mom was busy working from home, and Kiara was with me every day in the shop that she wasn't in class.

On Wednesday, Kiara finished dress number nine on our list, while I put the finishing touches on dress number ten.

"All done," Kiara said, straightening the hem of the Charlotte dress she was working on.

I got up to inspect her work. Putting my hands on her shoulders from behind, I nodded. "It's perfect. I, literally, couldn't have done any better myself. Nice job."

With a sigh, she raked her nails back through her hair. "I hope there aren't any more who chose those stupid beaded butterfly appliqués. That's some super-tedious shit, Grace. Can we please take them off the choices menu?"

I walked back to my desk. "They are a fifteen-dollar add-on each."

"Well...as long as we're getting paid for being tedious."

I pulled an envelope from my top drawer. "I have something for you."

She turned in her chair, and I handed it to her. She slid a finger under the flap to open it, and pulled out the check inside. Her eyes widened. "Grace, holy cow. Are you kidding me right now?"

"You've earned it. You saved my ass on Black Friday, and there's no way I'd be able to get all these done without you. Go. And enjoy your time in New York for both of us."

She got up and hugged me. "Thank you so much."

I laughed. "I'll remind you of that after the twenty or twenty-fifth order of the Charlotte with butterfly appliqués."

We called it a day after that. I was so exhausted that even my knuckles were tired. But it was scrimmage night, so I went up to my apartment, fixed a sandwich for dinner, and changed into my derby tights and practice jersey.

I should have known I was in trouble when I had to stop for water midway through our warm-up with Midnight Maven.

Monica skated over to me. "Are you OK?"

I was panting hard, but I nodded. "Just running a little slow today. I was up half the night finishing a dress."

"Are you going to make it through a scrimmage?"

The answer was no; I just didn't know it yet. Monica and I were sorted into different scrimmage teams. She was with Medusa, and Lucy and I were with Maven. *Great.* Maven started me as a jammer, and things went downhill from there.

I wasn't sure if it was punishment for slacking off during the warm-up or just Maven's twisted life mantra that one can never have enough cardio, but not once in the first half did she let me call off the jam early. And while two minutes doesn't sound like a very long time, when you're skating full-out at top speed, then slamming, pushing, and shoving your way through a wall of blockers, two minutes is a lifetime.

By my fourth jam, I had nothing left to give. Held up in the pack with no energy to push my way through, I ripped the star off my helmet and passed it to Lucy, the pivot for our team. As I stretched to reach her, Bad News Baroness, a blocker for the other team, knocked me sideways. I lost my balance and went down inside the swarm of skaters, taking Princess Die with me.

Her elbow came up and clocked me in the face. Then I landed hard with my right hip on her wheels. I screamed out in horrific pain. Four loud blasts from a whistle ended the jam as I rolled onto my back on the cold floor.

Maven appeared above me, her face blurry from the tears in my eyes. "Are you OK?"

I moaned in response.

"Doc!" she yelled.

Doc Carnage was suddenly beside me. "Yikes. Somebody's going to have a black eye."

"No shit," I said, draping my forearm over my helmet. "It's my ass that really hurts." I rolled onto my left side, and pulled my waistband down over my butt cheek.

Everyone around me cringed audibly. Maven said the F-word.

Doc covered it back up, gently. "The good thing is, there's a lot of padding back there."

"Hey!" I said with some offense.

"Be glad. If that were bone, you'd be heading out in an ambulance."

"That bad?"

"I can almost see the outline of the skate."

Oh god. The visual made the pain skyrocket.

"You need ice. Immediately," Doc said.

"I'm on it." Maven turned and skated away.

Doc touched my arm. "Can someone drive you home?"

"Give me a minute to rest, and I'll be fine to drive."

She offered her hand. "Come on. I'll help you off the track."

"Me too," Monica said, grabbing my other hand.

The two of them helped me back up onto my skates, but once I was vertical, it was obvious my right leg would be of little use. The pain was too great. It radiated from my hip all the way down to my toes.

Monica took my arm across her shoulders, letting me use her as a crutch over to the bleachers. "Want me to take you home?" she asked as I eased down onto the bench with my left butt cheek.

"No, I'll be fine. Get back out there and finish the scrimmage."

She hesitated.

"I'm fine, Monica. It's just a bruise."

Midnight Maven skated up behind her with two bags of crushed ice. "Dr. Hooker, practice isn't over."

She nodded and returned to the track.

Maven handed me the bags.

The smaller one, I pressed to the side of my right eye. "Thank you." I laid down on my left side and rested the other bag on my ass.

"What's going on with you tonight?" Maven asked. "You've been really off your game."

"I know. It's been a really crazy week, and I haven't slept much. Why have you been pushing me so hard all night?"

Maven crossed her arms. "Because I think you have what it takes to play this sport. My job here is to make you even better."

I wasn't sure whether to thank her or throw my ice pack at her.

"Leave the ice on your ass for fifteen to twenty minutes at a time a few times a day for the next twenty-four to forty-eight hours. And be prepared. I've fallen on a skate before. There's nothing like the bruise you're about to have."

"Or the black eye, I'm sure."

"Be sure to post pictures on the team app." She smiled. "None of us are going to want to miss it."

———

The perfect outline of a roller-skate wheel was imprinted in the center of my blackened ass cheek. By the next morning, the bruise had spread like a dark crimson stain from nearly my hipbone to my thigh. It was so glorious I snapped a picture of it in the mirror and texted it to Jason.

Me: *Day two, badge of honor.*

Jason: *Holy hell. You've got to be kidding me. Please tell me that's makeup.*

Me: *I wish it was makeup.*

Jason: *Think you should go to the doctor?*

Me: *Our team doc says no, for now. Just to keep ice on it for a while. Check this out.*

I took a picture of my face. My right eye was nearly swollen shut and a deep blackish purple.

Jason: *Geez, Grace! It looks like you were in a UFC fight last night.*

Me: *And it looks like I lost. LOL Kinda makes me look tough though, right?*

Jason: *I guess. Keep some ice...on all of that.*

Me: *I will.*

Jason: *This has been the longest week ever without you.*

Me: *I know. Is it Saturday yet?*

Jason: *Right? If I can get my aunt to come help Mom on Saturday morning, I think I'll come straight there after work and sleep. Maybe come crawl in bed with you.*

Me: *That sounds like heaven. But I'm going to go ahead and say this now...I have to work on Saturday!*

Jason: *Fair enough. It's been a week since I've seen you. I can guarantee what I have planned won't take long.*

Me: *Haha.*

Jason: *Heading to bed now. I'll text you when I wake up.*

Me: *Sleep well!*

All day, I walked with a limp, and by lunch, Kiara was calling me Boss Hobble. Sitting behind the sewing machine was torture, even after I repositioned my seat and foot pedal so I could sit halfway on and halfway off the seat. Still, I managed to finish one dress and start another by the time I finally called it quits near midnight.

On Friday morning, Ben Sinclair-Hoyt called to tell me that his mother had been discharged, and I was welcome to visit her at home if I "dared"—his word, not mine. When I closed the store that evening, I picked up flowers from the market and followed the GPS to the address he'd given me.

Sylvia lived in Belle Meade, the old-money neighborhood of Nashville. Her house was hidden at the end of a long driveway, which was protected by a stone gate and an armed guard. The historic three-story mansion was adorned with thick white columns and tall stone statues. The landscaping was meticulously groomed, and the Christmas lights were expertly hung. I gulped as I pulled up to the entrance.

The front door opened before I even knocked, and a woman about my mother's age stepped outside to greet me. "Grace Evans?" she asked, then did a double take when she registered my black eye.

"That's me," I said, not offering any explanation. I wondered if she would ask about my injury. She didn't.

"Come on in. Mrs. Sinclair is expecting you."

I followed the woman inside, and my breath hitched in my chest, standing in the massive marble foyer. Its walls were hand-painted with murals of white horses, and the largest crystal chandelier I'd ever seen hung over my head. "Wow," I whispered, feeling a bit like Orphan Annie.

The woman led me up a hand-carved wooden spiral staircase to the second level. Sylvia's other son, Andrew, greeted us at the top. "Ms. Evans, I'm so glad you could make it. Thank you, Marie. I'll take care of her from here."

The woman nodded and started back downstairs.

When she was gone, Andrew turned back to me. "It's nice of you to come." He was eyeing my face, obviously debating whether or not to ask.

"Roller derby," I said. I'd learned in the past forty-eight hours that seemed to be an adequate response for a black eye.

He nodded. "Oh, that's right. Brutal sport, isn't it?"

"Sometimes."

"Did you have any trouble finding us?" he asked as we walked down a long hallway covered in expensive crimson carpet.

"No. GPS brought me right to the gate. This place is spectacular," I said, admiring the framed paintings on the walls.

"Thank you. Our family's been here a long time."

"How is she?" I asked quietly.

"Better. It was a bowel infection that caused all the problems on Saturday. She was losing blood, and no one knew. They've gotten it under control now, they think. They wanted to keep her in the hospital for a few more days, but she was determined to come home."

"Is there anything I can do?"

"Would you mind sitting with her while I run out and make a phone call? I need to check in with my wife."

"Of course not. You can go home and rest if you need to. I don't have anywhere to be tonight."

"That's quite all right. I appreciate the offer, but she might cut me out of the will if I leave her for too long." He winked.

We reached an open door near the end of the hall.

"Who's there? Is that Grace?" I heard Sylvia ask.

I walked inside ahead of him, and Sylvia's head rolled along her pillow to look toward the door. There was a hospital bed in the center of the lavish bedroom, and Sylvia looked tiny in it, propped up with pillows and hidden beneath layers of blankets. She pressed a button, raising the head of the bed even more.

"Mom, I'm going to go call Lisa. Grace will sit with you until I get back. Do you need anything right now?"

"Yes. Will you bring me that album I said I wanted Grace to see?"

He smiled. "Sure. I'll be back soon."

When he was gone, I walked over and sat down in the over-stuffed chair beside the head of Sylvia's bed.

"Good lord, what happened to your face?" she said, reaching over to grip my chin.

"Roller derby accident."

She scowled. "You sure about that? You didn't let some man do this to you, did you?"

I smiled. "No. I promise. I got hit with an elbow during prac-tice. How are you feeling?"

"I'm dying, Grace. How do you think I'm feeling?" Sylvia sat back and laid her head against the white pillow.

"What are the doctors saying?" I asked.

"They say it could be three months. Six, if I'm lucky."

I swallowed. "What about treatment?"

She shook her head. "They think it would buy minimal time.

Not worth the agony of having to suffer through it, in my opinion."

"I'm so sorry, Sylvia."

"I told you to call me Sylvie, Grace."

I smiled. It may have been the nicest thing she'd ever said to me.

Andrew returned a moment later carrying an old black leather-bound photo album. She scowled at him. "Took you long enough."

His brow lifted. "It was two minutes, Mother."

She held out her hand for the book. When he handed it to her, her hand and the book dropped to her lap. "*Oof.* Andrew, are you trying to kill me?"

He just shook his head and walked out of the room.

"Come here, Grace." She opened the book. The first few pages were black-and-white professional photos of a young woman, richly dressed with a bright smile and jet-black hair. I didn't need to ask who it was. Sylvia had been stunning when she was younger.

The next photos were all from her youth: a beauty pageant she won in 1953; a newspaper ad for the family business she'd done when she was twenty; a picture of her first shih tzu, also named Miss Taylor. It was an odd walk down memory lane with her, to say the least.

Then she turned the page again. Three women, all wearing roller skates, were laying in a pile on a banked track. A fourth woman was jumping over them.

My mouth dropped open. I grabbed the book. "Are you in this?"

She laughed and it triggered a painful-sounding cough. "That's me," she said when the coughing subsided. She tapped her wrinkled, bony finger on the picture. She was one of the women on the floor. "This was in Chicago. 1953, I believe. That's

Charlotte "Basher" Bashburn flying over us. She was a real ball buster."

"You played roller derby?" I asked, still in disbelief.

"The word *played* might be a stretch. I skated for a few months while I was in Chicago. I was terrible at it, really. Not nearly as tough as some of the girls like Basher. I was much more suited to the fashion industry, so I left, came back to Tennessee, and got married." She smiled and turned the page. "Here's another one."

The next photo was of her skating. She was clotheslining someone on the track.

I was in awe. "Sylvie, this is incredible."

She chuckled and coughed again. "I was tickled when you mentioned it all those months ago. And now you play, just like I did. I'd like to live long enough to see you in action."

Sadness seeped into my veins like a poison. I forced a smile back on my face. "Well, we scrimmage every Wednesday. Maybe once you're stronger, Andrew can bring you."

"I'd like that."

Silence hung in the air for a moment between us. "You know who else plays roller derby?"

Her brow lifted in question.

"You know the young girl you recently gave the dress I made to? Her sister is on the junior derby team within my league."

She froze, like she knew she'd been caught.

I sighed. "Sylvie, why didn't you tell me about the dresses? About Lexi?"

She looked toward the window. "I don't like to talk about Alexandria."

"The girl you gave the last dress to wore it in the Christmas parade. I saw her in it. She looked like a princess."

"Her name is Chloe. She told me she was going to be in the parade. That's why I asked you to rush the dress."

The rare tenderness on her face made me feel like I was watching the Grinch's heart grow three sizes.

"Who did you give the others to?" I asked.

She shrugged. "A few I met at the children's hospital. The rest were other girls I met through Hope Haven."

"A good friend of mine works there. And, like I said, Chloe's sister is on our junior roller derby team."

She perked up. "Really? I didn't know there was such a thing."

"Yeah. It's open to girls eight to eighteen."

Her eyes sparkled with tears.

"Small world, huh?" I asked.

She nodded and looked down at the photo in her book.

"It's really sweet what you did for those girls in honor of your granddaughter."

"Not a day goes by that I don't think of Alexandria"—her breath hitched—"about Lexi."

I took her hand. "It's a precious way to celebrate her memory. Thanks for letting me be a part of it."

"She would've loved each of them, Grace. You're very talented. You've certainly found your calling."

My nose scrunched. "I don't know about all that. I feel like you're supposed to love your calling."

"You don't love making dresses?" she asked, surprised.

"I used to. But ever since I found out that I most likely won't ever be able to have my own children, it's been like rubbing salt in an open wound every time I sit down at my sewing table."

"I had no idea. I knew you were going through a divorce, but I didn't know about the children part."

"I don't talk about it much." *And I've always thought you hated me,* I added silently. "My ex-husband actually got another woman pregnant while we were still married and trying to conceive."

"No!"

"Afraid so," I said.

"Some men are such bastards."

"Agreed. As you can imagine, it's not too fun making princess dresses anymore. I honestly kind of hate it. But for now, it pays the bills." I smiled. "Thanks mostly to you."

She chuckled softly, avoiding another coughing fit. "What would you do instead?"

I shrugged. "I really have no idea."

"I have no doubt you'll figure it out. And if you're this good doing something you hate, I can't wait to see what you do with something you love."

SIXTEEN

IT WAS STILL dark outside when I heard my front door quietly open and close the next morning. I'd hidden a key for Jason outside in the hall, so I wouldn't have to get up and let him in at the crack of dawn.

Outside in the hall, he tripped over a potted plant by the door and swore. I laughed and hugged my pillow. "It's OK to turn on the light. I'm awake."

"Oh, thank God." He flipped on the light, and through the door, I could see him in his uniform.

Good lord, he was handsome.

"You all right?" I asked.

"Just a couple of broken toes, I think. I'll be fine." He came into my bedroom and unloaded his gun on my dresser. "I had a plan to sneak in here and slip into your bed without waking you up. Guess I shot that all to hell. What are you doing awake?"

"I rolled over the wrong way. My ass woke me up." I reached over and turned on my bedside lamp.

Taking off his utility belt, he froze. "Grace, your face."

"I told you it was bad. Wait until you see the other bruise."

He carefully placed his belt on the floor near the door. "I don't know if I want to."

"You won't be able to miss it."

He unbuttoned his shirt, revealing a black bulletproof vest over a white T-shirt.

I smiled. "And I thought your uniform was sexy."

The Velcro tore away as he peeled the vest off. Then he knelt down beside the bed to unlace his boots. "Let me see it."

I was only wearing a tank top and cotton panties. I pulled the comforter down, and he drew back in horror. He stopped untying his boot and covered his mouth. "Grace."

"Have you ever seen anything like it?" I asked, looking back over my shoulder.

Running his hand down his face, he nodded. "Yeah, I have." He reached up and pulled the blanket back over me. Then he stood, his boots still on his feet. "Mind if I take a shower? I'm gross."

"Of course not. You want some company."

"You stay in bed. I'll be quick." He turned toward the bathroom.

"Jason?"

He stopped.

"Are you OK?"

"Sure. I'll be out in just a second."

That was weird. Sure, the sight of my bruises was alarming. But was it a total turnoff? I got up and walked to the bathroom. I tapped my knuckle against the door and heard the shower running on the other side. "Jason?"

"Come in."

I pushed open the door and found him sitting on the toilet lid, his elbows balanced on his knees. "What's going on?"

He blew out a deep sigh. "The bruises." He raked his fingers back through his hair. "I didn't realize how much I would hate it."

"I sent you pictures."

"You did, and I thought I'd be prepared."

"I don't understand why this is such a big deal—" Then it hit me like another elbow to the face. I covered my mouth. "Your mom."

He stood and walked over to me. "Logically, I know this isn't the same thing. I just didn't think it would have such an effect on me."

I put my arms around his neck and hugged him. At least with my head on his shoulder, he couldn't see my face. "I'm so sorry. I didn't even think."

Gently gripping my waist, he pushed me back to look at him. "Don't apologize. This is my issue. You didn't do anything wrong. Does it hurt?"

"Not so much anymore. It just looks awful."

He nodded. "Yeah, it does."

I slid my hands down to his. "Come to bed. We'll turn the lights off, and you won't have to look at me."

"Come here." He cradled my face and kissed me. "I've missed you."

"I've missed you too. Now turn off that water and come show me just how much."

———

Kiara and I were at work in the back room when the front door bells jingled later that afternoon. "It's just me!" Jason announced.

"Ooo, loverboy is here," Kiara said with a teasing smile.

I looked at the clock. It was almost five. "In the back!" I called.

He walked through the doorway a moment later, and Kiara and I both turned our chairs to look. She let out a slow whistle. "Wow, you clean up well, Officer Eye Candy."

"Yes, you do." I got up to greet him with a kiss. He wore a gray suit with a white shirt and no tie. "You look handsome."

"Thank you. How's work been today?" he asked.

"We're getting there. Kiara, how many more dresses would you say we have to do yet?" I asked.

"Four thousand, three hundred and three," she said with a grin as she finished the hem of the navy gown she was working on.

I laughed. "It does feel that way. I'd say we're about a quarter of the way finished with the orders from Black Friday."

"That's great. They're coming along faster than you thought, right?" he asked.

"Yes. It helps to have four of us working on them, though I keep thinking about hiring one more seamstress."

"No more seamstresses." Kiara was shaking her head. "We've got this process down to a science. You bring in someone else and it'll throw a kink in the whole damn thing."

"Maybe so." I smiled. "Jason, let me finish this sash, and I'll be at a good stopping point for the evening. What time do we need to leave?"

"The party starts at six thirty, but we can be fashionably late and show up in time for dinner at seven thirty if you want."

"Where is the party?" I asked, sitting back down at my sewing machine.

"The Opryland Hotel."

"Fancy," Kiara said.

"Yeah, they went all out this year."

I finished sewing the edges of the white sash I was working on. "All done. Time to go change. Kiara, are you almost finished?"

"Yes, ma'am. And I have a hot date tonight too. Davion is taking me to your friend's restaurant out in East Nashville."

"Lettuce Eat?" I asked.

"That's the one. You keep talking about how good it is, so we're going to try it out."

I hung the tiny dress on its hanger. "Make sure you ask to speak to Olivia, and tell her you work for me."

"Is this the same Olivia you were with at your awards banquet?" Jason asked as I cleaned up my mess.

"That's the one."

"Kiara, make sure you tell her I said thank you," he said with a laugh.

I laughed too.

Up in my apartment, Jason laid across the bed while I got dressed. "What, no stockings?" he asked as I slipped my shoes onto my bare feet.

"Do you not remember ripping the elastic out of them last weekend?" I turned to check out my backside in the mirror.

"Oh yeah." He smiled and laced his fingers behind his head on the pillow, closing his eyes. "We'd better not talk about that, or we might not leave this apartment."

"Does my thigh look too bad in this dress if I move a lot?" I asked.

He sat up on the edge of the bed and looked at my skirt. "I can see it when your skirt moves, but you shouldn't worry about it. Your legs look so amazing, nobody's going to notice anything else."

"Right. I'm *so* sure that's true." I laughed and walked to the bathroom. "Let me touch up my makeup, and I'll be ready to go."

Touching up my makeup meant adding more concealer to my eye. Unfortunately, no matter how many layers I slathered on, I still looked like Rocky Balboa post-Apollo Creed.

Jason walked into the bathroom behind me. "I've given you a complex. I'm sorry. You look gorgeous, with or without the black eye and certainly with or without the makeup." He kissed the side of my neck. "Can we please go so I can show you off to my friends now?"

"Yes. Let's go."

The Opryland Hotel was arguably one of the most romantic spots in all of Nashville. With three football-field-sized garden lobbies filled with every exotic plant and tree known to man, the experience was breathtaking on an average day. But at Christmas? Holy smokes. Talk about a winter wonderland. I was on the edge of my seat as soon as we pulled into the parking lot. Even outside, Christmas lights were tacked onto everything standing still.

Jason valet-parked his truck and checked his watch when we stepped out onto the curb. "We've got a little time. Want to stroll through one of the gardens, maybe have a drink alone before we go to the ballroom?"

"That sounds amazing."

Smiling, he took my hand and led me inside.

The sound of rushing water cascading over rocks greeted us, as we entered the atrium from behind a two-story waterfall. Somewhere, "Carol of the Bells" was being played on a piano. I clung to his arm as we walked the shadowed winding pathway toward the indoor oasis.

When we emerged onto the main path, the vision took my breath as it always did. Christmas lights twinkled high above our heads. The lush greenery was dotted with countless bright red poinsettias. A Christmas tree—seven stories high—rose toward the glass ceiling. It was hard to tell where the lights ended and the stars began, looking up at the clear night sky.

"I love this place," I breathed, closing my eyes as we walked along the trickling creek. "We used to come here every year when I was a kid."

"I've only been here a couple of times. And never with my family."

I wondered what his childhood must've been like. The closest thing I'd ever experienced to violence at home was my brother holding me down and trying to fart on my head.

Jason pointed up ahead. "Looks like they're serving hot cocoa over there. I wonder if they can spike it for us."

"I say we waste no time finding out."

Sitting at a private bistro table, tucked beneath a light-wrapped palm tree, we drank our cocoa (spiked with salted caramel liquor) and watched the dancing-water-and-lights show. It was timed with a piano playing on a third-floor balcony above us.

"Grace, look at me." His arm was draped across the back of my hair. "You have a bit of whipped cream just here." He leaned in and kissed me.

With my eyes still closed, I rested my cheek against his. "This is already the most perfect night."

He laughed. "I know. I'm almost afraid to go the party and let my cop buddies ruin it."

I had almost forgotten we even had a party to go to. "Five more minutes?" I asked, kissing the corner of his mouth.

"Make it ten." He pulled me closer against him, and I laid my head on his shoulder.

———

We should have stayed at the lights show.

It felt like all eyes were on me when we entered the ballroom. His strong hand settled at the back of my waist. "You all right? You look nervous."

"I'm in a room full of cops. I *am* nervous."

He slid his hand around my stomach. "Let's make an appearance and leave. We don't have to stay." He leaned closer to my ear. "Or we could stay and check into a room."

A chill made me shudder. I felt him smile against the side of my neck.

"Is that Jason Bradley with a date?" a man asked behind us.

We turned to see a man in a suit and a woman in a floor-length navy dress. She blinked twice when we made eye contact, or rather when she made black-eye contact. The man laughed and nudged Jason's arm. "Been keeping this one in line, have you, Bradley?"

It was like all the oxygen had been sucked out of the room. I felt Jason go rigid beside me, and his fingers dug into my side. "She's actually a badass roller girl, Jamison. She could kill us both with a hip check."

The man offered me his hand. "Is that so? Roller girl, huh?"

"That's right," I said. "Grace Evans."

"Mitch Jamison. This is my wife, Wendy. It's nice to meet you. I don't think I've ever met a real roller girl before. And I know I've never seen Bradley show up to one of these things with a lady friend. Have you, Wendy?"

She was looking at Jason like most women do. "Not that I ever recall."

I bet she would know.

"How'd you two meet?" Mitch asked.

This conversation wasn't getting any better.

"We've been friends since college," Jason said. "Jamison, have they started serving food yet?"

"Yes, sir. The line starts over there in the corner," Mitch answered.

Jason nudged my side. "Shall we?"

"Please," I said.

When we were away from them, I groaned. "Well, that was a disaster."

"Eh, Jamison's a rare breed around here. Not all my buddies are imbeciles."

"Jason!"

Another man was walking toward us with a beer. He was tall with dark skin, black hair, and a goatee. The two of them greeted each other with a hug. Jason turned, smiling at me. He pointed to his friend. "Case in point, Jordan Wade is not an imbecile."

"Who's an imbecile?" Jordan asked.

"Jamison."

"Screw Jamison. His cornbread's not really cooked all the way through, if you know what I'm saying." Jordan smiled at me and shook my hand. "You must be Grace. It's nice to finally put a face with your name. Nice shiner. Roller derby, I bet?"

My whole body almost went limp with relief. "Yes. How'd you guess?"

"You kidding?" He gripped Jason's arm. "This guy hasn't shut up about you in a month. I told him, he has to take me to watch you play next season and introduce me to some of your roller derby friends."

I laughed. "We could certainly hook you up with that."

He clapped his hands together. "Hell yeah."

"Bradley!" another voice boomed.

A guy in uniform walked over to us. He and Jason shook hands. "Merry Christmas, brother," the man said.

"Merry Christmas to you too, Metcalf. You on duty tonight?" Jason asked.

The man nodded. "Working third. Just stopped by for the food." He turned to me. "Well, well. What happened to you, gorgeous? Somebody need to call in a ten-forty-one on this guy?" He slapped Jason's chest.

I had no idea what a ten-forty-one was, but I could guess.

"Metcalf, why do you have to be such a dick?" Jordan asked. "You remember what happened to his mom?"

The smile drained off Metcalf's face. "Shit, man. I'm sorry. It was a joke. A bad one." He looked at me. "I apologize to you too, ma'am."

"Forget about it," Jason said.

"No, I'm serious. Let me buy you a drink to make it up to you. I insist."

"Metcalf, let it go." Jason leaned into me. "Imbecile."

I chuckled.

"What'd you say?" Metcalf asked, raising his voice.

I gripped my temples.

Jordan put his hand on Metcalf's chest. "Come on, man. Get the hell out of here. You're embarrassing yourself."

Jason took a deep breath. "Well, I've had enough holiday cheer for one night. Wanna go?"

"Please."

We said goodbye to Jordan, then left without speaking to anyone else. I started toward the outside door, but Jason pulled me to a stop. "We don't have to go yet. Let's go find a table at one of these quiet, fancy restaurants and continue our evening. What do you say?"

I smiled. "OK."

Back out in the atrium, I hooked my arm through his as we walked toward one of the restaurants in the center of the room. "I'm sorry about the comments that were made."

He shook his head. "You weren't the one who made them."

"No, but it is my face. And, for that, I'm sorry."

He stopped walking and turned toward me, near the restaurant's entrance. "I don't want to talk about it anymore. It's Christmas. I just want to be with you."

I kissed him, long and slow on the mouth. He still tasted of chocolate and caramel. Smiling, I pulled away and licked my lips. "About that room..." I said, gripping the lapel of his jacket.

"Grace?"

We both turned at the sound of my name.

Clay.

The most romantic place in all of Nashville, indeed. Walking hand-in-diamond-studded-hand was my ex-husband and his *very* pregnant fiancé.

It was the first time I'd ever seen her up close. She was shorter than I expected, maybe because everyone was, with a tiny figure even into her third trimester. Her swollen boobs bubbled out of the deep V-neck bodice of her creamy mocha dress, and the silky fabric of the skirt clung to her perfect basketball baby bump.

I wanted to slap her.

I wanted to cry.

I wanted to run away.

But Jason held me close to his side.

"What the hell's going on here?" Clay demanded as they stopped in front of us. He looked at Jason, the angry vein pulsing in a V-shape between his eyes. "You said you weren't seeing her."

"I wasn't." Jason shrugged and wrapped his hand around mine. "But I am now."

Clay took a shocking step toward him. My eyes widened. So did Dr. Vagina's. She grabbed his arm. "Clayton, honey, don't make a scene."

Meanwhile, I was chanting in my head, *Make a scene! Make a scene! Make a scene!*

"How could you?" Clay hissed.

Jason shook his head. "No, man. How could *you?* Don't ever come near me or my girlfriend again."

Whoa. *Girlfriend.*

Clay looked at me. "My best friend? Really?"

I pointed at Ginny. "Someone else's uterus? *Really?*"

Jason stifled a laugh beside me. Several people from the restaurant were now watching us.

Ginny pulled on Clay's hand. "Come on. It's not worth it. Let's go."

Clay knocked shoulders with Jason as they passed, and for a second, I thought it might spark a fight, but Jason restrained himself. I turned and watched them leave. Ginny didn't even look pregnant from behind. Bitch.

"You OK?" Jason asked, pulling on my hand.

I tore my eyes away from her back. "Honestly? Can we go home?"

He nodded. "Of course."

"I've never really seen her before." My feet felt frozen to the floor.

"Grace," he said gently, taking my arms in his hands.

"Don't. Don't be nice to me right now, or I'm going to lose my shit in front of all these people."

"OK," he said very matter-of-factly. "Let's go."

With a shaky nod, I took his arm and walked toward the exit. It was a quiet wait for the valet to bring his truck. It was an even quieter drive back to my side of town. My thoughts were a dark and dangerous playground.

He was really having a baby.

He was really getting married.

He really didn't love me anymore.

The gravity of reality settled on me like a load of jagged bricks. Silent tears finally spilled over my eyelids, dripping off my chin and making the Nashville skyline a neon blur passing by my window.

I kept quiet until we reached my exit. It was a right turn to my house. A left turn to my parents'.

"Jason? Can you do me a favor?"

"Anything."

"Will you drop me off at my parents' house? I think I need to go there tonight. Is that OK?"

"Whatever you need. I turn left here, correct? They're still over near the mall?"

I nodded, unable to look at him.

We didn't speak again until I pointed out their street and then their driveway. He pulled in and put the truck in park. "I'll need to go by your house and grab my stuff. Do you mind?" he asked.

"No. You have my key, right?"

"I do. I'll leave it under your mat."

I turned toward him. "You know how you told me I'm not over it?" More tears flowed down my cheeks. "I—I think you were right."

He reached for my hand across the bench. "It's OK, Grace. Do what you need to do."

"I'm sorry."

He pulled my hand to his lips and kissed it. "Don't be. You didn't do any of this." He glanced toward the house. "Go on. I'll wait until you get inside."

The front-porch light came on when I slid out of the truck. I looked at him for a long moment before I closed the door. My mother met me outside in her maroon robe and slippers. "Grace?"

"Mom." I burst into sobs when I reached her.

SEVENTEEN

I SPENT the rest of the night at my parents' house in the throes of all the emotions I thought I'd gotten over in the past six months. God, none of it was fair. Cheating bastards are supposed to get crotch rot, not a beautiful replacement wife with the perfect tiny baby bump.

Early the next morning, I went home, showered, and changed my clothes before driving to Jason's to apologize in person. My hand was shaking as I pressed the doorbell.

His mother answered the door in her wheelchair. "Hi, Grace. My goodness, what happened to you?" Her face was horrified, and I suddenly felt guilty for showing up there unannounced, without giving Jason a chance to warn her. If Jason had some PTSD issues with my bruises, I couldn't imagine what it might do to her.

I covered my eye. "Don't worry about me. I took an elbow to the face during roller derby practice, and I have a perfect wheel imprint on my backside to match it."

She sat back in her chair, then cracked a smile. "You're pretty tough. I like that."

Oh thank God. My whole body relaxed.

"I'm sorry to drop by like this so early in the morning, but I was hoping to talk to Jason. Is he home?"

"Come in," she said, rolling backward out of the doorway.

I stepped inside. She'd been watching a church service on the television.

"Jason's asleep, but you should go down and wake him up."

I looked at the clock on their mantle. It was just after nine a.m., or past bedtime for day sleepers. "I don't want to disturb him."

She shook her head adamantly. "No. He would be very upset if he knew you were here and I didn't wake him."

That made me feel better *and* worse.

"Would you rather I call him on the intercom?" she asked.

"No. I'll go down." I turned toward the staircase, then hesitated. "Are you sure?"

She pointed. "Go."

"OK." I walked down the stairs to the basement. A small sliver of light was shining under the door to Jason's bedroom. I knocked on it.

"Come in," he said.

I pushed the door open.

He was laying on the bed, propped up against his pillows, reading a book by Stephen King. "Grace. I thought I heard your car pull in." He wore a white T-shirt and gym shorts.

"Hey. Aren't you supposed to be asleep?"

He closed the book and placed it on the nightstand. "Haven't done much of that since yesterday."

I grimaced. "Sorry."

"Not your fault. Want to come in?"

Nodding, I walked into the room and around to his side of the bed. I sat down on the edge beside him.

"What's up?" he asked, sitting upright beside me.

"I'm really sorry about last night. I don't know what came over me."

He reached for my hand. "I do. You saw Clay. That's a *big* deal."

"Yeah, but I wasn't expecting for it to rip out my soul again. I was a mess last night when you dropped me off."

"I figured as much. To be honest, I'd be pretty worried about your soul if it didn't affect you at all."

My whole body slumped. "You know, it wasn't even so much about Clay. The baby thing is just impossible for my heart to digest. It's so horrifically unfair."

I could have easily peeled off the fresh scab on all those feelings that had been ripped open again the night before, but I miraculously held it together.

He leaned his head against mine. "I wish I could fix it for you."

"Why are you so patient and understanding?" I smiled. "Nobody's this nice."

"It's easy to be patient and understanding when you care about someone."

I curled both of my hands around his. "I care about you too. And now, I'm a little worried I've broken my promise and made you the rebound guy."

"I guess I should've made you pinky swear on it. That's my fault." He winked at me, and I smiled. Then he lowered his voice. "But, if it makes you feel better, the sex was totally worth the possibility of having my heart broken."

I laughed. "That's a terrible thing to say."

He squeezed my fingers. "I'm joking. I mean, the sex was phenomenal, but my heart is fine. It's totally up to you what you want to do with it."

"What do you mean?"

"I mean, we both rushed into this. I knew better, but I didn't listen to myself." He stroked the side of my hand with his thumb. "If you think we should cool it for a while, you can take all the time you need. I'll be here when you're ready."

"I don't want to stop seeing each other. If you can be patient when my heart hits a speed bump, I'd really like to see where this goes."

"I was hoping you'd say that. Let's take it slow and see what happens." Smiling, he pulled me close and put his arms around me. "I can be patient. However long it takes."

I kissed the side of his neck, then his cheek. Then he pulled back enough to kiss my lips. He tasted like sweet spearmint and everything good in the world. When the kiss deepened and his fingers raked through my hair, I realized we were on his bed and he was already mostly undressed.

I broke the kiss but lingered close, our noses still touching. We were both breathless and smiling.

"So does 'taking it slow' mean sex is on or off the table?" His voice was deep, gravelly, and *oh*-so-sexy.

My toes were curled inside my shoes. "On the table, on the bed, on the hardwood floor...you name it."

He leaned in and kissed me again, and before either of our better judgments could kick in, he pulled me down and rolled on top of me.

Sometime later, my phone chirping somewhere in the room roused me from a shallow dream. He stirred beneath me. My head was on his bare chest, and his arm was curled around me. "Is that my phone or yours?" he asked groggily.

"Mine, I think, but don't worry about it. It's probably just my mom checking to see if I'm OK."

"I wonder what time it is. I fell asleep," he said, tightening his arm.

"I dozed off too, and I have to get up. I'm supposed to skate with Monica today."

My phone chirped again.

When it went off a third time, I felt along the comforter but didn't find it. He checked his side of the bed. "Bingo." He raised it over his head, and the screen lit up. "It's ten-seventeen." He paused. "And you have a text novel from Clay." He handed it to me with a frown.

I groaned as I read it out loud.

"Of all the people in the world, I can't believe you'd go out with my best friend."

I stopped reading. "It amazes me how he's so victimized by this."

"He called me last night and said basically the same thing."

I rolled my eyes and kept reading. *"What I did to you was unforgivable, but at least it wasn't on purpose."*

Jason laughed. "Is he kidding?"

"You're only with Jason to hurt me. Congratulations. Mission accomplished. I hope the two of you are very happy together, however long (or short) it may last." I turned off the screen and laid the phone on the bed between us. "Well, now I don't want to break up with you just out of spite."

Laughing softly, he rolled onto his side. "That's exactly what every man wants to hear."

"For the record, I'm not dating you to hurt him. Just in case you ever wonder."

He smiled. "That's good, I guess. Because if you were, what we just did might kill him wherever he's at."

I curled my leg over his. "Mmm, then maybe we should do it again."

"Spoken like a woman who's truly not on the rebound."

I laughed.

"That reminds me," he said.

My brow lifted in question.

He raised his pinky finger. "I want you to pinky swear it."

With a smile, I locked my pinky finger with his.

———

Later that day, I skated the park with Monica while Jason slept. After telling her all about the events of the weekend, she instructed me to make an appointment with my therapist first thing on Monday.

I took her advice, and Monday morning, I called and made an appointment with Dr. Cecelia Napier, a divorce-recovery psychologist. Thanks to a cancellation, she was able to work me in over lunch. I hadn't seen her since before the divorce was final, and on my drive to her office, I figured out why I was probably subconsciously trying to avoid her.

Dr. Napier's office was in my old neighborhood, about six blocks past Clay's.

And who was bringing the trash in from the curb when I passed by in my whistling chariot? Douchewaffle, himself.

I pressed the gas, which only made the car *whir* louder.

Clay looked up. I kept going, but not so fast that I missed the bright red "For Sale" sign in the front yard.

My phone buzzed with a new message as I turned into Dr. Napier's driveway. I killed the engine and pulled my phone from my purse.

Clay: *Did you just drive by the house??*

Two question marks like, *how dare I have the audacity to drive down the city streets in Nashville?* My jaw clenched.

Me: *Yes, on my way to a meeting. Not stalking you.*

Clay: *Where's Jason?*

God, I needed to have my windows tinted.

Me: *Not here.*

I restrained from adding that if he were really Jason's best friend, he would know Jason works nights and sleeps during the day.

Clay: *Did you see I'm selling the house?*

Me: *Didn't even notice.*

Sure, that was a total lie.

Clay: *Yeah. I think something died in the walls. There's a terrible stench I can't seem to get rid of.*

I laughed—really loudly—in my car.

Me: *Hate to hear that. Good luck.*

Clay: *Thanks. The movers are coming on the 31st. If I find anything of yours, where should I drop it off?*

I raised an eyebrow. Clay was fishing for information. He wanted to know if I was still living at home or if I'd moved in with Jason.

Me: *At my apartment.*

Again I stopped myself from adding a snarky comment about not all of us stomping on the gas pedals of our relationships.

Clay: *Good to know.*

"Let it go, Grace," I whispered to myself. I silenced my phone before dropping it into my purse.

Dr. Napier's office was located inside a renovated historic house at the end of the block. An alarm bell sounded when I walked through the front door. A moment later, she met me in her small lobby.

She extended her hand. That was when she registered my black eye with alarm.

I gripped her hand. "I'm OK." I gestured to my face. "This was a roller derby play gone wrong. I am not being abused by anyone, and this is not why I'm here, I promise."

She relaxed a little. "OK. After all you've been through, you can see why I'd be concerned, correct?"

"Yes. This is nothing like that."

She blew out a sigh. "OK. Then, let's start over. Hello, Grace. It's nice to see you again."

I chuckled. "It's nice to see you again too. I'm sorry. I need to start warning people. Problem is, I don't remember it's there until the horror flashes across someone's face."

"It looks like it hurts. I'm surprised you don't think about it all the time."

"It happened on Wednesday, so it feels a lot better."

"That's good. Come on back to my office."

I followed her down a narrow hallway to the room I'd become all-too familiar with over the past year. She closed the door behind me as I sat in an armchair near the window. After a few minutes of polite chitchat filled with my weak excuses of how busy I'd been since I'd last seen her, she folded her hands over her crossed knee. "So how have you been since the divorce was finalized?"

"Better. I think I've grieved the loss of my dog more than anything, so that must say a lot about my marriage."

I told her the whole story of how Clay had gotten Bodhi in the divorce, how I had dognapped him the night I moved out, and how I'd been sneaking dog visitations behind Clay's back.

"What prompted you to call me today?" she asked eventually.

My face fell. "I really thought I was over him. Then I saw him this weekend with the woman he had the affair with. She's *very* pregnant now, and they just got engaged." I took a deep breath to steel my nerves. "I sort of fell apart after that."

"Understandably," she said.

"I really thought I was getting past the baby stuff, you know?"

"I'm not sure that's something you completely ever get past. You're coming to terms with it, but the grief process of infertility is long. And so cruel a reminder of what might have been, would be unbearable for anyone."

"To make it worse, it happened while I was on a date with his best friend." Even to me, that sounded terrible. "I guess I should say his ex-best friend."

"How did that go?" she asked.

"Clay was pissed." I couldn't contain a smile.

She pointed her pen at me. "I see that grin on your face."

I ran my hand down my face to draw my lips back into a frown. "I know, but that's not the reason I'm dating Jason."

"What is the reason you're dating him?"

It was a good question. I thought for a moment so I could give it a good answer. "Because he looks at me like I'm the only woman in the world."

"That's always a good quality to have in a man. Why do you think it's the first thing that comes to mind for you?"

My shoulders sank. "Probably because of what Clay did to me."

She pressed her lips together and stared at me for a long while, probably to let my own admission sink in. "Give yourself some *grace*, Grace," she said with a gentle smile. "You've been through a lot this year. Be kind to yourself. Be kind to your heart. And be careful with this new guy. The last thing your divorce needs is any more victims."

———

I thought you were supposed to feel better after leaving your shrink's office. I plopped into the driver seat of my car and started the engine. Before putting it in reverse to pull out, I checked my phone.

There were no new messages from Clay, but there was a missed call from Sylvia's home number and a text message from my brother.

Garrett: *Call me when you get a chance.*

I dialed his cell phone.

"Hello?" he answered.

"Hey, it's me. Sorry I missed you. What's up?"

"So I finally made a decision," he said.

My brain was scrambling. "Decision about what?"

"A decision about letting the girls join the roller derby team." He sighed heavily on the other end of the line. "I think I'll let them do it. Can you help me get their gear? I want it to be a surprise for Christmas."

"Absolutely! This is so exciting!"

"Remember, it's a secret. So don't say anything and spoil Christmas."

"I won't. I have practice tonight, so I'll find a way to get in touch with their coach and figure out exactly what they need."

"Thanks, Grace. Hey, what's your plan for Christmas?"

"I was thinking about spending the night at Mom and Dad's on Christmas Eve. Why? What are you thinking?" I asked.

"I'd like for you to be there when they open their gifts. Maybe we'll sleep over there too."

"Mom would love it."

"If we do, we are ordering takeout."

I laughed. "No argument here."

"I've got to run. Let me know what the coach has to say."

"I will. Love you, brother."

"Love you too. Bye."

When I ended the call, I immediately redialed Sylvia's number. A woman answered on the second ring. "Sinclair residence."

"Hi, this is Grace Evans. I believe I missed a call from Sylvia."

"Yes. Hello, Miss Evans. Mrs. Sinclair would like to invite you to lunch tomorrow. Here, at her house, at noon."

I blinked. Lunch at Sylvia's? "Sure, I'd love to."

"Excellent. I'll let her know. Goodbye."

"Goodbye." I stared at the phone in my hand for a second, then finally dropped it into my purse and pulled out of the driveway. On my way back to the interstate, I passed my old house again.

This time, Clay was nowhere in sight.

—————

I walked into the Sweatshop a little later than usual for practice that night. Half the team seemed to be on skates, while the other half were still wearing their tennis shoes. Monica and Lucy were already skating the track, so I rushed to put on my gear and then skated out to join them.

Monica looked at the clock as I skated over. "Cutting it close tonight, aren't we?"

"I was desperately trying to finish an order before I left the store. Have I missed anything?"

"We're skating with Medusa tonight. The All-Star team is working out off-skates."

I looked around for Lucy. She was talking with eL's Bells from the marketing team.

"How did things go today with your therapist?" Monica asked.

I wobbled my head from side to side. "Not as well as I'd hoped, but I did get some good news afterward."

Her brow lifted in question.

"My brother is going to let my nieces play junior derby. Do you know how I can get in touch with Full Metal Jackie?"

"Actually, I had planned on taking Maisie to watch them scrimmage tomorrow night. Want to join?"

I thought about my schedule and how many more dresses I had to make. "What time is it?"

"Their practice starts at six, but the scrimmage doesn't start until seven."

"OK. I can do that."

A whistle blasted around the concrete room. We looked around and saw Medusa walking toward the track. "The Rising Rollers will be with me tonight!" she announced. "Let's get warmed up!"

After a decent warm-up on the track, Medusa divided the members of the B-team into four groups and positioned us at the four different corners of the track. Each group was assigned a position. Two groups were blockers. The other two were pivots and jammers respectively. The jammers and the pivots had to work together as teammates to get the jammers through the two opposing blockers.

It was a really great way to break down gameplay and hone our skills as each group rotated through each position.

When we were done, Medusa checked the clock. "27 in 5s!"

Monica's whole body slumped beside me. "Dammit."

With a grin, I slapped her on the back. "I'll count for you if you'll count for me."

"OK. But you're going first."

Neither of us had done 27 in 5s since we passed our skills test in October. The object was to skate at least twenty-seven laps in five minutes or less. The exercise was brutal, but crucial to building endurance for gameplay.

I skated just short of twenty-eight laps, which was less than usual, but my ass bruise started throbbing somewhere around lap fifteen. When I finished, I dropped to my knees beside Monica and plopped over onto my left hip.

She smacked my helmet. "Good job, Grace."

I was panting. "Your turn. You've got this."

She groaned as she got up, and she skated out to the track.

Lucy came over and sat beside me with her water. She was

even more breathless than me. "I don't think...I'll ever enjoy...that shit."

I smiled. "I know I won't."

When she finished what was left in her water bottle, she was finally able to speak evenly. "Hey, Olivia wanted me to tell everyone she's having a New Year's Eve party at Lettuce Eat. All you can eat and drink off a limited menu for fifty dollars from nine till midnight. I told Monica before practice, and I think she's coming. West and I will be there too, of course."

"Sounds like fun. I'll talk to Jason and let you know."

Medusa blew the starting whistle, and the girls on the track started to sprint. Monica started out strong but stumbled on lap thirteen just as Medusa yelled out the midpoint warning.

I sat up on my kneepads. "Push harder, Monica! That's fourteen!"

"Fifteen!"

"Sixteen!"

"Seventeen!"

Monica was back in derby stance with her head down and her eyes forward. Her stride was getting longer, a good sign.

"Eighteen!"

"Nineteen!"

"Twenty!"

"Twenty-One!"

"Twenty-Two!

"Twenty-Three!"

"Final minute!" Medusa shouted.

"Twenty-Four!"

"Twenty-Five!"

"Twenty-Six!"

"Twenty-Seven!"

"Twenty-Eight!"

The whistle blew.

I clapped my wrist guards together as Monica rolled toward me. "Personal...best," she said, lifting her arms in the air.

Lucy and I cheered.

————

At lunch the next day, I drove to Sylvia's house as promised. Her son, Ben, answered the door. "Hello again, Grace. Come in."

This time, from the foyer, I followed him to the dining room downstairs. It was a long rectangular room with hardwood floors and a large stone fireplace. The walls and ceiling were both painted red with stark white trim. A crystal—or hell, maybe diamond—chandelier hung in the center of the room over a table that could probably seat my entire derby team.

The end of it was set for three people.

"I feel like I'm in an episode of *Dynasty* every time I come over here," I said, following him to the table.

"They actually filmed some of that here."

"Really?" I asked.

He laughed. "No."

"Jokes, huh? You certainly didn't get that from your mother."

"That is the truth."

"Where is she?"

He pulled a chair out for me. "Her assistant, Marie, is bringing her down in the elevator."

My eyes widened as I sat down. "I don't think I've ever been in a house with an elevator before."

"You have now. What would you like to drink? We have tea, sodas, lemonade..."

"Water would be fine."

He walked over to a rolling drink cart and picked up a clear pitcher of water. He carried it to the table and filled my glass. "I hope we're not pulling you away from anything important."

"No. Kiara is manning the store. May I ask what this lunch meeting is about?"

Just then, Sylvia rolled into the room with the woman I had met the last time I visited. Miss Taylor was laying on the blanket across her lap. "Gra-ace, are you early?"

I looked at the time on my phone. "No, I don't think so."

"You must be early if you were here before me. I'm never late, especially in my own house."

My eyes narrowed as my head fell to the side.

"Mom, leave her alone," Ben said, pulling away the chair at the head of the table.

Marie walked around to the front of Sylvia's chair. "Ma'am, would you like me to take Miss Taylor?"

"Yes." Sylvia took her hands off the dog, and when Marie went to pick her up, Miss Taylor growled at her. At least it wasn't just me.

Ben rolled his mother's chair the rest of the way to the table. Then he poured her a glass of sweet tea and put a bendy straw in it, so she didn't have to pick it up. "Marie, can you let Paul know we are ready for lunch," he said.

"Yes, sir."

Sylvia's hand reached for her. "Marie, have you eaten? Would you like to join us?"

It was a surprisingly sweet gesture.

Marie shook her head, holding Miss Taylor close to her chest. "I'm going to grab a bite out with my daughter while you have lunch, but thank you for the invitation."

"Tell her I said hello," Sylvia said.

"You look well," I said to her when Marie was gone. "Are you feeling better?"

"I am today." She looked at Ben across from me at the table. "What is it the doctor gave me?"

"An iron infusion and codeine," he answered with a smile.

I chuckled. "I'll bet you do feel better."

A man, I assumed he was Paul, carried in a tray of three plates. He put one down in front of each of us. On it was a croissant stuffed with what looked like chicken salad, kettle-cooked potato chips, and some sort of red congealed salad on top of a lettuce leaf.

"This looks wonderful. Thank you, Paul," Ben said. "Grace, I hope you like chicken salad."

"I love it. Thank you."

"Grace, I asked you here today because I want to talk to you about making more dresses in honor of Alexandria," Sylvia announced.

Ben cleared his throat.

She rolled her eyes behind her glasses. "Lexi."

I smiled. "I'd love to. What did you have in mind?"

"Now that the cat is out of the bag with what I've been doing, Ben suggested that if I want to really honor Lexi, I should talk to you about how we might partner with agencies like Hope Haven to help young girls have something special."

"I love that idea. As I told you before, I have a few connections at Hope Haven. They could probably help us out."

"Think you could set up a meeting?" Ben asked.

I finished a bite of my sandwich. "Of course. How soon would you like to try to do that?"

"The sooner the better. I'm dying, remember?" Sylvia said with a smirk. "How about tonight?"

"I'm actually busy tonight. I'm going to go watch a junior roller derby scrimmage."

Sylvia parked in her wheelchair. "I would actually love to see that." She looked at her son. "Can we go?"

"You want to go watch roller derby?" he asked, his head tilting to the side.

"Grace, didn't you tell me that the sister of one of the girls who received a dress has a place on the team?" Sylvia asked.

"That's right. She does. Her name is Hellissa."

"Yes, Ben. I want to go watch Hellissa skate," she said.

He chuckled. "That's quite a name. Do you have a pseudonym too, Grace?"

"Britches Get Stitches."

They both laughed.

"Because you're a seamstress. That's funny," Ben said. "Of course we can go if you want to, Mom. Tell me, Britches Get Stitches, what time does it start?"

"The scrimmage starts at seven." I reached into my purse. "If you'll give me your number, I can text you the address."

Sylvia groaned. "It's rude to have phones at the dining table."

I froze with my phone midway out of the bag.

"Mom, do you want to go or not?" Ben asked.

With a huff, she picked up her fork.

Ben smiled at me. "Please send the address."

Relaxing, I pulled out my phone. On the screen was a missed text message from Clay.

Think we could talk sometime? Just us?

EIGHTEEN

I DIDN'T RETURN Clay's text until after I left Sylvia's. I almost didn't return it at all, but he could've needed to talk about the house or Bodhi.

That was a big mistake. I texted him as I sat in her driveway.

Me: *What do you want to talk about?*

Clay: *I don't know. It's just been a while since we've spoken without screaming at each other. I kinda miss that.*

My thumbs twitched over the digital keyboard. "One...two...three...four—"

The phone buzzed.

Clay: *I guess I miss talking to you.*

"Oh. My. God."

Me: *I really don't want to hear this. Please stop.*

Miraculously, he did.

At 6:30 that evening, I locked up the store and drove across town to the Sweatshop. A whole new set of cars were parked in the lot. I parked next to a minivan sporting a bumper sticker that read, *My roller girl could hip check your honor student.*

I laughed and got out of my car.

A siren behind me caused me to turn. I saw Jason's patrol car pull in, so I waited. "Hey, gorgeous," he said, getting out of the car.

"Hey, what are you doing here?" I asked as he greeted me with a kiss.

"I decided to get ready for work early so I could join you for a little bit. Is that OK?"

"Of course. I always love seeing you, especially in your uniform." I kissed him again.

We held hands as we walked into the building. Full Metal Jackie spotted me from across the room by the scoreboard. Her eyes doubled in size. She excused herself from the group of parents (I assumed) she was talking to, and walked over. About fifteen girls, all different heights, were circling the track.

"Britches! You're here!" Jackie said excitedly.

"Yes, but only to watch the scrimmage and talk to you."

She deflated a bit.

"My nieces want to join the team, and they're getting derby gear for Christmas. I need a list to give my brother."

She looked at Jason. "Did you need an armed guard?"

"Ha. No. Jackie, this is my boyfriend, Jason Bradley."

Boyfriend. I'd said it.

His hand tightened around mine. Thankfully, he was smiling. "Nice to meet you, Jackie."

"You too. Britches, I can get you that list. Come on." We followed her to the equipment cage in the back of the room.

As we walked, Jason lowered his voice. "Boyfriend, huh?"

"Shut up," I whispered.

"You know..." Jackie said as she looked through a file box on one of the shelves. "I started coaching junior derby because my nieces wanted to play."

My eyes narrowed with skepticism. "I feel like that's the politician coming out in you. Is that true?"

She smiled. "No, but it was worth a shot."

I shook my head as she handed me a sheet of paper. "You're terrible."

"Still, I think you'd be great at it."

"What's this about?" Jason asked.

I pointed at Jackie. "She wants me to coach the juniors' team this season."

"I think that's a great idea," he said.

"He's a Little League coach," I said to Jackie.

"And isn't it super rewarding?" she asked him.

"It sure is."

"I feel like I'm being ganged up on," I said.

He put his arm around me.

"Why don't you stay and watch practice? We're going to scrimmage tonight." Jackie said.

"That was already our plan. Monica is coming as well. So is another friend of mine and probably her son. I hope that's OK."

"The more, the merrier. Happy to have you. I've got to get back to it. Maybe we can chat afterward."

When she was gone, I noticed Monica had walked in with her daughters, Maisie and Ariana. I waved and pulled on Jason's hand. "Let's go find a seat with Monica."

Ariana squealed and ran to me. She had recently turned six. "Aunt Grace!"

I caught her in my arms and hugged her. "Hi. It's so good to see you!"

"I've missed you," she said, pushing her long dark hair out of her face.

"I've missed you too, kiddo."

She looked up at Jason. "Is this your new Clay?"

Oh wow.

Monica looked as mortified as I felt. She grabbed Ariana from behind and pulled her against her legs. "Sweetheart, his name is Jason."

She waved. "Hi, Jason."

He waved back. "Hello."

"Are you a policeman?" Maisie asked.

He knelt down in front of her. "I am. Are you the future roller girl?"

She blushed and ducked behind her mother.

"I'm going to be a roller girl too," Ariana said proudly.

Monica guided her to a seat on the bleachers. "Not for a few more years, you're not." As we sat down, she mouthed the words "I'm so sorry" to me.

I waved my hand to dismiss it.

Jason leaned against my shoulder. "So, I'm your *boyfriend*, the 'new Clay,'" he said, using air quotes.

I winced. "I'm sorry."

He chuckled. "I thought it was funny."

Sylvia arrived with Ben shortly afterward, and I made introductions all around. I sat between Jason and Sylvia in her chair. Sylvia was looking around the room. "Where's the track?"

Confused, I pointed to the center of the room. "See the lines on the floor that make two rings?"

"Yeah."

"That's the track."

"No, it's not. The track is a bowl." She made her hands into the shape of a bowl, in case we didn't know what one looked like.

"Most teams don't play on a banked track anymore. The flat track is easier to set up and cheaper for everyone to use."

She sat back with a huff. "Well, that's boring."

Jason laughed beside me.

"What do you know about a banked track?" Ben asked.

I turned to look at him. "Did you not know your mama was a roller derby queen once upon a time?"

His head pulled back. He pointed at Sylvia. "My mother?"

With a laugh, she nudged my arm. "Always keep them guessing, Grace. Always keep them guessing. Now, which one is Hellissa?"

Squinting my eyes, I watched the girls on the track. "See the girl in the black shirt and purple shorts? I think that's her. I've heard she's pretty good, so she should be interesting to watch."

They finally looked ready to begin the scrimmage, and Hellissa lined up to be one of the jammers.

"Do you all know how this game is played?" I asked those sitting around me.

"Only a little," Jason said.

Ben shook his head. "No idea."

Sylvia tapped her temple. "Refresh my memory. It's been a couple years since I've played."

I smiled. "Each team has five players on the track for each two-minute jam, four blockers and one jammer—she's the one with the star on her helmet. Blockers play both defense and offense. They try to stop the opposing jammer while trying to help their own jammer. Once the jammer makes it through the pack the first time, on her second lap, she collects one point for each opposing player she passes. The team with the most points at the end of the bout wins."

"Who's the player with the stripe on her helmet?" Jason asked.

"She's the pivot. If the jammer gets in trouble, she can take the star off her helmet and give it to the pivot, making the pivot the new jammer."

"How long is the game?" Ben asked.

Jason held up a finger. "First rule of roller derby is it's called a bout, not a game."

I clapped my hands together. "Good job, babe." I looked back at Ben. "The bout is played in two thirty-minute periods. I doubt they will play that long tonight though. Scrimmages are usually shorter."

A whistle blasted, and the two jammers took off down the track and pushed through the pack. Hellissa made it through the pack first. "See how the referee is pointing at Hellissa? She is now the lead jammer. She can call off the jam early if she wants. That's usually done to keep the other team from scoring."

"I think we only skated for one minute at a time," Sylvia said.

I laughed. "I think a lot of us now would have a hard time making it through to the second pass to score any points in just one minute." I pointed out to the track. "Hellissa just passed all the players on the other team including the jammer so she scored five points."

"How many points can you score in a two-minute jam?" Jason asked.

Monica leaned forward. "The world record used to be forty-five points, and it was held by one of the skaters on our team, Medusa. She lost the world record last year to a girl in Colorado who scored fifty points."

"Fifty points in two minutes?" Jason asked.

"Yeah, but I've never seen anyone actually do it in person," I said.

"There's an actual world record?" Ben asked. "Is this sport really that popular?"

"There are about two thousand teams around the world," Monica answered.

"Wow," he said.

"Grace, what position do you play?" Sylvia asked.

"Usually, I'm a jammer."

"A very good one," Monica added.

My cheeks felt warm.

"So you play as well?" he asked.

"Yeah!" Ariana said. "Her name is Dr. Hooker!"

Monica laughed and nodded her head.

"Do you get paid to play this?" Ben asked both of us.

"No. This league is actually a nonprofit. It relies on donations and volunteers," I said.

Monica looked back at him and smiled. "We actually have to pay dues to the league every month to play."

"No kidding?" he asked.

We both shook our heads.

"We have corporate sponsors, but that only covers stuff like our practice space, jerseys, insurance..."

He cringed. "I'll bet insurance for this sport is a nightmare."

"I have no idea," I said.

Sylvia sat forward in her chair. "Look at her go," she said, watching Hellissa collect more points. "And her family was part of Hope Haven?"

I lowered my voice. "I don't think that's supposed to be public knowledge necessarily, but yes. That's what I've been told. I heard her father is going to be in prison for a very long time."

Sylvia just nodded and watched the bout.

Halfway through the period, Jason reached over and squeezed my knee. "I've got to head to work. This has been a lot of fun though. I can't wait to see *you* play."

I cocked an eyebrow. "You have seen me play. You almost got me killed, or don't you remember?"

He chuckled. "That's right."

"I scrimmage again right here tomorrow night if you think you can refrain from distracting me."

"I'll be here." He smiled and kissed me. "I'll do my best to save all the distracting for this weekend."

"Mmm..." I kissed him again. "I wish you didn't have to go now."

He sighed. "Me too, but criminals won't catch themselves. I'll see you tomorrow though."

"OK. Be safe."

"Always." He stood up in front of the bleachers. "It was good to see everyone. I have to report to duty now."

Sylvia reached for him. "I don't suppose you could help me, Officer?"

"Help you with what, ma'am?" he asked, stepping toward her.

She motioned him closer, and then she lowered her voice. "I have some parking tickets..."

"Mother, leave the man alone. He's not going to fix your parking tickets," Ben said.

Jason laughed. "Goodbye, Mrs. Sinclair." Then he waved to Monica and the girls. "It was good to see you again. And very nice to meet you, girls."

"Bye," Maisie said.

Ariana waived. "Bye, New Clay."

Monica clapped her hand over Ariana's mouth. "Oh my god. I'm so sorry." Then she turned to her daughter and spoke in a hushed but stern voice.

I covered my face with my hands and cringed.

Jason leaned down and kissed me one more time. He was smiling. "Text me later."

"I will."

When he was gone, Sylvia reached over and grabbed my arm. "I like that young man. You should see what he can do about those parking tickets." Before giving me a chance to respond, she turned toward her son. "Ben, I've changed my mind."

"About what?" he asked.

She pointed out to the track. "I want to spend my money here. On these girls."

I shot up straight in my seat. "You want to do what?"

"You said this league relies on corporate sponsors, didn't you?" she asked.

"Well, I did, but —"

"This is helping those young girls more than any ball gown ever could. And look at them. They don't even have real jerseys."

"They wouldn't wear their real jersey's for a scrimmage," I said.

Monica had scooted over into Jason's empty seat. "When I talked to their coach, she said the team is so new they don't have bout-day jerseys yet."

She looked at Ben. "Didn't we do something with jerseys recently?"

"We created the material for the Vikings new jerseys last year," he said.

"The football team?" Monica asked.

He nodded.

"Wow," she said.

"We could do roller derby jerseys, couldn't we?" she asked him.

"I don't see why not. We've done everything from curtains to swimwear."

Sylvia was watching the track. "Watch them pushing on each other, Ben. See how the Velcro on their pads is sticking to their shirts?"

"Yeah, that's a problem when we're playing," Monica said.

"We could fix that." Sylvia snapped her fingers over her head. "You should call Leon."

Ben looked at his watch. "Leon's gone home for the night. I'll call him tomorrow."

"Who's Leon?" I asked.

"Leon works with the manufacturers that use our fabric. There are a lot of companies out there that make jerseys," Ben said.

"Grace, can you introduce me to someone in charge when this is over?" Sylvia asked.

My brain was scrambling to keep up. "Sure. I can do that."

When the scrimmage was over, I didn't have to introduce them to Jackie. She came to us. And after a five-minute conversation, Sylvia had promised to deliver brand-new jerseys to all the girls by the start of their season.

———

Kiara doubled over laughing when I told her the story the next day at work. "What's so funny?" I asked, as I pinned a zipper into the fabric of a dress I was working on.

"You just couldn't get enough of Sylvia here at the shop. Now she's in your extracurricular activities as well."

"Oh, shut up."

My phone on the table buzzed with a text message. I leaned to look at the screen. It was Clay again. "Good god. What now?"

"What's the matter?" she asked.

"Nothing. Except my ex-husband has decided this week that we need to be best friends again. Listen to this: *Have you seen my Cowboys jersey?*" I put the phone back down. "Why the hell would I know where his stupid jersey is?"

The phone buzzed again.

Clay: *Remember, I wore it to the Super Bowl party last year.*

I groaned but still didn't answer.

"Somebody's jealous," she said, snipping the silver thread she was stitching with.

"You think so?"

"Definitely. He saw you with his best friend last weekend. There is nothing in this world that will make a man see the error of his ways like seeing his woman with someone else."

"How do I get him to stop?"

"Give him what he wants." She laughed and pointed the scissors at me. "If he knows you'll take the bait, he'll leave you alone."

"I won't give him that satisfaction even to get rid of him."

"You could change your number."

The front door bells jingled. Smiling, I got up. "Now that's an idea."

Sylvia and Andrew came through the front door. Miss Taylor was on Sylvia's lap again. I didn't even bother to sigh or feel irritated. "Hello there. I wasn't expecting to see you today, Sylvie."

Sylvia clapped her hands together and laced her fingers. "I have a fabulous idea for you, so I had to come down here and tell you in person."

Behind me, I heard Kiara come into the room and mumble, "Oh, I have to hear this."

"Ben talked to Leon this morning about the jerseys. He has a few shops that can make them," she said.

I crossed my arms. "That's great news."

She shook her head. "No, Grace. *You* should make the jerseys."

I heard something *clang* on the counter behind me. It sounded like Kiara dropped a pair of scissors.

"You want me to *what?*" I asked.

"You should make the jerseys," she said again.

I gripped my temples. "I heard what you said. I'm just trying to figure out why you think I would want to make jerseys."

"You told me yourself that you don't want to make dresses anymore."

Busted. I had told her that. And that was the truth.

Kiara stepped over beside me. "You look like you need a chair, Grace."

"I'm fine. Sylvie, making jerseys requires a giant ass printer and a heat press." I looked around the store. "Not only do I not have either of those things, but I wouldn't even have anywhere to put them."

She waved her hand. "Details, details. You could do it, though, if you had the equipment, right?"

"Of course she could do it," Kiara said.

I glared. I wanted to hit her.

"You went to MacKay, same as me. I know it was a while ago, but sublimation isn't new. It's just easier now. You probably took a course on it, just like I did."

"Sure, I know *how* to do it, but there are a lot of skills involved that I do not have."

Kiara frowned. "Like what?"

"Like graphic design. I can't do that."

"It's called outsourcing, Grace," Sylvia said with an eyeroll. "You can hire people to do that part of it."

"Can I buy more time too?" I walked to the back and returned with our order book. I thumbed through the pages, counting the first twenty or so. "I've already got a backlog of dress orders that will keep me busy from now until spring."

Sylvia, possibly sensing I was going into panic mode, held up her hands. "Just think about it. Don't give me an answer right now. We'll talk again next week."

I sucked in a deep breath and nodded.

She reached for me, and I took her hand. She squeezed my fingers. "Sometimes, Grace, the fastest way to get to where you want to go looks like a blind jump off a cliff."

———

On Wednesday, Jason came to practice and watched the first part of my scrimmage before he had to go to work. Then I told him that weekend all about Sylvia's idea. I also ran it past my parents, Monica, and my big brother—the current best entrepreneur I knew.

Everyone was interested in the idea, at the very least. Garrett jumped all over it and started spouting off ways I could grow the business that I hadn't yet agreed to take on. After five minutes, he had me redressing the entire NFL lineup and creating band T-shirts for Maroon 5.

My follow-up lunch with Sylvia was scheduled for the following week. I promised her an answer by then.

Saturday was Monica's concert. Jason and I dressed up for the formal evening. He wore a black suit; I wore a dress I bought at the mall the day before (don't tell anyone). We had a delicious steak-and-crab-cake dinner at J. Alexander's downtown, and then he drove us to the Symphony Center.

The building was beautiful inside and out, like a wedding cake come to life and stuffed with the city's most beautiful people. Our seats were excellent. So was the wine.

It was the perfect evening...until I returned from the bathroom before the start of the show and found him holding the cell phone I'd left on my chair.

He looked guilty as hell when he looked up and saw me.

"What are you doing?" I asked, sitting back down beside him.

"I wasn't snooping." He handed it to me. "I was just trying to silence your ringer because you kept getting text messages and it was beeping."

My heart withered with the words *text messages*. "Were they from Clay?" As I asked I looked at screen.

Yes—*holy shit*—they were.

Clay: *Have you thought about us meeting up?*

Clay: *Ginny is on call Thursday night.*

Clay: *Doesn't Jason still work 3rds?*

Clay: *Grace?*

My insides twisted into knots. "This is *not* what it looks like." I swiped my screen open just as the house lights went down. "Read this."

He shook his head. "I don't want to."

I pushed the phone into his hands. "Please, read it."

"I don't want to," he said again.

Just then, the haunting sound of a piano began to play the single notes of the opening to "The Little Drummer Boy."

"He's been texting me all week. I haven't responded to any of them," I whispered. "Please look."

With a huff, he took the phone and scrolled through the messages. Clay had sent a handful of messages that week that I truly hadn't responded to. None of them had been as bold as these. I wanted to crawl in my seat and die.

Jason finally turned off the screen and handed me the phone. "It's fine," he whispered over the soloist who had begun to sing the melody.

But it wasn't fine. I could feel it in my bones.

NINETEEN

JASON and I barely talked about the text messages again. On our drive home he'd asked if I wanted him to deal with Clay. I'd said no. That was the end of it. Or, at least, I *hoped* that was the end of it.

Clay didn't text me again. Perhaps he'd gotten the message—pun intended.

The following week turned out pretty great, starting with roller derby practice on Wednesday. At our final scrimmage until the New Year, I helped my team win by forty-two points. Even Maven and Medusa were clapping for me when I finished the final jam.

And at work, I busted my ass to finish up all the last of the orders marked "would love to have in time for Christmas." With Mom, Margaret, and Carla all working from home and me working at the store, we finished every single one by Friday. All twenty-nine orders had been completed in just shy of a month. That was some kind of record for me.

Kiara was in New York. She sent me pictures every day from her trip.

Also on Friday, I drove to Sylvia's fully prepared to turn down the job of making junior roller derby jerseys. I'd already said as much in an email to Ben that morning when he'd suggested we could rent machines until I knew for sure if it was something I might consider doing long-term.

When I pulled up at the Sinclair home for lunch, Sylvia wasn't there. Marie was embarrassed that no one had called me. Sylvia had gone to the hospital for another iron infusion. "It was a last-minute sort of thing," she'd said. Because the doctor wanted to get the treatment in before the holiday.

She wanted to know if we could reschedule. I told her to have Sylvia call me on Monday.

Christmas Eve marked the fourth Saturday in a row that I woke up with Jason in my bed. He'd made a standing arrangement with his aunt to take care of his mom so he could spend the morning with me.

The alarm on my phone went off at nine. I switched it off, and he rolled over, curling his arm around me to prevent me from getting up. I gently scraped my nails down his forearm. "You have to let me go. We discussed this already."

He shook his head, his face buried in the pillow. His arm didn't budge.

I rolled toward him instead and scratched my nails across his back. "I promised Monica we'd skate today since tomorrow's Christmas."

He finally turned his face toward me. "But we'll see her tonight."

"I know, but we have to skate. It's our *thing*. We keep each other accountable."

"I'm trying to admire your commitment to this, but it's so warm under these covers," he said with a weak smile.

"I'm waiting for you to break out in a sleepy rendition of 'Baby, It's Cold Outside.'"

He groaned. "It *is* cold outside."

I nuzzled my nose against his neck. "Then you'll have your work cut out warming me up when I get back."

"What time are we going over there tonight?" he asked.

"Not sure. I'll find out from her this morning."

"Can you also find out if her kid is going to call me New Clay all night? If so, I was thinking of wearing my name badge."

I dropped my face onto his pillow and whined.

He laughed.

I propped my head up on my arm. "About him...are we OK?"

"Yeah, we're OK. Is he still bothering you?"

"No. I haven't heard from him since last weekend."

"That's good."

I snuggled against him. "You know what else is good?"

He smiled and rubbed his leg against mine. "I can think of a few things."

"*This* is very good. I like waking up with you here. Can't we do it again tomorrow? You're not *supposed* to work tomorrow."

He moaned and turned away from me, removing his arm and freeing me to lay across his smooth, muscled back.

I rested my chin on his shoulder and spoke into his ear. "Don't you want to wake up with me on Christmas Day?"

"You know I do, but I promised Jones I'd cover his shift." He rolled over underneath me and put his arm behind his head. "He has kids, and it's his little boy's first Christmas."

My hand slid below the covers. "But it's *our* first Christmas."

He squirmed and pulled my arm back up to his chest. "Stop trying to tempt me, woman."

"You're such a good guy."

"I know. It sucks sometimes."

I traced my finger along his collarbone. "You could still sleep over and go into work from here."

"I'd have to be up by four in the morning. You and I both

know if I sleep over, neither one of us are going to sleep before two a.m."

We both laughed.

"I'll go home after dinner at Monica's. You can go to your parents' house and wake up there on Christmas Day. Then I'll stop by when my shift ends before I go home to see Mom."

I sighed heavily. "OK. Do we have plans for New Year's Eve?"

"I was thinking about having a few of the guys over. Why? What did you have in mind?"

"Olivia is having a party at her restaurant. All my friends are going."

"We can do that." His smile turned wicked. "Depending on what it's worth to you…"

I giggled. "I guess that depends on what you want."

With a laugh, he pulled the covers up over our heads. "I want you to be *very* late for skating."

———

We had a wonderful Christmas Eve with Monica and Derek and the girls. Derek and Jason got along famously—something I could have never said about Derek and Clay—and Ariana called Jason by his *actual* name all night long. Monica had assured me during skating that she'd told Ariana there would be no Santa Claus if she called Jason "New Clay" one more time.

After dinner, Jason drove me home to get my car, and following a *very* long Christmas kiss goodbye, I drove to my parents' house alone. Garrett and the girls were already there. Hope lugged my bag up to my room and informed me that she, Gabby, and I were having a sleepover.

Before bed, we watched *A Christmas Story* and ate microwaved popcorn. Mom made hot chocolate—the safe, powdered kind from packets—and Garrett spiked ours and Dad's with salted caramel whiskey.

Hope fell asleep on my lap.

Garrett made Gabby, a nonbeliever, put out cookies for Santa.

Dad and Mom kissed under the mistletoe in the den.

Even though Jason wasn't there, and it was my first Christmas as a divorcée, my heart was full. And it was happy.

An elbow to my ribcage woke me up at six-thirty the next morning. As the ham in the "Aunt Grace Sandwich," I'd been kicked, elbowed, and rolled on all throughout the night by Hope. I finally gave up on sleep and reached across Gabby for my phone on the nightstand.

A text message was waiting from Jason. *Merry Christmas, beautiful.*

I texted him back. *Merry Christmas, Jason. Wish you were here.*

Jason: *Why are you awake so early?*

Me: *I shared a bed with my nieces. The younger of them is training to be a ninja when she's older, I think.*

Jason: *Rough night? LOL*

Me: *To say the least. How's work?*

Jason: *Wild. Christmas makes people nuts. I miss you.*

My heart fluttered.

Me: *I miss you too.*

Jason: *See you in a few hours?*

Me: *Yes! What time do you get off?*

Jason: *Around two.*

Me: *Can't wait.*

Jason: *Me either.*

Then Hope slung her arm across my face. I managed to snap a selfie and send it to him.

There was no going back to sleep after that. I climbed carefully over Hope and tiptoed out of the room. After brushing my teeth, I went downstairs and heard the familiar flutter of a sewing machine.

I found Mom at work in her sewing room. She was finishing the hem of a Sophia dress for me. Her foot came off the pedal when she saw me.

"What are you doing up so early?" she asked.

I crossed my arms. "Why are you working on Christmas?"

She smiled and slipped off her bifocals. "Old habits." She put her glasses down. "Want to have some coffee together before the rest of the crew is awake?"

"I'd love to."

She followed me back to the kitchen, and I made two cups of coffee with their single-cup machine. I handed her the first one while the second brewed.

"Why are you awake?" she asked as she accepted it.

"Hope. Garrett should really sign her up for martial arts. The kid has one hell of a butterfly kick."

Mom laughed. "Oh no."

"Oh yes. I think she's left more bruises than roller derby."

"Speaking of, your black eye is finally better."

"Yeah. My backside is almost healed too. Now it looks like a faint brownish-yellow stain in the shape of Wisconsin."

She chuckled and sipped her coffee as she walked to the kitchen table. I followed her when my cup was poured and I'd diluted it with half a bottle of hazelnut creamer.

"How are you doing, honey?" she asked when I sat down.

"I'm good. Staying busy at the shop, of course, and I went back to see my therapist."

"That's wonderful."

"Things with Jason are better now too than the night he dropped me off here in a puddle of tears. We have had a few other hiccups, though. Mostly because of Clay."

"What else has happened since you saw him at the hotel?"

"Clay's been blowing up my phone."

Blowing up may have been an exaggeration, but compared to how many times I'd heard from him in the last six months—and how *little* I wanted to hear from him now—it certainly felt like a lot. Not to mention, the content of his messages.

"What does he have to say?"

"He misses me. And he wants to talk."

"Talk about what? About how much of an asshole he is?"

I laughed. "Mom!"

"Well, he is." She smiled over her cup. "Do we still get to meet Jason today?"

My cheeks flushed with heat. "He'll be by after two."

"Did you get him anything for Christmas?"

"No. We agreed not to get each other anything this year. We're still supposed to be taking our relationship slow."

"That's very good."

"I think you'll really like him. He reminds me of Garrett."

She laughed quietly. "You'd better not let Garrett hear you say that."

"Let Garrett hear you say what?" Garrett asked, coming into the room.

Mom turned all the way around in her chair. "What are you doing up this early?"

Garrett, still in his flannel pajama pants and T-shirt, walked to the coffee maker and reached for a cup in the cabinet above it. "I fell asleep last night watching some reindeer horror movie and never put out the presents from Santa, so I had to get up early and do it. The girls will probably be awake soon. What are you two doing up?"

"Talking about the weaker sex," I said with a grin.

"I'm glad you're coming to terms with it, Grace. It's good you are finally conceding your place."

"If I had something to throw at you, I would."

He grinned over his shoulder. "You'd probably miss."

Mom got up and walked to the oven. "Don't you two start. You'll wake up the whole house."

Garrett put his hands up as Mom preheated the oven. "Mom, back away slowly and no one has to get hurt."

She laughed. "Oh, shut up. I'm baking frozen cinnamon rolls."

When Garrett's coffee finished brewing, he carried it to the table and sat down in his place across from me.

"Did you get the girls the skates and the gear?" I asked.

"I did. They're going to freak out." He pointed at me. "Your ass had better help me with this."

"You know I will. I'm even playing around with the idea of helping coach the team."

"Aren't you a little new to be coaching?" he asked.

I shrugged. "Their current coach doesn't seem to think so. She's been asking me to do it for weeks now. Even just last week when I went to watch that scrimmage."

"Right. With the old rich lady. Have you made up your mind about taking on those jerseys?" He slurped his coffee.

"I'm going to tell her no."

"That's stupid."

"Why?"

"Because you were just in here telling us how you hate your job, and now something new comes along, and you're not going to at least try it? Dumb."

"Garrett, if you only knew how busy I am at the dress shop."

"Then hire somebody to manage it for you," he said.

Mom returned to her seat. "What about Kiara? She has certainly proven herself these past few months. With a little direction from you, she could handle the store while you try something new."

"Kiara isn't going to stick around after she graduates. You and I both know we'll be reading about her in fashion magazines before too long."

"I said the same thing about you once upon a time, Grace. You won't know until you ask her. If she says no, you're no worse off than you are now."

"And you can always hire someone else," Garrett said. "Mom, for example."

Mom laughed a little too loudly for the early hour. "I'm retired, or have you forgotten?"

Garrett's head fell to the side. "Are you though? Did I or did I not hear a sewing machine at five this morning?"

Mom raised an eyebrow but didn't argue.

Garrett turned back to me. "And once you have someone to help you really manage Sparkled Pink, you can diversify. You can let the dress shop pay the bills while you get the new thing off the ground."

"How would I ever find clients?"

"Hell, if you get into the screen-printing business, I might even let you make all the T-shirts for the brewery." He tapped his chest. "Insta-customer."

I held up my hands. "What do you mean you *might*?"

"You'd have to give me the family discount," he said, smiling.

"Let's say I did decide to try it. What if I rented equipment for a few months just to do it for the juniors' team and to see if I liked it. Where would I even put the machines?"

"You could borrow some space at my warehouse," Garrett said with a shrug.

I sat back in my seat. "You'd let me do that?"

"If it's for the team my kids are going to be on, I guess I'd better start supporting it."

Heavy footfalls pounded the steps in the foyer.

"Speaking of your kids," Mom said.

Garrett stood, stretched his arms over his head, then patted his flat stomach. "Enough work talk for the day. It's time to go play Santa."

———

The squeals were deafening when the girls opened their Christmas presents. Garrett bought them skates (that were nicer than mine), nice indoor and outdoor wheels, full sets of pads, and shiny black helmets. I bought them enough crazy knee-high socks to last a lifetime and got them each a poster of my team, signed by most of the skaters.

For the rest of the morning, I answered a bazillion questions. I could see why Garrett had begged me not to encourage them. They didn't need it.

Gabby had her derby name already picked out: Gabzilla. Hope had hers narrowed down to Cinderolla or Hope U. Fall. My dad said she should be called "Toothless," and Hope launched a full-blown, sugar-fueled assault against him that made Garrett take the Christmas ribbon off the tree and wrap it around his ears.

Finally, I showed them how to change their wheels and took them outside to skate around the driveway. Mom called us in around lunch, and I made the girls a deal: if they would go play with their other new toys and leave me alone for an hour, I'd take them to the skating rink one day that week. Thankfully, they agreed and went upstairs.

I collapsed onto the sofa.

"See what I mean?" Garrett asked from where he was laying on the floor, trying to watch television.

"Holy smokes. Think they're excited?" I asked with wide, exhausted eyes.

"Welcome to my world for the past few months."

Mom stood up. "I need a nap after all that."

"I'll come with you," Dad said, getting up to follow her.

The doorbell rang.

I looked at my clock. 2:12 p.m.

"Who could that be on Christmas Day?" Dad asked with a knowing smile.

"I'll get it!" My heart pounding with excitement, and I jumped up and ran to the foyer. I threw open the door, and froze.

It was Clay.

"What are you doing here?" I asked, looking behind him to the empty street.

He shrugged and stuffed his hands into his coat pockets. "It's Christmas. I wanted to see you."

"Why?"

"Can we talk a minute?"

Suddenly, I felt someone behind me. "You've got a lot of nerve showing up here," Garrett said over my shoulder. "What the hell do you want?"

"I want to talk to Grace," Clay said.

"I don't think Grace wants to talk to you," Garrett fired back.

He was right. I didn't want to talk to Clay, but this nonsense needed to stop. I turned and put my hand on my brother's chest. "I've got this under control. I'm going to talk to him, so maybe he'll go away."

"I'll make him go away."

I was sure he would. "Wait here." I stepped outside and tried to close the door behind me, but Garrett blocked it with his foot.

It was sweet he was so protective. I grabbed Clay's jacket and hauled him halfway down the sidewalk for some privacy. "Now, why are you here?" I asked, crossing my arms.

He looked down at the ground, and when his eyes met mine again, they were glassy. "It's Christmas. I miss you."

"You don't get to miss me!" I threw my hands into the air.

"You lost that privilege when you knocked up somebody else and divorced me."

"I'm sorry—"

"You're sorry. You're sorry. You're sorry. Why weren't you sorry when you caused this mess? Why weren't you sorry the first time you felt guilty because of her? You haven't always been a dick, Clay. I know you must have had a moment where you could have stopped it if you'd wanted to."

He covered his face with both his hands. "I don't know, Grace. It was like I forgot what it felt like to have a woman attracted to me."

"What are you talking about? I've always been attracted to you!"

"No you haven't. Not for a long time. I was simply the other half of the equation on your fertility calendar. You didn't want *me*."

I swallowed hard.

"Somewhere in all that, we lost us," he said, his voice breaking.

As much as I hated to admit it—and, actually, would never admit it out loud to him—Clay was right. "That doesn't excuse what you did to me. I never went looking to anyone else to fulfill what I wasn't getting from you."

He reached for my hands, but I jerked them away. "You're right, Grace. You are so right. What I did was inexcusable. And I'm sorry. If I could take it all back—"

"You can't take it all back! It's done. It's over. You're engaged to marry someone else, or have you already forgotten about her too?"

"I don't want to marry anyone else. *You* are my wife."

I laughed. "I have a stack of paperwork and an attorney's bill that say otherwise." I gripped my forehead because it felt like it might explode. "Where is all this coming from? Is it from seeing me and Jason together?"

"Seeing you with him made me crazy, but it's more than that. Packing up the house, boxing up our whole life together. I hate it. I hate it more than you can imagine."

"I *very* seriously doubt that. I had to leave everything behind. Even my dog, Clay. Even my dog!" Angry tears were pooling in my eyes. "If you really cared about me, if you were really sorry, you'd let me have Bodhi. But you're not sorry. You're just disappointed that the grass really isn't greener on the other side."

"Grace, want me to end this?" Garrett asked from the front stoop.

I shook my head. "No, we're done here."

"Grace, please," Clay begged.

"This madness ends here." My voice was even and stern. "Goodbye, Clay."

As I turned back toward the house, I caught a flash of a blue-and-white car passing by. Then Clay grabbed my arm, spun me around, and pressed his lips against mine.

"You son of a bitch," Garrett was saying as the world spun back into focus around me. I released Clay's jacket that I hadn't realized I had grabbed and shoved him backward as the tail end of the Metro police cruiser disappeared around the corner.

I touched my mouth. "What did you do?"

Tears spilled down Clay's cheeks. "What? Are you afraid of what Jason might think?"

Just then, Garret stormed past me. I clotheslined him with my arm as he went for Clay. "Stop! He's not worth it."

My brother's face was red, his jaw was set, and his fists were clenched at his sides. I looked him in the eyes. "He's not worth it," I said again. "Let's go inside."

As I pulled Garrett toward the house, Clay let loose a sob behind us. "I love you, Grace. I'm sorry. I love you!"

I stopped. Turned on my heel. And walked back to him.

The tiniest flicker of hope twinkled in his eye.

"Say you're sorry one more time."

"I'm sor—"

I balled my fist and knocked him out cold.

TWENTY

I WAS lucky I didn't break my hand.

My knuckles swelled immediately. So did Clay's face. He left without much more to say after that except for a few choice words that almost left him at my brother's mercy once again. When he was gone, Garrett took me inside and put a bag of frozen peas on my right hand. I tried to call Jason, but he didn't answer.

That night, once I was back at my apartment, he finally returned my call. I answered on the first ring. "Hey, I've been trying to reach you all day."

"I know. I was really exhausted after my shift, so I came home and passed out. Merry Christmas."

His tone was difficult to decipher. I couldn't tell if he was sleepy or sad. Had it even been him that drove by the house that day? If it wasn't him, why hadn't he come by or called?

"Merry Christmas." On my couch, I pulled my knees up to my chest. "Did you drive by my parents' house today?"

"Yes."

I swallowed. "So you saw what Clay did?"

"It still isn't over, Grace."

"It's over enough that I punched him in the face for kissing me."

There was silence on the other end of the line. "You punched him?"

"Yeah, and I almost broke my hand."

He was silent again, but I could hear him breathing on the other end of the line. "Do you understand that feelings still have to be pretty intense to punch someone you were once married to in the face?"

I slumped to the side against the arm rest of the couch. "OK. I guess you have a point. But I didn't kiss him. I need you to know that."

"I believe that. And I'm not mad at you. I think we just need some space."

"What do you mean?"

"I mean, it's been nothing but drama since you and I got together. The hotel, the text messages, now this. I really like you, Grace, and I thought I could be patient and handle it because of how much I want to be with you, but this shitstorm is making me crazy. It's going to ruin everything if I don't back off for a while."

Tears drizzled sideways across the bridge of my nose as I laid against the armrest. "When will I see you again?"

He sighed on the other end of the line. "You'll know when you're ready. Until then, I need to step back."

"I understand. I'm sorry this is so complicated."

"It's not your fault, Grace."

"It kind of is. I pinky swore."

He chuckled softly. "I'm fine. We'll talk soon, OK?"

"OK."

I hung up the phone and cried.

———

Monday morning, I went back to work.

I heard nothing more from Jason. Nothing more from Clay either, which I wasn't shedding any tears over.

Kiara came into the store around nine, all smiles and excitement, talking about her trip to New York. She described it like I'd never seen it for myself, about the beauty of the Christmas lights and the overwhelming feeling triggered by the soaring skyscrapers. She talked about the food and the museums. How sad the 9/11 Memorial was, and how she'd spent six hours wandering the Met. She was mostly impressed by how unexpectedly nice the people were, and how great Uber service was in the city.

She showed me all the pictures of the store windows she'd seen. And I could honestly say, her design was right up there with the best of them.

We were in the back workroom, chatting in the breaks between the whirring of our sewing machines. "Kiara, what are your plans after you graduate?"

"I really haven't decided yet. Right now, all I want to do is pack up my bags and move to Manhattan."

I remembered that feeling.

"Why do you ask?"

"The semester is over now. You're done with this place if you want to be," I said, cutting off an extra strip of satin.

She stopped pinning the piece of lace she was working with. "I thought we had agreed I could keep working here."

My eyes snapped up. "Of course you can. I didn't mean it to sound like I was anxious to get rid of you. Quite the opposite actually."

Gripping her chest, she laughed. "You scared me. I thought I was getting fired."

"Not at all. Do you remember Sylvia asking me to make those jerseys?"

"Yes. Are you thinking about doing it?"

I dropped my hands into my lap. "Maybe, but I can't do it alone. Not while running this place too."

"I'll help in any way I can."

"OK. I think I'll tell Sylvia I'll at least try it."

Kiara's eyes doubled as the gravity of what I'd just said sank in for us both. I raked my nails back through my hair. "Ahhh! Am I actually going to do this?"

She laughed. "Would you be working for Sylvia?"

"I don't think so, but I'll know more after lunch tomorrow."

———

On Tuesday at lunch, Ben met me at the door to Sylvia's house. "Grace, come in! So good to see you again. How was your Christmas?"

"It was nice. Yours?" I asked as I walked inside.

"Quite lovely. The whole family gathered here."

"I hope Sylvia was feeling better for the holiday. Marie said she needed another iron infusion on Friday."

He stopped walking and looked at me. "Really?"

"That's why she had to cancel lunch with me," I said, my head tilting to the side.

A thin smile spread across his face. "OK."

"What?"

"My mother lies. I told her you didn't sound like you were interested. I don't know anything about another iron infusion." Laughing softly, he started walking again.

I sighed and shook my head.

Sylvia was waiting for us in the dining room, where the food was already on the table. More color was in her cheeks than I'd seen on her face in weeks.

"Merry late Christmas, Sylvie," I said as we crossed the room.

"You are supposed to say happy holidays during the days between Christmas and New Year's Day," she replied.

I sighed and unbuttoned my coat. "Whatever you say."

Ben laughed. "You're learning, Ms. Evans."

"Let's get down to business, shall we?" Sylvia asked as Ben and I sat across from each other. "Grace, have you made a decision?"

"I have, but I'd like to hear what you propose."

Sylvia and Ben exchanged a glance. Then Ben spoke first. "Regardless of your decision, our company is going to pay for and donate a full lineup of jerseys for the Music City Rollers Junior Derby team. Our proposition to you is this. We will rent all the equipment necessary for a period of one month for you to complete the twenty jerseys necessary for the team. We will also provide the fabric, which we've already begun the process of creating."

"You're creating new fabric?" I asked.

"That's right. It's a special blend of spandex and polyester that will help with the Velcro-sticking issues. Antimicrobial agents have been incorporated into the fibers to help control odor, and it features wicking to help the athletes stay dry," he explained.

I waved my hand. "You had me at controlling odor. Continue."

"We will also pay you a small amount per jersey for the work," he said.

"It seems like doing it this way would just cost you more in the long run. We're all business people here. What's in it for your company?" I asked.

His head tilted from side to side. "We'll be able to expand this fabric into new markets, as well as get the tax write-off for helping the nonprofit."

"But you'd do that anyway if you already used a manufacturer that was up and running in this line of work. Why me?"

He looked at his mother.

"Because I like you, Grace. You want to do something new? Here's your chance," she said.

Ben opened a notebook in front of him. "I've done a lot of research this past week. There *are* thousands of teams around the world. Once word of this new fabric starts to travel, other teams are going to want it."

He handed me a sheet of paper. "After the trial run with the juniors' team, should you choose to stick with it, this contract states only you and your company will be allowed to use our fabric in the world of roller derby."

I cradled my head in my hands. "Wow. I don't know what to say."

With a huff, Sylvia leaned toward me. "You say thank you, dear. Goodness, Grace. It's really not that complicated."

———

By the end of the week, arrangements had been made for the jersey project. The first week of the new year, all the equipment and a few extra sewing machines would be moved into my brother's storage building behind Battle Road Brewing.

In exchange for the use of the building, I agreed to help drive the girls to and from junior-derby practice. Like I wouldn't have done it otherwise. (Eyeroll.)

Mom also agreed to help out wherever I needed her. She'd said to me in private that Garrett was right—but not to tell him that.

Still, I didn't hear from Jason.

On the morning of New Year's Eve, I skated the park with

Monica, and that night, I took an Uber alone to Lettuce Eat for the party.

Olivia was with the hostess near the door when I walked inside. "Grace, you made it!" she said, coming over for a hug.

"Ready to ring in the new year and all that. This is a great idea."

"Thank you. I knew the restaurant had to be open, and I wanted to celebrate with my friends, so this was a nice compromise." She turned toward the hostess, a bubbly redhead with a lip ring. "You can mark Grace Evans off the list. Where's your beau?"

"I have no beau."

Her face fell. "Tell me later?"

"Yeah." I reached for my purse. "Do I pay here, or will you bring me a bill?"

Olivia waved her hand. "No way, José. My guests are on the house."

"Olivia, that's really not necessary. There's no telling how much I'll end up drinking tonight."

With a laugh, she looped her arm through mine. "I fully expect it. In fact, it's mandatory. You are my new favorite person to get drunk with."

"How are things with you and Styx?"

"Things are good. She's around here somewhere."

"Good. I'm really happy for you."

"What happened with the guy?"

My nose scrunched. "Nothing good. I did, however, punch my ex-husband in the face last week."

She laughed and gripped my arm. "Well that, sure as hell, is something to celebrate. Come on. Monica and Lucy aren't here yet, but Zoey and Maven are."

"Maven?"

"Yep. I hear Medusa might be coming as well. Styx invited them."

"That's cool. Are Lucy and West still coming?"

Olivia smiled. "Yep. This might get interesting."

I followed her through the maze of old wooden tables with mismatched chairs. The exposed rafters were draped with white twinkle lights and silver streamers overhead. Near the back wall, two rectangular eight-tops were pushed together. Zoey and Maven were sitting at the end of it.

"Grace!" Zoey said, getting up from the table. She came over and gave me a hug. Her hair was now long enough for her dark-brown bangs to be pinned to the side. "Happy New Year!"

In my arms, she didn't feel as frail as she used to. "Happy New Year, my friend."

Maven smiled across the table as I pulled out a chair. It was the first time I'd seen her outside of the Sweatshop at a non-derby event. She wore a deep crimson sweater with matching lipstick, and her thick black hair hung in tight curls around her shoulders.

I peeled off my jacket and hung it on the back of the chair. "Happy New Year, Maven."

"Happy New Year, Britches." She raised her glass toward me.

Olivia touched my shoulder. "What would you like to drink? We have a few New Year's specials, the New York State of Wine and Hoppy Brew Beer."

I chuckled. "What kind of wine is it?

"Our house red. It's a cabernet this month."

"I'll take that. What are the food specials?"

She pointed to a menu card on the table. "Everything's right there. Let me know if you have questions."

"Cool, thanks." I sat down and picked up the menu.

As she turned, Styx approached our table. They exchanged a quick peck on the lips, and Styx sat down beside me with a full glass of beer. "Hey you," I said.

"Hey. When did you get here?"

"Just now."

The specials for the night were: Midnight Toast, which was basically bruschetta; Thyme Square, a flatbread with white cheese sauce and fresh thyme; Auld Lamb Syne, lamb kabobs with grilled zucchini, mushrooms, and pineapple; and New Year, New Meat, beef tenderloin sliders with an orange-cranberry relish.

Zoey had a half of a slider left on her plate. "Do those taste as good as they sound?" I asked her.

"They're delicious."

"The flatbread is great too," Styx said.

"Good to know. It's really good to see you here. I was worried about you guys after the Slammy Awards."

She nodded. "Things have been rough, but I decided there's always going to be drama, and I'm not going to let that stop us from being happy."

I thought of Jason.

"Britches, are you ready for the B-Cup?" Maven asked, saving me from a downward spiral of sadness.

"Ready? No. Excited about it? Absolutely," I said.

"You're going to kill it out there," Styx said.

"Thank you." I split a glance between her and Maven. "Do you really think we might have to skate against Richmond?"

Styx nodded. "It is possible."

I groaned.

"Don't worry. The biggest one you really have to watch out for on their team is Demoness, and she won't be skating because she's on their A-team. You guys will be fine," Maven said, picking up her glass.

That made me feel only slightly better.

Styx slapped the table in front of Zoey. "Fresh Meat starts back soon. You're coming, right?"

"Wouldn't miss it," Zoey replied with a smile. "Are you guys missing practice yet?"

Styx sipped her beer. "A little."

"Not me," Maven said. "I'm thankful for the break this time of year. You know, it's our busiest season at Hope Haven."

"I'll bet it is." I looked at Maven and Zoey. "Hey, do either of you know a woman named Sylvia Sinclair?"

Maven straightened in her seat. "I do. She's one of Hope Haven's biggest supporters. How do you know her?"

"She's a regular customer of mine. I recently found out she donated some dresses I made to girls in your program."

Maven and Zoey exchanged a glance. "I know exactly what you're talking about," Zoey said.

"I do too. I wasn't aware that you made the dresses though," Maven said.

"The light-blue dresses, right?" Zoey asked.

"Periwinkle," I said with a smile.

"Wow, small world. Do you know how she's doing? I heard she was in the hospital," Maven said.

"She's at home now. I've seen her a lot lately."

"It's cancer, right?" Maven asked.

"Leukemia. They're not doing treatment."

Zoey's face fell. "I had no idea. Please give her my best wishes when you see her."

"And mine," Maven added.

"I will. She's just signed on as a sponsor for the junior derby team and hired me to make their team jerseys."

"Jerseys, huh?" Styx asked.

"Yeah. The woman owns a textile company, and they're developing a stretchy athletic fabric that won't stick to the straps on our wrist guards," I said.

Styx and Maven both looked impressed.

"That would be awesome," Styx said.

"Yeah. Can't wait to see them," Maven agreed.

Olivia put a glass of red wine down in front of me. "New York State of Wine for you, my love. Do you want anything to eat?"

"I'll take the sliders," I said, smiling back at her.

She scowled. "You have to order them correctly."

I laughed and picked up the menu. "Excuse me. I'll have the New Year, New Meat sliders please."

She winked at me. "That a girl. Anybody else want anything?"

Maven raised her hand. "I have a question for you."

Olivia leaned on the back of Styx's chair. "OK."

"Why the hell are you not skating?" Maven asked.

I glanced back over my shoulder. "Because she's a quitter."

Olivia rolled her eyes. "I have no time for skating."

"You're just as busy as me." I started counting on my fingers. "I usually skate four days a week, and I'm a business owner too."

"You need to figure your shit out because you're too good to not be out there with us," Maven added.

"Agreed," I said. "Maven, did you and the other veterans really call her The Prodigy?"

Maven laughed. "Yeah, I think Medusa started that one."

"Is she coming tonight?" Zoey asked.

"She said she'd stop by, but she's on a date right now."

Zoey smiled. "Good for her."

Olivia sighed behind me. "That might be a good thing. Lucy texted me a second ago with some news. She'll be here soon with West."

"What news?" I asked.

"I'll let her tell you. They should be here any minute."

Something waving caught my eye out the window. It was Lucy's arm. "Looks like they're here now."

Lucy was waving on the other side of the glass. Her smile was bigger than I'd ever seen it. She pulled West toward the front door.

"I wonder what's gotten into her," Zoey said.

Lucy practically skipped across the restaurant to join us. I had turned all the way around in my seat to watch them come in. West took her coat when they reached us, and she couldn't pull her arms from it fast enough.

Olivia walked over from the bar.

"What's going on?" Zoey asked.

Lucy looked around. "Where's Monica?"

"Not here yet," I said.

"I'm too excited to wait!" Lucy held up her left hand high in the air. A huge, sparkling white diamond glistened on her finger. My mouth fell open. "Shut up," I said.

She was beaming as she draped her arms around West's neck. "He asked. I said yes!"

"Congratulations!" Zoey cheered.

"Congratulations," Maven said, picking up her phone again. I wondered if she was going to text Medusa with a warning.

Olivia grabbed Lucy and kissed her on the cheek. Then she pointed a warning finger at West. "I know where you live, and I know how to use a meat cleaver."

He laughed. "Warning received."

I stood and grabbed Lucy's hand. "Good lord, Lucy. You'd better never go swimming with that thing. You'll drown!"

"Isn't it beautiful?" Lucy asked.

"*Beautiful* doesn't do it justice." And it didn't. It was the biggest rock I'd ever seen on anyone, including Sylvia Sinclair. "Congratulations, you guys."

Lucy was still hanging onto West. "Thank you. He asked my dad over Christmas."

"When did he ask you?" Zoey asked, coming around to hug her.

"About an hour ago," Lucy answered as she hugged her.

"I know it's fast and some people will think we've rushed into it, but I don't care." West put his arms around Lucy's waist and gazed at her, his eyes full of love and happiness. "I'd originally planned to ask her at midnight, but I couldn't imagine starting the new year with even one second of her not knowing how I feel."

All of us whimpered at his sentiments.

Tears dampened my eyes, but not just tears of happiness for my friend. And I was *truly* happy for her. All of a sudden, I couldn't figure out what the hell I was doing in East Nashville alone on New Year's Eve when there was a man across town waiting for me to get my shit together and be with him.

Zoey must've noticed the shift in my demeanor because she put her hand on my arm. "You OK, Grace?"

I nodded. "What time is it?"

She looked at the time on her phone. "Almost nine."

I stood and picked up my jacket.

"Where are you going?" she asked.

"Across town to Crieve Hall. Tell Monica I'm sorry I left before she got here."

"Everything all right?" Olivia asked.

I laughed through my tears. "Everything's great. I just figured out where I'm supposed to start the new year. Thank you, West."

He looked confused. "You're welcome?"

I hugged Lucy and Olivia, then blew a kiss to Zoey. "Happy New Year, my friends."

"Happy New Year, Grace!"

———

It was the longest ride ever across town to the south side of the city. We pulled into Jason's driveway at nine thirty behind several other cars and trucks. Jason wasn't home alone. I gulped as I held onto the door handle.

"Everything all right?" the driver asked, eyeing me in the rearview mirror.

"Yeah." I forced open the door. "Thank you. Happy New Year."

"Happy New Year to you."

The sky was clear with faint stars twinkling through the distant neon lights of the city. A wood-burning fire was smoldering nearby, and laughter and men's voices floated on the breeze from around the back of the house.

Jason's driveway seemed a thousand miles long.

A small path led behind the house and through a gate in the tall wooden privacy fence. When I opened it, everyone on the other side turned to look. A handful of guys were gathered around the fire pit sitting on camping chairs and drinking canned beer. Jason wasn't anywhere.

One of the men stood up. I recognized him from the Opryland party. He walked over with a smile. "Grace, right?"

I nodded nervously as I reached to shake his hand. "Yes. Jordan?"

"Yes, ma'am."

"Good to see you again. Is Jason here?"

He jerked his thumb toward the house. "Inside helping his mom. He'll be back down in a second. Want something to drink? We have cheap beer and cheap beer."

I laughed, my nerves beginning to settle. "I guess I'll have a cheap beer."

"I knew I liked you." I followed him toward the fire pit. He gestured toward me when we reached the other guys. "Gentlemen, this is Jason's roller girl. Mind your manners."

They greeted me with "hello"s and handshakes, and Jordan handed me an ice-cold can of beer from the cooler.

"Grace?"

I turned as Jason walked out the sliding-glass door.

"Hi," I said with a small wave.

He looked around. "What are you doing here?"

Chewing on the side of my lip, I looked at his friends and then back at him. "I was hoping to talk to you."

Jordan loudly cleared his throat. "Party's over, guys. Pack up your shit, and let's give them some space."

"That's not necessary. I don't want to spoil the party," I said.

With a smile, Jordan shook his head. "We've all got to work first thing in the morning anyway. Consider this your service to the City of Nashville, keeping a bunch of cops from being hungover on New Year's Day."

The men stood and began closing their chairs and picking up their cans.

"Thanks, guys. Happy New Year," Jason said.

I went over and stood beside him. "I'm so sorry. I should've called."

"It's OK. He's right. They weren't planning on staying much longer. It was an impromptu gathering because none of us had any plans."

He didn't have any plans because he should have been with me.

"Is your mom OK?"

"Yeah. She was ready to go to bed."

A few minutes later, we were alone and standing in the cold. He stuffed his hands into his jeans pockets. "What are you doing here, Grace?"

The cold beer can was freezing my fingers. I put it down beside the grill. "I came by because I miss you."

He looked at the ground. "I miss you too, but—"

"Jason, hear me out."

After a second, he met my eyes.

"This divorce has been the messiest thing I've ever gone through. I'm not going to lie and say that it's over, that nothing will ever happen again, or that I've been miraculously healed from it." I took a deep breath and a step toward him. "But I have no doubt in my mind about what I want. I want to start over. And I want to start over with you."

"Why? Why me?"

My therapist had asked me something similar, and I had spent the last couple of weeks thinking about my answer. "Because I admire you."

He lifted his head.

I started to count on my fingers. "You're thoughtful. You're protective. You *love* your mother. You're kind to dogs, and you're loyal to a fault. I love you for all those things."

"You what?"

I let out a deep sigh and dropped my hands to my sides. "I love you. And I know it's too soon and I know I've got a lot of baggage and I know I'm probably—"

He grabbed the back of my neck and kissed me.

Startled, I froze.

After a second, he pulled back. "Stop talking. You've said enough." I swallowed as he took my hand and leaned his forehead against mine. "I love you too, Grace."

We were in his bed when the clock struck midnight.

Our ringtones had chimed in the new year, but our well-wishing friends had gone unanswered. Because as the rest of world was turning the calendar from one year to the next, we were ending an old lifetime and beginning a new one together.

I had dozed off on his chest sometime around daybreak, our

naked limbs still tangled in his sheets. His arms were curled around me when we woke up to the sound of the doorbell.

He groaned and sank further under the covers with me. "Who the hell could that be?"

"Your aunt?"

"Nah. She doesn't ring the bell, and I'm sure she's already here." He rolled toward me, and I moved my head to his pillow and draped my leg over his hip. Smiling, he ran his warm hand up my thigh. "Good morning."

"Yes, it is. Aren't you going to get the door?"

"My aunt can get it. I asked her to come over early so I could sleep off the hangover I planned to have this morning."

"I thought you said it was an impromptu party?"

"It was. That doesn't mean I wasn't sure I'd get drunk." He pushed his hips further between my legs. "I missed you. Bad."

"I'm here now."

Smiling, he hooked his hand behind my knee. "Yes, you are." We kissed as he rolled on top of me again.

Upstairs, someone pounded on the door.

Jason stopped, and his eyes whipped toward the ceiling. "I don't like the sound of that."

He moved over, sat up on the edge of the bed, and grabbed his jeans off the floor. As he stood, he pulled them up over his bare ass. Then he took his phone from his pocket and looked at the screen. "Shit."

I sat up. "What's the matter?"

"I have a bunch of missed calls from Jordan and the station."

"What's that mean?"

"I don't know, but I'll bet that's who's here. You'd better get dressed."

He put on a T-shirt as he left the room. A moment later, I heard muffled voices upstairs as I dressed in my party clothes. The voices got louder as I walked up the stairs.

When I entered the room, Jason was talking to Jordan, who was in full uniform at the front door. His mom and his aunt looked worried in the living room.

They all turned toward me.

Jason ran his hand down his face as Jordan stepped around him.

"Grace Evans, you're under arrest."

TWENTY-ONE

CLAY HAD FOUND THE EGGS.

The arrest warrant was almost comical. I was being formally charged with vandalism and destruction of property over $1,000. The probable cause was stated (by Clay) as follows:

Upon moving into my new house, two rotten hard-boiled eggs were discovered underneath the wooden drawers in my desk. The eggs, now partially liquefied and crawling with maggots, were each marked with letters (C & K) written in blue marker.

After conducting a thorough search of other pieces of furniture that had begun to smell, more eggs were discovered inside my sofa, inside my recliner, and inside my mattress.

A photo (which I kept) was found the day after my ex-wife moved out of our house—a photo of her posing with a bunch of eggs, all marked with blue letters. The same eggs that have ruined my furniture.

By the time Jason finished reading it out loud, I was laughing through my tears.

"Grace, this is serious," Jason said, holding up the sheet of paper. "It's a felony."

"A conviction could carry a sentence of up to twelve years in prison and five thousand dollars in damages," Jordan added.

I gulped. "What do I do?"

"You're going to have to get booked in the jail." Jason raked his hand back through his hair. "I'll come down with you and either post bail or see if I can get you released without it."

Jordan shook his head. "They won't do an ROR. Not for a felony."

"I'll post her bond then."

"Everybody knows who she is by now," Jordan said hesitantly.

Jason sighed. "Of course they do."

None of it was funny after that statement. This was an embarrassment for him, on top of it being more drama with Clay. "Jason, I'm sorry."

He shook his head. "We'll talk about that later. I need to change clothes."

———

Jason wasn't allowed in the room when they were booking me into jail. It was the most humiliating experience of my life. While the female officer was tactful, I was given a pat down that registered on the invasive scale somewhere between TSA and foreplay. Then I was fingerprinted, photographed, and put into a holding cell while I waited for Jason and the bondsman to get me out.

How the hell could Clay do this to me? I knew he'd be pissed. But actually have me arrested? Not in a million years. I'd bet my life it was Dr. Vagina who'd made him do it. If only she knew about his behavior the past few weeks.

Jail was miserable. It was cold, loud, and it smelled funny, like old pee and sadness. Finally, one of the officers opened up the cell I was in. "Evans?"

I stood.

"You're free to go now."

But Jason was gone by the time they released me. My brother was waiting in the lobby. He stood when I walked out and took a deep breath of freedom.

I looked around. "Where is he?"

Garrett shrugged his shoulders sadly. "He paid your bond but left when I got here. He said to tell you he was sorry."

I couldn't say I was surprised.

And I couldn't say I blamed him.

———

Roller derby was fun that week.

Not only did Monica, Lucy, and I get to skate again with Zoey at Fresh Meat practice before our practice, as a hardened criminal now, I was able to bring some serious street cred to the track. That first scrimmage back on Wednesday, I scored thirty-two points all by myself. The whole team had cheered. Maven even hugged me.

After practice that night, we took Zoey out for drinks at Lettuce Eat to celebrate being back at the Sweatshop. While we were there, I had a chance to talk to the soon-to-be Mrs. West Adler about designing some jerseys for the juniors. Lucy happily agreed. We were set to start production sometime the next week.

To say the least, there was a lot to distract me from my legal woes and Jason. For that, I was thankful. I had texted Jason to thank him for his help the day I was arrested and had never heard back. I wrote him a check to repay the amount of my bond, and I considered delivering in person. It was obvious, however, he didn't want to see me, so I put the check in the mail instead.

The next Tuesday night was my nieces' first roller derby practice. Garrett couldn't go because of a meeting at the brewery, so I picked them up after work. They talked a thousand miles an hour all the way across town.

Full Metal Jackie was coming through the parking lot when we got out of my car.

"Full Metal Jackie!" Hope cheered, running over to give her a high five.

Jackie laughed. "Let me guess. Your nieces?"

"Yes, ma'am," I said, smiling proudly.

Jackie knelt down. "And what are your names?"

Hope stuck out her hand. "Cinderolla. *Pleathed* to meet you."

Jackie shook it. "Great name." She looked at Gabrielle. "And yours?"

"Gabzilla"

"That's fierce. I like it." Jackie winked at her. "Are you girls here to skate?"

Hope raised both fists in the air. *"Yeth!"*

Gabby nodded her head.

Jackie stood and looked at me. "And you?" She cocked an eyebrow.

I put my hands up in resignation. "I'm here to watch, but I will volunteer if you need to put me to work."

"I need you to coach," she said, leveling her gaze with mine.

"Yeah, Aunt Grathe." Hope was clinging to my waist. "She *needth* you to coach!"

"I can't coach *and* make your new jerseys. What do you want from me?"

"We want you here," Gabby said.

"I like these girls already." Jackie straightened and turned toward the entrance. "Come on inside and get warmed up, girls. We'll wear your aunt down later!"

———

After lengthy training sessions with technicians from both the printer company and the heat-press company, followed by more wasted material and ink than I could've ever imagined, actual jersey production finally began. Lucy had come up with a beautiful design in the league's signature teal and black, and had even designed a brand-new logo just for the juniors.

All in all, it was a little over two weeks of trial and error (on my part), but we finally started printing, pressing, and sewing. Kiara and Mom handled the store, Margaret and Carla finished the rest of the Black Friday orders, and I worked around the clock making the jerseys.

Garrett came out to the warehouse a few days later to see me. He brought a six-pack of beer and opened one with a bottle opener on his keychain.

"I can't drink that. I'm working," I said when he sat it down on my worktable.

"You're probably going to want it when you hear what I have to tell you."

I sat back in my chair. "I don't like the sound of that." I picked up the beer. "What's going on?"

"Guess who I ran into today?" Garrett opened a beer for himself and pulled a chair over to the table beside me.

"Jason?"

He shook his head. "Clay."

I slouched.

"One of my servers broke a glass and cut his hand pretty bad, so I drove him to the emergency room."

"Is he OK?"

"He had to have a few stitches. While we were there, Clay came in with the other woman. She was in labor."

I tilted the bottle up—way up—to my lips and drained a quarter of it before putting it back down. Then I burped. "Good for him." I took another long drink.

"I wanted you to hear it from me instead of somebody else."

"Did you talk to him?"

"No, but it was all I could do to keep my fists to myself. Had we not been in a hospital, it would've been a different story."

"He's a lucky guy." I sighed. "I guess it's a good thing though. Both of us don't need to go to prison."

"Have you talked to your lawyer lately?"

"Yesterday. We go to court on Valentine's Day. How ironic is that?"

Garrett chuckled. "OK, now that's funny."

I peeled the purple-and-black label on the bottle. "You know, if I get convicted, I'll be a felon.

"Surely you won't be convicted."

"My lawyer hopes to get the charges lessened to a misdemeanor with probation time and restitution via a plea deal. She should find out next week. If it goes to court, she's sure I'll be convicted. He has the picture."

Garrett shook his head. "Why the hell did you take pictures?"

"Sorry. The next time I commit a felony, I'll be sure to consult you first."

"You'd better. I can't believe you did that shit without letting me participate."

I laughed.

He pointed at me. "I talked to Mom and Dad the other night, and Dad said the same damn thing."

We both laughed harder.

When the laughter subsided, my brother took a drink of his beer. "Have you talked to Jason?"

"No, and he never cashed the check I sent him for the bond money."

Garrett sighed. "I can't believe he'd just go MIA like that."

"I can. It was a really tough month when we were together. Dating me wasn't easy."

"Now that, I can believe."

I held up my middle finger.

"You gonna be all right, sis?" he asked, putting a hand on the back of my chair.

"Yeah. It's time to move on. Let my heart heal, and all that. From Jason, Clay, the divorce..." I sighed. "And the baby stuff. Thanks for telling me about it."

He stood. "Why don't you come over for dinner with me and the girls tonight?"

"I'd love to, but I have practice."

"Tomorrow?"

"Your girls have practice."

"I knew that"

I snapped my fingers. "Hey, speaking of practice, you should plan to come next Tuesday. Sylvia and I are presenting the jerseys to the team. It's kind of a big deal."

"I'll be there. Call me if you need me?"

"I will. Love you, brother."

Garrett kissed the top of my head. "I love you too."

TWENTY-TWO

"GRA-ACE!"

Even though we were friends now, the sound of my name on Sylvia's lips still made my insides quiver. I got out of my car and closed the door behind me. Ben was wheeling Sylvia and Miss Taylor—*great*—across the parking lot of the Sweatshop. Andrew was with them, along with two other women and three kids I'd never seen before, a boy and two girls.

"Did you bring the whole family?" I asked Sylvia as I walked around the trunk of my car.

"You think I'm picking up strangers on the highway now?" she asked.

"I assume nothing with you, Sylvie."

"Grace, you know Andrew and Ben." Sylvia gestured toward Andrew and the woman he was walking with. "This is Andrew's wife, Brandi, and their two kids, Luke and Ellie. And this is Ben's wife, Jeanine, and their daughter, Mia."

Mia looked a lot like the pictures I'd seen of Lexi.

"It's nice to meet you all. And it's good of you to come." I opened my trunk and pulled out the large cardboard box inside it.

Andrew stepped forward. "Need some help with that?"

"That'd be great." Before he took it, I pulled out one of the jerseys and held it up for Sylvia to see. "Well, what do you think?"

Sylvia reached for it, rubbed the fabric along the back of her hand, stretched it a few times, then held it at arm's length. "It's fine, Grace."

Fine.

The word no longer irked me the way it used to.

Ben nodded his approval. "I think it looks great."

"Me too," Andrew agreed.

"It would have been better in periwinkle," Sylvia said handing it back to me.

With a laugh, I took it from her. "Of course it would." I turned toward the building. "Come on. Let's see what everyone else has to say."

Gabby and Hope ran to me when we walked inside. Garrett was there. So were Mom and Dad. I waved to them. All the juniors skaters and their parents were seated in the bleachers. A few of my teammates were there as well: Monica, of course; Doc Carnage with her daughter; Madam Veruca because she helped with the team; and Susan, our faithful president.

Jackie came over, excitedly clapping her hands. "It's time! It's time! It's time! We have a table all set up for you." She led me to a folding table draped with a teal tablecloth.

Andrew set the box on top of it. I thanked him and opened it.

Careful to hide it behind the flaps of the box, Jackie lifted out one of the jerseys. "Oh, Grace, these are amazing. Are you sure you haven't done these before?"

I laughed. "Trust me, it was a *lot* of trial and error."

"You can't tell. I've played roller derby for a long time now, and these are the best jerseys I've ever seen. Just wait until Susan and the rest of our team sees these."

"Come over here, Jackie. I want you to meet the Sinclair family." I leaned close to her and lowered my voice. "I hope it's OK she brought her dog. She doesn't go anywhere without her."

Jackie waved her hand. "Dogs come into the Sweatshop all the time."

We walked toward the bleachers where Sylvia and her family had settled near my family. "Everyone, I'd like for you to meet Full Metal Jackie, the head coach and president of the Music City Junior Rollers," I said.

Jackie beamed at all of them. "Thank you all so much for coming. We really appreciate your support, and we are so excited to finally have our jerseys."

"It's nice to finally meet you in person," Ben told her. "I'm Ben Sinclair-Hoyt. We spoke on the phone. This is my mother, Sylvia Sinclair."

"Hello, Sylvia. Welcome to the Sweatshop," Jackie said, shaking her frail hand.

"We recently found out our mother used to play the sport," he added with a smile.

"Yes. She skated on a banked track," I said.

"Really?" Jackie asked, surprised.

If I didn't know any better, I'd swear Sylvia Sinclair was blushing. They continued to chat while I went over to greet my family and Monica. She and Derek were there with both girls.

"Maisie, how are you enjoying junior derby?" I asked, sitting down beside her.

"It's really fun."

Monica leaned toward me. "It really is. And the extra prac-tice? Don't even get me started on how great that is."

"Really? You're skating six days a week now. Aren't you tired?" I asked.

She laughed. "I'm exhausted. But it's great. I still think you should try it."

"You and everyone else." I looked over at my nieces. "I am seriously thinking about it. We'll see."

Finally, Jackie returned to the table. "Good evening, everyone. Welcome to the Music City Rollers' Sweatshop. We have a lot of new faces here tonight, so in case we haven't met, my name is Full Metal Jackie, and I'm honored to be one of the coaches of this fabulous team. Thank you all for coming to our very first jersey presentation!"

Everyone clapped.

"Before we get started, I'd like to thank a few people who made this evening possible. As most of you know, our team relies heavily on the generosity of its supporters. Tonight, we are honored to have the Sinclair family, who have donated our new jerseys in honor of Lexi Sinclair."

Clapping my hands, I smiled over at Sylvia. She caught my eye and motioned me over. I happily obeyed.

"I'd also like to thank one of my fellow Music City Rollers, Britches Get Stitches, who has been working tirelessly the past few weeks to create our new look," Jackie said.

I waved to the group as they applauded.

"Who's ready to see your new jerseys?" she asked.

The whole room cheered.

"When I call your name, please come up to the front." Jackie reached into the box. I knew which name was on top. "Hellissa! Unlucky number thirteen!"

Sylvia reached up and took my hand. I smiled down at her and squeezed her fingers.

———

When the ceremony was over, and all the girls (and coaches) had changed into their new jerseys, we took a huge group picture with the whole Sinclair family. Sylvia and Miss Taylor were right up front.

Afterward, I said my goodbyes to the family.

"Lexi would've loved this," Ben's wife said, looking wistfully around the room.

Ben put his arm around her. "Yes, she would have."

Their other daughter, Mia, smiled. "I think her name would have been Lex Lethal."

Her parents smiled.

"Or Lexplode!" The boy, Luke, fanned out his fingers dramatically.

We all laughed.

"No," Sylvia said.

We all turned toward her. I expected some defiant variation of Alexandria.

There were tears in Sylvia's tired eyes, and her hand trembled as she brushed them off her cheeks when they fell. "Her name would have been Lexceptional."

———

The next night, I was gearing up with Monica and Lucy when Susan and Shamrocker skated over. "Britches, got a second?" Shamrocker asked.

I double-knotted my laces and stood up. "Sure."

"Last week, Doc Carnage told us about those new jerseys you made for the junior's team," Susan said. "That's why I showed up last night when they were handed out."

"Yeah. Thanks for coming."

"Of course. They are amazing, Britches. That fabric is so soft and cool. Does Velcro really not stick to it?"

"That's right. It's a fabric the Sinclair family created specifically for roller derby."

"We want it," Shamrocker said almost before I could finish speaking.

My eyes widened. "Really?"

"Really. The board has been discussing updating our jerseys for a long time, and after last night, I called an emergency board vote. Your jerseys are lightyears better than what we have now," Susan said.

I smiled. "I think so."

"Shamrocker needs to order new jerseys for you and the other newbies to be here for the B-Cup Tournament in March. If we give our business to you, think you could have them done by then?" Susan asked.

I was surprised my skates didn't slip out from under me. "Wow. What date is today?"

Shamrocker looked at her phone. "Today is the eighth, so you'd have about five weeks to do them. I know that's cutting it close. Would it be enough time?"

I held a bubble of air in my mouth while I did the math in my head. "How many skaters do we have in the league?"

"Sixty-two this season," Susan answered.

My mouth dropped open.

Shamrocker jumped in. "But we'd only have to have the jerseys for the B-team skaters who are going to the tournament by then. The regular season wouldn't start until our first home bout on Saturday, April first."

"How many are going to the B-Cup?" I asked.

"There are fifteen of you, but we might need a couple more just in case someone has to fill in," Susan said.

"So less than twenty by the third weekend in March?"

They both nodded.

"I think I can do that. Can I give you a definite answer next week? Monday, maybe sooner?"

Before committing to anything with anyone, I needed to

make sure I wasn't going to jail. A meeting was scheduled with my lawyer on Friday to see about the plea bargain.

"Monday would be perfect," Shamrocker said.

"OK. I'll let you know."

———

On Thursday morning, I drove back to the warehouse to pack up the rest of the supplies I'd left there in my scramble to finish the last jersey the day before. When I was finished, I carried the box of stuff out to my car. That was when a familiar silver SUV pulled into the parking lot.

I turned my face toward the sky and closed my eyes. "Are you kidding me?"

Clay pulled up behind me and rolled down his window. "Hi, Grace. Wasn't expecting to see you here."

He looked better than the last time I saw him. His face was clean shaven, and his hair was meticulously groomed the way it used to be. Looking in the car, I could see he was alone. But in the middle of the back seat, a car-seat carrier base was strapped in with the seatbelt.

My eyes darted away from it and back to him. "Pretty brave of you showing up here. You know my brother wants to kill you."

"I was in the area. My attorney's office is just down the road."

My hands twitched at my sides, but I refused to ball them into fists. Silently, I was counting, *One... Two... Three...*

"I wanted to get a message to you. It seems you've blocked my phone number and my email address," he said.

"Why would you need my phone number? You're trying to have me thrown in jail."

"I'm not trying to have you thrown—"

"Whatever. My attorney has advised me not to speak to you. I suggest you go talk to yours."

"Grace, I just wanted you to know I'm sor—"

"You're sorry?" I asked with wide eyes.

"Ginny was pushing me to press charges. It wasn't me."

"Clay, your signature was all over that document."

"Yes, I know. But the baby was due any day. We were so stressed out from moving. I knew I wasn't thinking clearly, but Ginny insisted we call the police. I never thought it would get this far. And I never thought they would charge you with a felony."

"Well, they did. Or, I should say—*you* did."

He stared ahead over his steering wheel off into the distance. That was when I noticed the sun glint off a ring on his left hand that was draped over the window frame.

"Nice ring."

After a quick glance at the wedding band, he pulled his hand back inside. "How's Jason?" he asked with a smirk.

I crossed my arms. "I honestly don't know. He's not speaking to me thanks to *you*. Do you know what that did to him? He works there, Clay."

He took a deep breath and was silent for several minutes. "I am really sorry, Grace."

"Tell it to somebody who gives a shit." I opened my car, got in with a huff, and slammed the door behind me.

———

My attorney's office was in downtown Franklin, Tennessee. I drove there on Friday after a morning meeting with my therapist.

Garrett was waiting in his truck in the parking lot when I pulled in. I got out, almost melting at the sight of my big brother. "You came," I said when he got out.

"Of course I came. You shouldn't have to do this alone."

I hugged him. "Thank you, brother."

"I figured we could go out and get drunk after this. Either way this goes, you're probably going to need it."

"Probably. I'm still planning on pleading guilty, or no contest, whatever they recommend."

He stuffed his fists into his jacket pockets as we walked toward the building. "Hypothetically, if Clay were to meet an untimely demise before the hearing on the fourteenth, would you still be at risk for going to jail?"

I laughed. "I am a thousand-percent positive that the new Mrs. Clayton Byron Maxfield the Third would see to it."

He sighed. "I thought it was a pretty good idea."

"Oh, no one is questioning that it's a *great* idea."

"So has he already married her then?"

"Yeah."

"How'd you find out?"

"He showed up at your bar yesterday when I was leaving the warehouse."

Garrett stopped walking. "Seriously?"

"Yep. He said he was going to see you so he could get a message to me."

He laughed as he started toward the door again. "God, he is stupid. What was the message?"

"He wanted me to know he was sorry and that it was Ginny's plan to have me arrested for the eggs. Not his."

"What's his deal? Does he have a penis ring that she's got a chain hooked up to?"

I laughed. "Who knows? I think he was feeling guilty yesterday because he was on his way to his attorney."

Garrett held the door for me as we walked inside. "What a dick."

"I know."

The lobby was bright and airy, furnished with expensive chairs and a leather sofa I'd sat on plenty of times before. My new defense attorney was within the same legal group as my divorce lawyer.

I had jokingly asked about a two-for-one discount. Nobody but me thought that was funny.

I walked up to the receptionist's desk, and the woman looked at me expectantly. "Grace Evans to see Frank Holbrook, please. I have a meeting with him at one thirty."

She glanced toward the waiting room. "Have a seat. I'll let him know you're here."

Garrett fixed a cup of coffee for each of us at the table full of refreshments. He poured mine full of creamer and carried it over to where I'd made myself comfortable on the sofa.

I smiled as I accepted it. "I really appreciate you coming."

"I'm surprised you didn't want Mom or Dad here."

With the sigh, I curled my hands around the warm paper mug. "There's something about criminal charges that makes a girl not want to look her daddy in the face."

He nodded. "I get that. For what it's worth, they wanted to come."

"It's worth a lot." I shifted uncomfortably. "Can we talk about something else?"

"Sure. When are you going to get your shit out of my warehouse?"

I laughed. "I'm not sure. The Sinclair's said they have the lease on the equipment for two more months. They said I'm welcome to use it if I want to."

"Do you want to?"

That was a good question. "Maybe. My team asked me last night if I'd be interested in making their jerseys this season."

He turned toward me. "Really? That's awesome. Look at you getting clients without even trying."

"If I do it, I might need to stick around as a squatter for a little while longer. Is that OK?"

"You know it is. I'm just giving you shit about it. Why wouldn't you do it?"

"Well, I might be going to prison."

He rolled his eyes. "Grace, you are so dramatic."

"Grace Evans?" the receptionist said. "You can go on back to Mr. Holbrook's office now."

Garrett and I stood. "Thank you," I said and took a deep breath. "Here goes nothing."

Frank Holbrook's office was the first door on the left. It was sad how well I knew that building. We walked in and sat down in the padded chairs that faced his cherry desk. Frank looked up from the stack of papers he was reviewing.

He offered me his hand. "Hello, Ms. Evans. Nice to see you again."

"You too. This is my brother, Garrett Evans."

The two men shook hands also.

I sat back in my chair. "Well, Frank, what do you have for me? Am I headed to the big house?"

He laughed and closed the folder in front of him. "Not hardly. I worked out a nice deal with the district attorney for a year of probation and the cost to have the furniture cleaned and the sofa replaced."

I straightened. "That's great, right?"

"Not as great as your ex-husband dropping the charges."

If I hadn't been sitting, I would have fallen down. "Clay dropped the charges?" I reached and grabbed my brother's hand.

"His attorney called me this morning."

Garrett squeezed my fingers. "Yes!"

"How? Why?" I asked.

Frank smiled. "Does it matter?"

I covered my face with my hands and squealed. "So what do I do now?"

"Pay me and get out of here."

"Really?"

"There will be some paperwork for you. Janice will take care of it. Aside from that, I suggest dating better men."

"Amen to that," Garrett agreed.

Frank leaned toward me. "Or if you don't, at least leave the camera at home."

TWENTY-THREE

I ACCEPTED the job of making the Music City Rollers' new jerseys for the season. Production began the next week.

Surprisingly, I heard nothing more from Clay.

Or Jason either, *not* surprisingly.

B-team practices were grueling as we neared the B-Cup Tournament, even more so now that the new class of Fresh Meat had started. Medusa had made their practices mandatory for Rising Rollers like me, who were headed to Indiana.

It was fun, though, being part of Fresh Meat again, especially since Zoey was back skating with us. And there was something bizarrely satisfying about being the veterans around the newbies.

They all looked at us like we looked at Medusa, Maven, and the others.

At Fresh Meat on Wednesday night, two weeks before the B-Cup, we were about to start the weekly 27 in 5s, when I stopped for some water and to check my phone. I had a missed call from Ben Sinclair-Hoyt and a simple voicemail asking me to return his call.

Maybe it was his tone.

Maybe it was intuition.

But I knew before he answered, Sylvia was gone.

———

I took a break from making jerseys and made myself a new dress for the funeral. It was a simple black wrap-around with tiny periwinkle stars.

Kiara and I attended the funeral on Saturday together. She picked me up at the store, and we drove across town to the largest church I'd ever been inside. There was a closed casket visitation with the family before the service, and we waited in line for over twenty minutes just to see them.

When we finally reached Ben at the end of the greeting line, he was holding Miss Taylor. When I went to hug him, she didn't even growl at me. She just laid her head in the crook of his arm and stared somewhere across the room.

I'd held it together pretty well until then.

Ben hugged me as I burst into tears. "I'm so sorry for your loss," I said, as I pulled away, sniffling.

"Thank you. And thanks for coming. You meant a lot to my mom."

"I can't believe she's gone."

"It was fast in the end. I'm glad she didn't suffer."

I dabbed the corners of my eyes with a tissue. "That's good."

"Yeah. Is it okay if I bring some things by your place soon? Mom wanted you to have something."

"She did?"

"Yeah. I think you'll like it."

"Of course. Anytime. Text me or call and let me know when. I'm working outside the office a lot these days."

"Will do." Another man in a black suit came and spoke

quietly to him. Ben turned back to me. "Please excuse me, Grace. The service is about to begin."

Kiara and I found two empty seats together in the crowded sanctuary. There must have been a thousand people there, at least. It wasn't a particularly long service. A choir sang a few old hymns. Andrew delivered the eulogy. And a pastor gave a short message.

While the choir sang another song, a photo slideshow scrolled on a screen that hung from the ceiling. There was a picture of her at the beauty pageant. There was a recent picture of her and Miss Taylor.

There was a picture of her on her skates.

At the end, the pastor invited everyone to a graveside service.

"We can do what you want, but I'm not gonna lie," Kiara whispered. "Graveyards freak me the hell out."

I chuckled softly and looked at the time on my phone. It was almost three o'clock. "You know what? I have a better idea. Something I think Sylvia would appreciate."

"Girl, anything but tombstones."

"OK. Let's go."

We walked out the back doors of the sanctuary and through the lobby that was filling with people. Near the exit, I spotted a familiar smile.

Jason.

"Well, well. If it isn't Officer Eye Candy," Kiara said quietly. She touched my arm. "I don't want any part of the awkwardness that is about to unfold right now, so I'm going to take my ass to the bathroom. I'll be back in three minutes. Got it?"

"Got it."

She went to the left and I continued on toward the door. He met me halfway. "I was hoping to catch you. I saw you come in and sit down."

"You came to her funeral?"

"She's an unforgettable lady. Plus, I thought I might bump into you."

God, that smile.

He reached up and ran his fingers through the ends of my shoulder-length hair. "You cut your hair."

"And bleached it," I added with a smile.

"I like it. You look great," he said, looking down at my dress.

"So do you." Did he ever. I let my eyes drift over his charcoal slacks and fitted gray button-up, then higher to his square jaw dusted with golden stubble around his full lips—

No. No. No! Geez, Grace. You're at a funeral. What on earth would Sylvia think?

My head tilted.

Actually, Sylvia would probably agree...

"Grace?"

My eyes snapped up to see that his brow had crumpled, and he was grinning. "Sorry. It's been an emotional day."

"It's all right. How have you been?"

I hugged my arms. "Well, I didn't go to jail, so that's good. Clay dropped the charges."

"I saw that. I've been following your file."

I lifted an eyebrow.

He put up his hands in defense. "Not in a creepy way. I just wanted to make sure you are okay."

"You could have called."

"Trust me, I wanted to." He looked down at the floor, then shook his head like he was trying to clear it. "How's derby?"

I nodded. "It's going well. Our big tournament is next weekend in Indiana."

"Oh right. What's it called? Something really funny..."

"The B-Cup Tournament."

"That's it." He laughed and cupped his hands under his pecs. "Golden-bra trophy."

"That's the one."

"Sounds like fun."

"How are you?" I asked.

"Good. I got moved back to the dayshift, so I'm no longer a night walker, which is excellent."

"I'm sure you're happy about that. And your mom is well?"

"She's great. Thanks for asking." He looked past me. I turned and saw Kiara crossing the room. "I guess I'd better let you get going. It was really good to see you, Grace."

I forced a smile. "You too, Jason."

He opened his arms, and I gladly stepped into them. Then he held me for a moment past the "this is really over" time mark.

My fingers curled into his shirt.

Finally, he pulled away and disappeared out the door.

———

The car ride was silent until we reached the interstate. "Girl, if you don't start talking soon, I'm going to pull this car over and beat it out of you. What did he say?" Kiara asked, gripping the steering wheel so hard I could see the whites of her knuckles.

"He really didn't say anything. Asked how I was doing. That was about it."

She laughed and changed lanes. "Judging by that goodbye hug, I'm calling bullshit."

"Call it what you want. He said nothing important."

"That man loves you. It's all over his face."

I leaned my elbow against the window, cradling my head in my hand. "Sure doesn't seem that way."

"Grace Evans, will you please stop being Negative Nancy? I'm one of the most positive people I know, and you're going to make me depressed."

That got me to laugh. "Oh, Kiara. What will I ever do when you're gone?"

"Gone? Am I going somewhere?" She turned toward me. "Are you firing me?"

"No, but I'm sure you won't stick around here forever. After you graduate, I assume you'll—"

"You assume I'll what? Because if you know, you're way ahead of me."

"I figured that you couldn't wait to get out of this place. You know, go somewhere fabulous like New York City and soak up the fashion scene."

"Nah. I think I'd like to visit New York City more often, but I don't want to live there. Have you seen how expensive rent is in Manhattan? I could live like a Sinclair for that in Tennessee."

I nodded. "That's true."

"Davion wants me to stay here too. He'll inherit his family business someday."

Her story was beginning to sound a lot like mine.

"Think you'll marry him?"

"Hell, not anytime soon. Not until that boy learns to do his own laundry. You know his mama still washes his underwear? I love him, but I'm not about to marry that mess."

I laughed.

She pointed at me. "If he ever does get his shit together and I do marry him, when he inherits that hobby store, I'll have all the satin and tulle in the world. So you know, one tick mark in the plus column."

"You're too funny. So you think you'll keep working for me for a while?"

"I like working for you. Besides, Professor Sleight called me yesterday. It looks like the school is going to pass the city-wide competition next year for decorating store windows. She's asked me to help run it."

"Kiara, that's amazing. Congratulations!"

"Thank you. So simmer down, cupcake. I'm not going anywhere anytime soon."

"That's excellent news." I pointed at the next exit sign. "You need to get off on Wedgewood."

"What are we doing here again?" she asked, taking the exit.

"Last year, when I went through Fresh Meat training, I became friends with a girl named Zoey."

"Oh! I know Zoey. She helped me on Black Friday."

"Yes! I forgot all about that. When we were going through training together, she had just finished cancer treatment. Her health wasn't really good enough then to let her play. Today, she's taking the test again. I'm hoping we make it there in time for them to announce who made the team."

"In that case..." Kiara pressed down on the gas pedal.

The parking lot at the Sweatshop was nearly full when we pulled in. I checked the time on my phone again as we got out of the car. "I hope we didn't miss the announcements. I'm sure it's almost over."

We hurried to the door, and I pulled it open with a loud *creak*. Everyone inside turned to look at us. Most everyone was seated in the bleachers, except Styx, Shamrocker, Medusa, and Maven, who were down front.

Lucy and Monica were standing in the corner. "Hey, guys. What did I miss?" I asked quietly when I dragged Kiara over to them.

Monica pointed to where Zoey was sitting nervously on her hands in the middle section of the bleachers. "She passed her skills test and her 27 in 5s trial."

I made a victorious fist. "Yes."

"And they just finished calculating the written test."

"You made it just in time," Lucy whispered.

"If I call your name, you can come get your test and your new skater packet. If I don't call your name, you'll be eligible for the next round of Fresh Meat this summer."

Lucy, Monica, Kiara, and I all held hands. The girls in the bleachers were doing the same.

Shamrocker held up the first test. "With a written test score of ninety-six percent, Pow! Mia, number 8oo8!"

Everyone in the bleachers cheered.

"With a score of ninety-four, number .o1, Penny Pinch 'er!"

More clapping as the girl walked down to claim her test.

"Also with a score of ninety-four, number 29, Rhea Volt!"

I leaned over to Monica. "I'm more nervous now than when we were up there."

"I know! Me too!"

"And with a score of ninety-two percent..." Shamrocker paused. "I'll let Maven do the honors on this one."

Monica and squeezed my hands even tighter. Lucy squealed. Maven held the test high in the air.

"Her derby number is"—Maven's voice broke—"stage zero. Chemosabe!"

TWENTY-FOUR

MOST OF THE NEXT WEEK, I spent at the warehouse working on jerseys while managing the chaos of the store from afar. With the Easter season right around the corner, the dress business had been crazy again, so the jerseys were taking longer than I'd expected.

On Thursday, I had no choice but to pack up early and head home to get ready for junior-derby practice. I'd promised my nieces I wouldn't miss it. It was their very first scrimmage.

I stopped first at the store to check on Kiara. She was in the back, printing off online orders. "Just popping by to see if your offer still stands," I said with a grimace.

She scrunched her nose. "You didn't get them finished?"

"I ran out of ink. I was able to get some more, but he didn't show up until about half an hour ago."

"How many more do you have to do?"

"Only three. We can do that many tomorrow, right?"

"What time do you have to be there?" she asked.

"Worst case scenario, as long as I'm there by Saturday morning, I can still skate."

She nodded. "We'll get it done."

I glanced at the clock. It was already five-fifteen. "I've got to run. My nieces are having their first scrimmage tonight."

"Oh fun! Tell them I said good luck."

"Thanks. I'll see you tomorrow."

I walked back through the store and outside to my front door. I punched in the code and pulled it open. Bodhi jumped up with all fours and slammed them against my chest.

I screamed.

He barked.

We tumbled out onto the sidewalk together.

Immediately, I burst into tears. "Bodhi! Bodhi, what are you doing here?" Then I launched into my high-pitched dog-speak as he bounded happily around me.

Kiara ran out the store's front door and skidded to a halt when she saw me. She was grabbing her chest. "Sweet Jesus! You scared me to death. I heard you scream."

"Look!" I was holding Bodhi by his collar. "How did he get here?"

"I have no idea. I didn't see anything."

"Come on, boy," I said, tugging him back inside.

Kiara walked into my stairwell. "Here's a bag of his stuff." She dug around inside it. "I found a note." She handed it to me.

I unfolded the half sheet of notebook paper and immediately recognized the handwriting as easily as I would recognize my own.

Dear Grace,

I hope now you know I'm truly sorry. For everything I did to you. For everything I did to us. I hope someday you'll be able to forgive me. And I hope with all my heart that you'll find someone who loves you as well as I should have.

Take care of him for me,

Clayton

PS Tell Jason I'm sorry too. Had I really cared about anyone other than myself, I wouldn't have tried to keep him away from you. He's a good guy. You'd be lucky to have each other.

Now I was really going to be late to practice. I didn't even bother to change clothes or grab my skates' bag. I just put Bodhi in the car and we left. I need to say that again...*I put Bodhi in the car and we left!*

My dog was back. And I'd never let anyone take him away again. His tongue wagged in the passenger's seat our whole drive across town. Thankfully, we made it to the Sweatshop in record time. There was an empty spot next to Garrett's truck, so I parked beside him and led Bodhi inside.

Mom and Dad and Garrett were helping to set up for the scrimmage. Monica was on her skates in the middle of the track with a few of the girls. She skated over when she saw me.

"Look! A dog!" one of the girls yelled.

Several of them followed Monica over.

She did a quick tomahawk stop. "You can pet the dog later! Back to the track!" She turned toward me and raised her arms. "Look at you, screwing up my practice. What's Bodhi doing here?"

"He was waiting at my apartment when I got home today. There was an apology note and everything from Clay."

"No way. Are you serious?"

"I never joke about my dog." I looked down at my clothes and pointed at my sneakers. "I didn't have time to get my skates today. Sorry I won't be much help."

"Don't worry about it. We'll talk after the scrimmage, OK?"

"You bet!" My phone buzzed as I walked across the room to see my family. My heart dropped half an inch, worried that it might be Clay changing his mind. I pulled out my phone. It was a message from Ben Sinclair.

Is now a good time?

I tapped out a quick response. *Only if you want to come to the Rollers' Sweatshop. I'm at juniors' practice right now. You're welcome to join us.*

He sent back a thumbs-up.

For the scrimmage, I sat on the floor with Bodhi. As a new level-three, Gabby was able to jam. Hope, still a level-two, was only allowed to block with limited contact. Gabby scored seven points in the first half of the scrimmage. A hell of a lot more than I ever scored the first time I played.

Behind me, my brother laughed and cheered for his girls.

The bout ended, and I didn't even see which team won because Gabby was skating toward me with her fists pumping the air. I caught her in my arms. "I'm so proud of you! You should have seen yourself out there!"

Hope came next. "Aunt Grathe! Did you *thee* me? Did you *thee* me?"

"Of course I saw you. Wow, you're both so very good!"

Jackie walked—err, waddled—over. Her "baby bump" was now a full-blown mountain. "Congratulations on your first scrimmage," she said to the girls, slapping high-fives with both of them.

"Good job to you too, coach. They look really good out there. How are you feeling?"

She took a deep breath and rested her hands on her belly. "Like I'm going to explode any day now."

I didn't realize mom was standing behind me until she spoke. "How much longer do you have?"

"About six more weeks."

I rocked back and forth on my tennis shoes. "Then I guess you are going to need a replacement around here."

Her eyes doubled. "Yes...?" she said, drawing out her answer into a hopeful question.

I looked at my nieces. "What do you say, girls? Think Aunt Grace is good enough to coach?"

"Yes!" Gabby said.

Hope folded her hands in the prayer position. "Oh *pleathe*! Oh *pleathe*! Oh *pleathe*!"

I laughed. "I'll start next week."

Hope squealed and threw her arms around my waist. Gabby raised two victorious fists in the air.

Jackie put her hand on my arm. "You're going to be great."

"I guess we'll see." I grabbed my purse off the bleachers. "I have something for you."

"For me?" Jackie asked.

I nodded, reaching in to the bag. Then I handed her the newborn onesie, printed like the juniors' jerseys.

She covered her mouth and laughed before accepting it. "Oh my god. I love it!" She hugged me. "Thank you so much."

"Your little girl will officially be our tiniest member."

"She must have heard you. She's kicking!"

I gestured to her stomach. "May I?"

"Of course." She put my hand on her stomach. There was a *thump thump thump* against my palm.

I smiled and hugged her. "I'm so happy for you, Jackie." And for the first time, I truly meant it.

Mom tapped me on the shoulder. "Grace, I think someone's trying to get your attention." She was pointing toward the door.

I looked over and saw Ben Sinclair-Hoyt. "Jackie, excuse me for a second. Girls, I'll be right back."

Bodhi and I walked to meet Ben at the entrance. "Hi. You made it," I said.

"I hope I'm not interrupting."

"Not at all. The girls just finished a scrimmage."

"Is this your dog?" he asked, leaning down to scratch Bodhi's head with his free hand. In the other, he carried a thin box.

I smiled. "Yes, he is. Bodhi, say hi."

Bodhi barked.

Ben laughed. "That's pretty good. Grace, I won't keep you. I wanted to give you this." He handed me the box.

I took it and carefully opened the lid. Inside was the album Sylvia had shown me at her house. Immediately, tears filled my eyes.

"We made copies of all the photos for the family, but she wanted you to have this," he said.

The tear slipped down my cheeks. "Thank you. I'll treasure it always."

There were legal papers underneath the album.

"We've transferred ownership of the sublimation printer and the heat press to you."

"I thought you said they were rented?"

His head bobbed from side to side. "My mother lied sometimes." He chuckled. So did I. "She was afraid you would object to us purchasing them."

"I would have. I know how much those machines cost."

"You can still continue the jersey business or not. There's no pressure from us. But if you do, the contract guaranteeing you exclusivity in the roller derby market is in there as well. We've already signed it. There's also another agreement in there guaranteeing you a discount on all our fabric for as long as you are in business."

I covered my mouth with my hand. "Ben, I don't know what to say."

He grinned. "I think my mother would say, you say 'thank you.'"

I nodded. "Probably followed by something snarky."

He laughed. "Probably."

Closing the box, I held it to my chest. "Thank you, Ben."

"You're very welcome. Mom also designated, in her will, a sizable donation to this team. Part of it, she intended to be a scholarship fund for girls who might need it to pay for skates, gear, or whatever they might need to allow them to play. Our attorneys will spell that out for the league's board. I just wanted you to know."

"I know it will be put to good use."

He offered his hand, and I shook it. "Thank you for being a friend to my mother. It's truly been a pleasure to meet you."

Bloomington, Indiana, didn't know what hit them when the Music City Rollers rolled into town. Our entire league showed up and took over the hotel. And most of us, at least the ones who were skating in the tournament, brought an entourage.

It took Kiara and me both to finish up the jerseys that morning. We packed up the very last one, and literally drove straight to the tournament. Thankfully, the hotel was dog-friendly, so Bodhi came with us. Kiara had even made him a bandana to match the team's colors.

There was a note stuck to our hotel door when we checked in.

All Music City Rollers in the lobby at 8 p.m. for jerseys and team meeting. If you're skating tomorrow—NO PARTYING TONIGHT.

Kiara ripped it off the door. "That doesn't apply to me. Bring on the booze."

"Did someone say booze?"

I turned and saw Garrett coming down the hall behind us. He was carrying a case of his brewery's beer.

"Are you kidding me? Your kids are here," I said, shaking my head.

He pointed the corner of the box at me. "Correction. My kids are bunking with Granna and Pops. I'm bunking with *you*. Hey, Bodhi." He scratched my dog's head.

"You're sleeping in our room?" I asked.

"Oh hell no." Kiara was shaking her head as we walked into the room.

He followed us inside. "You've got two beds. You don't want me to sleep on the floor, do you?" He grinned and put the beer on the dresser. "Better yet, you don't want me to sleep with one of your *teammates*, do you?"

"Oh my god." I put down the box and my skates' bag, then let Bodhi off his leash. I looked at Kiara for help. "Do you mind?"

She rolled her eyes. "I guess not. But he can sleep with you."

"Girls night! Girls night!" Garrett chanted in a high-pitched voice while opening up a beer.

"You're an idiot," she told him. "Give me one of those."

He handed her a beer, then flopped down on the bed where I put the box of jerseys. "Does your team have corporate sponsors? I feel like roller girls would draw in my core demographic."

"You're probably right. And yes, we do. Remind me and I'll introduce you to Medusa. She works with all our sponsors."

"Is she the chick with all the tattoos and the purple in her hair?"

"Yeah."

"I saw her in the lobby. She's hot."

"I know. Don't get any ideas."

"I think I've met her before," he said, raising his beer to his lips.

"Probably. She used to be a bartender."

He nodded. "That would make sense. What time does this shindig get started?"

"The tournament starts tomorrow at eight," I said.

"In the morning?" Kiara asked, her voice jumping up a few octaves.

"Yes, but my first bout isn't until nine forty-five."

"Oh, thank God," she said.

"Garrett, what time is it now?" I asked.

He looked at the silver watch he was wearing. "Seven thirty-two."

"Hey, Grace. I'm starving. Can we get something to eat?" Kiara asked.

"You guys can go. I've got a team meeting downstairs soon."

"Mmm, roller girls. Maybe I'd rather stay here with you," Garrett said.

I pointed at him. "You need to stop."

Garret laughed and stood up. "Come on, Kiara. Let's get some grub."

"You buying?" she asked.

"Yeah. I'm buying. Since I'm kicking you out of your bed and all."

She followed him to the door. "I told you. You can sleep with your sister."

"We'll see about that. See you later, Grace!" Garrett called as they walked outside.

"Bring me back a burger or something!"

"You got it," he replied as the door closed behind them.

I had just stepped into the bathroom to fill Bodhi's bowl with water when someone knocked on the door. "Grace, open up!" Monica yelled.

I walked back into the room and pulled open the door. All my girlfriends were standing on the other side. Monica, Lucy, Olivia, and Zoey. They were all wearing their bras outside their clothes. Olivia held a pizza box. Lucy held a six-pack of beer.

"Happy tournament weekend!" Zoey announced as I moved aside for them to come in.

Monica greeted me with a hug. "We just bumped into your brother in the hallway. I canceled your burger order, and he yelled at me about our beer."

I looked at the six-pack. "I can see why. What are you guys doing here?"

"Celebrating. Duh! It's your very first bout against other teams!" Olivia said, putting the pizza on the bed.

Lucy passed the beer around to everyone. "We figured we wouldn't have much of a chance to hang out tomorrow, so we decided to have our party in here tonight instead."

"You know we have to be downstairs in about twenty minutes, right?"

Olivia cocked an eyebrow. "Are they going to present the jerseys without you?"

I laughed. "Good point."

Monica rubbed her hands together, standing over the box. "Is this them? Can I peek?"

"Yes. But you have to let me do it," I said, moving her out of the way.

She was hyperventilating. "This is so exciting."

The jerseys were folded neatly inside the box with the numbers facing up. I searched through them until I found Monica's. "Dr. Hooker," I said, handing it to her proudly.

She squealed as she held it up in front of her.

"Oh my gosh, Grace. That looks amazing," Zoey said with wide eyes.

"It feels amazing too. Check it out." Monica handed it to her.

Zoey and Lucy rubbed the fabric.

I looked in the box and found Lucy's. "Lights Out Lucy, here you go."

She clapped and reached for it. "This doesn't feel real."

"I know, right?" Monica asked.

"And Chemosabe," I said, handing Zoey hers.

Zoey covered her face with it. "But Grace, I'm not even skating this weekend! I love it so much!"

"You've certainly earned it, Zo." I dug around in the box some more. "And last, but never least...The Prodigy."

"What?" Olivia asked, her head tilting to the side.

I pulled out a T-shirt I'd made with her honorary derby name on the back of it and our logo on the front. I held it out of her reach. "Someday, I expect to make you an actual jersey."

She laughed. "We'll see."

Monica let another squeal loose. I pulled them all in for a group hug, and Bodhi barked in the middle of us.

———

Monica, Lucy, and I skated out into the arena together the next morning. The three of us held hands. "Good luck today, my friends. I hope we all survive," I told them with a laugh.

"There are so many people here," Lucy said nervously.

Monica pointed across the room. "Look! There's our group!"

My eyes followed her finger across the room until they landed on Bodhi. My brother was holding his leash. My mother waved. Hope and Gabby held up a sign. It had my name and jersey number.

I blew out a nervous sigh. "Okay. Let's do this."

We skated out to the track and began to warm up. The people in the stands cheered.

Monica skated beside me. "Don't forget, when they introduce

our team, your name is Britches Get Stitches. Say it with me. Britches Get Stitches."

I shoved her sideways and laughed. "You're a jerk, Dr. Hooker."

She did a 360-degree turn. "I'm just looking out for you."

"Grace!" A woman was yelling somewhere. "Grace!"

I looked in the direction of the sound. Near the door, Kiara was waving her arm over her head. Her other hand was holding onto a man's arm.

It was Jason.

"Holy shit." I took out my mouth guard and hooked it on the front of my jersey.

Not looking where I was going, I slammed into the back of Goldie Knocks. We both went down in a tangled heap.

"Britches, what the hell?" she asked shoving me off of her.

"Sorry. My bad." Several people around the track saw it and were laughing.

I quickly pushed myself up and skated toward the door. Kiara's eyes were wide as I approached. "Look who I found wandering around the lobby," she said, looking up at him.

I slowed with a T-stop.

"I'll let you guys talk." Kiara grabbed my elbow pad. "Good luck. With *everything*," she added in a whisper. Then she scampered back toward the bleachers.

"Jason, what are you doing here?"

With his delicious smile cemented in place, he looked around the room. "I heard there's some badass roller girl debuting today. You seen her?"

"I think there's a few of them."

"Hey, is that Bodhi over there with your brother?"

"Yeah. Clay gave him back to me."

"Good. Glad the asshole finally came to his senses."

"Me too. Seriously, why are you here?"

He reached for my hand. "Why do you think I'm here?"

"Jason, I'm obviously not so good at getting things right with us, so I'd rather not guess if that's OK with you."

"Grace, I haven't been able to get you out of my head since I saw you last week. Hell, I haven't been able to get you out of my head for the past five months...or maybe even longer, if I'm being honest."

"Longer?"

He looked down at the concrete floor. "I had planned to ask you out in college. Then everything happened with Mom, and Clay beat me to it."

I bit down on the insides of my mouth. "Does Clay know that?"

"Clay doesn't have a whole lot on his radar outside himself."

He could say that again.

"Well, you'll be glad to know all these years later that he finally apologized for keeping us apart. Though I kinda doubt he meant all the way back to college."

"Clay told you then?"

I nodded.

"You know that was the only reason I stayed away, right?"

I turned my ear toward him. "What was the reason?"

"I only stayed away because Clay said he'd dropped the charges if I did."

My eyes doubled. "He did what?"

His head pulled back. "You didn't know?"

"He just told me he was sorry for trying to keep us apart. That's it. He said he'd drop the charges if you broke up with me?"

"That was the gist of it. I went to his place the day you were arrested. I broke his nose, and we made a deal."

"Why would you agree to such a thing?" I rolled back a few inches.

"Because I love you. If I can ever keep you from becoming a

felon, I'm going to. Besides, I knew a little distance wouldn't hurt us. If we kept going the way we were, we'd probably ruin everything."

I couldn't argue with that.

He pulled my hand, rolling me closer again and rested his forehead against mine. "Can we try us again?"

My heart was hammering in my chest. "Yes."

With a relieved sigh, he pulled me into his arms. "I do love you, Grace."

"I love you too, Jason."

Then he kissed me, and somewhere on the other side of the room behind us, I heard a group of people break out cheering. Bodhi barked, telling me it was *my* people.

"May I have your attention please?" a familiar voice boomed over the loudspeaker. I turned to see Medusa in the center of our track holding a microphone. "The Music City Rollers seem to be missing a skater. Britches Get Stitches, please stop making out with your boyfriend and get your ass over here!"

––––––––

We won our first bout against the Hotlanta Brawlers, 164 to 144.

We won our second bout against the Chi-Town Rollergirls, 112 to 108.

I had scored a total of sixty-eight points so far that day.

After a short dinner break, we returned to the arena to find out who we'd be playing in the championship bout, the Silicon Beach Babes...or Richmond. The score from their last bout was still on the screen.

Silicon Beach, 82.

Richmond Vixens, 209.

"Holy moly," Lucy said with a sigh as we all stared at the board.

Monica nudged my arm. "Is that...?" Her question faded into a gulp.

There was a lone Richmond skater wearing the number 6VI6 circling the track. Her face was painted with a solid black stripe across her eyes. "Demoness," I whispered.

"Why is she in uniform? She's not a B-team skater," Lucy said.

"Isn't that cheating?" Monica asked.

Jason looked at me. "What's the matter?"

I groaned. "We're gonna get creamed."

"Excuse me," a woman said, walking up to us. She was wearing a Chi-Town jacket. "Are you Britches Get Stitches?"

"I am."

She stuck out her hand. "My name is Bad Ghoul. I'm Chi-Town's league president. I just talked to Susan about your team's jerseys. She said you made them."

"That's right."

"Everybody's talking about them. They're amazing. Do you do them for other derby teams?"

I smiled. "Possibly."

"Here's my card. Let's talk sometime next week."

"OK. Great. Thank you," I said.

She waved as she walked off.

Lucy pointed at her. "You know, you could do T-shirts and jackets and lots of other stuff on that machine of yours. The new business could offer more than just jerseys."

"You have a jersey business now?" Jason asked.

"Sparkled Pink is going to start offering athletic wear, so it seems," Monica said.

"Not Sparkled Pink," I said, shaking my head. "I'll start a completely separate clothing line. Thinking of calling it *Lexceptional Ink*."

Jason's head tilted. "Lexceptional?"

"It's a long story, but now it looks like I'll have plenty of time to tell you all about it." I leaned in and kissed him.

"Music City!" Medusa yelled. "Locker room. Now!"

"Wish me luck," I said.

He shook his head. "You don't need luck. You're a badass."

"Thanks. Pray I don't die."

In the locker room, we all gathered around Medusa.

She paced back and forth with her hands on her hips. "It's been a long day, ladies. It's been a good day, but a long day. For some of you, this is the most roller derby you've played in your entire career collectively. You're tired. You're sore. Some of you are even injured." She gestured toward Rocksee Rolls, who had suffered a busted lip in the first bout. "But this next bout is what you've been training for. This is why we're here.

"I know some of you are freaking out right now, thinking, *Oh my god we're playing Richmond. Oh my god they're letting Demoness skate...*well don't. The only people who matter out there are the girls standing around you right here, right now. You're going to give every shred of energy you have left, not to Richmond—no, screw them. You're going to give that last drop of sweat and blood to your sister. To your family. *We* are your family.

"You've already blown out two games tonight." She held up two fingers. "Two games! And for some of you, this is the very first time you've played against another team. That's incredible! That's phenomenal!

"Well, listen up. You haven't come this far to *only* come this far. You've got the heart to win this. You've got the skills to win this. You've got the balls to win this. Now let's get out there and shut their shit down!"

Everyone clapped and cheered.

"Bring it in, bitches!" she yelled.

We all crowded in the center of the room and put our hands together in the middle. "On three!" she said.

Then we all yelled our team's motto together.

"Be brave! Be strong! Be badass!"

———

"Call off the jam! Call off the jam! Call off the jam!" Medusa was screaming from our bench.

I double-tapped my hips, and the jam whistle blasted four times. Heaving and in pain, I skated back to the bench. I gave Lucy a weak high five as she skated by to replace me as jammer. Someone threw me a bottle of water, and I plopped down and ripped the star off my helmet.

I looked at the scoreboard. Richmond was up, 154 to 151. It was closer than any of us would have believed before the start of the bout. There were less than eight minutes left on the clock.

Sweat poured into my eyes, and I splashed my face with water, then dried it with the tail of my jersey.

Medusa's hand came down hard on my shoulder. "Don't get too comfy. You're going back in."

My head fell back toward the ceiling as I tried to catch my breath.

"Hooker, I want you on offense!" Medusa yelled down the bench. "It looks like Demoness is jamming again next, and Britches, we need points!"

No shit.

The jam ended, but not before the Vixens added seven to their score. 161 to 151. Richmond.

I skated back out, and Demoness lined up with me at the jammer line. On the starting whistle, we bolted forward and began fighting our way through the pack. We both made it out about the same time, and Demoness cut toward me. But Monica came from behind, intercepting her with a huge hit that sent Demoness flying out of bounds.

Screaming and laughing as the ref signaled I was lead jammer, I skated around the track.

Pushing my skates as hard as I could, I rounded the final turn before the pack. My blockers divided to allow me to pass. Then Monica skated like a bowling ball toward the Richmond blockers and busted them apart. I slipped through the center, claiming four more points.

With wild and flailing arms to get my attention, Medusa was striking her hips on the sidelines.

I double-tapped mine to end the jam. The whistle blasted. I turned and saw Demoness reach our blockers without scoring. She stayed on the track rather than switching out with another jammer.

I'd gained four more points. The score was now 161 to 155. Richmond.

Everyone on our team was standing. So was everyone in the crowd.

I spun to a stop at the bench beside Monica. "Oh my god, that was awesome!" I screamed.

She was laughing.

"You good?" Medusa asked as we sat down.

I gave her a thumbs-up.

She gripped Monica's shoulder. "Hooker, that was badass."

"Thanks," she said, panting and tilting her water bottle up to her lips.

Lucy was jamming against Demoness. The jam started, and after a struggle, Lucy made it out of the pack first. Demoness caught her in the next turn but came in too far behind for the hit. She made contact with Lucy's back, and the referee's whistle blasted. He signaled Demoness to the penalty box. One of Richmond's blockers was already there as well.

The announcer jumped up behind his table. "Power Jam for Music City!"

With Demoness in the penalty box, Lucy was free to score as many points as she could.

Medusa grabbed my arm. She was looking at the clock. There was less than two minutes left in the period. "Demoness will have to start the next jam from the penalty box, but she won't be in there for long. Britches, you have to win lead jammer, but don't end the jam until the period clock runs out. You'll need to hold Demoness back for about forty-five seconds to keep her from scoring."

"How am I going to do that?"

Medusa grabbed my arm and Monica's. "Girls, it's time to eat the baby."

I caught a glimpse of Maven in the stands and smiled.

Lucy scored ten points before the end of the jam, putting us in the lead by two. Music City, 163. Richmond, 161.

All we had to do was keep Demoness from scoring.

My heart was pounding against my breastbone as I rolled to the jammer line alone. Demoness was standing in the penalty box, which meant she had ten seconds or less to come back on the track.

In other words, I had ten seconds or less to claim lead jammer.

The Richmond defense was lined up in front of me when the starting whistle blasted. I skated straight for the tiniest gap in their wall and hit them with everything I had. One of the blockers stumbled forward, giving Monica an opening to sweep in and knock her out of my way. I ran on my skates through the hole.

Lead jammer!

As fast as I could, I sped back around to catch Demoness. She had already reentered the track and was trying to pass Monica.

Electra Cal barreled through Richmond's blockers as I neared the pack. Then I caught up with Demoness in turn three.

Bam! I knocked her sideways over the outside line. Then I spun around and sprinted back to the pack where my blockers were waiting.

Demoness reentered behind me, and Monica, Goldie Knocks, 5 Scar Jeneral, and Electra Cal swarmed around her. I skated away.

Medusa was screaming. "Call off the jam!"

I struck my hips twice and ended the bout.

The Music City Rising Rollers had won.

TWENTY-FIVE

OUR ENTIRE TEAM, both on and off the playing floor, had rushed the track, colliding in the biggest and sweatiest group hug known to mankind. Monica, Lucy, and I had been in the center of it, crying in each other's arms.

When the ceremony concluded, the Music City Rising Rollers carried the Golden Brassier back to our hotel. Everyone gathered in the hotel ballroom for an informal presentation, and Susan took the stage.

"Wow! Have you ever seen a B-team tournament that exciting?" she yelled into her microphone.

Everyone in the room cheered. Standing with my family and Monica and Derek, Jason put his arms around me from behind. I couldn't imagine what I must've smelled like, but it was obvious he didn't care. Bodhi was sitting on my feet.

"After each bout, our league votes to hand out a few player awards. Most Valuable Jammer, Most Valuable Blocker, and Most Valuable Skater Overall. We also have a tradition, if ever our Rising Rollers win the B-Cup Tournament, we award the

Most Valuable Skater Overall with a position on the All-Star team for the coming season." She looked offstage. "I'd like to invite the coach of the Rising Rollers, Medusa, up here to present those awards now. Didn't she do an excellent job today?"

The room erupted in applause again as Medusa walked up onto the stage.

"Thank you, Susan. First, I've got to say, that was one of the best damn games I've ever seen played. All of the Rising Rollers deserve another round of applause. Give it up, you guys!" She clapped her hands over her head.

Maven walked up beside her, carrying three glitter-encrusted rollerskate wheels, each hanging from a long loop of ribbon. Two of them were teal. One was shiny gold.

"And now I'd like to present the award for Most Valuable Blocker," Medusa said. "Number one-hundred dollars, Dr. Hooker!"

I screamed and hugged my best friend. She was covering her red face as she walked on stage. Maven put one of the teal skates around her neck.

"And the award for Most Valuable Jammer...Britches Get Stitches!" Medusa yelled.

Jason kissed my cheek. My nieces and my brother hugged me. My dad gave me a high five. My mother blew me a kiss.

I handed Jason Bodhi's leash and walked on stage. Maven put the other teal skate around my neck. She laughed as she did it. "Eat the baby, Britches?"

"All thanks to you!"

"Congratulations."

Monica and I held hands as Medusa continued.

"Normally, we would have three separate winners. But tonight, one of these fine skaters unanimously claimed the award for Most Valuable Skater Overall. We have watched this newbie bust her ever-loving-ass—sometimes, literally—to improve her skills, to support her league, and now, so I hear, to help teach the next generation of Music City Rollers on our juniors' team. Let's hear it again for...Dr. Hooker!"

Monica gasped and gripped my hand. "It's supposed to be you!"

"No, Monica." I hugged her neck so tightly I worried her head might pop off. "It's supposed to be you."

———

We all dispersed after that, and my crew headed to the bar-slash-restaurant in the lobby. Jason and Garrett pushed together the biggest tables they could find, and we all gathered around them. We were short on chairs, so I happily volunteered to sit on Jason's lap.

After receiving our first round of drinks, I clinked a silver knife against the side of my glass and stood. "May I have your attention for a second?"

All my friends and family stopped talking and looked up at me.

"As most of you know, the past year has been—kids, cover your ears—absolute hell for me. So many of you have been there for me in ways I can't even begin to show my gratitude for."

"We love you, Britches!" Olivia shouted.

"I love you too." I held my drink in the air. "Now, I don't know if it's because I'm newly single, or because Lucy and West just got engaged—congratulations, you guys—but I'm feeling *very* romantic tonight."

Everyone "Ooo"d and looked at Jason.

He blushed and covered his face.

"I have a very important question to ask someone so very

special to me." I gazed at Jason. He looked excited, nervous... maybe nauseated.

Then I turned toward Monica. I put my drink down on the table, and I got down on one knee.

Taking her hand and looking lovingly into her eyes, I smiled. "Dr. Monica Hooker, will you be my derby wife?"

★ Want leaked chapters of new books?
★ Want the first look at what's coming soon?
★ Want to win some awesome swag and prizes?

Join HYDERNATION, the official fan club of Elicia Hyder, for all that and more!

Join on Facebook
Join on EliciaHyder.com

Book 0 - **The Detective**
Book 1 - **The Soul Summoner**
Book 2 - **The Siren**
Book 3 - **The Angel of Death**
Book 4 - **The Taken**
Book 5 - **The Sacrifice**
Book 6 - **The Regular Guy**

ABOUT THE AUTHOR

Bestselling author Elicia Hyder played women's flat track roller derby with the Nashville Rollergirls under the skater name "eL's Bells." After a black eye, a broken finger, a severely pulled groin, and two knee injuries, Elicia hung up her skates to focus on a safer hobby—writing.

She has fictionalized her experience in the Music City Rollers series. She also writes the bestselling series, The Soul Summoner.

Elicia still lives in Music City with her superhero husband, five (loud) children, and two co-dependent dogs.

www.eliciahyder.com
elicia@eliciahyder.com